# Tell Me Who You Go With

Darla J. Michaels

**To Michael and James, for knowing I could write this story before I did.**

Cover design by Kristina Bates Design

## Content Note

The story of Micah and Hadley involves polyamory, the practice of, or the desire for, romantic relationships with more than one partner at the same time, with the informed consent of all partners involved. Please note brief references of sexual assault do appear in some of the storylines, however, explicit details of the assault are not included in this novel.

I'd rather live a life that others don't understand than a life I can't stand.

Micah A. Stevenson- Brotherhood Co-Founder

# Prologue
# **Hadley**

I roll my eyes up at him, stunned at the document in my hands. He simply nods. His silent confirmation that he is in fact serious about the terms written here. Terms that he expects me to follow if I'm to continue in this relationship. A relationship with him and the brotherhood, or his brothers as he calls them.

**Brotherhood Rules**

1. Your body belongs to the brotherhood. You will not touch another outside of the brotherhood, nor allow another outside of the brotherhood to touch you. Doing so will end your agreement and involvement effective immediately.
2. Maintain an agreement that is true and accurate at all times.
3. Be a willing, enthusiastic and fully reciprocating participant in all interactions with the brothers. Specifically, sexual favors will be returned in kind and requests for sex will be granted without hesitation. No outright refusal of sex will be tolerated as this is seen as a means of control or manipulation. Denying the brothers your body will only be allowed in cases of illness or injury. Additionally, members of the brotherhood will not attempt to involve you in acts that are not in your agreement and/or disrespect or shame your sexual preferences or practices.

4. Safety is of utmost importance and ensuring your safety is at the discretion of your owner. As such, you will not participate in unsafe actions as determined by your owner.
5. You will not disclose the identity of those in the brotherhood unless given permission to do so.
6. Follow orders thoroughly and without hesitation.
7. Make yourself available when called upon or scheduled, wearing only the items you're gifted for each occasion.
8. Pleasure will be granted at the discretion of your owner.
9. Concerns within your relationships will be discussed and resolved immediately. The silent treatment, withholding information or shit tests of any kind will not be tolerated.
10. Information is given to you on an as needed basis. Gossip will not be tolerated.
11. No phones on dates. No exceptions. Period.
12. Access to any member of the brotherhood will be granted at said owner's discretion.

Should violations occur, suitable punishments will be decided and carried out by the brotherhood.

All parties may cease their agreement at any time, thus forfeiting their right to any and all possessions gained during their commitment with the brotherhood. Upon ending your commitment, all communication with brotherhood members will come to an immediate and end.

I lay the document down on his glossy dining room table and look down at his hands, holding both my bare feet, stroking the tops with his thumbs, waiting for my decision. First, I think this man who made me fall for him harder than I've fallen for any other owes me some answers.

# Chapter 1
# Hadley

**December 27th 6 p.m.**
(Present Day)

Tell me who you go with, and I'll tell you who you are. My grandmother used to say this to us a lot when we were in high school. She was reminding us to make friends with the good kids. I'm reminded of this tonight as my eyes wander the room. My grandmother would not like my friends at all, God rest her soul. It's not that the people I spend my time with aren't good. It's that she just wouldn't approve of how they are. How *we* are. How *I* am.

I look around at the men in fancy suits and coats each with a beautiful woman at their side. It's winter out east and I'm surrounded by broad-shouldered powerful men. Their suits cost more than my monthly mortgage payment. If you were an outsider, this scene would look completely normal. Except that these men are model worthy. The most beautiful specimens of the male gene I have ever laid eyes on. Not a hair out of place, unless it's on purpose. Perfectly straight, blindingly white teeth. Chiseled jaw. Eyes that captivate you. Fuck. I'm one lucky woman.

Every man here, including my own, touches their girl possessively. Theirs. For now. A hand on our back. Some snake an arm around our waist. And one in particular, has his hand on Linea's cheek.

Linea's the first of the women to belong to a member of the brotherhood. The First Lady, I think, smirking to myself at the comparison. The legendary golden-haired princess out in public but likely a sexual deviant in private.

She looks up at Braden like he is her one and only, and he looks down at her the same way. Their lips meet and even from across the room I know that kiss is filled with love and adoration that he'll only give to her.

My heart swells for her. I can't resist a good love story. And although Micah has told me the story is epic and I wouldn't believe it when I heard it, he refuses to tell me himself.

*It's her story to tell. Remember the rule? We don't share about others. If you want to know, go ask her yourself.*

Ah yes. The rules, my owner, Micah, reminds me. Rules I once thought were impossible to live by. Some I thrive on. Some I think are completely ridiculous. Others perplex the hell out of me. But the rules are not an option. Not up for negotiation. No exceptions. Not even by the men.

Each man gets to make one. They enter our circle with an understanding of the rules, get acquainted with all of us and voila...a new rule is born.

There are twelve rules. None made by the women...unless you count their agreement, which only impacts the men. The woman's agreement is the playbook for their sexual preferences. Just like the men, we're expected to be honest about what we like. If we like it, it's noted in specific detail. No deviations allowed. All the men get a copy for their reference.

Being the last woman in the circle, I often wonder who made which rule. Despite my inquiries, Micah is tight lipped. He simply says... *Let's not focus on things you can't change, hmm?* He's right. We get a say in almost nothing.

I remember the day Micah was waiting for me at his house. *Come over.* It was an order, not a request. I was raised to be respected. Not ordered around. Generally, being spoken to like that would have earned a man a first-rate spot back on the dating market. But Micah? That order hit me right between the legs. My response? I submissively said, "Okay."

When I arrived on his doorstep, he opened the door before I could even ring the bell and created just enough space for me to slide between him and the frame. I could feel the sexual tension radiating off him. It felt amazing. Like what existed between us had shifted. We couldn't get enough of each other as it was, but this? This was different. It made the hairs on my arms stand up and my heart race in the most unnatural way. He hadn't even touched me yet.

When I was through the door, I dropped my head when he looked at me like a predator stalking his prey and I picked up my pace through the entryway. Before the door shut behind me, his strong hand wrapped around my bicep, stopping me dead in my tracks. He merely looks down at me and shakes his head. I start to open my mouth to...apologize? But nothing comes out. How could it with those steel grey eyes looking back at me?

Micah smiles like a wolf, releasing my arm, his open hand following my skin up to my shoulder, then throat where two fingers rest under my chin. He steps toward me, and I instinctively take one step back and then another. My escape ends as my backside bumps into the wall.

He lets out a long breath and runs his tongue over the bottom of his top teeth before sinking them down on his lower lip, pressing his lips together...just waiting. Searching my face.

"Micah." I practically pant his name. This is a little different. Good different. But different all the same. I had suspected he was holding back with me. It had been just over a month that we'd been dating. I mean, we all hide things in relationships this early. Why would it be any different with him?

He leaves his fingers under my chin and leans forward, bracing his forearm against the wall at the side of my head. Then he plants a gentle kiss on my lips. His woodsy smell and soft lips cloud my brain. He tastes like whiskey and Cuban cigar.

"Hadley." His lips are millimeters away from mine. Just enough space to say my name clearly.

I lean forward to kiss him. That's my answer. Yes. Whatever you want it's a yes. I'll do it. No questions asked.

I huff out a breath when my head doesn't move forward. I hadn't even realized he shifted his hand to weave his fingers through my hair and those fingers were keeping me right where he wanted. He smiled the devil's smile, and chuckled.

Leaning forward to bring his mouth next to my ear he says in a low voice, "Let's try this again." Then he releases my hair and props my chin up with the same two fingers, lips almost touching mine once more. "Hadley."

"Yes." I breath the word out because I'm desperate for him. This is torture. He smiles, clearly pleased with my response.

"I want you to be mine. If I promise to take very good care of you, will you be mine? Completely mine to do with as I please?" His voice sounds calculated and sinister, but I can't help but believe every word. I will be his. He will take very good care of me. I've experienced his care. So far, it's been first rate.

"Yes."

"Hmmm…". He hums his approval. "Your mind is saying yes, but let's see what your body says." He moves his hand from my face, not moving his lips an inch from my mouth. "Stay." He had read my mind. I wanted the kiss I was after moments ago. I gave him a meek nod and he smiled again. "So obedient. Tell me, have you touched yourself today?" I whisper the word *no*. We hadn't even had sex yet and I was dying to feel him inside of me. Because if he could take care of me without even having sex…I couldn't even imagine what tricks he had up his sleeve with his cock.

His hand slides down my thigh, easily finding the hem of my knee length summer dress. The warmth of his strong warm hand traveling up my thigh so painfully slowly makes my heart race. But when his fingers find the edge of my panties, I'm pliable to do whatever he wants with. He pinches the edge of the fabric, two fingers just underneath and his thumb on top, following the fabric down to wear my legs meet. When he gets to my sweet spot, he runs his thumb over the center of the fabric and a whimper escapes from my lips.

I knew what he would find. My panties are soaked. If he continued this torture for much longer, I think my own arousal would be running down my legs.

"This is mine." He rubs the pad of his thumb over the fabric, stroking my throbbing clit. I pant in response. It's all I have the presence of mind to do. "To do what I want with." He slides his thumb under the fabric, stroking me, spreading my wetness everywhere. "Whenever I want…with whoever I want. I'm going to share you. All of you." My eyes dart to his in surprise and he stops rubbing me.

"What?" I'm not even sure what I'm questioning more. That his hand left my panties or he's going to share me. Maybe I misunderstood.

He straightens my panties and pulls his hand from under my skirt, bringing his fingers to his mouth. He hums and closes his eyes as he savors my taste, then pushes off the wall, leaving me there needy and confused as he walks into his home. I'm left there standing in the foyer in complete and utter shock.

"Beautiful, isn't it?" Micah's question snaps me out of the memory. He nods at the grand entryway of the hotel. It's decorated for Christmas. Classic. Whimsical. It's like being dropped into a Hallmark movie with the shimmery lights, vibrant green pine, and red velvet bows. The hotel is Graham's. He owns the chain and is rich as sin. "Elena arranged all of this. She mentioned it at lunch today. She didn't give herself enough credit." I search the room as casually as I can, trying to remember which one she is. "Tan coat. Brown wavy hair." He nods his head in her direction. Micah can read me like a book.

"You haven't asked for any of their numbers yet. I think if you got to know them, you'd like them. Most of them, anyway." He looks down at me, a small smile tugging at his lips.

I can't help but to smile up at him, but I purposely give him no verbal response. This life is still new to me and seeking any of the women or the men out just feels strange. The day after Introduction Night, the men came to visit me. Before they left, they put their contact information into my phone. I was expected to call them any time I wanted to see them. Or even if I just wanted to talk. Just like I would in any other ordinary relationship.

I hadn't called any of them because it felt like cheating to me. I knew if I called one of them, they would let Micah know. They let Micah know everything. It was one of their rules. No secrets among the men. If I were to ask any of them to meet up, they would check with Micah first. Micah had the ultimate say. And not only did Micah decide if I could see one of them, he also got to decide if we would be intimate including to what extent. I had to admit, there was something about Micah pulling the strings that was kind of hot. I never knew what was on the menu sexually. Of course, I could ask for what I wanted but even then, I was still at the mercy of the men.

If I called one of them, I didn't think I could look Micah in the eyes at night. I would feel like I had done something wrong. Because the belief system I had grown up with until about four months ago said you're with one man and one man only. Not a dozen.

But Micah wasn't talking about the men. He was talking about the women. To get to the women I would have to go through the men. I'd have to ask one of them for their girlfriend's phone number or ask them to give her mine. Either way, becoming friends with the women in this group is a process. The men are insanely protective of us. But our everyday partner takes protective measures to no end. I've never felt so safe and honored in all my life.

I can still hear the authority in Micah's words when we were drafting my agreement. *We work in the city. You still live in the city. Tell me something. Would you just leave the most important thing to you on a park bench for twelve hours and hope that it's still there when you return in the same condition you left it in? That one thing that is so important if it were damaged or stolen it would turn your whole world upside down and positively wreck it?*

This was Micah's opening and closing argument the night I began drafting my agreement to enter a relationship with him and his friends.

Micah and I spent an entire weekend ironing out the details of our relationship after I had agreed to this lifestyle. It was so hard for me to concentrate that Friday night as he leisurely paced back and forth in his formal dining room, crystal glass of whiskey in hand, dress shirt sleeves rolled up to reveal his tan corded forearms. He was doing his lawyer thing. It was like he was dropped from the set of a television show but better. Because he was real, and he wanted me. I had no defense. So, I shook my head, knowing he had won this round.

*Neither will I. When you are out in the city, you will be accompanied by me, one of my friends or your security detail. This is non-negotiable.*

So, I conceded. Any man would be a fool to try and harm me next to one of these men. They're huge. Tall. Muscled. Handsome. And completely menacing if pissed off.

I saw Braden grab a guy by the collar and shove him against the wall once because he made a lewd comment about Linea in passing. Micah calmly moved Linea and I out of the way, walked up to the men and rattled off how much time Braden would get if he cleaned the guy's clock. Not to mention jeopardizing his medical license. All the guys are sweethearts but there is one thing they will not allow. Do not disrespect their women.

So, every morning when I leave for work, I am, much to my irritation, escorted by my security detail. I try to think of him as a quiet friend. Or my driver. Even though my upbringing was such that I would never have had a driver much less security following me.

Micah literally pays a man to hand me off to at the start of each day and then hand me back to one of them at the end of each day. I wonder if the other men do the same thing with their girl. But that would require me to reach out to one of them and in all honesty, I'm not sure what I would even say.

"Pick one. Any one of them within the next week." Micah wasn't asking. He stood in front of me now, unbuttoning my dress coat, his signature ring as a brotherhood member shining in the light of the lobby. He was gently nudging me forward. I knew why. I was alienating myself. He wanted me to be a real part of their family and the more I fought some aspects of our lifestyle the harder it would be to assimilate. When I don't answer, he puts two fingers under my chin and tilts my head up to meet his gaze in the way that has become customary to us. Micah lets nothing he says go unacknowledged.

"Okay." Even I could hear how meek I sounded. He laughs in response, exchanging my coat for a ticket.

I'm at his mercy. I love how he loves me. How he knows what my body needs even if I don't or am too ashamed to admit it. I love how he controls me. And I know that sounds fucked up, but I do. He sets my heart on fire and makes me never want to leave him. And when he tells me he loves me, it's not just a habit. I feel that he means it in every fiber of his being. And what's crazier is that I mean it too. I fucking love him. I love him for this life he's let me experience and for every dominating thing about him. He twists me inside out and takes care of me until I fully submit to his will. Because he is all powerful Micah. His name literally means *who is like God,* and I gladly worship him every day because he worships me in return.

"They're women. They won't bite", he says, turning back to me, sliding the ticket into his breast pocket. He bends down and brushes his lips against mine.

"Beautiful." The way he looks at me when he straightens makes my heart stutter. Not only because he looks absolutely divine in his suit, but this man adores me, like no one ever has. He places his hand on the small of my back, guiding me to the doors of the hall the men have taken over. That warm strong hand makes my core ache for him in the most unnatural way. But I can't help it. It's my body's involuntary response to him.

When we step through the doors I'm stunned. The place looks like a living room in a Norman Rockwell painting. It's adorned with all the traditional Christmas trimmings. Wreaths, bows, Christmas trees, platters of cookies on coffee tables in front of plaid covered sofas and chairs, stockings, fireplaces... Wow. Just...wow. Actual candles light the room with the exception of the chandelier hanging from the ceiling. Off to the side is the dining table, set as if we were royalty.

Micah passes me a glass of champagne and I look up at him with that love-struck look that I can tell melts his heart. Because he *loves* me.

"You like it?" He wears his sly smile, and I answer *yeah* and take a sip from the champagne.

Who wouldn't like this? I've been dressed in the most stunning holiday gown that's the most beautiful shade of fir green. It's something I would have never had the courage to select for myself. It's like a walking peep show, which I suspect is the reason Micah selected it. Except that if I hold completely still, I'm covered. But the moment I move I become an advertisement for sex.

The satin fabric cuffs around my neck and the back is completely open. The back is cut so low I wasn't sure the panties Micah provided would be covered by the fabric. But Micah is precise. They fit without so much as a thread showing. The skirt has slits up the sides. They are indecently high but remain closed if I stand straight and perfectly still. The front of the gown has a slit in the fabric that starts at the collar and ends at my waistline.

The sleeves have a similar cuff as the neck but are closed at my wrists with a delicate gemstone clasp. The sleeves also have slits up them. There is no area of my body that isn't accessible.

I'm an average height, but the shoes Micah selected, a gold satin strappy heel, almost make us equals in the height category.

I scan the room, taking in the men who have now rid themselves of their coats. All in black suits, even spread out with drinks in hand, I can feel their command over us. They don't show it though. To the wait staff, they look like a bunch of wealthy men having a nice night out. And that would be true. But what the wait staff doesn't realize is that they own us. We've all made a commitment and we're theirs until one of us wants out, which hasn't happened. Over six years and no one has bailed. Impressive.

Micah brings me back to him, tilting his head to the mock living room, signaling that he'd like time with me there. It looks like no one is over there, but I know Micah has something slightly devious up his sleeve.

He guides me to the couch, takes my glass and sets it on the coffee table motioning for me to sit. He sits beside me and drapes an arm around my shoulders as we watch the fire in the fireplace dance in front of us. His fingertips stroke the bare skin on my arm lazily and I relax at his touch and his heavenly scent.

My heart skips a beat as Braden enters the living room. Alone. He looks stunning as well. The opposite of Micah, he has beautiful brown eyes and blonde hair. He smiles at us, showing off a predominant dimple in each cheek. After shaking Micah's hand, he has a seat next to me.

"Hey Sweet Hadley." He leans in and gives me a brief kiss on the lips and settles his hand on my bare leg. Micah's arm is draped over my shoulders once more, paying no attention to Braden's advance.

This is one of the fundamentals of our relationship that I can't seem to wrap my head around. Micah just let his friend kiss me and touch my bare leg. He is okay with this. If this would have been any other man I had been with before Micah, punches would be thrown, and I can guarantee an argument would have followed between us about it not being okay that I let another man touch me. But to these men, me letting them touch me is expected.

I'm hyper aware of them and what this situation could mean for me. One of my hard limits is no sex in front of others. I have a feeling they want something in this living room and that this living room was designed for all of us to have fun in at some point during the evening.

"Rough day?" Braden turns towards me. He must have felt me stiffen slightly. I didn't think my angst was obvious but then again, that's why they call me Sweet Hadley. Because I am sweet. Everything about me is kind.

"No. Long. How was your day?" Perhaps if I distract them with conversation this will turn into nothing more than a few touches and a kiss here or there. It has to. Hard limits are hard limits. And one of my hard limits is that I will not have sex in front of the women. That's why the agreements exist. I have Micah's and all twelve men have mine. Like the twelve rules, the agreement is non-negotiable unless I make changes to it.

"Busy." Braden's hand moves up my thigh and when I start to protest, he interrupts me. "Relax. No one is coming over here and no one can see us."

I glance down at his lap. His erection is huge. His unbuttoned jacket allows me an unobstructed view of him straining against his pants. I look to Micah for help. He gives me a lazy smile, shifts in his seat, and presses his lips to mine. And just like that, I lose the fight against them.

Maybe the word fight is a poor choice of words. There is nothing they're doing that I don't want them to do. But doing this in an area where anyone could walk in here unannounced makes me nervous.

When I shift in my seat to kiss Micah more comfortably, my legs part and Braden's hand slides between them. I moan as Braden's fingers find my sweet spot. The thing is, Micah and I had sex earlier this morning, but it wasn't enough. I wanted to spend the day in bed with him. I wanted to skip right to Sunday, where we have a lazy day planned together at his house. I think clothing is optional. I want to spend the day pleasing each other on every surface in his house.

I was keyed up and chasing an orgasm. I needed this. It would help me relax and I desperately needed to relax. I know they won't violate my hard limit. I remind myself that I'm safe.

Micah breaks the kiss and drops his hand to my thigh, spreading my legs further apart for Braden. "Stop fighting it, Hadley Joanna."

He used my nickname. My middle name is not Joanna, but that's a story for another day. I wanted this but deep down inside it still felt so wrong. Micah's letting his friend get me off and he's loving every minute of it.

"Feel this. Didn't you take care of her this morning?" Braden was being cute. He knows Micah and I start and end every day with sex. I can't think of one day where that's been different, and I hope it never is. Micah laughs and takes Braden's place.

"She was very well taken care of. Weren't you, Hadley?" His fingers stroke me under my panties. "She's always had a hungry little pussy." My breath hitches at his dirty words and how he strokes me. "Is your pussy still hungry Hadley?"

"Oh god." It comes out as a moan. His touch and his dirty words are enough to send me over the edge. Micah slips his fingers from my panties.

"Finish her off. Then I'm going to fuck her." My head whips to Micah and he captures my mouth with his while Braden's hand takes his place between my legs. Micah isn't giving me time to think. He kisses me relentlessly as Braden strokes me and I fall apart between them.

As if nothing happened, Braden adjusts my panties and hands Micah a key card. Braden doesn't bother adjusting his hard on. He simply buttons up his suit coat and leaves the living room.

Micah stands and holds his hand out to me. I pause. Everyone will see us leave. They'll know what we're up to. Micah cocks his head to the side, steeling his gaze at me in challenge. I am to obey unless I have a good reason not to. Being concerned others will notice our exit is not a good reason.

"Good girl", he praises me when I take his hand and rise from the couch. When I look back at the group as we make our exit, I note Jonathan and Grace moving into the living room in our place. "Looks like I'll have to work to keep you focused tonight." My head snaps back to Micah and my mouth falls open at the devious smile on his lips. I've just poked the bear.

Graham's office isn't far from the dining hall. He owns The Lux and is hosting this holiday celebration for us. Micah pockets the key card after swiping us in, shuts the door behind him and wastes no time hoisting me up against the wall.

"I'm going to fuck you harder than I've ever fucked a woman in my life. And when I'm done, you're going to thank Braden for getting you ready for me." He waits a moment in case I'm going to speak up to refuse and then he wastes no more time, taking me hard. I burry my head in his neck to muffle my cries. Micah is a big guy. I thought I'd never get used to his size. But now I love it. He's always been careful with me and has never taken me like this. I think I can feel him in my throat he's going so deep.

"Fuck! You feel so...Hadley. Are you going to come?" He continues slamming into me not so much as breaking a sweat, sounding in awe of my body's response to him. I can't answer. I just burry my face in his neck and bite him as I convulse on his length.

I just bit someone. I had never done that before. I must have lost my mind. He doesn't seem to mind because he answers my indiscretion with a groan as he releases inside of me. He holds me there for a moment, waiting for me to unbury my face from his neck. His ice blue eyes bore into mine and my breath stutters in response.

He withdraws himself from me and gently puts me on my feet, not bothering to tuck himself back in, which I note as odd. Instead, he slides my panties back in place, leaving his cum right where he deposited it. Then he smooths my dress back down as if nothing had happened and gives me a brief kiss on the lips. He leans forward and whispers in my ear, "Anyone who wants you tonight will have to smell me on you first." Fuck that's hot. He just marked me as his, even though he knew it would deter none of them from having me if that's what they really wanted. I knew he had given them all permission based on his comment. The thought of any of them having me tonight made me nervous and excited at the same time. There wasn't a bad lover among them.

Micah's steamy demeanor changes as he pulls back to look in my eyes. "I love you Hadley. You know that don't you? My heart belongs to you like it has never belonged to anyone before." He looks so sincere. No different than any other time he's declared his love for me. I nod and he kisses me long and hard.

"I'm going to get cleaned up while you thank Braden." I know what he means. Give Braden head. And I'm good with that. He's a perceptive lover and to be honest, it's no chore. I have no idea what the man's diet consists of, but he tastes great.

That's also a difference between my past and present lovers. I dreaded swallowing. I dreaded giving head altogether. But not with these men. Besides, it's a rule. We are expected to take everything they give us. I believe they refer to this as *fully participating*. That expectation is made very clear on Introduction Night. Just thinking of them lining up for me to service them gets me excited to have Braden in my mouth.

When Micah moves out of my way, I see Braden standing across the room, waiting patiently for me. Some towels are folded in front of him, for me to kneel on. The bulge in his pants tells me he's ready whenever I am. I didn't even hear him come in. That's what Micah does to me. He consumes me.

My gaze shifts to Linea who is kneeling on a similar set of towels roughly an arm's length away from Braden. Realization and panic slam into me as I watch Micah cross the room to where Linea waits. I'm frozen where I am but I look to Braden for...help? He just holds his hand out to me, but I can't move. This can't really be happening.

I let out a harsh breath when Micah stands in front of Linea, a partial hard-on glistening with my arousal and his. My hand is already covering my mouth when Micah asks Linea to clean him off. And as soon as her head bobs forward and ecstasy floods across Micah's features, I stumble backward.

I don't even realize Braden has crossed the room until his hand grabs mine and he's leading me to my set of towels. Micah praises Linea, looks at me and grips the back of Linea's head, moving her to a new rhythm that causes him to toss his head back and let out a groan. And I fall. The fuck. Apart.

I'm not naïve. I knew Micah would fuck whoever he wanted whenever he wanted after my Introduction Night. We discussed it. It's a fundamental part of the brotherhood. But there's a big difference between seeing and knowing. And for some reason I never thought I'd see it. Maybe I had hoped I wouldn't. Or maybe I thought I'd be the exception. That he loved me differently than he did the others. Regardless, I can't watch this.

I tug against Braden's grip as I sob, but it's child's play to him. I'm so tiny compared to Braden. Compared to all of them really. It takes him no effort to move me to a chair in the corner that gives me a perfect view of Linea giving Micah head. No amount of struggling will free me. He has me in a backwards bear hug, holding me there to watch. I sink against Braden, breaking more and more with every passing second.

Micah moans her name. I should close my eyes. But I don't. Closing my eyes won't escape the sound of Micah's pleasure and the sound of her slobbering all over his cock. I cry the words *let me go*. Never in my life have I sounded so wounded and heartbroken. I'd beg Braden if I thought it would help.

"Almost done, Hadley.  Linea sucks cock like a pro." Braden sounds so reassuring. I imagine him talking with his patients in this tone when he's doing something that causes pain or discomfort to them. I cry harder. "Shh, shh, shh, shh. Breath Hadley. Just breath. Look at how good this makes Micah feel. What he's doing isn't about you sweetheart. You have to remember that." I struggle harder in his arms and then I hear Micah.

"Oh, honey. Swallow every drop for me", Micah carefully reminds Linea. He stills her head shoving farther into her mouth and releases into her with a groan. Even from across the room I can see his thick cock pulsing with his release. She gags a little, and Micah reaches down to wipe a tear from her cheek. That's what he does to me too.  The gesture is so loving even though it's paired with something so dirty, I secretly wish he'd gag me every time.

Linea bobs up and down on his cock a few more times, her hand milking every last drop from him. And when he's satisfied, she says, "All clean, Micah." Her voice is so innocent. Like she just finished wiping down the kitchen counter for him.

"Thank you." He's sincere. They all are. She notices his cock dripping and licks it up. He silently praises her by laying his hand on the side of her face. She continues to catch drip after drip with her tongue until Micah is satisfied. When he's finished with her, he simply holds out his hand and helps her to her feet. After tucking himself back in, he kisses her on the lips. The kiss is sweet. A thank you of sorts. And when Micah turns to look at me, I'm crushed...and he knows it.

A new round of sobs erupts through my chest and this time when I struggle Braden releases me. I stumble at first, forgetting my heels won't exactly make it easy for me to make a quick getaway. When I recover, I rush to the door. As I exit, I hear Braden telling Micah to let me go but I pay no mind to if he's listened. My only goal is putting distance between us.

I've never been here so I have no idea where I'm going. For a fleeting second, I think about hailing a cab. But my purse and cell phone are at Micah's. I am stuck here.

When I round the corner, I'm in the restaurant that's attached with a full-service bar. It's either this or I walk home. It's December on the east coast. A fresh abundant layer of snow covers the streets. Even if I wanted to walk home I couldn't. Micah has our coat check ticket, and I don't even have keys to my home on me. They're also on Micah's kitchen counter. I was planning on staying with him for the long weekend.

Defeated, I walk up to the bar and sit, wiping my face haphazardly with the back of my hand. I have no money on me and at this point, my only prayer is that I can charge a drink to the party. The bartender is young. In his mid-twenties, I'd guess. He's dressed in standard bar wear. Black shirt, sleeves rolled up, black pants and a black apron.

"What can I get you?" I waste no time placing my order. He on the other hand takes his time filling it. He pulls out his phone, taps the screen a few times and looks me over. Then he sends a message. "It'll be a minute." He looks uncomfortable. Clearly this isn't his normal routine with patrons. He checks his phone when it buzzes and fills my order. "Enjoy", he says as he leaves the bar unattended.

The whiskey burns as I swallow a mouthful. The bartender gave me a generous pour. He must have taken one look at me and knew I needed it. I appreciate his candor. He probably figured I wouldn't be able to talk anyway. When he finally served me, I was still wiping fresh tears from my cheeks.

I sit at the bar quietly, sipping my drink and wondering how long it will take Micah to find me. I don't have anything to say to him. What's left to say, really? I just watched him get head from someone else. And it broke my heart.

I should have expected this. It was bound to happen. I just didn't think it would shatter my heart into a million pieces. I thought I was prepared for this.

I hear heals clicking behind me on the marble floor. I knew it was one of us for sure, but never expected it to be Linea. She has a lot of nerve coming after me. I can't even look at her. She makes me sick.

She sits down on the bar stool next to me and the bartender appears out of nowhere. She places her order and there's no delay. No phone checking or texting. He just fills her order and makes himself busy in the background.

We sit there in silence for a few minutes. What could she possibly have to say to me? Sorry you had to see that? Micah tastes great but you probably already know that? I know she didn't come find me to have a drink in silence together, but I can't talk. I'm too raw. Too emotional. And I don't know her well enough to care about preserving our relationship, but I also don't want to ruin any chance we have to build one. She seems like one of the nicer women. The least territorial so far. Silence will do me just fine. It's better this way.

"I know it's a lot...What we do can be a lot." She lets it hang there and I make no move to encourage her.

"I remember the first time I saw Braden with Lexi. I fell apart. Like...literally fell apart. I went full on ugly cry and then started to run up to them. I had no idea what I was planning to do but I never got the opportunity. The guys kept a watchful eye out for my reaction and the second I started to move toward Braden and Lexi they were scooping me up, despite my thrashing and screaming to be put down." She chuckles and then takes a sip of her drink. "It was silly to think I'd have a chance to do anything more than watch. Micah helped carry me off. He told me to breath and reminded me that Braden loved me. That his heart belonged to me always. And I remember looking at Braden while I was being carried off kicking and screaming. Sadness was etched all over his face for a moment. But when Lexi brought her hand up to his face, he tore his gaze away from me and slid right inside of her."

She swivels her chair towards me, and I instinctively look at her. "I have an idea of what you're going through, Hadley. I could help you if you want." She says it like she wasn't the one to help shred my heart to pieces. Movement in the distance catches my eye and I notice Braden standing against the wall, assessing if he should intervene. I look back at Linea and then flag the bartender down for another. I'm emotionally spent. She'll get no response from me. I won't even waste the effort.

"They do it on purpose. This isn't a life anyone is brought up in. Certainly not women. They help guide us through what it means to be with them as best they can. I get the feeling they strategize about it sometimes. It's different for all of us. Why mine was public and yours wasn't I'll never know. But it won't be the last time he'll test you because he needs to get you to feel comfortable with the lifestyle. With all of us."

I listen as I watch the bartender pull out his phone once more, taking longer to fill my drink. What the fuck is this guy's problem? When he finally serves me, I thank him because I'm not so broken, I can't be polite. I also want him to keep giving me alcohol.

I sit there, staring out the window, watching the snow swirl around in the glow of the streetlights. Linea had left. I heard the click of her heals retreating. I assumed Braden had left as well.

I had finally stopped crying when I heard familiar footsteps come my way. And then smelled the mixture of cologne and shampoo that make up Micah's delectable scent. I reach for my glass of whiskey but have to set it down. My hand shakes so badly from the heartbreak and rage that boils inside of me I couldn't take a drink on my own if I tried.

Micah takes the seat Linea vacated. I can't even look at him. He grabs my glass and brings it to my lips, tilting it so I can get a drink. This is exactly how he is...how they all are. They break you and then put you back together. And every single one of us comes running back like we have amnesia. Because it's that fucking good.

But this time I'm not so sure. This time feels different than the others. This time feels like disrespect. Betrayal even. We'll never be the same. He'll never be the same to me. And I realize I'm out of my league. Too strait laced to play with the big boys. So why do I still need a fix? Why do I want him to fix this? A part of me feels like I died back there. And I desperately want him to make it better.

He raises the glass to my lips once more and the damn breaks open. My whole-body shakes as I sob, barely even able to take a drink. He stands and shrugs off his jacket, telling the bartender to close off the room. Then he swivels me around, lifts me out of my chair and settles me on his lap.

I take one look at him and bury my face into his chest to cover up the sound of my sobs. I don't know why I'm seeking comfort from the man who broke my heart. It doesn't make sense. But I desperately want him to fix this. He says nothing, one hand steadying me on his lap and the other stroking my back. When I'm spent, I sit up straight, pulling myself out of the cocoon he created for me. He takes a napkin and dabs at my face, looking calm and sure of himself as always.

"Why?" I couldn't get out anything else. It was such a broad question? Why her? Why here? Why in front of me? Why? Why? Why? Why? Why?

Before he answers me, he holds my drink up for me to take a sip. I'm grateful for it. In fact, I want more. But when I grab for the glass, Micah pulls it out of my reach and simply shakes his head. "I'll do it for you." He gives me one more sip before answering my question.

"Now, tell me why we have the agreements? Who are they for?" He's doing his lawyer thing. Answering my question with a question to lead me down the right path.

"The person writing the agreement", I whisper.

"Tell me why", he gently coaxes me along, breaking this down for me into easily digestible parts.

"So we don't change ourselves for anyone else." I look at the glass tumbler and he allows me to have another sip.

"That's right. People change for others and the point of the agreement is to clearly outline what you want and your intentions, for yourself and no one else." He takes a sip of his own drink and shifts me on his lap so he can get a better look at me. "What I did with Linea, in front of you, is in my agreement, which you have your own copy of. I'm not sneaking around. If I want to fuck one of my girlfriends, I'll do it, regardless of who is watching...unless it violates her agreement. Linea has no limits. Her agreement is blank, with the exception of the standard language all of you have in your agreements. And nothing I did today, violates your agreement." He runs his fingertips down my bare shoulder, and I shiver. I love how he touches me, but I'm not sure if the shiver is because of his touch or finding out Linea has no limits.

I cannot even imagine what allowing anything to be done to me would feel like. Why would someone want that?

"Linea sucking my cock...is that the precise thing that bothered you?" He asks me the question gently, like he's trying to coax something out of me to teach me a lesson. I shake my head. Because it isn't her. If it were any of them, I'd be this upset. "Did it seem like cheating to you? Like I was disrespecting what we have?"

I had to think about this for a moment. I knew him having sex with the other girls without hiding it was in his agreement, so it's not like this is a surprise to me. He wasn't hiding anything. And while I don't have the other guy's agreements, it wouldn't surprise me if all of them had this little detail in theirs as well. No. No, it did not. He wasn't rubbing it in, he was just getting his cock sucked. And he had asked me to suck Braden's, which is who Linea belongs to.

"You looked...like you were in heaven." He looked like he was getting relief. So relaxed. Like this was common between the two of them.

Micah laughs. Tears well up in my eyes because it's not funny. Not to me.

"Oh sweetheart, I was." I look away but he won't allow it. He gently grabs my chin and turns my face to him, wiping yet another tear away without a second thought.

"The way you looked at her. Like, you were cherishing her. She was the most important thing in your world." It was hard to even get the words out because it hurt so badly. He nods in understanding.

"How do you feel when you're with Jonathan, Tyler, Graham...any of them? Do you think they're just filling a quota? Checking a box? Or do you feel as though they truly care for you like I do?" He gives me another sip of my drink while I think about this. And I hate that he's right. I've never once felt like they were obligated to see me or just going through the motions.

"No. But it still doesn't make it feel any better. Why did I have to see it?" I sob again, not bothering to wipe this fresh stream of tears. "I mean, I know that you're with them." I pause to suck in a few rapid breaths before sobbing loudly once more. "And after time without you I decided that I could accept I wasn't the only one. I just never thought you'd show me. I need...to go home. I can't be here. I can't look at you. And I certainly can't go back in there and pretend everything is okay. Because it's not. I'm calling Steven. He can take me home. Can you get my coat?" He nods and I slide off his lap, spotting a ladies' room in the corner that I can take refuge in. Without a word, I turn and walk away from him. Normally I'd show him some affection. It's customary with us. But now...I can't bring myself to pretend...especially with him.

I'm the only one in the ladies' room. That's what happens when your big shot boyfriend closes a hotel bar. You get the whole place to yourself. I was thankful for it. Looking back at myself in the large mirror, I note Micah did a nice job of cleaning my face. My eyes are still red, making my green eyes even more brilliant. A few pieces of hair from my updo had come undone during my struggle with Braden. I removed the clip and the few pins that held my fiery red hair in place and watched it fall in waves, down my shoulders. I note that Micah loves my hair down. I should have worn it down tonight.

Turning this way and that in front of the mirror, I wonder why Micah chose me. I don't have big, beautiful breasts or a big plump behind. I'm just...average. An average, slender redhead. Nothing to see here folks. Just a young woman, crying over something that she shouldn't be surprised about. A laugh escapes me at the observation. This is such an unusual situation yet such a usual reaction to dating. Relationships suck sometimes.

A knock on the door startles me and without warning, Micah walks into the ladies' room. I am stunned that he would just waltz into such a sacred female space, but then I remember, we're the only people at the bar.

He's wearing his dress coat with his scarf draped around his neck, holding my coat out for me to slip into.

"What are you doing?" I'd like to think he misunderstood, but he didn't. Micah does what he wants without apology. All twelve of them do.

He sets my purse down on a nearby table and holds my coat out so I can put my arms through. I consider yanking my coat from him and putting it on myself, but I don't. Because despite my anger, I like the chivalry. He's never treated me any different. Even the moment I met him he was a perfect gentleman.

"You're coming home with me. Steven has the night off." I doubt it makes one bit of difference whether Steven is on call tonight. He hands me my purse and adds that this isn't a discussion. Normally when he says things like that, I find it wildly attractive. Now? I want to punch him in the face.

"You're unbelievable." I walk out the bathroom, leaving him on my heals. I don't care that it's disrespectful and I don't care that he's probably seething. Good. I hope he is. I want to piss him off. To break that calm exterior.

# Chapter 2
# Micah

**Over 6 years ago**

"God damn Braden. How high are you?" I've been here a total of ten minutes and can't believe what I'm hearing.

"I'd do it", Tyler volunteers.

"Why not", Jonathan chimes in.

"Are you all high?" They nod in unison and hand me the joint. "There is no woman on this planet that will agree to that. You know that, right? They want marriage", I tell my best friends, almost gagging on the word.

Divorce is one of the few cases I won't litigate because my personal belief is that marriage is useless. Find someone you think loves you for who you are, and you don't have to take them for half their assets when you find out they don't in fact love you for who you are.

I take a drag on the joint, reveling in the immediate peace it brings, but when I open my eyes, my three best friends are staring at me.

"Bullshit", Jonathan tells me, taking a long pull from his bottle of beer.

I take another drag, not in the mood for his scrutiny. Jonathan and I are nothing alike. He'd try anything once where I'd look at it from one hundred different angles before I made a decision.

"You're telling me that if we found women that were willing to fuck any of us, you wouldn't do it?" He pauses to let me answer. I do not answer. "That's what I fucking thought. So, what we do is we find the most beautiful women with questionable morals that want to get laid."

"No. Jon. C'mon", Braden cuts in. "No questionable morals. I don't want someone who's easy. I want someone who's right. You know...the marrying type but without the marrying?"

"You are really high, aren't you? There's no way a woman is going to hook up with four men. Women are programmed to marry and have babies. Don't they teach you psych in med school?" I grab a slice of pepperoni pizza with one hand and undo my tie with the other.

"Women sleep with me all the time", Jonathan volunteers.

"It doesn't count if you pay them." He shrugs and takes another hit from the joint.

Jonathan is a trauma surgeon. He spent his youth studying medicine and as a practical means to sex, decided to pay escorts to help him "focus". It's fine, I guess. I'm not going to judge him. But because of Jonathan's dating history, he can't exactly claim he dates. In fact, I don't think he's ever had a girlfriend...at least since I've known him.

"How much worse could it be? I mean...I can't stay with one woman", Braden declares, unnecessarily.

We've been friends since college, which is almost a decade ago. He hasn't had one relationship that has worked and most of the time, it's because he can't date one woman at a time.

"I'm fuckin' busy", Tyler interjects. "A rotation seems easier. Plus, she'd never get bored. Well, she might if she were with Micah." Tyler and Jonathan laugh at his jab.

"You think I'm boring?" I'm not mad. Just curious.

"All I'm saying is you should live a little. Everything isn't an opportunity to get sued."

Tyler is right. Everything isn't an opportunity to get sued. But he of all people knows I'm not boring. I get plenty of women who hit on me. Plenty of sex. Plenty of requests for more sex. I just won't go out with the same woman twice. Nobody gets tricked. Everyone agrees. But the problem is that after one night, women think they can change my level of commitment which is absolutely nothing.

"I didn't say I wouldn't participate. I said I don't think you'd find a woman to participate. Also, I'm not even sure I'd want to be in a regular relationship with a rotation of women. Sharing or not sharing, it's still a commitment of some kind."

"That's why I pay for it. I don't have time just like Tyler, but I also never think of it. Like, I never look at a woman and think...*wouldn't she be great to settle down with? To be the only person I ever sink my cock into for the rest of my life*?"

This time, we all laugh. Braden's the romantic of the group and even he has never thought those things. In fact, he's the worst of the three of us. He looks at these women all dreamy and these women start doodling their names on their notebooks only using his last name instead of hers. And the minute things start to get serious, Braden cuts it off or starts fucking some other woman.

"Alright. So, what I hear you all saying is that you're in?" Braden scans the room. He's serious about this plan.

"Yeah man. Sounds like a solid idea", Tyler commits to the group.

"Why the hell not", Jonathan agrees, the most relaxed out of all of us would never pass up an opportunity for pussy.

"Micah?" My best friend zeros in on me from across Jonathan's living room.

"I'll tell you what…if you find a woman willing to date all four of us at the same time, I'll organize the whole God damned thing."

# Chapter 3
# Hadley

**June 6th**
(6 Months Earlier)

"I'm sorry. I have plans tomorrow", I tell my boss, even though I don't. It's an unusual day that I've gotten out early from work on a Friday, however, I cannot seem to escape work regardless of how hard I try. In about five minutes, I'll be having drinks with Madison, my best friend since grade school, so I won't care about requests from inappropriate clients or eager to please bosses.

"He'll pay you double", my boss counters, trying to entice me. And although I could use the extra money, there is no price worth paying for my dignity. Out of all my clients, this one has the most accidental brushes and touches. He's asked me to dinner. He's asked me about genital massage and the benefits to which I told him about the place down the street and that they would probably do it for him, but we don't do that kind of work here and in professional massage school, they don't teach that. He is undeterred.

"I'm sorry. I simply cannot come in tomorrow."

"Hadley", my boss starts to protest but I don't allow it.

"He's a creep. You're lucky I'll still work on him. I have to go. Have a good weekend."

Downtown is officially alive and the nine to fiver's are officially off work. The streets are crowded, traffic is starting to get backed up and the smell of pizza and fried food waft through the air with each footstep I take to my destination, Bottles & Bites.

Madison insisted we meet at the new restaurant and bar earlier this week and I'd be lying if I said the idea didn't sound appealing. I work five days a week and occasionally on the weekends as a massage therapist.

My reputation precedes me, which is why I get a lot of requests to work longer or add an extra shift. It's flattering but exhausting. I like what I do. It's physical and relaxing but the best part is that I totally make someone's day. Well, most people's day. Clearly, I don't provide *those* kinds of services. In fact, I try to avoid talking about my occupation altogether. It's the first thing that crosses a man's mind when I tell them. Truthfully, there hasn't been one man I've even considered doing *that* for.

My parents thought I'd be something more prominent. When I announced I wasn't going to college after graduation but was going to massage school, I thought my dad was going to have a stroke. And I get it. His beautiful young daughter touching all over strange men?

Even though my job is nothing like my dad's worst fears, he still isn't a fan. He puts my line of work right up there with grocery bagger or grounds keeper. His daughter was supposed to make more of herself. That's how he and mom raised me according to him.

I do alright. I make a modest living but it's my modest living and I like it. I'm twenty-four and I own a house. I have enough money to feed and clothe myself. And I still have money left over to save and go out on occasion. So tonight, I'm going to relax and have fun. Mostly because I deserve it but also because I don't teach at the massage school tomorrow.

You would think teaching would bump me up higher on my dad's list of responsible occupations but as it turns out, to him, teaching someone to do a job less than I should be doing is also not how he raised me. I stifle an eye roll before opening the door to the new restaurant.

I had heard this was the new hip place in town to go, but I wasn't prepared for the sheer volume of patrons at this early hour on a Friday. It was exactly five o'clock and the place was packed. I had hoped to snag us a table, but there's no way that's going to happen.

There's standing room only and I feel like I could suffocate in this space. What does one who comes alone even do in this situation? There's no room at the bar. No tables. I have no one to talk to and am not looking to pick up a guy tonight so chatting someone up is not going to happen.

But I understand why it's so busy. It smells fantastic in here. Not like regular bar food fair, but like grilled meat and meticulously prepared dishes with fresh herbs and lots of butter. What I wouldn't give for a plate of food like that right now. I'm starving. Skipping lunch to take an extra client will do that.

As my eyes wander, looking for the slightest hint that someone is planning to vacate their table or bar stool, I lock eyes with the most beautiful man I have ever seen in my life. He's tall, thin but muscular, has dark hair, is wearing a white button-down dress shirt with the sleeves rolled up and collar undone and has the most kissable mouth I'll never consider kissing.

That's right. I can't. He's a bartender. Bartenders look for a quick hookup. I'm just not interested. The truth is, I've barely had sex. Mostly because it's been awful. Unskilled. Selfish. Thoughtless sex. And I know I shouldn't be so picky because let's face it...I don't have the job or the education to demand a millionaire, but I can't imagine myself sharing my body with someone over and over again who takes it for granted and uses it for their own pleasure alone. And that guy behind the bar is no exception. In fact, he's the worst kind of guy. The kind of guy you have a one-night stand with and never see again. The kind of guy who makes up some lame excuse about the gym or some vague early morning commitment to get you out of his house.

I can't be here right now because I need Madison as a buffer. Between the two of us she's the one who engages in conversation with random people on the street. Not me. I'm the introvert. She's the extrovert. *This was a mistake.* I turn around, heading for the exit. Only making it half-way into the establishment, I start to jockey my way through the crowd back to the door. That guy will be my undoing. Just the way his lips tilted up in a half smile, he knows he has me. And if I spend any amount of time with him, I won't leave with my dignity intact. He's too good looking and if he's a bartender, he knows how to play people.

I'm not sure if people are too into their conversations to notice me trying to move through the crowd to get to the door or if they just don't care, but getting out of this place literally takes me placing a hand on each human obstacle in front of me to get them to notice I need through. Most of them are men looking for a quick hookup themselves. How can I tell? The attention I get with each touch is unwanted. A suggestive smile and then elevator eyes. It's funny how I feel more disgusted by these stranger's looks than I did Rico Suave's behind the bar.

And then time stops. Not literally. But you know those old movies where there's a record scratch or some sound or event that happens and the screen freezes? Yeah. That happened. The whistle equivalent to how one would call a dog pierces through the room, silencing the patrons immediately.

I pause. Why did I pause? Because that's why the sound was made. To get absolute attention. Mission accomplished owner of said piercing whistle.

"Stop that beautiful red-haired woman heading for the exit." That masculine voice...a voice of pure power. I'm not hard to find. Redheads aren't a dime a dozen so it's very obvious who the owner of the voice is referring to. A few men stand in front of me with what looks like no intention to move, as I weigh my options. Everyone is staring and I realize I'm holding my breath. Because I know who that authoritative, masculine voice belongs to now, and I also know the choice to spend any amount of time with him will lead to heartbreak. "Turn around."

A shiver runs through my body as I slowly turn on my heel and swallow hard, noting how the patrons are parting on cue, so the bartender and I have a clear view of each other. He's even more gorgeous than I gave him credit for. I want to walk right over and just stare at him...but I also don't. Men like that know women think they look good. Men like that know how to manipulate women.

He looks at the man sitting in front of him. I can hear his deep voice murmur something to patron about a stool and a tab. The bartender extends his hand to the man, they shake hands in that firm way confident, strong men do. No actual pumping of the arm up and down but a firm grip, holding onto the other's hand, exchanging a brief smile or a few words. The man grabs his drink and gets up. When the bartender meets my gaze, he points down at the chair.

It's not a suggestion. It's a silent order. And I'm stunned.

The restaurant is still quiet, patiently waiting for my next move. I'm the girl that's in the background, not on stage. And right now, everyone is watching me. They're invested in my decision.

I shouldn't take that seat. It's like walking up to a lion and knowing you're going to get eaten. So I stand there, my gaze shifting from the chair to the bartender in contemplation. But when my eyes meet his again, his brows are raised in challenge and once he sees I'm still not moving forward, he pulls the towel down from his shoulder, places it on the counter and exits the bar.

With each step he takes, I can feel all reason leave me. Because if I thought he looked good behind the bar, he looks so much better from head to toe.

His slacks are perfectly tailored. And when I say perfect, I do mean perfect. His slim waist is accentuated with what looks like a very expensive leather belt. The dark fabric covering his muscular thighs is rich and expensive looking. For a moment, I wonder what it would be like to be one of those massage therapists who had questionable morals. What the fabric of those pants would feel like under my fingertips as I knelt in front of him, fully clothed while he fucked my mouth mercilessly. Those are the pants of a powerful man. Not a bartender. And his shoes give it all away. Probably more expensive than his pants by far. Shined to perfection. Each measured step he takes toward me, carries a weight and cadence that my mind will never be able to forget.

In some twisted way, I want to hear those footsteps come up to me without seeing him. God the anticipation of what a man like that could do to a woman like me. I smirk at him, and he cocks his head. *A woman like me.* I muse to myself. A woman who hasn't seen pleasure and a woman who doesn't exactly know how to give it. A man like him, and a woman like me would be fire and ice. Oil and water. Gasoline and matches.

When he reaches me, I have to tilt my head up because even in heels, he's tall. A brute of a man. And looking into those grey crystalline eyes causes me to swallow hard with fear. I don't fear him personally. No. He doesn't seem like a serial killer or anyone that would intentionally harm someone. I swallow hard because I know I'm done for. The big bad wolf is standing in front of me. And he's going to eat me right up.

He smiles and I clutch my wallet. His beautiful smile hits me in the heart, and I know this is my last chance to get the hell out of here before I'm no longer thinking clearly. Before I become Hadley, the love-drunk idiot who believes every word that comes from this man's mouth regardless of the evidence staring me right in the face.

The God in front of me extends his hand and without another thought, I place my hand in his. Game. Over.

He smiles because he knows he has me and that irks the hell out of me. But I also don't pull back. I relish in the feel of his warm firm skin against mine. How strong his hand is and the possibilities of everything he could do to me...everything he could make me do to him.

Once we're a few steps in, the bar erupts with clapping, hooting and hollering. Mr. Bartender doesn't react. He simply looks down at me and gives me a small smile at the way my skin has heated from the attention, no doubt. I'm not used to being called out in a public space. Attention embarrasses me.

Once he has me at my stool, he quickly rounds the bar and turns his attention on me.

"What can I get for you..." He drags out *you*, waiting for me to give my name.

"Joanna." I lied. I shouldn't have done it, but I did. My lie was a means of protection. He was jaw-droppingly gorgeous with his high cheekbones and eyes that looked like they could be equally as wicked as they could be kind. And I knew he wasn't really a bartender. My job is to read people for Christ's sake. He was something more.

"Joanna", he repeats tilting his head and narrowing his eyes just a fraction as if he could tell I was lying to him.

"I'll have an old fashion, please. Sweet", I clarify. Again, he narrows his eyes slightly, pushes away from the bar and begins to fill my request. I watch him work. He's neat. Exact. And I squirm in my seat a fraction at the thought of having him zone in on me like he is my drink order. There's no way he's like the others. I've never seen another man put so much focus and quick concentration into a single task as he is.

He slides the drink across the counter to me and waits. I smile at him and huff out a breath. He wants praise for his work. Figures. I indulge him and take a sip. I hate old fashions so it's perfect. Perfectly disgusting.

"Now, do you want to tell me what you really want to drink or are you going to sit here and choke that thing down and order another?"

"Limoncello please." He raps his knuckles on the table and offers me a beaming smile as he swipes my drink away and ceremoniously pours it down the drain.

"The truffle fries are amazing. Especially with this drink. If you're meeting someone, you could also order a bottle of champagne. That would be even better", the man offers.

"You're not a real bartender, are you?" He smiles and chuckles in response but continues making my drink. As it turns out, he's not the only one comfortable with calling people on their bullshit. "You act like a real bartender. That stunt you pulled to get my attention...what was that about?"

He simply shakes his head and presses his lips together while assembling my drink.

"It's tough being caught, isn't it. Hot bartender gets woman's attention in a crowded bar..."

"Restaurant bar", he interrupts me, giving me a stern look as if it matters.

"The point is, I'm on to you. And your charms won't work on me. So whatever you thought you were getting from me, forget it. I'm not interested." God was I interested. I'd kill to have his naked body on top of mine. But I wasn't willing to go through the torture of it all. He was probably a liar or a douche like all the others.

"You think I'm hot", he asks with a smile as he slides my new drink to me across the shiny bar top. I glare at him and take a sip. Clearly, he missed the most important point of what I told him. When he sees my glare, he pulls his phone from his pocket, swipes the screen and begins tapping. I have no idea what this guy is trying to prove but now, I'm curious. He lays his phone down on the bar top, face up.

"Duty calls. Look...", he leans on the bar, his forearms supporting his weight so he's at eye level with me. "I don't normally quiet a bar for a woman, but for you, I'd do just about anything." He brings his hand up to his mouth and runs his thumb across his bottom lip a few times, never breaking eye contact with me. With a long exhale and him mumbling something I can't quite make out under his breath; he backs away from the bar and heads to the first patron who gets his attention.

I can't hear him, but he seems like he's enjoying himself, talking to this woman while he makes her drink. He doesn't seem like he's flirting. In fact, if I didn't know better, he seems like he's being a nice guy.

I look down at his phone and see a man's name.

**American License Registry**
**Micah A. Stevenson**
**Bartender License: B-37469**
**License Originated: 1/14/2023**
**License Valid Thru: 1/14/2026**

I look back at Micah A. Stevenson and watch him work the room. I guess the question was never whether he was a bartender. Clearly, he could make a good drink, and he knew how to connect with people. But there's no way I believe he's only a bartender.

"Oh my god, Hadley! You got a seat, and you didn't get one for me?" My body stiffens hearing Madison's voice behind me. "Jesus you're jumpy." She hugs me from behind and looks down at the phone still in my hands. "Who's Micah Stevenson?" She looks up and follows the bar straight to Micah. In that moment, Micah winks right at me and I close my eyes, shaking my head while Madison starts peppering me with questions so quickly, I can't answer one before she gets to the next.

"Is that Micah?"

"Is this his phone?"

"Wait, did he hit on you?"

"He's hot. Let me see that." She swipes his phone, and I grab it back, suddenly feeling the need to be protective of anything having to do with this alcohol God behind the counter. "Did he get you this seat?"

"Ladies." Micah seems to appear out of thin air and looks right at Madison, paying no mind that I still have his phone.

"Micah Stevenson. And you are?" He holds his hand out for Madison, and she takes it without delay.

"I'm Madison", she tells him with stars in her eyes.

"Madison. It's great to meet you." Micah looks at me as though he's considering something, and then he addresses

Madison again. "Did you know, your friend Joanna's go to drink is not an old fashioned?" He looks between us as Madison turns to me, question written all over her face while I give her a small smile that hopefully says *just go with it.*

"I did know that Joanna's favorite drink is in fact not an old fashioned", she tells us both and gives me a similar squinted look as Micah gave me while she drums her fingers on the back of my chair.

"Allow me to get you a drink and a seat, Madison." He punctuates her name as though he's calling me out on my lie and giving me one last chance to come clean.

Madison laughs and looks around. "Yeah. I'll take a French Martini but how are you getting me a seat?"

Micah holds up a finger and begins assembling Madison's drink. He uncorks a bottle of champagne with a flourish, once again calling attention in my direction. The unused bottle is set in front of me, and the French Martini is placed next to it. Micah gets the attention of the man sitting next to me.

"Sir. Want a free tab today? Give this lovely lady your seat and your drinks are on me."

"All of them? Even from the table", the guy qualifies, still in shock a bartender would pay someone for their seat.

"Tell you what. If you're a gentleman and give Madison your seat, I'll comp your drinks and your meal." The man wastes no time getting out of his seat, even pulling the chair out for Madison. I laugh at the grand display. Madison sits down in complete shock.

"Thank you", she tells Micah.

"My pleasure." Then Micah turns to me and extends his hand, palm up. I place the phone in his waiting hand, screen side up and then he walks off to serve another patron.

"Joanna", she questions me, before taking a sip of her drink.

"I work with creeps all day. And guys like him are the worst kind of creep. I mean come on…" I nod down to the end of the bar where a woman slips him a napkin, no doubt with her phone number on it.

"Just because he's being polite doesn't make him a creep", she says, taking another sip from her drink.

"Whose side are you on", I grumble.

"Hadley's. That girl hasn't gotten laid in over a year. So I'm on Hadley's side. And I think that hot bartender could set you straight." She gives me a knowing look and I have no argument. He could set me straight. For one night. That's all I would allow him. One night.

Micah looks over at us while he's pouring a beer. He caught me checking him out and satisfaction spreads across his gorgeous face. I blush and turn away. I'm not slick.

"Get it together Joanna. You might accidentally send him a signal you're not the ice queen."

I laugh at Madison. I'm not the ice queen. It's just that I want something genuine. I haven't found it and I'm reluctant to believe that I found it behind the bar of a busy new restaurant and bar. A server hands Micah a basket and some plates.

They exchange a few words and Micah heads down to our side of the bar. Setting the basket and plates in front of Madison and I, he rearranges our small space, so everything fits in front of us.

"Oh my God those smell amazing", Madison tells him.

"I didn't order those…", I start to object. I don't exactly have deep pockets so ordering a bunch of food and drinks tonight wasn't in my plans.

"I did. You've had a long day. We'll get into that in a moment, but first, I thought you could use something delicious to eat." He plucks a fry out of the basket and holds it up to my mouth. I take a bite of the steaming fry, and he pops the other half in his mouth. He smiles as he chews at my surprise.

"You just ate the other half of my fry", I challenge him playfully.

"I promise I'll make it up to you later", he banters back.

Madison slams her hand down on the table. "That's what I'm talking about, Hadley."

The color drains from my face as Micah quirks a brow at me. "Hadley, huh?"

"I am so sorry", Madison starts to apologize to me, but I'm distracted by Micah and my own humiliation from being caught in a lie.

Micah holds another fry up to my mouth and I take a bite. He finishes this fry too. I chew as he studies me. "Madison, how do you spend most of your time", he asks my best friend, turning his attention to her.

"I own Sinful, the cupcake place down the street", she answers proudly.

"No way. My brother, Archer, loves that place. I'll have to stop by sometime."

"Thanks. Whatever you want is on the house", Madison offers. He shakes his head, not hearing of it and turns his attention back to me.

"I'm going to take care of a few needy patrons down there. When I come back, I'd like to hear about how you spend most of your time." He holds another fry out to me, and I decide in that moment that I never want to feed myself a single fry ever again. I nod my head and try not to melt into the floor.

The second he's out of earshot Madison is falling all over herself to make things right between us.

"I am so sorry. He's just so hot. And he clearly likes you. I was excited. I mean, I think you have cobwebs down there", she says, trying to plead her case. I laugh at her reference to my lady parts. There probably are cobwebs down there.

"How much trouble do you think I'm in with him?" I lied and haven't even been in his orbit for an hour. He must think I'm the worst.

"I'd say you're in the best kind of trouble." Madison laughs when my mouth falls open in surprise. Leave it to her to dirty everything up.

I watch him work the bar, chatting up the patrons and filling drink orders. Maybe he's some rich pretty boy who works as a bartender but doesn't really have to. No. That doesn't make sense. Rich pretty boys probably don't work. They're probably on islands licking whipped cream off the nipples of models.

"I wonder what the catch is", I comment to Madison as I grab a fry, a little heartbroken that I'm not eating it from Micah's fingertips. "I mean..." I take a bite and chew thinking of a logical explanation for him. "...he could really be a woman." Madison cackles next to me, already feeling the effects of her drink. "Or an illegal alien." I snort this time. "Or just an alien."

We're both laughing at the thought. He's simply too good to be true. We're almost half done with the basket of fries when he joins us again.

"We need glasses for this", Madison informs him, pointing to the lonely champagne bottle on the bar. He steps back to grab glasses behind him as we wipe the tears from our eyes.

"What's so funny", he asks pouring our drinks.

"Hadley thinks you're an alien." Madison can barely get through the statement with a straight face before she bursts into laughter once more.

"Like an illegal one? Or a *take me to your leader* one?" He slides my glass over to me and leans in for my answer. Meanwhile, Madison is laughing manically next to me.

"I'm sorry." He smiles at my response, and I know he's got me. "I shouldn't have lied."

"Then why did you?" I can see the glimmer in his eyes. He's waiting to see if I'll tell him the truth.

I contemplate my answer. I want to be honest. I really, really do. But I also know that sometimes honesty comes with a price. In this case, I'd have to defend my answer, and I wasn't sure I wanted to do that. Getting into your past with a guy is a sure-fire way to kill something before it's even started.

"In my line of work, men get handsy because they think they can. You're a bartender. My experience with bartenders has shown me that they can really rack up the one-night stands." He clutches his heart as though he's just been shot by me. "It's easier if you don't know anything about me because then you can't come looking for me and spin your sad tale of horse shit to get me to waste time with you." He grips his heart once more, dramatically wincing. "You asked." I take a sip from my drink and wait for his response.

"I don't have a sad tale to tell you. I haven't dated anyone for the last six months. No one nightstands either. To be honest, I'm a little pent up right now. I'd like to get to know you. But I can't do it if you keep lying to me." I nod, caught up in his spell.

"Yeah Hadley. Nobody likes a liar", Madison mock chastises me. Micah laughs and pushes the basket of fries closer to her. His silent hint for her to be quiet.

I laugh at his sense of humor even though I still feel awful about lying. Normally, I don't feel guilty, but there's something about him that seems different. Like he might actually care about more than getting off.

"Madison here is a cupcake genius. What's your genius?" I shake my head. I do not want to talk about my work. This perfect human will no longer be perfect when I do. He'll insinuate I do sexual favors for money like most men do when I tell them I'm a massage therapist.

"I don't want to tell you." At least I'm being honest.

"Why?" He feeds me another fry and I feel my resolve getting weaker. "Can I guess?"

"Yeah, sure." He wastes no time grabbing my hand and inspecting it. He runs his fingers down my palm.

"Too soft for manual labor", he says to himself. Then he flips my hand over and runs his fingertips over my fingers, checking the sides for callouses. He repeats the process with my left hand, but this time, he stops on my ring finger. "Not married. Or not married in a long time." Then he looks my face over. Its unnerving being under his gaze. He's observant. "You sleep well. He tips my chin up with his fingers and tilts my head up and to the side. "Stand up", he orders as he releases my chin. I comply immediately imagining him ordering me around in the bedroom. I bet he does a fantastic job at that.

Micah rounds the bar once more and looks me over from head to toe. His display once again catches the attention of the patrons, and I can feel the blush spread across my face as I stand there just for him.

"Toned legs and arms. You do something physical, or you do a lot of yoga or Pilates." He stops in front of me and swipes his thumb across his lower lip once more. "But you're embarrassed about being put on display. I think I'll embarrass you more. The blush on your cheeks is beautiful." I blush harder and he laughs. "Long hair that you leave down, but you wear a hair tie on your wrist so maybe you have to tie it back for work. You wear casual well considering your frayed jean skirt and casual t-shirt, but you aren't sloppy because you tucked your t-shirt in. Let me see your foot."

"No", I protest in shock. He tilts his head to the side and cocks a brow at me. With a heavy sigh, I sit back down on the stool and raise my leg straight out. He grabs my calf and gently removes my slip on casual athletic shoes revealing my unstockinged foot. I cover my face with my hands but before I can explain how I don't like people touching my feet which is why they aren't manicured he slides my shoe back on and gently lowers my leg.

"Well, you don't work in an office and if you do, you don't wear heals. So, office work is out. Manual labor is out. You aren't the center of attention so you must work one on one with people. Or you don't work with people at all. Maybe you're an accountant. A home accountant."

I laugh at his assessment as he returns behind the bar to wash his hands, then signals for me to wait a moment for him to fill a few more drink orders. I can't help but to revel in the feel of his skin on mine. How he was so curious and took so much care. Not like I expected him to be rough, especially in a room full of people. But come on, there was something different about this guy. I just wasn't sure what it was.

I look away when I notice Madison's stare is fixed on me. Her smile saying, "you're so screwed Joanna". Another man walks behind the bar and grabs a glass. He must work here because he seems to know where everything is. Jesus, he's a looker too. Dark hair. Dark eyes. Similarly dressed as Micah, he's got a white button-down shirt rolled up at to the elbows and slacks on. He's a muscular guy, just like Micah, but bigger. He kind of reminds me of the Brauny paper towel guy. Brauny mixes himself a gin and tonic and takes a sip before walking over to a patron and shaking his hand. They exchange a few words, laugh at something and then he claps Micah on the back. Micah looks back at him and smiles while he completes the drink order. When he's done with the patron's order, he pours a finger of whiskey and raises his glass to the man behind the bar with him. They take a drink and shake hands. They seem genuinely happy.

Micah leans in and says something to the man and they both turn and look our way. The man looks right at me, and I feel my face blush again. They walk over to us and Madison nudges me with excitement. I give her a look that hopefully says knock it off, but she doesn't.

"You could do them both! Can you even imagine?!" The guys must hear her because they both laugh but neither disagrees.

"Mav, this is Hadley Joanna and her friend Madison", Micah introduces us to his friend, and I shrivel up on the inside when he uses the fake name I gave him. Mav shakes our hands, exchanging pleasantries. "And Madison, not right away. Hadley Joanna would have to be thoroughly vetted before that could happen."

Mav's brown eyes glint mischievously as he smiles at us. He doesn't look like he's kidding at all.

I'm mortified by Madison's behavior. She's totally outgoing but she's never actively called me out about sex before. "I'm so sorry. This is two drink Madison", I apologize to them for my friend's behavior as Madison starts fumbling through her purse. She pulls out her phone and swipes the screen.

"No", she wines. We all look at her curiously. "I have to go to the bakery and call maintenance. My refrigerator quit working." She hops off the bar stool and shoves her phone in her purse looking thoroughly pissed off. I get up from my stool to accompany her, but she quickly puts me in my place. "Oh no. You've got cobwebs down there. You're staying." She turns to Mav and Micah. "And you two can go ahead and vet her.

Don't let her leave here until she has a good story to tell me tomorrow or those cobwebs are gone." She pulls out her wallet.

"Not necessary, Madison. It's on me", Micah tells her.

"Thank you." She looks back and forth between them. "Please don't be serial killers, okay?" The men laugh at her while she throws her arms around me whispering that I should call her later.

Now it's just me, Mav and Micah. They're smiling at me, and I instantly feel self-conscious.

"Are you the manager here", I ask Mav trying to make conversation.

"I'm the owner", he corrects me.

"Oh. And Micah works for you?" They both laugh and suddenly I'm lost. "Do you both own this place?" Micah shakes his head.

"I'm doing my brother a favor. I'm licensed. I keep my license good so I can serve my employees and their wives every year for our annual celebration. Other than that, I don't do much with it."

I do a quick comparison of Mav and Micah. They have to be adopted because there isn't one feature they share.

"So you both own a business. What kind of business do you own", I ask him. He shakes his head at me.

"You tell me yours and I tell you mine", he teases. "Are you with the IRS or something? Taxidermist? Stripper? I could believe stripper." I laugh at him and shake my head.

"Maybe I'll show you sometime", I offer. He smiles and nods his head, accepting my answer for now.

"Hadley Joanna, it was a pleasure to meet you", Mav says as he rounds the bar and bends down to give me a hug. He kisses me on the cheek and tells me to enjoy the place. I'm nervous to look at Micah. His brother just kissed me on the cheek and clearly, Micah is interested in me. Where I come from, brothers don't do that sort of thing. But when I look up at Micah under my lashes, he's smiling.

"Your brother just..." I can't finish the sentence. Micah just nods and smiles as though he's proud of himself or maybe he's proud of me.

"Hadley Joanna with the secret job. You are now mine to watch over until your friend returns. You may be closing the bar down with me. Can you handle that?" I nod because I can handle that. I really, really can.

It's almost three in the morning and we're just leaving his brother's restaurant. Madison never came back. She texted that she had to move a bunch of her supplies to her home refrigerator. I have no idea how she did it. I've seen her refrigerator space at home. Even there it's packed and she's only one person. If she has refrigerator space, she will fill it.

The night is muggy, and I've got that thin film of sweat covering my body as a result. Tired from the late hour, I'm so grateful I decided to go for drinks in casual attire. I could have dressed up, but I decided against it. I like dressing up every once in a while, but really, why bother? I'd rather be comfortable.

Even still, I sway a little as I walk, longing for sleep.

"You okay, Hadley Joanna?" Micah says next to me, suddenly throwing his arm around my shoulders and pulling me close to him.

He's so incredibly male. And smells like whisky and whatever those smells are that make men so damn masculine smelling. Outdoors? Spices? I don't know, but I want to burry my face against his warm hard body and just smell him.

"How far is your house from here?" I let out a yawn and he laughs. "Do you want me to carry you?" Now I laugh. I bet he would. He kept me company all night long while attending to his patrons. Feeding me. Watering me. And spending more time with me than anyone I've ever dated has cared to before him.

"My house is a few blocks away. Are you going to tuck me in", I ask him as suggestively as I can but then I punctuate my sentence with a yawn.

"Yes. But I'll give you a better tuck in tomorrow night." I can hear the smile in his voice. And I'm not sure if it's because I'm flirty with him, I'm tired, or because I've agreed to go out on a date with him.

My home is just on the cusp of downtown in a small residential area. I got my tiny house for less than what it was worth. The owners needed to make a fast sale to get out of town and I came looking to buy at just the right time.

The houses on my street are all older. They have charm. The block looks like a classic neighborhood straight from the 1920's or 1930's. It's really a pretty little house, and I'm beyond proud that it's mine.

We don't talk much as we walk. I think he's tired too, but he just hides it better. I still have no idea what he does for work, and he has no idea what I do as well. The secrecy isn't an issue for me. I like him just how he is right now, and I don't want the little details to ruin how my heart flutters when he looks at me or how my pussy throbs when he touches me. I want those cobwebs to be cleared so bad by him that I just might try to muster up the energy for sex tonight. After all, he did tell me he's pent up. And six months? What man goes six months without sex?

The glow of my porch light is like a beacon to me. Roughly six houses to pass before we're there. I think I may just fall right into bed with all my clothes on...unless Micah takes them off for me.

"May I show you inside?" Micah patiently waits for me to fumble through my keys for the one that opens my front door. I look back at him and even after a long day, he looks gorgeous.

His hands are in his pockets. He's completely relaxed. And I realize my body misses his warmth. I want to lay with him. Not just sex but to really just lay with him. I bet he's a fantastic snuggler.

I turn the nob and shove the door open, waiving him inside after me while I flip on the light in the living room. Everything is as I left it. Neat. Tidy. Perfect.

The moment his shoes hit the hardwood floor, I get goosebumps. Even though it's just a few steps, it's the same powerful cadence he used to usher me to my seat at the bar tonight.

His hands are on my arms, rubbing away my goosebumps as he stands behind me.

"Hadley Joanna?" I suck in a breath, loving how his name for me sounds in his deep authoritative tone. "I'm going to leave you here because you're tired…because I'm a gentleman…and because I'm picking you up for dinner tomorrow. But tomorrow…" He turns me around to face him, and cups my face with both hands, tilting my head up to him so I have nowhere else to look. "…you won't be tired…"

He leans down and brushes his lips over mine. I lean forward as he pulls away, opening my mouth to him for more. He chuckles and smirks.

"I want to know you. All of you." He lets his declaration hang there and then ever so gently, kisses my lips again.

"Micah, please." He smiles against my lips.

"That's it. Do you want more", he asks me, his voice becoming slightly sinister.

I put my arms around his neck and try to pull him closer, but he doesn't budge.

"How do you ask?"

And right there, I see the devil. And I want to be all his. "Please, Micah." I lean my forehead against his. I can hear the quiver in my voice from just a kiss. "Please."

"Just one more kiss and then off to bed you go." It was an order mixed in with a suggestion. I nod frantically, needing a real kiss from Micah like someone who's been dieting needs a soda and peperoni pizza. Just give it to me!

Micah wraps his arms around me and kisses me slowly at first. He is absolutely intoxicating. The sheer strength of him alone has my head spinning. He holds me as though I'm his. As though I'm precious and he's taking care of me. Giving me what he knows I need. And he's also taking from me as his hands slowly roam down my back, never landing on my ass but dangerously close. My mind is chanting for him to continue but he doesn't. Instead, he moves one hand into my hair and grabs a fistful. I moan into his mouth at the pain and erotic pleasure of it all.

He walks me back until I'm against the wall and releases my hair. I'm hoping he lifts me up to wrap my legs around him for the promise of more than just a kiss, but he does not. Instead, his kisses slow and the voice in my head is screaming at him not to stop.

He's released his hold on me but plants his hands against the wall on either side of my head, giving me short kiss after short kiss as if he's having trouble stopping himself. Then he leans his forehead against mine and the only sound in the room is our heavy breathing.

"I'm awake now", I break the silence, and he laughs.

"So am I", he says, looking down at the front of his pants.

My eyes follow his and I my mouth falls open in surprise. The tent in his trousers could clear out my cobwebs from across the room. Oh my god.

"I'm nothing to you right now, Hadley Joanna." He tilts my chin up to make eye contact instead of me drooling over his hard dick.

Not true. In the last few minutes, you became everything to me, and you have no idea.

"But I have expectations. And I expect you to follow them if we're going to continue this. And those expectations start tonight." I start to nod, but he cups my chin to stop me from moving. "No. You will think about what you agree to with me. Don't agree because your pussy wants attention. Do you understand?"

"Yes, Micah." The words come out of my mouth breathy and rushed. He gives me a stern look, warning me that my consent may have come too quickly.

"Are you wet?" I nod. I am soaked. "Are you throbbing?" I nod once more. "Do you ache?"

"Yes, Micah." I can hear the tension in my reply. I'm like a rubber band wound so tight it's about to snap.

"You need relief. I can hear it in your voice", he says to himself. "All from a kiss." Then he looks me in the eyes. "It would be so easy to take care of it for you", he says, thinking out loud again. I nod frantically and he smiles. Words have escaped my brain. "I bet it would take just a few kisses...just a few strokes."

"Yes", I breath. No time at all. We could both be ready for sleep in minutes.

"Would you like that? Would you like to come?" A small smile plays on his lips and when I nod, he brings his thumb up to his bottom lip, considering the situation while he runs his thumb back and forth against the plump flesh.

He steps up to me once more and kisses my lips. "Maybe tomorrow", he says, breaking the kiss and leaning his forehead against mine.

"What", I whine.

He steps back and looks me over once more. I can feel his gaze everywhere. It makes my skin hot and tingly because he isn't ogling me even after his kisses and dirty talk. He sees me.

"No touching yourself without my permission." I let out a huff of air. "Hadley Joanna, this is a rule. You will be rewarded if you follow it and punished if you do not. Understood?" I nod and he chuckles. "Don't look so upset. You'll thank me tomorrow. I'll pick you up here at six. Wear a skirt. Good night, Hadley." And with that, he sees himself out and the next fifteen hours are the longest hours of my life.

# Chapter 4
# **Hadley**

**June 7th**
(6 Months Earlier)

My phone rings obnoxiously at my bedside. Madison. Unable to open my eyes from shear exhaustion and denial that I might need to join the living, I fumble for my phone. I crack one eye open long enough to answer the call.

"Tell me everything", Madison's giddy voice greets me.

"I'll call you later", I tell her, just about to hang up when I hear her yell about the spare key. I grumble into the phone. Only Madison would threaten to use my spare key to get details about a man if I hung up on her.

"Has he called you yet?"

"What time is it", I groan, unwilling to look for myself.

"It's six thirty. So has he?"

"No." I pull the covers over my head and contemplate hanging up anyway.

"Hmm..." I can hear her wheels turning as if this is a true mystery for her.

"You're the only one calling people right now. In this entire city, if the phone company looked up records of who's talking on the phone right now, it would only be you and I Maddy", I tell her sarcastically.

"That's it. I'm coming over." And with that, she hangs up the phone.

So, I did what any real best friend would do. I went back to bed and made her use her spare key to get in. And she did. About thirty minutes later, she's whipping my blankets off me with a hot cup of coffee extended out as a peace offering.

"You are so lucky I love you", I tell her as I sit up begrudgingly and take said peace offering.

Grabbing a white bakery box from my nightstand, she sets it in the middle of my bed and climbs in, sitting Indian style and grabbing a pillow for her lap.

"You know, we could have had sex in this bed. You could be sitting in his splooge right now", I tell her, opening the bakery box with my free hand to inspect the treats inside.

"He's so good looking I wouldn't even care. Also, I know that's not true because it only smells like you in here. I know what sex smells like. You still have your cobwebs", she accuses. "Did you mess it up?"

I grab a braided glazed donut and glare at her.

"All I'm saying is that you're too picky. There is *nothing* wrong with him. *Nothing*." She grabs a chocolate frosted donut with sprinkles and licks some of the topping off before taking a bit. She's such a child sometimes it cracks me up. "Did you at least kiss him?" Her voice raises an octave, and I shrug, toying with her a bit. She snatches the partially eaten donut out of my hand. "Joanna?" Now she's using my nickname too?

I heave a heavy sigh of defeat, mostly because I want my donut back. "Yes, we kissed." I hold my hand out for my donut.

She arches a brow at me. “A lot. It was good. He’s good.” She takes a bite out of my donut. “Madison”, I raise my voice in surprise and grab for my donut, trying not to spill my coffee but she pulls it back.

“I want details.” She punctuates her demand with an even bigger bite this time. “Mmm…this is good”, she says with her mouth full. “Talk quick or I’m going to eat the whole thing”, she threatens with a full mouth.

“He’s a gentleman. But he talks dirty. Like…so dirty it makes me want to do dirty things with him because I really believe he can do those dirty things well.” Madison hands me back my donut and this time I take a bite, then hold a finger up for her to wait so she knows I’m conceding.

“Like what kind of dirty things? Spanking? Tying you up?” I shake my head as I swallow the bite and disappointment flits across her face.

“He uses words like pussy and cunt.” She looks at me like I’ve lost my mind. “I know they’re nothing special, but the way he says them… It’s like they should start with a capital letter. They aren’t filthy sounding. They just sound like words Micah owns. Just thinking about it makes me want his hands between my legs.”

“Oh my god, did he get you off?” I shake my head. “So it was just talking and kissing?” I bite my lip, nervous to tell her more. “I will tackle you for the rest of that donut and shove it in my mouth, Joanna.”

“Okay! Okay. He told me he has rules. And he’d punish me if I didn’t follow them.” Her eyes light up like a child’s on Christmas morning.

“What kind of rules? Don’t leave anything out.” She’s leaning in, elbows supported by the pillow on her lap as though this is the most enthralling tale she’s ever heard.

"He told me I couldn't touch myself unless I had permission." Her eyes light up even more. "And that if I was a good girl, I'd be rewarded but if I didn't follow his rule, I'd be punished."

"Yes! So, which one are you? Please say you were a bad girl, Hadley." I shake my head, and she throws her head back with a heavy sigh and looks up at the ceiling. "When does he pick you up for dinner?"

"Six."

"Well, you have a little less than twelve hours to change your status. Friend to friend, be a bad girl", she advises. I laugh hard and then shake my head. "Why", she whines.

"I want to see what being rewarded by Micah is like. He told me it would be worth it. Every guy I've ever been with claims to be a God in bed. All of them were liars. I really don't think he's going to be a liar", I explain, the only defense I have.

"Fine. But if he comes through on his promise of being good in bed, promise me you're going to find out what it's like to be a bad girl." I can practically see the horns forming on Madison's head and I chuckle as I take another bite of my donut, looking over the open box for my next pick.

# Chapter 5
# **Micah**

**June 7th 6:30 p.m.**
(6 Months Earlier)

I'm a lawyer. Being in the business of reading people, there are some things that I just know. It's a useful skill I've acquired over time. One that levels the playing field when honesty is of utmost importance. It's my superpower. And it will take every ounce of self-control I have not to call Ms. Hadley Joanna out tonight. Instead, I'll play oblivious. It's more fun this way. Because if she followed my rule, she'll want me to ask her. She'll want the credit of doing something so utterly difficult.

*No touching yourself without my permission.* Hadley thinks I'm just being kinky, and I am, but that's not the reason for my rule. No one touches what's mine without my permission. And after that kiss, nothing is more mine than Hadley Joanna. Even the thought of her defiling herself without an order from me makes me irrationally irritable. *Mine.*

Every brother gets a rule. This one is my rule. And the ladies are going to be pissed. Because the way we do things is nothing if it isn't unusual and clipping their wings further by adding this rule to the long list they must already abide by will surely end in some shit tests. I haven't told my brothers what my rule will be yet, because it won't go into effect until Hadley has her physical with Braden and gets her birth control. Not one of my brothers will be against this. They love pulling the strings as much as I do.

I wonder if she obeyed me, my heart a flutter at the mere thought of it as I drive to her house to pick her up for our first date. If she did, it's going to be hell to look at her and know her pussy is dying to be touched. To know she is so wet she won't even be able to taste her food because her impending orgasm has consumed her. If she did not, I'll have to punish her. And boy do I have ways of punishing that are so impactful she will never disobey me again.

Pulling up in front of her tiny home I can see her through the curtains. She's pacing, so it seems. Nerves. This could go either way. My heart sinks at the thought of not being able to reward her. There is nothing more that I want tonight than to hear the sounds she makes when she comes. I shove the image out of my head and focus, thinking of my latest shit show of a client at one of my local firms so I don't knock on her door with a raging hardon. The tactic helps and in no time, I'm able to leave my car and walk to her door.

It's humid out, which means her skin will be dewy with sweat. She'll have that flushed look that women get when they've just orgasmed without even so much of a drop of pleasure. I really have to focus on something else or I won't make it through this date without rewarding her early. I have to remember that she has no idea what she's in for with me. This date is one of many that will establish trust with her. If she doesn't trust me, she'll never agree to what the brotherhood does and if that happens, I'll simply be settling for someone else.

She answers the door almost immediately, hurrying to let me in, looking me over. Her eyes dance with delight and I can't help but to smile at her. She reminds me of a child on Christmas morning but with a hunger in her. A hunger that tells me she's a very good rule follower.

I shut the door behind me and close the distance between us. "I missed you, Hadley Joanna." Using two fingers under her chin, I tilt her head up from her submissive downcast look to face me, and then I brush my lips against hers. She whimpers. She. Fucking. Whimpers.

Stepping back out of her reach, I openly admire her outfit. It's nothing flashy or overly sexy. It's simply Hadley. Similar to the jean skirt in style, it's a dark floral pattern that comes straight down ending above the knee. Her top is white. It shows no cleavage and has sleeves that come down mid-way to her bicep. But there's about an inch of skin showing between her skirt and shirt, exposing her toned stomach. A stomach I want to make jump with pleasure because she comes so hard.

She bites her lip as I assess her. And boy do I assess her. "Hold still", I order her and circle around her like a predator would circle its prey. When I stop behind her to admire her backside, she looks over her shoulder and the pure look of submissive vulnerability in her eyes is enough to tempt me into canceling dinner out and eating Hadley instead.

"I wasn't sure if this would be fancy enough", she attempts to explain. "You didn't tell me where we were going." I say nothing, making my footsteps deliberate and powerful. "I can change", she offers as I appear in front of her, simply shaking my head at her offer.

"You're perfect." A smile spreads across her face. God this woman wants to please me, and I love it. And while that's half the goal, the other half is making sure she gets what pleases her. That's where I come in. For both of us to get the things we need, implicit trust must be given, and rules must be followed to the letter. She follows rules quite well. At least in this initial test anyway. But this evening we'll see how much work we have to do in the trust department.

I motion for her to follow me out of her house so we can get this date started. She follows my lead but stops at an end table and grabs her phone and the same clutch she had with her at Mav's place yesterday.

"Will you be paying?" She looks up at me, shock written all over her face as she stammers, attempting to respond appropriately.

"I...um...can pay", she tells me.

And. I. Laugh. Hard. There is no way she will ever spend one cent when she's out with me. The mere thought that I would even allow her to have that burden is ridiculous. Her brows are furrowed when I stop, and I think I may have offended her. So, I use myself as a weapon against her to gain compliance and take care of any offense I may have caused.

Stepping up to her, I tilt her chin up to me. She looks wary and I understand. We don't know each other yet. But we will. And if I have her follow this rule early, it won't be so hard for her later.

I take her clutch from her hands and deliberately place it on the end table where she picked it up from moments ago. And when she starts to object, I simply shake my head and kiss her. Again, another whimper. Those whimpers make me want to do dirty things to this woman.

"You won't need that", I tell her, my lips still hovering over hers, at the ready to kiss away any more objections.

"Okay", she says, like she's just been hypnotized.

"Leave your phone", I challenge her. She pulls away from me.

"I...what if someone needs to reach me?"

I give her a questioning look. We won't be gone for days. It's just dinner. That's a weak excuse.

"You could be a weirdo", she says.

I smile at this, furrowing my brow and tilting my head to the side for theatrics.

"I'm serious."

"And what exactly would a weirdo do with a woman like you that would require her to keep a lifeline on her?" This I have to hear.

"You could steal me. And no one would ever hear from me again. Like Ted Bundy", she clarifies.

I shake my head at her. "What's Madison's number?"

Hadley lets out a heavy sigh but gives it to me and I send her a quick text.

Micah- Hi Madison. This is Micah. I've asked Hadley to leave her phone behind. This is my number in case you need to reach her in the coming hours.

Bubbles immediately appear across the screen as I read the text I sent Madison about Hadley. When I receive Madison's reply, I can't help but to smile as I read it back to Hadley.

Madison- If I hear from her tonight, it will mean you didn't clean out her 🕸 with your big 🍆 and I will have underestimated you ☹.

Hadley covers her face with her hand in embarrassment. "You told her I have a big eggplant?" I can't help to embarrass her further. She's gorgeous when she blushes. She nods her head and bites her lip.

"Shall we go", I urge her. This time, she very willingly leaves her personal belongings behind and after locking up, hands me her house key to hold onto. My heart warms at the gesture even though it's clear to me that trust will need to be earned with Hadley. She doesn't give it freely. She's smart.

Once in my car, I can tell she's nervous. She has no escape. No lifeline. Everything she has is either at home or with me. And as I ease away from the curb, I can feel her become more nervous as the seconds tick by.

"Tell me what you're thinking", I gently order her.

"I know who you are", she tells me, without hesitation. I nod, figuring she had looked me up. I'm everywhere online so it probably only took her one query to find me.

"And who am I", I nudge her forward.

"You own not only the major law firm in this city, but many others across the country. You're a shark. At least that's how the articles describe you." She seems sad when she says this. As if the public's description of me somehow bothers her.

"Do you dislike sharks", I ask playfully as we drive into the city.

"No. You do your job well. That's something to be proud of. It's just that...I'll always just be a little fish. And I think your world might eat me up." I glance over at her, and those wide eyes look at me with so much sincerity, I know this woman is putting all her cards out on the table so we're on level playing field.

"I would never allow my world to eat you up, Hadley Joanna. And I have no intentions of changing you. In fact, I want quite the opposite."

"It doesn't bother you that I live in a tiny house? That I'm just a..." She doesn't finish her line of work even though I already know it. There aren't many people in this area with the name Hadley. It took me almost no time at all to learn she's a massage therapist, and a good one at that.

"Go on. You're what now?" I want to see if she'll tell me herself.

"It's not important", she mumbles. "Where are we going for dinner? Back to your brother's place?"

She's so innocent. So guarded. It makes me wonder about the experiences she's had. Who has mistreated her and how? And she seems to be clueless about her beauty which makes her even more attractive to me. Or maybe she's not clueless. Maybe she just doesn't care.

"We will not be returning to Mav's restaurant this evening, although I'm sure he'd love to see you again." I dangle the bait out there, curious how she'll respond. She looked so nervous when Mav kissed her on the cheek last night. It was cute. I should savor that memory. With little time and effort, I'm hoping she'll kiss him freely regardless of who is watching. Me included.

"I have reservations for us at Lorenzo's." The food there is fantastic. I know the owner. He was a client of mine and since he prevailed, I've gotten the best tables from him as a lingering thanks.

"I don't think I'm dressed for Lorenzo's", she starts, once again doubting herself in comparison to the life I live.

"No. You're not. You're dressed for me. And from this point forward you'll dress for me. And when I allow it, you'll dress for you." She turns to me, and I can almost see the question forming above her head. *Are you serious?* So I answer it. "Hadley, for a moment, can you imagine what it would feel like to just give up control? To have someone take care of you?

Get to know you? Love you? Spoil you?" She doesn't answer me, so I continue. "Monday night, I have an after-hours event. I'm going to have your clothes delivered. I want you to wear only what I send you." She chuckles at the audacity of my request. "You'll never know if you like something until you try it."

I pull into the valet and two crisply uniformed men promptly greet us. One opening Hadley's door and the other opening mine. I slip him a hundred-dollar bill and shake his hand. I come here often so the staff and I know each other well.

"No baseball tonight", I ask Samuel.

"Missing it tonight. I'll catch tomorrow's game though." I can see in his eyes that missing his son's game truly bothers him.

"I'm sorry about that. I have a good feeling about tomorrow", I tell him. Because I do. Tomorrow is the day Ms. Hadley Joanna will completely fall in love with me and tonight is the night she will understand I'm not a man who runs around misrepresenting what he is and is not good at. True to my word she will be rewarded tonight.

Dinner is phenomenal as usual. The company was even better. Hadley isn't one of those women who is afraid of eating in front of people. It drives me crazy when a girl picks through her food when she's clearly starving. Though I did decide to remind Hadley to eat here and there. The conversation was so natural. It was obvious that she was becoming more comfortable with me as the dinner progressed and I liked that. I liked that she was interested in me and not my job or my money. Yes, those things are a part of me but that's not who I am, it's what I have and what I do.

After dinner, I made sure we took our time getting back to her place.

"You're doing this on purpose", she accuses me as she takes a sip from her champagne. I squeeze her hand and wink at her as I steer her around the corner of the rose garden. The attraction is open at night as well and it's just as beautiful now as it is during the daytime.

"I was good", she tells me, raising her brows expectantly.

"I know you were." I take a sip of my champagne and say nothing more as we continue our stroll.

"Tell me you're not another big talker."

I don't answer her.

"You are, aren't you?" I could hear the disappointment in her voice. She thought I was like every other man out there. Now was as good a time as any to show her that I was many things, but average has never been one of them.

"This way", I croon to her, guiding her toward a wooden door that led to tall trellises covered in roses. It was private enough that passersby could see people moving but couldn't make out anything significant. Once in the space, I give the heavy wooden door a tug and it swings freely. Once shut, I close a thick wooden latch over the door. No one is coming in.

"Do you want to find out?" Hadley's mouth falls open in shock. I point to the cement bench in the middle of the small space. "Sit at one end", I order her curtly. She scrambles to obey, almost spilling her drink. As she seats herself, I take a seat on the bench as well. "Turn", I order her to sit as though she would be laying her legs down on top of the bench. She follows my order well, her back ramrod straight as she waits for me.

Sitting behind her, I have one foot planted on the grass on either side of the bench. I lean forward, extending my glass to her. "If you wouldn't mind." She grabs the glass. "Now, would you like your reward?" She nods her head. "Out loud, Hadley."

"Yes. Please."

I love the quiver in her voice. She's cute when she's nervous.

"Don't spill", I warn her, pulling her back and holding her against me so her back is resting on my chest and I'm looking down the front of her body. Her skirt is hiked up a bit in this position but not nearly far enough for me. So I take my free hand and touch my fingertips to her knee, gently sliding the fabric of her skirt up her leg until I expose her panties.

The rapid rise and fall of Hadley's chest is delightful as I look down at the damp spot waiting there for me.

"You're going to have to be quiet", I whisper in her ear as my fingertips slide over her navy satin panties, right over her wet spot...right over her clit.

Hadley doesn't make a sound, but she does let her head fall back, the champagne sloshing dangerously close to the edge of our glasses.

"You have no idea who you're dating, Hadley." I plant a kiss on her neck and hear her breath hitch as I strum her between the legs. "Can you do it this good?" She closes her eyes and lets out a sharp breath. "Or am I better?"

"You", she whispers.

I stroke her for a few moments more and when I feel her hold her breath, I push her over the edge. I want this woman so badly if she tells me no, I don't know what I'll do. Never in my wildest dreams did I think I would be desperate for another, but I am. She's been a constant distraction since I laid eyes on her.

After I'm satisfied she's finished, I slide my fingers in my mouth to taste her. She is perfection. And I celebrate this perfection by taking my glass back from her and holding her there for my viewing pleasure while I take a drink. This is all she'll get from me tonight. I want her so strung out tomorrow it hurts.

# Chapter 6
# **Hadley**

**June 8$^{th}$ 1 p.m.**
(6 Months Earlier)

Where in the hell is she? Madison wanted to meet at the park for a walk, but she isn't here and she isn't answering her phone. I stalk off, ready to head home when a deep voice calls my name.

No.

She.

Didn't.

I turn on my heel to find Micah strolling toward me looking casual in some shorts and a polo shirt that hugs his muscular arms to perfection.

"I'm glad you're here", he greets me, wrapping his arms around me for a hug.

"Are you two working together or something?"

"Or something", Micah answers, sliding his hand into mine and leading me down the paved path. "I'm leaving for Houston tomorrow. Business", he clarifies. When he sees the stunned look on my face he explains further. "I have a few firms in Texas that I make quarterly trips to. It's that time. A rather poor time", he laments, looking over at me, "...but duty calls."

I want to ask when he'll be back, but we've only been on one date. I have no right to this information.

"I know it's short notice, but I was hoping to spend time with you before I fly out."

Micah sounds different. Not like the Micah from last night or even the night before at the bar. If I'm not mistaken, I can hear a little vulnerability in his voice. Like he thinks I might turn him down, which is absolutely absurd.

"What do you have in mind?" I try to sound casual, but he swivels his head, looking down at me and the side of his lip twitches like he's trying not to smile. I laugh at his reaction, and he joins in.

"Ice cream at Scoops." He nods when he sees my eyes widen with excitement.

Scoops is a local ice cream shop that was my guilty pleasure every day for about a month when I moved here. I've been so busy I haven't been there in quite some time. "And then we go back to your place", he hedges. I raise my brows, waiting for what we'll do there. "...and I make you a delicious dinner and then I tuck you in for the night."

He sounds like he really means he's going to tuck me in. I want to ask him so badly if that's code for something or if there will be more, but I hold back. He must see the disappointment in my eyes because he laughs and takes me with him this time.

"It sounds like Scoops is a yes but what about dinner?"

"You'll be cooking in my kitchen", I state the obvious.

"Yes. I will need to cook dinner in your kitchen if I'm cooking you dinner at your house", he gently clarifies.

"Ha ha. I get that. What I mean is, my kitchen is pretty basic. I'm pretty basic when it comes to cooking. You talk about truffle fries and champagne. Your kitchen is probably three times the size of mine…" He nods. "With all the gadgets. I don't know."

"Ramen."

"You're planning on making me ramen for dinner?"

"That's the first thing I learned how to make. My mother caught me making ramen and almost had a stroke. She treated it like I had opened a package of pesticide and was about to boil it and eat it right up. She taught me how to cook. My mom is a great cook. What my mom didn't teach me, Mav, my brother who owns the restaurant did. Why don't we start with what you like to eat. Then I'll surprise you."

I consider his offer. If I let my pride stand in my way, I could really be missing out on a nice gesture. A man has never cooked for me. What's the worst thing that could happen?

"What's the worst thing that could happen?" He clutches his heart like he did at the bar two nights ago in mock injury. "I'm sorry. It's just…I think you're too good to be true."

"I know the feeling, Hadley Joanna." I give him the stink eye for using my fake name.

"You're going to keep calling me that aren't you?"

"That'll teach you to lie to me now, won't it?"

"I didn't even know you", I argue back.

"Well now you do. And you know I don't like lies. So, from this point forward, if you lie to me, that lie will haunt you." I let out a heavy sigh. "I'll promise you the same. If I lie to you, you can do whatever you need to do to ensure my lie haunts me." He arches that beautiful dark brow at me.

I roll my eyes and shake my head. "Fine."

By the time we're done with our banter about honesty, we're at Scoops and I'm practically drooling. They serve the best custard around in the most delicious flavors. My favorite is German chocolate cake.

Micah motions for me to order first and I order my favorite.

"Nice choice", he tells me right before he orders. "I'll have a black forest please."

"I've never had that one."

"Well, it looks like today is your lucky day. I like to share", he says suggestively.

I blush at this. It's not even that dirty but my mind goes to all the filthy places just by the way he said that. And what's worse is I can't stop looking at him. He's so remarkable. Tall, dark hair, tan skin, muscular, five o'clock shadow, full lips light grey eyes... The list could go on.

"What?" He catches me checking him out.

"I'm just...taking you in before you leave." I say it like he's a mirage. Like he's going to disappear before my very eyes.

He doesn't say anything but grabs our ice cream and leads us to a table. He slides a napkin across the table at me along with my dish of ice cream and then meticulously prepares his first spoonful.

"Open", he orders me. I roll my eyes up to look at him and he knows what I'm thinking. I sink my teeth down on my lower lip, trying to decide if I want to say something sexual. Right now, all I'm thinking about is if that's how he'll sound when he wants me to suck on him. Normally, I'd be turned off. I've given blow jobs before but could probably count them on one hand. They've all been awful experiences. Either the guy tastes disgusting, he's a little too rough or both. I bet he wouldn't taste disgusting. I also bet he wouldn't be too rough with me...unless I wanted it.

"Hadley?" He gives me a knowing look when I open my mouth, and I roll my eyes up at him suggestively.

"Mmmm. That's good", I murmur around the cold treat and blush when I realize I sound like I have a mouth full of cum.

He laughs, knowing where my mind has been, taking a taste of his own ice cream.

"Want some of mine?" I take care to make the perfect first scoop, just like he did for me.

"Oh yes. I want very much to taste yours." He makes no secret hiding the double meaning and I try my hardest to keep a straight face.

"Here", I hold the spoon out to him. He opens his mouth and those damn white teeth and that devilish tongue...

He leans forward and takes the bite, watching me as he rolls the ice cream around in his mouth. I watch him, holding my breath as his hard jaw moves and his lips follow, savoring the spoonful.

He can't be real. He's a dirty talking gentleman who knows how to find a woman's clit through her panties and gets her off in public after wining and dining her without her having to pay a single cent or get him off.

And he actually wants to get to know me. After a lull in conversation, he asks me about my family and moving here. Where I was from and how did my family feel about me moving. Did I leave siblings behind. All those types of ordinary getting to know you type of things.

And as I tell him how I left my hometown a few hours away because I needed space and my family was not supportive of my move at all and even less supportive of my job choice, we fall into an easy back and forth rhythm of conversation.

We learned we have some things in common from a familial standpoint. Neither of our parents were in favor of our moves and while they recognize we're good at what we do, they don't fully support it. We also both have sisters. I'm the oldest of three and he's the only boy but the youngest of four.

The conversation is easy as we offer each other tastes of ice cream between questions. We're still talking when our treats are long gone and Micah is answering a question about why the 4th of July is his favorite holiday when a mother of three little kids comes in, clearly struggling.

He looks between her and me as he gives a very fragmented answer and finally stops to address what's bothering him.

"Excuse me for a moment please", he says to me as he gets up from the table and walks straight over to the lady with the kids. They're little. If I had to guess, I'd say the oldest is five, the middle is about three and the one she holds in her arms is just over a year.

I can't hear what he says to the lady at first, but she shakes her head, refusing what he offers. Then he holds his hands out and nods to her.

"She'll make a mess of your clothes. He's all covered in chocolate ice cream", she counters.

"It's fine. My drycleaner hasn't been challenged enough these days. What's life without a little challenge here and there?"

She must decide he's not a weirdo because she laughs and then hands her daughter over to Micah. The little girl looks surprised for a moment but when Micah smiles at her, she smiles right back and puts her chocolate covered hand right on his face. He doesn't even flinch.

"You're going to make me a sticky mess, aren't you?" The little girl babbles loudly, trying to say the word sticky but it just comes out as icky.

I notice the mom quickly working to clean up the ice cream on the floor. I wasn't turned their direction, but Micah got to watch what was going on behind me. That little girl must have grabbed the top of an ice cream cone getting it all over her mom and the floor. Meanwhile, her boys must have run through the ice cream on the floor while eating theirs. Yes, that woman needed help and Micah came to her rescue.

"Go clean up", he tells the woman. When she looks at him with uncertainty he follows up with, "I'll stay right here. Your kids will be fine." When she doesn't move towards the restroom, he steps over to the napkins and grabs a bunch for her. "I get it. Just, use these at least?"

When the mess is clean and she's wiped the wet ice cream off her clothes, Micah hands her back her daughter and the woman thanks him profusely. He waves off her thanks and holds the door for them while they exit.

Micah just stole my heart. If he's a fraud I think he might ruin me for every man out there. God, I hope he doesn't ruin me.

We walk to my house, and he wears his ice cream like a prize. I think he does it because I can't stop swooning over him.

"It's not a big deal", he'll says when he sees my gaze linger on the chocolate fingerprint on his bicep a little too long.

"I didn't think you'd be a kid person."

"I love kids, actually. I like kids more than I like most adults." We both laugh and I nod my agreement. Adults can be real jerks sometimes.

I pause at the end of my street. There's a black car sitting on the street in front of my house.

"It's Steven. With groceries."

"Steven?"

"My driver. He picked them up for me when we were having ice cream."

This guy is next level. I know he's rich, but he has a driver…who picks up his groceries.

"Hadley, I have help because my life is so very different from the norm. It's nothing to be concerned about, that I assure you. To me, it's normal. Someday, I'm hoping it will be normal to you too."

Someday. Wow. He's planning on us having a someday together. And so soon. We barely know each other.

A man who I assume is Steven steps out from the black car. He's dressed in a suit and sports a hat with a shiny black bill on it. As we get closer, I watch him as he opens the trunk and pulls a few shopping bags out, closing the trunk with ease. He's older than Micah, that I know for sure because I can see his grey hair peek out from the hat.

"Thank you, Steven", Micah greets the man taking the groceries from him in one hand and using the other to shake his hand. "Hadley", Micah turns to me. "This is Steven. He's my driver. My right hand." He turns to Steven. "Steven, Ms. Hadley Joanna. She's..." He pauses to think and I'm hanging on his every word. "...mine."

Steven raises his brows, looks at me and extends his white gloved hand. Reluctantly, I take it. I don't want to dirty up his gloves. I didn't realize drivers really wore those. I thought they only did that in the movies.

"Sir, shall I have your car dropped off?"

"That'll be fine, Steven. Go ahead and arrange for it and then take the rest of the day off. I'll see you tomorrow morning, bright and early to head to the airport."

"Yes sir", Steven nods with his agreement. "Ms. Hadley Joanna, it's a pleasure to meet you." Then he turns on his heel and gets back in his car and drives away as I silently look after him.

"Shall we", Micah asks, breaking my daze.

When we get inside, Micah won't even allow me to wipe the chocolate from his arm and face. He simply tells me to sit while he cooks, and I swear the smudges of chocolate make him even more charming.

It only takes him a quick inspection of my kitchen tools before he's all set. Before he begins, he pours me a glass of wine and I once again have the luxury of getting to know him.

"You were telling me about your favorite holiday", I prompt him.

"Oh yes. Fourth of July. Hands down, it's the best."

"I don't get it." I shake my head in disagreement. There are several others I'd name as my favorite before that one.

"When I was a kid, my parents would host this fourth of July celebration at our cabin. People would come from around the area to celebrate with us. It was a huge party. Our cabin was on the lake, so we had a dock. We'd grill for everyone, set off fireworks, roast marshmallows...we did it all."

"That sounds pretty normal to me. You aren't making a good argument counselor", I goad him.

"Alright, so those things only had me interested for so long. But one year, I got a tent for my birthday. And I devised a plan. You see, around the time I got a tent, it was very apparent I was interested in girls, and it was also very apparent they were interested in me. So I set off to find the perfect place to camp out. And after some exploration earlier that summer, I had found a place. So I swiped some drinks and invited some girls back to my tent."

"What?! No you didn't."

"Yes I did. And let me tell you, it went very, very well." He winks at me and my mouth falls open. "I got to see boobs, kiss girls, I even got my first blowjob that summer."

He slides the tray of chicken and potatoes in the oven and then pours himself a glass of wine.

"And", I prompt, wondering about the end of this adventure.

"And I put that tent up every year until I graduated high school, thus, the fourth of July being my favorite holiday." He clinks his glass against mine and we both take a sip.

"Can we sit while dinner cooks?" I nod and he leads us to the living room which isn't but a few steps from the kitchen but it's sweet none the less. When we sit, he takes my glass and sets it on the coffee table next to his. "I missed you", he tells me before kissing me.

He tastes like chocolate and chardonnay, and I hum my approval against his mouth. He pulls me on top of him and I gasp in surprise.

"Are you going to have your way with me like those girls in the tent", I playfully ask him.

"No ma'am I am not", he tells me before pulling me back in for a kiss. I'm feeling a little deflated until he finishes sharing his intentions with me. "My plan is to get you all pent up and hot for me. Then I'm going to Houston. And when I come back, I'm going to surprise you and make you even hotter for me." He kisses me again, his hands running down my back, landing on my rearend. "And I won't even let you touch yourself while I'm gone."

True to his word, before Micah tucks me in, I'm well fed and slick between my legs. The last contact I have with him before I shut my eyes is another kiss and a reminder about his expectations.

He whispers in my ear before he lets himself out. "It you're not a good girl for me Hadley, I'll know." Then he leaves my bedroom and lets himself out.

# Chapter 7
# Hadley

**June 16th 11:30 a.m.**
(6 Months Earlier)

Here it is. Micah is going to fuck this up big time, I think as I look at my schedule for the day. He's my noon appointment.

I contemplate switching him with another therapist but it's just me and another girl today. I heave out a heavy sigh as I walk away from the computer at the front desk. It wouldn't matter anyway. If a man is going to silence a bar full of people and figure out what I do for a living without me telling him, he's going to end up on my table. That's motivation if I've ever seen it.

His efforts should be flattering. So why do I have this pit in my stomach about him laying on my table? This should be business. And with most of my clients it is. But there are some that make it their business to get in my business. Whatever lengths Micah has taken to solve this mystery is concerning. He's in my business. And I don't want him to dirty up what I do because then he wouldn't be perfect. And I rather like the perfect version of him I've created in my mind.

"Did you get overbooked or something", Danielle asks as she watches me from the doorway of my therapist room. I realize I'm aggressively changing linens on the table and right myself by taking a deep breath.

"No Dani. I'm just...I've got some tough clients today is all."

"Oh. Well, we can switch. Who do you want to trade?" I adore Dani, I really do, but she has not a care in the world about turfing her clients. They get pissed when they can't have her, and I know some have complained to our boss. I'm not sure I really want to give Micah up anyway. Perhaps this is the test. If he can't be decent then that's the end of us.

"No. I think I just needed more sleep last night. It's fine", I concede. She eyes me suspiciously once more and then leaves me to my grumpiness.

It's funny that every other day goes so slowly...except for today. Noon arrives in what seems to be the blink of an eye. Reluctantly, I walk into the lobby to see if my client has arrived.

"Your client is weird", Stephanie murmurs to me behind the front desk. She hands me a clipboard with his personal information and required medical releases for the massage, arching an eyebrow and nodding to the papers in my hand.

Micah's stare brushes over my skin, calling me to look at him, but I don't relent. I keep my gaze focused on the task at hand. Review the paperwork, greet the client, room the client, complete the body work, wish the client well and on to the next. Micah can be no different.

I flip through the papers and don't see anything unusual at first. Then I get to the last page and see that he has marked up the liability release for his massage with his suggested legal edits and slid his card under the clip. At the bottom he wrote...

*Who did you pay to put this together for you? Call me next time.*

I turn my gaze on him and press my legs together. He chuckles. I breath out a frustrated breath.

"Micah", I ask, trying to keep up the rouse that I don't know him. Gracefully, he rises from his seat on the plush lobby chair and crosses the small space, so he stands in front of me.

"Hadley. You came highly recommended", he greets me, extending his large well-manicured hand out to shake mine, understanding that I want to keep our relationship thus far private.

The moment I lay my hand in his, it has the same effect on me as it did just weeks ago when we met at the bar. I want to run because guys like him make girls like me look foolish. I don't want to look foolish at my job, especially with another man.

Micah follows me through the studio to the massage suites. He does not go unnoticed by the patrons, male and female alike. Women in foils tilt their head his direction. A woman getting color rinsed out of her hair shifts her eyes to the side, letting out an *oh* when Micah passes by and a man getting a trim follows Micah's image in the mirror with what can only be described as admiration painting his face.

These people have seen him for approximately ten seconds or less. He touched my pussy mere days ago and I'll be trapped in a private room with him for an hour, rubbing his naked body. Panic creeps up my spine because I realize that now, I'm not worried about him. I'm worried about me. How can I do my job and not appreciate him sexually? We had a whole course on this in school. I *teach* part of this to my students in their externships. How sometimes guys get hard, and you can't help but to notice and that your reputation will carry with you wherever you go. That touching someone in their most private places could be considered sexual assault even if it's an accident. And on, and on, and on...

And what's worse is that I can feel his eyes on me. I can feel his gaze caress over my backside. He probably knows I'm wearing a thong because underneath these scrubs is no panty line. Suddenly, I'm not sure whether I want him to behave in there. And I'm not sure whether I want to either.

When I turn to indicate the room we're in, I can feel the professionalism drain from my face. I'm thirsty and the smirk on his face indicates he's fully aware of where my mind is at.

"We're in here", I confirm unnecessarily, further confirming my thirst by the wistfulness of my voice.

He crosses the threshold, but I can't bring myself to enter quite yet.

"There's a hook for your jacket." I point behind the door. "And a basket for your clothes." I nod at the basket on a small table in the corner of the room. "Please dress to your comfort level." I clear my throat after I beg to the universe that his comfort level is only enough for a foot massage, so I have no choice but to be professional with him. "Face down under the sheet to start. You can call my name when you're ready." I avert my gaze once more and then turn back to him to make sure he has everything he needs. It's then that I see a troubled look come and go. It's not worry. There's something else there. Acknowledgement, maybe? I don't have time to give it much thought. I need to keep my schedule today, so I exit like I would any other client, pulling the door closed behind me with a quiet click.

But this isn't any other client. This is a man who is my undoing. A man who is more. More to me. More to me than he realizes. The new standard by which I hold every male.

"Hadley", I hear my name through the door, and I feel my face heat. My God I feel like I'm a student and he's the principle. It's deep and confident. Even a little commanding.

Like he's summoning me. Well...he is summoning me but it's more than that. Like he knows exactly what will happen in this room. Anything he wants.

I fill my lungs with a deep breath and turn the knob to find him just as I've instructed. Face down on the table, his lower body covered with the white sheet. I swallow loudly. Jesus he's perfect. I haven't gotten to see an inch of him, until now.

He's like a male model. Even laying there, his muscles are defined under his tan skin. My pulse skitters in my veins as I realize I'll get to touch him...almost everywhere. Or maybe everywhere.

"Comfortable", I ask as I walk up to him, my voice higher than normal from the stress of my fantasy.

"Yes. Very."

I wash my hands trying to focus more on this task than I have anything else during the day because that's what it will take to get through this as a professional. Focus. Not on who is on the table or how beautiful he is, but on the task.

"Are there any areas that you want me to focus on today", I ask while drying my hands and looking over the oils. I love the way Micah smells, and I can't imagine changing that with an oil. But's it's necessary for the task.

"Legs. Glutes. I worked them hard at the gym this morning."

"Okay then", I agree, looking at him as though a curse will befall me if I touch him. "Anything I should avoid?"

"Not a thing", he says, with a smile in his voice.

I could run my hands over his taught muscular body for hours. It's funny because I love my job. But right now, I don't think I've ever loved my job more than I do in this moment. Until I slick him up with oil and then I think I may love it even more...which is beyond inappropriate.

Micah doesn't move a muscle when I drizzle the warm oil down his spine. He's unflappable, I think, as I return the bottle to the warmer and begin my work there first.

I've never had a moment where I've been aroused working on a client. Body work had always just been the vocation I chose. I gave people something most could not. Intentional relief that was near divine if they relaxed. But seeing Micah on this table and knowing he was naked underneath that sheet...feeling his warm, firm, powerful body...I couldn't help my mind from wandering about the possibility of him. About how his body could be my reward in the not too distant future.

I've never thought of a man like this. Everyone I'd ever dated was just average. Average build. Average height. Average weight. Average life. But there's something about the man laying on this table that's extraordinary. Like he was forged from the heavens above, perfectly put together for all to admire.

All three nights I was with him I wanted to scream, beg and bargain for him to come back, but I couldn't form words. He had played with my body so well...better than anyone had before him... He left me wondering how he did it. In such a short time, how could he make my body so undeniably his? The only thing I could come up with is that he was put in my path as a test. Or maybe a lesson. Maybe he would be the one who would do the most damage. A man like this had to be able to accomplish that.

Micah lets out a groan from the table. That sound is like a lightning bolt between my legs. Is this how he sounds when he finishes? We haven't been in here long. I want to ask him to be quiet, but I can't. The truth is, many of my clients make sounds of enjoyment. It's such an ego boost. I pride myself on the reactions that are involuntary during my time with them on the table. But all Micah's moan makes me want to do is turn him over, uncover him and stroke him there.

I wonder if he's hard. God if he turns over and he's hard what will I do? *You will be a professional, Hadley. You will pretend he doesn't even have a cock. He's like everyone else who's been on your table. Untouchable. You are here to provide a service. A non-sexual service.*

And then I do something I have never done in my entire career as a therapist. I moan. It's almost imperceptible but I do it, and I know he hears me because his muscles tighten for only a moment. His reaction is so brief I question if I've imagined it, but then he speaks.

"Hadley." I don't answer him. Instead, I focus on the measured long strokes down his back. On the skin that's begun pinking under my touch. "I can feel the war under your fingertips." I let out a harsh breath. War? War?! No. He is mistaken. This is an atomic bomb. We're counting down to detonation and right now, no one in this room has the code to stop it.

"Are you wet?"

"Oh..." The expression is clipped and as painful as the pulse between my legs. It's all I can say. I can't lie and I certainly can't be honest.

"I hope you're wet. I rather like you like that. Ready for me at all times. Hmm..." The way he hums makes pleasure run down my spine. "I shouldn't talk to you this way. It's inappropriate. My apologies."

What?! No! You can't just say those things and then stop. I'm okay with inappropriate. From you I'll take inappropriate anywhere.

"I..." Permission to continue dies on my tongue. A constant war between professionalism and pleasure. And when I pull the sheet to the side to reveal his left glute and leg, it almost brings me to my knees. He could have been carved from stone and turned into man.

"Do you have a policy about massages in the nude, Hadley?"

Oh. My. Fucking. God. We don't. My boss hardly has any policies. Show up. Don't piss people off. That's pretty much it. We haven't even had sex yet and God is dangling this opportunity in front of me, and I'd be getting paid for it. I cannot even believe I'm thinking about this.

"I find with my physique it's a bit more challenging for therapists to work me properly with a barrier", he explains. When he doesn't get a timely response from me, he becomes more direct. "Unless you're uncomfortable and this request or act bars me from receiving therapy from you in the future, I'd like the sheet removed."

Does it make me uncomfortable? With anyone else I'd say yes. But with Micah? No. The problem I'm having is this will be the first time I've seen him naked. This is my job. And the only thing I want from him are the only things I can't have at my job.

"I'm not uncomfortable, it's just that..." I can't tell him why I want that sheet to stay firmly in place. Can I? Not as a therapist. Not here.

"Thank you."

And we're in a silent standoff. Me, hands hovered over his backside and him completely aware of my pause. He says nothing and at this point, I'm surprised he isn't ordering me to shift the flimsy barrier. I wait, watching the steady rise and fall of his back, then finally, I slide the sheet from his body and lay it on a nearby chair.

I struggle to look at him but yet I need to. God I need to take him in. Especially while he's facing the floor.

"Glutes and legs?" My voice is a little hoarse and I could really use some water but that is far from an option right now.

"Glutes and legs."

My oiled hands drop to his lower back and the God before me doesn't respond in the slightest. I rarely get called to massage a glute. The only reason I can do this is because I train on it. I look because I have to if I want to avoid inadvertently touching between his legs. And yet I know when I start massaging the other direction, muscles will be flexed, skin will be shifted, and I will know whether he waxes or not.

Micah groans and I stop breathing. I'm sure what I'm doing does feel good, but I can't help but to fantasize about what else I could do to him that would feel better. When you're a therapist for so long, many times you can just move by the feel of your client. Their muscle response guides you more than what you see. But what I see is that he does in fact wax and I have so, so, so many questions for him about this.

"I missed you when I was in Houston", he shares as I work my way down his leg. "I hope that's okay to tell you", he hedges.

"Yes", I tell him, trying my best to keep it professional while I work the sculpture that has missed me so.

I am nothing but the model therapist as I work over his muscular body. However, my ethics and professionalism are challenged as I ask him to roll over. I study him as he turns to his side, his back facing me at first for the turn and when he lays on his back, I huff out an audible breath of air. He's hard, huge, and dripping.

Instinctively I turn away, but his hand catches me by the wrist, stopping me. I can't bear to look at him.

"It's too early to be finished, is it not? Or does my body make you uncomfortable?"

"I'm sorry. I shouldn't have looked. I shouldn't have done that", I panic, still unable to look at him.

"I'm waiting for my massage, Hadley." He sounds like an entitled prick right now and I face him to tell him, but his eyes...they don't look back at me in challenge. They're darker. Dilated with lust.

"I can cover..."

"There's no policy and I prefer to be nude", he challenges before I can finish my offer. "I believe you start with my legs", he prompts.

Reluctantly. I begin again, glancing his direction time to time to see if he is watching me. He seems to be enjoying my touch which was a partial distraction from his hard, leaking cock.

"I'm sorry", I whisper, when I graze his sack.

"Don't be." He leaves it at that. His tone tells me there's no discussion necessary. I swallow, thinking about how much he'd let me get away with. How much I'd want to get away with.

Suddenly my mind is racing with the possibilities. I don't know for sure, but I'm pretty certain he'd let me please him. At the very least, he'd let me clean him off. And God do I want that. I want to know what he tastes like. What he feels like in my fist and how soft he is on my tongue. I want to know how he likes it. If he expects me to swallow and if it turns him on to make me gag.

It's funny how I've never had the desire...no I've been thoroughly repulsed to even think about putting a penis in my mouth. It's never been enjoyable. Always the guy's idea. He finishes without warning, and it tastes like salty metallic tasting chicken broth but thicker and not warm enough to be safe for consumption. I bet he wouldn't taste like that at all...

"Hadley." He calls my name, and I drag my gaze up to his face. I'm so distracted by the possibility of touching and tasting him; I was on autopilot with my massage. "It's not shameful to want to touch it." My mouth falls open at his comment. "Or to taste it." I shake my head. "I'm not asking. I'd never belittle what you do. I'm simply stating a fact. And the thing is, Hadley...even if you wanted to, I wouldn't allow it."

"Why?" I cannot believe I just asked that. What in the ever-loving hell is wrong with me?

"Because that would make me like every other man out there. And I said I'd never lie to you. I'm not like every other man. You deserve the best and you will receive nothing less. It's simply not my turn yet."

And with that, Micah relaxes, closes his eyes and we finish the massage in silence.

# Chapter 8
# Micah

**December 27th 8 p.m.**
(Present Day)

I had been dreading this day. Almost every woman who has become one of us struggles with seeing...no...knowing they aren't the only one we're with. You see, being told something is entirely different than witnessing it. For almost everyone, seeing is believing. Hadley is no different than most of our women.

I watch her sitting on the couch, sipping from a glass of whiskey she shakily poured herself when we arrived at my home. The full weight of what she had agreed to months ago was threatening to crush her.

In truth, I wanted to do much more to Linea. She's an absolute dream when it comes to sex. She thrives on being possessed. Owned. Fucked. And I wanted nothing more than to do those things to her in front of Hadley, all to come back to Hadley and possess, own, and fuck her just the same. But even I knew that would be a long shot. Hadley needs more time. More training. More trust.

"Stand up." She gives me a teary chuckle and sets her glass down on the coffee table in front of her, slowly rising to obey my order.

"Tell me what you're thinking." I can't fix it if I don't know. And my job is to make adjustments to what I do…to give Hadley a different perspective that's grounded in reason and logic, not customs and expectations of society.

"I…I…can't watch you do that. I mean I know…I know what you do when you aren't with me. But I…" She sobs openly but I make no move to comfort her. I need to hear what she has to say, and I don't want to cut her off with my reassurance, because I have none. None of this is changing. And the sooner she understands that the sooner we can move forward.

"You're mine", she looks at me, tears streaking down her face. "You're supposed to be *mine*." She wipes her face with the back of her hand. "You gave yourself to her." She hiccups back her tears. "In front of me. And she took what you gave her and loved it." More hiccups. "…loved you." Her voice cracks at her next revelation. "And you love her."

I nod and it breaks the dam wide open once more, but still, I don't comfort her. I was honest about this too. The night I told her what I wanted from her, she asked me this question and I told her that our love would be different but in many ways, it would be just the same as my love for the others.

I cross the room to throw another log on the fire so I can think about what I want to do next. I don't want Hadley going to bed like this and I'm surely not letting her leave as she is. But when I turn to her, she looks so utterly shattered. And despite my openness and my need for her to be open with me, even I can't be comfortable with her so upset. In fact, I never want to see her like this again.

"I never thought you'd show me that I was just like the others. Nothing more special or more important even though I'm yours."

"Let's go", I tell her as I walk through the living room to the hall. I read somewhere that a walk in nature or a shower helps to reset a person when they're not feeling their best. A walk is clearly out of the question now, but a shower is beyond doable.

Hadley sobs openly but follows. I'm surprised. Immediate compliance isn't normally her way. If I had to guess, her sudden obedience is coming straight from defeat. As I pass my office, I think of Linea. She went through defeat, but it was different. It was trauma. Paralyzing and terrifying trauma. I'm glad Hadley and Linea do not have this in common.

"Why are we in here", Hadley asks, sniffling and squinting at the bright bathroom lights.

I hang my jacket on one of the towel hooks on the wall and grab a washcloth. My cuff links clink on the marble counter while I consider my answer. Rolling up my sleeves, I observe Hadley. She's stopped sobbing but tears still fall in silence down her beautiful cheeks.

"Am I being punished?" She hiccups in a few breaths, fighting another crying spell. Still, I don't answer her. I wet the washcloth, wringing out any extra water. "I'm not apologizing." Her face crumples again as she beings to sob.

"Hadley Joanna, we're going to fix this. That's why we're in here." I press the hot cloth against her face, and she nuzzles into my hand. "And I expect no apology from you. Close your eyes", I gently order her as I do my best to wipe away her eye makeup. She relaxes at my touch, and I take in this beautiful angel standing before me. She's stunning. Even when her emerald-colored eyes open, makeup smudges and all I want to press my lips to hers and get lost in her.

The green satin gown I selected for her is fit for a goddess. “I love the way you look in this gown. Now I want you out of it.” She shakes her head in silent protest, but she knows she doesn’t really get a choice. “Turn around, Hadley.” She opens her mouth to protest and then closes it, thinking better of whatever she was about to say. I don’t tolerate sass. She’s gotten leeway tonight because her response to Linea and I was expected. But I’m still expecting compliance. It’s a rule, she’s bound by the agreement to follow it, and I’m bound by the agreement for punishing her if she does not.

She reluctantly turns around and I take a moment to admire her. How the gown hugs her beautiful body. How that beautify body is all mine. Wasting no more time, I move her hair off to the side to find the zipper.

“This feels like pity”, she remarks.

I laugh. I don’t pity people. I help them. But pity them? No. That’s not my style. “Which part?” I have to know precisely the thing that makes her feel like I’m tending to her because I feel sorry for her. She’s got me curious. It will help me understand who Hadley is even more with this piece of the puzzle.

“The way you’re taking care of me as if I can’t do it myself. And then layering something dirty on top. Like you’re trying to get me to believe that you love me as much as you love her.”

I contemplate her statement. But before I respond, she continues.

“We don’t get a say on anything. Meanwhile, you and your brothers run around doing whatever you like with whomever you like, and we just get to take it. Like it’s nothing.”

My hand stalls on her zipper and I feel her body stiffen. “Tell me more”, I prompt her. This time she laughs. Her laugh is a bit sinister mixed with some frustration.

"I can't. I don't know what you do every day...or should I say who you do every day...because it's a rule. And here I am, left to play within these tiny borders of my agreement."

I tug the zipper down and push the garment from her shoulders. She helps the cuffs of her dress slide over her hands without any prompting from me. Right now, she's so caught up in her anger, I'm not even sure she realizes what she's saying. But I do. And with every passing second that ticks by, my perfect little world starts to crumble down around me.

"Stay." It's one word laced with tempered anger. An order I give her as I cross the space to turn on the shower. My pulse is pounding in my ears as I try not to come unglued at the reality of what I'm going to be faced with. *Tiny borders of my agreement.* That sentiment echoes through my mind as I try to focus on the sound of the water hitting the tiled floor. *Tiny borders of my agreement.*

The agreements were designed to give everyone *more* of what they love. Not trap them. No one has *tiny borders*. And the only reason Hadley would make that comment is if there were things she left off her agreement that she wanted to experience.

I take meticulous care in disrobing, so I don't lose my shit. Looking at Hadley, standing in the middle of the bathroom in only her panties as I count each button I undo on my dress shirt only fuels my anger. When our eyes meet, the worry in them tells me she's well aware that I know she lied. Her agreement is a sham.

"Micah." She lets my name hang there. The plea of just my name bouncing around the room. She's unsure of how to proceed. That makes two of us.

"Turn around." Her shoulders slump at my order. She thinks I don't want to look at her. The truth is, I need a distraction. Her pretty little cunt will do just fine to temper my anger. "Take off your panties." I stand still, watching her slide the insignificant piece of fabric over her hips and then down her thighs until she finally bends to give me a look at what I want to see. No. What I *need* to see.

"Stop. Stay right there." She's wet with my seed. The whooshing sound in my ears gets louder because in this moment, the reality is, she could be out. She could be done in this group for the infraction she made. My woman committed one of the biggest violations of all. She lied in her agreement. The only infraction worse than this one is if she were to touch another outside of our group. The latter is grounds for immediate dismissal the former hinges on votes from my brothers.

I'm painfully hard right now. Partly because of Hadley and partly because I'm enraged and want to claim what's mine. Especially if it won't be mine for much longer. At the thought of all my lasts with Hadley, I discard the rest of my clothes on the floor and stand behind her, considering my options. There are only two. Let her go or fight like hell to keep her. The latter may tear the brotherhood apart. The former may tear me apart.

I slide a finger through the wet mess glistening on her pink pussy and she whimpers. Satisfied with her response, I slide her panties the rest of the way down and tap on her leg, signaling she should lift her foot up and repeat the gesture with the other leg.

"You will shower." I grab her by the shoulders and turn her around to face me. "Everything gets cleaned but your cunt." She huffs out a breath at my crass language, but I ignore it. "You will wear a robe to wait for me. The living room is where you will stay until I come for you. Do not leave unless you have permission. You do not get to speak to anyone unless I allow it." Her eyes start to tear up at my stern orders, but compassion has left me now. I grip her chin hard. Much harder than I should, and she winces. "Do. You. Understand."

"Yes, Micah", she says with trembling lips, and I release her immediately.

"You held back with your agreement." I arch an eyebrow when she doesn't answer.

"Yes." The first of what will be many tears start to fall and I realize, I can't be here for this. I can't even be in the same room with her because the cloud of rage mixing with lust will make me do things I'll regret. And the one place I do not want to have a regret is with Hadley. The thought alone is too much already, and I don't even have the specifics from her.

I leave her without another word, closing the door behind me, stark naked. Finding my phone on the kitchen counter, I pull up my brothers' group text and then decide against it. They aren't through with dinner yet and I need to get everyone on the same page quickly, so I call Braden.

"Hello." He sounds like he's at the dinner table. "Micah?" I hear the conversation dissipate and then a door close.

"I need all the men here in an hour. We need a vote." I want to throw up just saying those words.

"A vote? For what? Jesus. What happened?" I can hear the thread of panic in Braden's voice. We've never had an emergency vote. Almost six years of being together and all the changes we've been through and now we need a vote?

"She lied, Braden." There's silence on the line. "About the agreement. She lied." I'm seething.

"Oh shit. What are we talkin' here..."

"I don't know. I just asked if she was holding back on her agreement. If she wasn't truthful. And she said yes."

"Sonofabitch", Braden fumes on the line with me.

"I know. I know. You have to bring Linea. Everyone else goes to Mav's and Grace is in charge." Since Linea and Grace were the first two in the group of women to join us, they know a little more by proxy. The trust we place in them is much different than the others and we only call upon them to help in this way when absolutely necessary. This is necessary. "She's the extra vote. Unless you can think of something better."

Braden lets out a heavy sigh. "No. I can't think of a better way to do it. Where's Hadley? I don't want them interacting."

I grind my teeth at him treating her like a criminal. It's not like she's going shank Linea or something. "In the living room. She does not have permission to interact with anyone. She knows there will be consequences if she does."

"Okay. Alright."

"Have everyone come to the dining room." I hang up the phone, not waiting for a reply already on my way to pour myself a stiff drink. How could this have happened? I'm not wearing clothes walking around my house with the hardon of the century. This was not how I saw my night ending. Crying? Yes. Confessions of epic proportions on accident? No.

It explains so much, though. She was so much farther behind the others in acclimating to the lifestyle. I just chalked it up to her being overwhelmed. Being the last of twelve women can be hard.

There's no way around what will happen tonight. I'll either be drowning myself in alcohol and pussy or punishing my girl. What she did put us at risk, and I imagine the guys will want to hear her explanation. I take a sip of my whiskey and hear my name. She sounds terrified. She should be.

Tossing back the rest of the drink and pouring myself another, I head to the hall where I hear her calling me once more. She looks me over, shock on her face at the sight of me walking around my home naked, as I barrel towards her. But I stop, just out of arm's reach.

"Come here." I barely recognize my own voice because it's vibrating with anger. So much pulsing anger at the betrayal I can barely see reason. She reluctantly steps forward, her eyes downcast. "Look at me." She does, but this time, she doesn't have tears in her eyes. She's too nervous to cry. "I want to shove my hard cock down your throat until you lose that gag reflex of yours." She takes a small step back. I shake my head, partly at her and partly at me. I don't threaten people, especially women, but my cock is hard, I'm angry as hell and she's so fucking tempting.

"But that would be wrong. Using you to take care of me like this...it would be wrong. And I respect you more than that. So I have to know, do you want out?"

"No", she shakes her head, tears forming in her eyes once more.

"So you want me to fight for you? Fight for us?" I put all my focus into not to getting choked up over this. The thought of losing her is pure agony. The thought of keeping her is pure bliss because now I know she was holding back which means what we have will be so much better than it has been, which up until now, I thought was pretty damn great. She nods and I've never needed to hear words more in my entire life than in this moment.

"Why?" I'll call this whole thing off if her reason is flimsy, because if I'm being honest with myself, I'm hurt that she didn't trust me enough to draft an honest agreement.

"I fell for you in that bar." She hiccups. "I was not supposed to fall for anyone, especially a guy like you." She chuckles and it sounds like the chuckle of someone who's sanity might be slipping a little. "You're the honest guy. You're the lawyer who bartends for his friends. You were supposed to be a sleazeball. And yet through all this, you managed not to be. And I knew you were a good guy the moment you helped that mom at the ice cream shop." She chuckles again and wipes her face. "Because what single, lawyer, pretty boy bartender does that?" She wipes her face with her fingertips and looks me in the eyes. "I liked you when we met but I didn't realize how much I loved you when I walked away. I don't want to be without you. Because the truth is, I was so much more miserable without you than I was watching you get head tonight." She hiccups a few sharp breaths, trying to stifle a new crying fit and then glances down at my cock, still standing at attention. "I could..." She sobers quickly at her offer.

I won't let her finish. "No, you will not. Not like this. Trust me. If I fight for you and win, I have big plans for that mouth of yours." She shivers at the thought. "Go sit", I tell her, as I give her a gentle kiss on the forehead and walk past her. Now is not the time for talk. Now is the time for planning, thinking, and strategizing and I can't be around her while I do these things. My anger and worry are too distracting. I have to think like a lawyer and not like a lover.

The hour passes quicker than I would have liked it to. I work very well under pressure; however, this deal is important to me. When deals are important to me, I like more than an hour to get together a presentation, an argument and legal documents. But by the time the first brother files into my dining room, it doesn't matter. It's show time and my best under the tight timeline will have to do.

When Braden and Linea enter, my pulse skyrockets. I can already see the answer on Braden's face. He's going to vote *no*. We shake hands and he can barely look at me.

"I'm sorry, man", he tells me, confirming my worst fear.

I simply nod my head and fight the urge to plead with him to change his mind. If I could play the best friend card, I would, but that's not how tonight will work. Braden will get a chance to explain himself. He'll be honest which is a foundation of trust and the only way in which the group can operate well.

I nod at Linea, but she walks right up to me and hugs me. "I'm scared for you", she whispers against my neck as she hugs me tight. I chuckle at her admittance, but I can't be dismissive. I'm scared for me too. Instead, I hug her back and just relax for a moment. I release her when I hear other footsteps filing in and greet each of the guys before they sit.

Once everyone is seated, I take a steadying breath and begin.

"There's no easy way to say this, so I'll get straight to it. Hadley's agreement is a lie." The guys mumble under their breath and shake their heads. "We have safeguards in place for this which is why I called you here tonight."

"Which parts are a lie", Callan asks with curiosity.

"I don't know. To be honest, I was so angry, I wasn't in a place where I was thinking clearly enough to get those details." He nods in response, and I continue.

"While I don't know the details of what she lied about, or even really why she lied, I do know that she wants to continue with us and wants to make things right." More grumbles come from the men and my heart sinks. "Before we vote, I think we owe it to Hadley to allow her to speak."

"*We* owe it to Hadley", Braden looks at me incredulously.

"We also owe it to ourselves. When we started this brotherhood, we agreed to always do the right thing." Jonathan glances at Linea and she gives him a small smile. There were many times when we had to make this hard choice, and it sucked...and we fought about it. "We owe it to the brotherhood to hear from Hadley so we can understand. We'll make a poor decision otherwise."

"Before I bring her in, remember how you would want your girl to be treated if she were in Hadley's shoes." I give this reminder because it's easy to treat others like shit when they betray your trust. Out of all these men, my wound is far greater than theirs on so many levels. But what you aren't as close to, you can easily give away and I cannot let that happen tonight.

The men nod in agreement, and I leave to get Hadley. As soon as she sees me, she rises, looking more terrified than she was earlier. "The men would like to hear from you. They have questions." If it were possible, she pales at this. "I know you're nervous, but you have to represent yourself. If you do not, I'm afraid tonight will be your last night with us."

"I'm scared." Her voice quivers and I understand. I'm scared too, just for different reasons.

"Do you know what I tell my clients when they're on the stand?" She shakes her head. "Nothing matters but the truth. Let the jury hear your voice. Be honest. Answer the question. There is no room for anything else. And if there is ever a moment when I think you need help, I'll be there. Just trust me." I lean in and brush my lips over hers. "Can you trust me?" She closes her eyes and nods. "Good girl."

# Chapter 9
# Micah

**July 7th 6:20 p.m.**

I hear her heels click down the hall slow and steady. She didn't run...or call me a pervert...yet. My guess is that she's curious. I can work with that. Curiosity is good. It means she isn't closeminded. That there's hope I'll still have her after tonight.

"Scotch", I ask over my shoulder, as if what we're about to talk about is as commonplace as a grocery list when I hear her stop in the threshold.

"Yes, please", she quietly answers me, but doesn't step into the room quite yet.

"You didn't run out of here screaming", I acknowledge with a chuckle. When she doesn't say anything, I look over from my second pour. She's leaning against the doorframe biting her lower lip. "But you look like you're considering running out of here now", I muse.

She steps into the room as I turn to her, seeming to find her confidence to face me and have this conversation.

"Why did you follow me, Hadley?" It's a simple question but there is no doubt the answer is complicated. She accepts the drink, and I clink my glass against hers and take a sip. She does not. She's too focused on me telling her I want to share her with my friends. That's good. She's smart that way. This isn't just some perversion. It's a way of life. And if she agrees, it will be her way of life too. I just hope she remembers how quickly she ran over here after I ordered her too. How wet her panties were. How she was willing to let me finger her in the foyer upon her arrival all because she knows what I give her is without question better than she'll ever get in the average dating market.

"Were you joking?"

I laugh. Hard. "No. I am not joking." This time she takes a sip of her drink. "In fact, I'd draft your agreement with you right now if you were willing. Then we'd spend the weekend reviewing all the rules and expectations."

"Like...a fifty shades agreement?" I shake my head.

"Would you like to see mine?"

"You have an agreement?"

"All of us do."

"How many of there are you?" She says this as though we're a species of mythical creatures, which she wouldn't be too far off about this. What we do isn't exactly normal and if there are many groups like us, they don't advertise it, that's for sure.

"I'm the last man of twelve. You would be the last woman of twelve.

You would share me with all of them?" Hadley's voice gets higher at the end of her question, and I simply nod, motioning for her to sit with me at the table. But instead of allowing her to sit in a chair, I pat the top of the table, indicating that is where I want her. She looks at me reluctantly and I know what she's thinking. She thinks I want to touch her. I do, but not right now. I simply want to give her the feeling of power and authority, while we talk about the areas where she'll have none. I don't want her to start getting defensive and shut down.

I take her drink and nod for her to sit where I've indicated. Reluctantly she does so.

"Your haste is something that will be frowned upon going forward", I tell her, handing her glass back.

"So, this is a dom-sub thing?" She looks insulted. "I won't be ordered around." She takes a drink, her hand shaking on the way up to her mouth.

"No. This is a *rules*, thing. We don't negotiate our expectations. And yes, you will be ordered around", I tell her, resetting the expectation as I take my seat in the chair, below her but clearly in charge of her even though she looks down on me. "But to answer your question about me sharing you, the answer is no. Not with the women anyway, unless you'd like that", I remark, dangling bait I hope to God she takes while I grab her ankle and work at the buckle on her shoes so she's barefoot before me. "Would you like to know how it works?" I let one shoe fall with a thud and work on the other foot.

"Yes."

Thank fuck. "I help you with your agreement that outlines your sexual preferences. Once it's finalized, I take it to my brothers. They have an opportunity to ask questions for clarity's sake only. I take those questions back to you. We finalize the agreement and then I take you to see our doctor. He gives you a birth control implant. And then no later than the minimum required time that it takes for that magic implant to work, I'm going to fuck you. A lot. Because Hadley, thinking about my cock in your tight cunt has been a constant distraction." She sucks in a breath as I place her bare feet on my thighs and continue. "After that long day of fucking, I start making plans for Introduction Night, where you will meet all the men, and take their seed in the form of their choosing. And finally, I schedule a double date with us and each man and his girl before you start going off with them by yourself."

She watches my fingers as I move her skirt up over her knees, just a bit to create the silent promise of more. Or maybe it's incentive. I'm so nervous she'll turn me down at this point, I'm not exactly sure what my motive is with this move.

"You want me to have sex with them? All at the same time?" She's shaking her head, and I can tell she's starting to panic.

"You'll be with us for the evening. But yes. Sex is required. When the bedroom door shuts, they have two goals. The first is to make you feel good. The second is to make you theirs. You become theirs once they cum inside you. Think of it liked being marked." She sucks in a breath and shakes her head, lifting her foot off my leg to hop down from the table. But I won't allow it. Not yet. She doesn't have all the information. So I grab her ankle and she looks at me, with wild eyes. "What you're imagining isn't it."

"How do you know what I'm imagining", she fires back, clearly terrified of what she may have gotten herself into.

"Because the only reference most people have are dirty videos where a woman is treated like a fuck doll for a group of men's pleasure. That's not what this is. You will be worshiped. Coveted. It's really a beautiful exchange. On this night, you make a commitment to obey me, even through the will of my brothers. And we make a commitment to always treasure you in the ways you most deeply desire." She squirms on the table and allows me to plant her bare foot back on my thigh. She's aroused. This is going to happen.

"What about disease?"

"Anyone outside the group is off limits. If you touch someone outside of the group in a sexual way, you're out. There are no exceptions. No second chances. You'll be tested when you get your implant. We have already been tested and to this day remain clean because of our strict adherence to this rule."

"We haven't even had sex. How do I know this is real? That you're even any good at it? How do I trust a bunch of strangers on top of that? And what if they don't find me attractive, or me them?"

I smile, my hand moving from her ankle up her calf and then resting on her knee. I stroke the inside of her knee with my thumb and think about how I want to answer her. It won't do any good to make her an empty promise about my prowess. Men make empty promises about their skill all the time just to get into a woman once. So instead of telling her all the reasons she'll never want to leave my bed, I tell her a truth based on nothing having to do with my skill but instead, having to do with my sincerest wishes for her and all the women I date.

"I want you to let me serve you. I would consider it the greatest of all privileges if you let go and gave your body to me. And the others...they've already seen you. They agreed to you without hesitation." My finger lightly strokes the inside of her thigh, and I see her breath kick up a notch. "I think you'll find your other boyfriends quite charming and easy to love, though, some take a little more getting used to than others." I consider telling her more but decide against it because I don't want to scare her off. I can tell she's an overthinker of the worst kind.

"I need time to think. This feels like a game. I wasn't expecting this from you." It's a reasonable request. But even though it's a reasonable request, we won't see each other again until I get my answer. And if she doesn't agree, we won't see each other again at all.

"I can assure you, this is far from a game, Hadley. It's my way of life. And I think you're perfect for it. Take all the time you need."

# Chapter 10
# Hadley

**December 27th 9:55 p.m.**
(Present Day)

It's so quiet when we approach the dining room, one would think it was empty.

"Are you ready, Ms. McAfferty?"

I nod in response.

"I should warn you, you may have decisions to make and almost no time to make them. This is a test, Hadley. Likely one of many from this point forward."

"Okay." I feel like I could throw up. I've had to face down these men stark naked and I was terrified. Now, there are no words to describe how tortured I feel. I lied. I hurt them. And I'm on trial for it.

Micah shows me in, and all eyes are on me. Everyone is dressed just as they were at the dinner. I stand out like a sore thumb in my satin robe. The same robe I wore on Introduction Night. Micah did this on purpose. This is a strategy. This robe connects me to these men. It's the robe they took off me to expose my naked body for their pleasure.

When Micah ushers me to the head of the table, I notice the men aren't the only ones here to ask questions of me. Linea sits off to the side, not at the table, purposely excluded from the group of men. She looks like an angel. Virtuous. A virtuous cock sucker.

I feel my face heat with anger as I look her over, then I turn to Micah, looking for an explanation.

"She's the tie breaker if there is one. We'll vote right here. She'll get a vote if it comes down to it." He spends no more time explaining. It's clear she doesn't get a say and neither do I. "Gentleman, who would like to ask the first question?"

"What's missing from your agreement", Cooper asks. He thrums his fingertips on the table, and I can't tell if he's nervous or if he's bored.

"Hadley? I think we'd all like to know." Micah looks at the men. "Keep in mind, she won't be able to name everything. Cooper, let's have her name two or three things, shall we?"

"Sounds good. I just want to know how far off her agreement is to what it should be", Cooper clarifies.

"Hadley?" Micah looks at me expectantly and when I open my mouth to answer, he redirects me. "This is Cooper's question. You'll answer to Cooper now."

I swallow hard. He's not making this easy for me on purpose. He's teaching me a lesson. *I can do this. I can do this. I can do this.*

"Sex with a woman." I look at Micah and he waives me on. "What is it called when you're tied up?"

"Bondage", several men say at the same time.

"I'd like to be forced to have sex against my will." This one makes my face turn beet red. Women aren't supposed to want this. What does this say about me?

"Consensual non consent or a rape fantasy? There's a difference", Emerick asks, leaning forward, truly curious about the workings of my mind and what turns me on.

"Both." There are hums of approval in the room and Micah waits for the room to quiet before he addresses Cooper.

"Cooper, does that answer your question to your satisfaction?"

"Yeah. Thank you, Hadley." Cooper does not look pleased, and I notice Emerick write something down on the small slip of paper in front of him then turn it over and set his pen down on top of it.

"What spooked you, darlin?" Archer's the only one who has ditched his suit coat and rolled up his sleeves showing his heavily inked forearms. He leans back with his fingers laced behind his head, elbows fanned out as if this is just another meeting among the men.

"I was scared." Archer unlaces his hands and waves me on to continue. He's giving me the benefit of the doubt, while Braden and Tyler begin writing on their papers.

"I was afraid of being judged. If I put too many things I liked in my agreement, you might think I was a freak. If I put too many hard limits, you'd think I was a prude." Archer holds up a finger when Micah opens his mouth to move on, signaling that he should wait. He knows there's more and he's giving me one more chance. Landon begins writing on his paper, and the sheer pressure of it all forces me to come out with it. "I didn't even know you. How could I be sure you'd be careful. I mean, the things I had fantasized were just that...a fantasy. The thought that I'd just trust a bunch of strangers I'd never met before because someone I had only known for a few months told me I could seems a little naive."

Jonathan and Mav start writing and I can't keep my question to myself any longer. "What are those? What are you writing about me?" I don't even look at Micah because I feel like I'm having an out of body experience. I'm nervous, angry, heartbroken, sad, and in love all at the same time.

"Those are the votes", Micah says in a detached way that sends chills down my spine. Does he not care?

"The votes. You're voting before I'm finished? How is that fair?" I turn to Micah for support. He gives me a pointed look, his brows furrowed, and his lips pressed into a thin line. I have angered him, but how, I have no idea.

"Anyone else have any questions for Hadley before we vote?"

"Why didn't you come to Micah when you realized you were safe", Graham asks from across the room. He's a businessman. I should have expected this question from him. There is no way he's going to like my answer.

"Because I was scared that Micah would leave me." It was a shit answer, but it was truthful. "Who wants to be with a liar? Especially someone who's job is arguing with liars every day."

"What about the rest of us? Did you care about us", Harlan asks. He's the bleeding heart of the group. This one cut him deep. I can see it in his eyes.

"Yes. I care about all of you. That's why coming clean was so hard for me." My voice starts to quiver as Graham and Harlan begin writing.

"How can we trust you if we let you stay? What will you do differently?"

Callan is the second bleeding heart. Tied with Mav. They must hate me. "I don't know, but I'll do anything you want."

"Do you mean that", Archer asks, and my heart falls to my feet. "You know me, darlin. I'm not trying to be an asshole, but anything is big. Is it really anything or is it anything with conditions?"

"It's anything. Anything you want, I'll do. I swear it. Just give me one more chance." I beg and I hate it. I don't think I've begged a day in my life, but I'd get down on my knees if it means they'll keep me. I don't know what I'd do without these men. I know it sounds weak. It *feels* weak. In this short time, they're family to me. Being without them would leave huge holes in my life and I'm not sure I could ever fill them.

These men show me they care without getting anything in return. It could be a Sunday; early afternoon and I'm getting a call from one of them just asking about my day. Or one could pop up while I grab a drink at this tiny little pub down the street I go to sometimes just to clear my head. And at that pub, it's no bother at all when he pulls up a chair beside me and participates in mindless chatter about wherever the conversation takes us. Then he dismisses my driver and walks me home, leaving me with nothing but a sweet kiss as a goodbye.

They don't shower me with gifts. They shower me with affection and attention. And of course, we go to nice places, but we also do casual things like pick apples and make pies or go on long torturous runs with the promise of long showers and relaxing in bed afterward.

As filthy as these men are, these are real relationships. And if I lose them, I'm not just losing Micah. I'm losing all of them. Twelve breakups at the same time. Twelve of the best men I've ever dated will be gone, just like that.

Archer and Callen write on their papers and flip them over.

Micah's hand finds the small of my back and I jump at the contact. This earns me another furrowed brow while he addresses me. "Is there anything else you'd like to share before the gentlemen share their votes, Hadley?"

"I'm sorry", I tell the group, keeping it short and sweet because I feel like I could just throw up. A public breakup. Losing twelve men instead of one. The most intimate relationships with the best sex I've ever had in my entire life just gone in a matter of moments.

"Okay then. Let's begin. Tyler."

"She stays." I let out an audible sigh of relief. "Conditionally. She'll test my buddy's prototype for a year. Anything less than full commitment on this turns my vote into *she goes*."

I look at Micah, having no idea what that means. Prototype? He doesn't look happy but nods in understanding and moves on. Emerick and Graham flip their papers back over, scratch off their original decisions and rewrite them. I think I'm going to pass out. This is a community. All the men sport the same signature brotherhood rings. What would happen with Micah's if I was voted out? Would he still be able to participate? Would he have to give it back? Shame floods me as these questions whirl around in my mind. This must feel like pure betrayal to Micah and I'm about to find out who else.

"Harlan", Micah prompts.

"She goes."

I feel gutted. Harlan is the sweetest and he no longer wants me. I fight back the urge to break down just hearing the words.

"What we do is hard, Hadley. The reward is so great because the trust is so hard to give. You care more about protecting yourself than you did about trusting us to protect you", Harlan clarifies. I understand where he's coming from, but it hurts like hell.

"Landon?"

"She goes. It'll be hard for me to make a liar come", Landon says, looking right into my eyes when he says it. And that did it. Congratulations Landon. He earns the first new tear. When I go to wipe them away, he speaks again. "No, no.

You've hidden long enough, Hadley. You leave those tears alone. I want to see them fall."

"Enough", Micah's voice cuts through the room, and I jump at his authority. "She is still ours and until we finish this meeting. You will afford her the same respect as you would your own." I fight back a sob because of Micah's rescue attempt for me. Micah cares but it is beyond clear that Landon does not.

"Callen, your vote?" Micah lets out a heavy exhale beside me.

"She's out. Lying was wrong Hadley. You crossed a line", he says quite simply. At this point, I'm gasping in air while tears slide down my cheeks.

"Cooper", Micah prompts, wanting to move on as my chances of staying are looking more dismal by the moment.

"She's out. We could have given her everything she named. And she should have come forward. Damn, Hadley. I really cared about you."

I'm openly sobbing at this point and don't even notice Braden left his seat to give me water. He gets my attention with his outstretched hand, the glass tumbler meant for booze but filled with ice water held out in front of me.

"Thanks", I hiccup and take a sip.

"Braden?"

"She's out." I sob harder. "Hadley, baby, I can't take a risk of someone in the group that isn't one of us and you're simply not. You could expose those of us who want to stay hidden, and that shit destroys businesses. We've worked hard to get where we are and some of us depend on that anonymity", he explains with all the kindness he can muster. For a moment, Braden glances in Micah's direction. "I'm sorry, man. I can't do it. I can't risk my business or Linea's future business", he apologizes to his friend.

"Jonathan?"

"She stays", Jonathan says, flipping over his paper. "She didn't have all the information. People make the best decision they can with the information they have. Now she has all the information, and she'll make different decisions." He winks at me, and I give him a smile between sobs.

"Graham?"

"She stays. But my vote is conditional too. If she doesn't get the implant, my vote changes. We need to have some assurance that she's being honest until our trust is earned."

I don't know what that is or where they want to put it, and I don't care. All I know is that if it keeps me here, I'll wear whatever they want. I nod, showing my agreement as Micah continues around the room.

"Emerick?"

"She goes. She could have had all of that. I could have given her two of the three on her short list." He just shakes his head at me, disappointed in my decision to keep some of my deepest sexual fantasies a secret.

"Mav?"

"She stays. She's had it the hardest of all of them." Some of the men grumble in disagreement but Mav won't have it. "You think coming into a group of over twenty swingers is easy? You don't think people are watching and judging? Christ, I was nervous the first time I did any of this and I wanted it just as much as I did my first restaurant. Think about your insecurities when you started. Cut the girl some slack."

I mouth the words *thank you* to Mav, and he nods in acceptance and waives Micah on to continue.

"Archer?"

Archer grabs his paper and walks around the room, handing it to me to read. I suck in a loud breath at the words.

"Go on, baby. Read it aloud for me", he croons, wrapping his arm around me.

"She stays", I gasp more air in as a new wave of crying washes over me. Archer would have torn me apart. To think he wouldn't have wanted me...I can't bear the thought of it.

Archer hugs me close, then he kisses me on the cheek. "I need five minutes with you before I head out, darlin." I nod, not sure what to expect in the next vote. It's Micah's and he is so mad. He could have very easily changed his mind about me after hearing what I had to share. Archer shakes Micah's hand says something to Micah that I can't make out, but I hear my name for sure and Micah nods.

"She stays." I heave out a sigh of relief. Micah wants me. I don't think I have enough votes to stay but I throw myself at him, wrapping my arms around his neck, begging for his comfort. "Conditionally", he tells me sternly. "You will have an open agreement from this point forward and you will give everything you own to me. You will sign your house and car over to me. The money you earn at work will go into a new account and be held there for you should this arrangement not work out. You will stay with me, use my transportation, use my money. Everything you do...everything you don't do...I will know about it."

I can't speak. All I can do is process his expectations bouncing around in my head. He wants me to give up everything to be with them. Literally.

"This is where you reaffirm your promise to do anything it takes to stay with us, Hadley. There will be more. This is just the tip of the iceberg." His cool eyes look down on me and my heart is beating out of my chest.

"I will. I do. Okay."

Very good." Micah pries my arms from around his neck and turns me to face the group. "We have a tie. Linea, are you prepared to share your vote?"

Although I can't see my face, I'm sure any color it had has drained from it. The woman who sucked my boyfriend off in front of me is going to determine my future with these men. The woman who I ignored. I treated her like vapor. This...this right here is why you treat everyone with respect because you never know when someone who is nothing to you becomes everything to you.

Linea stands and all eyes are on her. She looks like a goddess. Tall, slender, long blonde hair, perky full breasts spilling out of her cream-colored suit jacket. She looks like a winter queen. She's their queen. And she's voting on me.

"What we do is hard."

I stifle an eye roll. It's the same speech she gave me at the bar earlier this evening.

"Not everyone is cut out for it."

I want to crawl across the table and scratch her eyes out for even inferring I might not be able to do this.

"It's hard for me to question someone's devotion when they stand in front of all of us and bear their soul. I'm surprised at those of you who said she goes. I would have never expected that from you." She gives Braden the side eye and he shakes his head in return. "I think Hadley is brave. That bravery is exactly what will get her through this tough time. She should be admired and not scorned. My vote is yes, conditionally."

"Oh god", I gasp, my palms resting on the glossy table. "Yes?" Linea nods her head at me, affirming I had heard her right.

"You don't get to make conditions, Linea. You belong to me so I say what you will and will not do. You've done your part and that'll be all", Braden interrupts her.

"Braden, with all due respect, let's hear her out." I watch Micah and Braden exchange a look that says *back of*, but for entirely different reasons.

"Thank you, Micah." Linea gives Braden the side-eye once more. "Let me help you. I can help. I want to help. This is hard and you need an ally. A friend. A friend who does what we do that isn't a man", she pleads with Micah and Braden.

"You don't get to give conditions and that's the end of it." Braden turns to Micah. "Is there anything else you need from us? Because if you don't, I'm going to take Linea home and review our rules with her." Linea rolls her eyes, and Braden clenches his jaw so hard I think he's cracking teeth.

"No, gentlemen. Thank you for your time and participation on such short notice. Please drive carefully. I'll be in touch." All the men shake Micah's hand, except for Braden. Clearly, Braden is angry with his friend and my heart sinks again, knowing I caused a divide between them and probably many others.

"Micah", Archer greets Micah, going in for a hug instead of a handshake. "That was a nailbiter, man."

"Yeah. Thank you for your support. It means a lot." Micah's thanks drips with relief.

"Hadley's a good girl. She'll come around", he remarks as if I'm not standing right next to them.

"I'll have Hadley meet you in the living room when she's done going over paperwork. Make yourself comfortable. Pour yourself a drink. I'll have her out as soon as I can."

"Limits?" Archer checks in with Micah on what he can and cannot do with me tonight. Micah shakes his head and I'm so relieved. Spending time with Archer is the absolute best. Archer winks at me and then leaves the room. Now it's just me and Micah.

I turn to Micah and there's anger in his stare. I wither a fraction in front of him. I know he'd never hurt me but punish me? Yes. Yes, he would.

"Sit." He punctuates the t as he pulls out a chair from the table, indicating where he would like me to be seated. I comply immediately.

In front of me, he lays a leather folder and rests a pen on top, diagonally, just under the gold embossed letters of his law firm. Then he steps away.

I look back at him and see him fixing a drink. I'm relieved when he sets the drink down in front of me. I need this whiskey. I've earned this whiskey.

Micah pulls a chair out next to me at the head of the table. He sets two glasses down. One is identical to mine and another holds ice water. He seats himself and dips the white cloth napkin in the water glass.

"Look at me." His voice is still stern. It's angry and tense and I resign myself to whatever punishment he's going to lay out for me. Because as upset as I am at him, what I did to him, to all these men, is far worse.

I close my eyes as he blots my face with the cool wet cloth. Every touch from him I hold as a true privilege. A gift that was almost taken away.

"These documents are legally binding. There are many that require your signature." He continues wiping my face and I keep my eyes closed, just listening to his voice. *Privilege. Privilege. Privilege.* "I strongly recommend you read through them and ask any questions you have before you sign. They are non-negotiable documents. All agreements will be fully executed and followed to the letter. Any refusal on your part after signature will result in all your things being returned to you as they were, and you will go back to the life you had prior to us."

I open my eyes, and he stops wiping my face. For the first time this evening, I see sadness and not anger in his eyes. I hurt him and the fact that I did one of the worst things a partner in this group could do makes me feel like the lowest of the low. I am the lowest of the low right now. But not always. I'll make sure of it.

"I'm sorry, Micah", I tell him, grabbing his wrist to pull his hand from my face. He just looks at me and waits. "I love you. I did it because I didn't want to lose you." He lets out a laugh laced with frustration and shakes his head. "I'm not going back. I'm not backing out. And I'm not saying no", I tell him, picking up the pen and opening the portfolio.

I tug the substantial pile of paperwork out of the folder and zero in on the signature lines. None of the things in here matter. I'm signing, consequences be damned. And with that, I put pen to paper and sign on the line.

"Hadley, wait." I ignore him and flip the page, signing another line without reading the document. "You should read these. What have I taught you?"

"Read everything you sign. Line out the things you won't agree to and initial near the line-out. That's for people who provide a service for you. You aren't providing a service for me. None of your advice applies here." I look up at him and he's glaring at me again. "Well, do you provide a service for me", I challenge him.

"Watch your tone, Hadley Joanna", he warns, and I can't help but smile at the use of my nickname. It warms my heart that he still uses it. I continue to sign blindly as I explain myself further.

"All I'm saying is that I don't get to negotiate any of these terms. And if I'm supposed to trust you blindly to do what's best for me sexually and otherwise, there really is no point in wasting time reading through the fine print", I clarify, turning another page and signing.

"You'll be held accountable for everything in this paperwork. Which means if you so much as make a mistake, at the very least you will be punished. My recommendation is to read through these documents in your spare time, so you understand what you need to do to remain compliant."

"Okay", I tell him, without looking up.

"That's yes, Micah, from now on", he corrects me. I roll my eyes up to look at him and he's not smiling. He's never told me to address him in a specific way until now and I have to admit, it makes my belly warm at the thought of saying it.

"Yes, Micah." It comes out more breathless than I intend it to, which earns me a smile from him.

The minutes tick by. The only sound in the room is pen scratching against paper. I haven't stopped to read a single word, glance up at Micah or take a sip of my drink. When I'm finished, I lay the pen down and reluctantly look over at him. I can't tell if he's pleased or not. He doesn't look angry, but he also doesn't look satisfied.

Micah rises from his seat and stands behind me. He leans over me and all I can smell is the delectable scent of him as he flips over page after page to ensure I've not missed a signature anywhere. So male. So powerful. So mine. When he gets to the last page, he runs his nose across my cheek and presses a gentle kiss there. I reach up behind me and lay my hand on his neck, urging him to continue.

"Archer is waiting for you." He plants one more kiss on my cheek and then steps back. His warmth and scent immediately vanishing in his wake. "Meet me in the kitchen when you see Archer out."

"Okay", I answer him, and he shakes his head. "Yes, Micah."

"That's better", he tells me, his voice laced with something sinister. I shiver at the thought. I'm being punished. Shit.

"Go on", he prompts me and pulls my chair out for me to stand, then holds his hand out for me to take in his typical fashion. I'm not the lowest of the low. I'm still his queen. Even with all the rules I'm still his queen.

I pad out of the dining room, hating leaving Micah there alone. But I only have five minutes with Archer, and I intend to make all of them count. When I enter the living room, Archer is there on the couch, legs spread wide, hands behind his head with his arms fanned out, just like at the dining room table earlier. He gives me his signature mischievous smile when he sees me, and it makes my heart swell. When he pats his leg, indicating for me to sit, I all but run to him.

He throws his head back and laughs, unlacing his fingers from behind his head and holding his arms out to me.

This feels like home. It's so utterly perfect. So perfectly me. And the thought of not having this lifestyle is unthinkable. As terrified of it as I am, I want it in equal measure.

"The last time I saw you in this robe..." He unties the satin belt and opens the front of my robe, exposing my breasts all the way down to my pussy. "I remember it looked so much better on the floor", he tells me with a smile and a twinkle in his eye as he pushes the robe off my shoulders, and it pools on his legs behind me.

I rest my hands on his shoulders, needing to touch him. Needing to be anchored to one of the men who still want me to be here. His eyes roam my body. Under his stare, I feel cherished, not nervous. "Are you going to be a good girl from now on?" I nod. "I want to hear it, baby. Tell me how good you're going to be."

"I'll be good. I'll do anything. Whatever needs to be done. I'll follow all the rules." He smirks at me, and I smile back at him. "You have no limits", I remind him, keenly aware that the small amount of time we've been granted it quickly flying by.

"I don't have enough time to fuck you, baby. Lord knows I want to." I look down and it's clear he's hard.

"Can I suck on you?" He smiles at me and without another word, I slide off his lap and seat myself between his knees. With shaking hands, I unzip his pants and pull him out.

"Don't be nervous", he tells me as I wait for permission. He stands at attention, full, hard, and pierced. I simply look up at him. I am nervous. I'm nervous because things are different now. Even though Archer voted for me to stay, things are different. There's no getting around it.

With a brush of his fingertips to the side of my jaw, I begin by kissing the head of his cock. Just a gentle kiss right on the end as he slides his hand through my hair and behind my head pulling me forward to shove himself into my mouth.

He isn't violent or mean, but he doesn't let me control the depth, sliding right down my throat as I gag. "Relax, baby", he says, his voice strained with pleasure. This is new. He hasn't gagged me like this before.

Determined to please him, I grip his leg but don't fight him. And as soon as he releases my head, I pull back and gasp for air.

"We've got to work on that gag reflex of yours, hm?" He smiles at me, pleased at me for not fighting him.

I nod and wipe the dripping saliva from my chin and then the tears from my eyes. "Deep breath baby. Relax your throat", he tells me once more as he slides in until my nose is touching the little hairs above his cock.

This time I fight it. "Ah ah ah", he corrects me. "Focus, baby."

When he finally releases me, I'm gasping for air unsure of what to wipe off my face first. The tears or the spit. "Look at me." I roll my eyes up to him, unable to help feeling like I'm being punished. "I almost lost you today. That is unacceptable. I never want to see you like you were in that dining room again, understood?" I nod, swallowing thick with emotion. "Again", he tells me calmly as he guides my mouth back to his erection and gags me once more.

Each time he slides his cock down my throat, it become slightly easier to handle, but I still hate it. I wanted to make him feel good. I wanted to feel the power of making him lose control. Instead, I've unleashed a monster who's looking to tame me just like Micah. He's angry and he's showing me only a fraction of what he can do with that anger.

"Want help", I hear Micah's voice behind me, and I stiffen.

"Nah, man. We're almost done here. I need a few more minutes", Archer says as he slides back as far as he can go but then pushes my head a little further, bumping my nose up against his flesh even more, repeating the move a few more times. When he lets me up, I'm grateful. I gasp for air, tempted to beg him to stop. "Finish me off, baby", he tells me, and then lets his hand off my head.

I give him the best blow job I've ever given a man for fear he would gag me again. I'm sucking on him, making sure my tongue flattens against the underside of his crown. I can feel his piercings on the roof of my mouth and lips, careful not to use my teeth for fear of chipping them. Archer hates it when I use my hands, so I keep them firmly planted on his thighs.

"Look at me, Hadley", he rasps. And when I do, he's aiming his phone right at me, no doubt taking a video. "Good girl. That's right. Don't you dare spill a drop", he orders me in a tight voice as he erupts inside my mouth groaning with pleasure.

I swallow, and swallow and swallow, taking great care to follow his instructions of giving him a nice clean finish. When he's done, he runs his hand over the crown of my head but doesn't tell me to stop sucking him, so I don't. This is a standard expectation among the men. They tell you when to start and when to stop. And you do not start or end earlier than the permission they give.

"Look at how she takes care of me boys. Fuck...she can suck a cock. I've got some training to do but damn she'll get there in no time." His words send a shiver down my spine. This is not the end of Archer's newfound interest in owning my mouth. This is just the beginning.

His fingertips brush along my jaw, signaling I can stop. I slide him out of my mouth, kiss his tip to finish the act of affection and sit back on my haunches, waiting for further instruction.

"You did good, Hadley", he praises me as he tucks himself back into his dress pants and makes himself decent again. "You did real, real, good, darlin", he tells me, extending his hand out to help me up. I take it and he pulls me onto his lap once more and kisses me, despite the tears running down my face and the saliva around my mouth that I haven't wiped away yet.

We're out of time and I hate it. Kissing Archer is the best. It's right up there with kissing Micah. He's all stubble and a roughness that's a little unhinged but somehow relaxed. It's a perfect combination and I must admit, I'm a little sad that we only got five minutes together.

"You need to find Micah and I'm going to pick up Bethany over at Mav's." He leans his forehead against mine. "Be. Good." It's a warning laced with a desperation I never thought Archer had in him. I nod and kiss him once more. With a gentle pat on the backend, he signals that I need to get going and I reluctantly climb off him and grab my robe.

"Archer?" I pull on my robe, suddenly feeling cold now that his warmth is gone. "Do you think I can do this?"

"Do you?" It's all he says as he reaches around me to grab the belt to my robe, tying it shut for me before I go to see Micah.

I hope so.

# Chapter 11
# Hadley

**December 27$^{th}$ 10:45 p.m.**
(Present Day)

Bad girl. That's what I am right now. I've been a *verrrry* bad girl. I'm alone with Micah and I'm scared. He was so angry with me. I get it, kind of. What I did to deserve his glare in the dining room, I have no idea. But I'm sure I'll find out before the night is over.

I pad through his quiet home, every step bringing me closer to Micah. I have no idea what to expect because I didn't bother reading the agreements, but surely, he'll give me some grace. I had faith in him when I signed. Blind faith. That has to count for something in his eyes.

As I get closer to the kitchen, I smell food. We missed dinner this evening and whatever he's making smells divine. As I enter the kitchen, Micah looks like a king, standing behind the island, focused on whatever he's typing on his phone. He looks up momentarily and then glances back down, continuing to type. My heart sinks when I don't get a welcome greeting from him.

I walk up to the island and rest my hands on one of the high back stools, waiting for instruction. I feel like I no longer have the free will to roam around and do as I please. It's uncomfortable and strange. I feel the pressure to be a good girl. I want to be a good girl.

"Did you enjoy your time with Archer?" He sets his phone down and flips a grilled cheese on a frying pan.

"Yes." Micah glares at me. "Yes, Micah." I bite my lip, nervous as hell. I can't let the pressure of messing this up get to me. All I have to do is follow his rules. *Their* rules.

"You're nervous." I nod in response. "Don't be. Everything we're doing is for you. Even if you don't like it, it's for your own good." He grabs a plate, and my eyes follow his hand. My breath stops at what I see. Sitting on the counter is a glass butt plug. Next to it is a small container of lube.

"That is your punishment for not following my order." Micah pulls the dish towel from his shoulder and hangs it up.

"I...I don't understand. What did I do?"

Micah walks around from the island, grabs the plug and the lube and motions for me to follow him. I do not want this. This was a hard limit for me. At least it was a hard limit for me. Until I signed the agreement that no longer allows me to have limits. Even still, this is truly a punishment.

Micah sits down in the middle of the living room couch. "Lay across my lap. Your dinner is getting cold, and I'd like you to eat it while it's still warm. This won't take long", he informs, me with a coolness to his voice that I don't care for. He arches a brow when I don't comply immediately, and suddenly I find myself scrambling to lay on his lap.

The position is erotic and somewhat degrading. It makes me feel like a child about ready to get a spanking for putting gum in my sister's hair. His strong legs underneath me make me long for him on top of me, but there's no doubt in my mind that I won't be getting that tonight.

Micah's hand brushes up my backside and takes my robe with it. My ass is bare to him, and I squirm a little, nervous about what's next. I hear the cap to the lube open and I turn to look, needing to see what's happening next.

"Head down", Micah orders me, with the same cool detachment. Then his fingers are sliding between my cheeks, massaging my no-fly zone. "When I tell you that you may only speak to me, I mean you may only..." He slides a finger into my backside, and I grimace at the sensation. "Speak to me." He buries his finger to the last knuckle, and I let out a wince of discomfort. "What do you say?"

"Yes, Micah", I breath as he lazily pulls his finger out and slides it back in.

"Fuck, Hadley. I cannot wait to get inside this hole." I can hear the smile in his voice and feel his erection pressing into my belly. He's way too big for that. I can't even think about it. I shake my head, but don't verbalize my dislike of the idea. "You'll have no choice, Hadley Joanna. All your choices from this point forward belong to me."

I hear the cap of the lubricant open once more. "Open your mouth", he orders me, and I turn my head to the side, opening wide for him, without delay. "Good girl", he praises me as he slides the glass plug in my mouth. He continues to slowly fuck my backside as I suck on the plug. I groan around the glass implement with each pump of his finger, praying he'll change his mind.

"Despite your infraction, I'm proud of you. You were honest. You showed your fear and sadness quite genuinely. I don't take pleasure in seeing you like that, Hadley, but I needed to see something genuine. Something that was so very different than the restrained version of you that I've known. I never want to see you cry like that again, Hadley Joanna. Open."

He gently takes the plug from my mouth and in seconds, he's removing his fingers and lining the plug up with my tight hole.

"Relax. It will feel better if you relax." He tells me, using some pressure, but not enough to breach my barrier with the toy.

"I'm scared", I tell him.

"Of what?"

"It's going to hurt", I tell him.

"Deep breath", he gently orders me. "Exhale", he says once more. I tense waiting for the intrusion on the exhale, but instead, he has me repeat the breathing exercise to his liking, finally sliding the plug inside me on an exhale without warning.

I groan loudly at the intrusion, and I could swear I feel him get harder beneath me. Then he twists the plug and gives it a little tap on the end with his fingers.

"Beautiful. I love your new agreement, Hadley Joanna. This is going to be so much fun." He twists the plug, and I groan again. Then his hands are massaging my backside, causing the plug to move with each touch and change of pressure. "Up you go", he tells me, and then helps me onto his lap so I'm straddling him.

Every move I make shifts the plug inside me. But I suddenly forget about the foreign object in my backside when I look into his eyes. "I'm sorry", I tell him, choking out the words. He just looks me over in this new, cool way that he has about him when it comes to me. When I reach for his face in an attempt to try and soften it, he grabs my wrist and stops me.

"I gave up everything for this life. And when I say everything, I do mean, everything. I helped build a system that would honor the differences and preferences among us. Helped create a society where we all get to be free to experience new things and like what we like without fear of reprisal or scrutiny. The reason lying is met with the most severe consequence is because lying means you're a fraud in our world. You're an outsider. And as much as I'm angry that Braden voted you out, he has every right to protect him and Linea against someone who isn't one of us. You won't ruin my business. I don't give a fuck who knows about my involvement in this brotherhood we've created. My law firm wins. If my sex life matters to my clients then the risk is on them, not me."

"What I do care about is rebuilding us. I'm angry at you." I look down, unable to face him. "No, Hadley. You don't get to do that. Right here, sweetheart", he gently coaxes me to look up at him. When I look into those crystalline eyes, I see the sadness of the past few hours. It's new and raw and must hurt him something fierce. "I want you to want this life like I do. I want you to want us like we want you. And the moment I suspected you weren't honest about your agreement, that meant you didn't want us. You didn't want me."

I try to tell him that I do, but he silences me with a shake of the head. "Show me. Show us." I'm nodding and wiping tears from my cheeks once more. "Your dinner is cold. Let's see if we can salvage it", he tells me, moving me from his lap.

I let out a small groan as the plug shifts inside me once more. He smirks.

"I'm not hungry. Even if I were, I don't think I could eat it." Micah walks up to me and tugs on the belt of my robe, completely disregarding my comments about food. Just like Archer, he pushes it over my shoulders letting it fall to the floor. I shiver at the change in temperature, but don't cover myself. His eyes roam my body and when they meet my eyes, their smiling. My heart flutters at his acknowledgement because I feel like he's coming back to me. Like I'm not a total disappointment to him.

"You will eat. Then I'm taking you to bed. And if you're a good girl and follow all my instructions, I'll let you come tonight. But you have to be really, really, good." I nod and he lowers his lips to mine, tasting me for the first time since we've arrived home.

It's heaven. I want more. I need more. But he doesn't let me have it. He straightens, splays his hand on my lower back and leads me into the kitchen.

With every step I take, the plug shifts inside me. It doesn't hurt but I can't say it feels good either. It's just there and I don't like it. I cannot imagine someone putting their cock in there. I shiver with fear. That has to hurt. A lot.

Micah points to the exact stool he'd like me to occupy just like he did that night at the bar. He smiles when he hears the glass in my backend clunk on the top of the stool while I seat myself. "You're really enjoying this aren't you?"

"I am", he remarks, simply as he reheats my sandwich on the griddle and then begins making another, which I'm hoping is for him. We sit in silence for a few minutes before he speaks. "I want you to know that what you signed up for isn't designed to be a punishment. Even the plug you're wearing isn't really a punishment. My hope is by the end of the night, you'll miss it." I wrinkle my nose, taking a small bite of my sandwich and he laughs.

"As restrictive as my terms are, I'm giving you your life back. You may not see it that way at first, but you will, eventually", he tells me while he layers the cheese in between the bread. "You have an early day tomorrow." I frown at the thought of facing day one. I'm worried about what's to come and I'm suddenly aware of how important those documents are. I should probably go back and read them.

"What about Madison?" I wonder if my day has been canceled with her. I haven't seen her in months and was really looking forward to a day catching up.

"You keep your plans with Madison. You'll have an early start to your day tomorrow to get the prototype inserted. Then you're going to suck Braden's cock." He doesn't say *like you were supposed to do tonight*. He knows I know I failed to meet an expectation. The rule is if I get an orgasm I give it. "And finally, you'll be off to breakfast with your friend." He says all of this like it's a list of errands.

"Insert?" I pale at that word. Insert it where?

"Yes. It's a simple procedure", he tells me while lifting the corner of the sandwich up to check that it's browning appropriately on the hot griddle. When he lets the sandwich rest without flipping it, he looks up at me as though he just reported out on tomorrow's weather. "You're worried."

"Yes." He arches a brow at my snappy and now disrespectful way of reply to him. "Yes, Micah", I correct myself.

"What about?" He leans against the counter, crossing his arms against his chest, creating the most wonderful view of his muscles stretching in his shirt.

"What is it for?" I take a small bite of my sandwich and focus on chewing and the cheesy goodness on my tongue instead of the new butterflies in my stomach.

"It measures pleasure. We'll know exactly what you like and what you don't without you even having to say a word."

I'm sure I'm paling in front of him. This device means I'll have no secrets. No sexual secrets anyway.

"We'll all have an app that can track your pleasure. Think of it like an electronic sexual journal", he tells me, deciding to flip his sandwich over casually like this is no big deal.

"Where does it go?" I'm terrified to know but I have to ask.

"I don't know exactly but I can tell you we won't be able to fuck for a few days." He leans over the counter and palms my face, then he swipes his thumb over my lower lip. "But this mouth...mmmm...you're going to spend a lot of time on your knees until I can get back into your pussy." I close my eyes at the thought of it. There's nowhere I'd rather be for Micah than on my knees with his cock in my mouth. But in light of recent events, I suspect he'll take his anger out on me far worse than Archer did.

Micah makes a display of looking at my partially eaten sandwich. Deciding not to poke the bear any further, I start focusing on eating. I'll worry about tomorrow when tomorrow comes. Right now, I have bigger things to worry about. Like what's going to happen after we eat.

Neither one of us are too chatty and I'm glad. My mind is racing with the events from today. And I don't want to think anymore. Right now, talking with Micah is like thinking really, really hard. I know he doesn't want me to be guarded but how can I not be? I barely have anything left to guard.

When we're finished with our quick dinner, Micah helps me off my stool. "Let's go to bed", he tells me, as he ushers me toward the stairs. "Ladies first", he sweeps his arm out gallantly as I take the first step and feel every bit of that plug in my backside. "You. Are. Stunning." He's enjoying the view behind me. I want to glare at him but decide against it.

When we're in his room, he closes the door behind him and guides me to the center of the room. Then he circles me like a predator. Slowly looking me over while I stand there, helpless under his gaze. I can feel his eyes on me like they were his own hands.

"I want you to be clear about my expectations, Hadley." I meet his eyes and they're downright devious. "I want to know every little thing about you." He takes a lock of my wavy hair in between his fingers and rubs them together as he looks into my eyes. "But there's a fine line between understanding you and owning you. We will walk these lines every moment of every day. And while I do not expect you to kneel for me like some of the others will, I do expect compliance. Compliance will be rewarded. Anything less will be punished."

He stops next to me. "Touch your toes." I bite my lip and bend forward, touching my toes, trying to remember to breath. Micah's hand, warm and firm, rests on my backside and then runs down the back of my thigh only to sweep in between my legs and slide his fingers through my folds. I'm dry as a bone.

"Stand up." He faces me once more as I right myself, brushing my long hair out of my face and feeling embarrassed for not being turned on. This has never happened with us. I don't think I've had one day with Micah or any of these men, where I haven't been aroused until now.

He steps up to me, leaving no space between us. My nipples brush the fabric of his designer t-shirt. I can feel his body heat on my naked skin as he leans forward and murmurs in my ear. "Your body is being just as stubborn as your mind." He brushes his lips against my cheek. "I think, I'm going to teach you a lesson tonight." He drags his nose across my skin and when his lips find mine it's explosive.

I need Micah in the most visceral way. His kiss is like coming up for air and I've been deprived of it for far too long. How I could ever leave this man would be beyond me. I don't know what it would take but my God...he's *my* God. And even though I still feel betrayed by him for what he did with Linea, I want him so much more. He has never lied to me. I went into this full well knowing what he was doing when he wasn't with me. It was just so much better to pretend it wasn't happening. Except, really, it wasn't. What we had wasn't as real as it could have been, and I realize I've cheated not only myself but everyone in the brotherhood.

He's walking me back to the bed while I'm trying to take off his shirt…or at the very least, feel him up. On the way to our destination, I slide my hand down to palm his erection through his pants, but he catches my hand at the wrist as I moan my protest into his mouth.

"Get in bed", Micah is breathing so hard. He's shaking when he pulls his shirt over his head and tosses it on the floor. "Did you wash it?"

He's talking about my cunt. I shake my head as I scoot back on the bed. He gives me a wicked smile. "Spread your legs and open your mouth", he tells me as he climbs on the bed and spreads out on top of me, his face level with my pussy and his cock in my face. He turns his head to the left and kisses the inside of my thigh and then turns his head right and repeats the gesture. "Fuck. That God damned plug." He groans as he runs his finger through the center of my slit which is now soaked. "You do not have permission to come." And with that strangled declaration, his mouth is on my pussy and his cock is shoved deep into my mouth.

I'm going to orgasm. Oh my god this is bad. SO bad. He's fucking my mouth while he tongues me, and the experience is like being on drugs. I'm hyper aware of everything. His hot heavy weight on top of me, pinning me to the mattress. Him eating my pussy, sounding pleased with the taste of himself mixed with my own arousal. His cock is thick and hard, and I swear with every thrust, he slides into me a fraction deeper. It leaks on my tongue like it's been waiting to be in my mouth all day and the taste of him drives me absolutely wild.

"Let's see how close you are", he says, his mouth so close to my sensitive flesh I feel his warm words on my wet cunt. I'm close but I can't tell him that. I can't tell him to stop or to wait because my mouth is fucking stuffed with him.

He slides two fingers inside me and that does it. I'm moaning around his cock and strangling his fingers as my orgasm radiates throughout my body. I try to grind onto his hand, but he won't allow it. He simply slides his fingers out of me, moves his head away from my desperate heat and watches me fuck the air looking for friction to heighten my pleasure.

When I've stopped clenching, he pulls out of my mouth and turns himself around, so we're face to face. I don't need to say anything because I'm sure he can see the apology in my eyes. I'm not sure what my punishment will be, but I know it's coming.

"What happened", he croons to me, caging me beneath him holding himself up with one arm while he explores my body with his other hand. "Talk to me, Hadley."

"I couldn't tell you I was close", I begin, but it's not what he's looking for.

"Before you disobeyed me." He takes one of my nipples between his thumb and forefinger and rolls it between his digits, then pinches. The gesture sends a signal to my pussy, and I clench with pleasure one more time.

"I liked it." I bite my lip at the admittance. What we had done was so dirty. I want to do it again.

Micah laughs and then kisses me. I taste us on his tongue as I run my fingers over his muscular arms and up to his shoulders.

"Hadley, why do you make this so fucking hard", he asks me, frustration all too clear in his voice now. He kisses a trail down my neck, and I focus on his firm wet mouth. "What did you like about it, sweetheart?"

Knowing is easy. Telling is a whole different thing. When it comes out of my mouth, I'll feel dirty and then remorseful that I'm such a freak. He must see the war within me, and through his kisses, I can actually feel him trying to figure me out. As if physical contact with me will tell him everything he needs to know.

"You're scared", he tells me, and then slides inside of me to the hilt. I writhe beneath him because the pressure of him competing with the plug is too much and not enough all at the same time. "Settle, Hadley. Come on. Submit." His lips are on mine once more and when I press up into him, he smiles, leaning his forehead against mine. "What are you afraid of, sweetheart?" I bump up against him once more and he leans his forehead against mine.

"I shouldn't like this." This time I kiss him. He's intoxicating and I do like this. In fact, like isn't even the appropriate word. I need this. Having sex with Micah and the guys is an event, not an obligation. They perform for me and have me perform for them and I crave it every fucking day.

Micah starts pumping inside me, slow but deep and I moan against his lips. "Why? Why wouldn't anyone like this", he prompts me.

"It's dirty", I pant, trying to kiss him again, but he pulls back, not allowing me to access to his mouth. "Women shouldn't like dirty sex." He increases the speed of his thrusts a fraction, sliding in deeper. "But I do. Oh, Micah."

"Don't you dare fucking come, Hadley Joanna. We're talking this through, and you will not finish unless I allow it." He sounds angry and frustrated, and it turns me on even more.

"And that. God, the fact that you own me turns me on and terrifies me in equal measure." I close my eyes, and he pinches my nipple, hard. I gasp and look up at him.

"You do not get to close your eyes. You look at me. My face". Thrust. "My chest." Thrust. "My cock." Thrust. "But you do not get to float off into your own world when you're with me.

"I want to come", I tell him, knowing he's going to deny me. He shakes his head.

"Do you think I'm going to hurt you?" I shake my head and gasp his name. I'm so close to erupting around him I'll tell him anything he wants to know if he just stops. "Are you scared of the others?" I shake my head once more.

"Stop. Oh god, I'm going to come, Micah." He doesn't. Instead, he pumps into me faster. He's trying to make me fail. When he sees the panicked look on my face, he kisses me. Hard. And I become so tight with arousal there's no turning back. I clench around him and moan against his mouth as he gives me what I need, continuing to pump inside me.

"Such a naughty girl", he says when my orgasm slows. "Are you going to answer me?" I look at him in confusion. What did he ask me? "The others. Are you afraid of them", he repeats himself.

"Not afraid of them. What they'll make me do. That's what scares me." He kisses me as a reward and then pulls back as if to say *and?* "I feel shame at liking it." That earns me another kiss and more thrusts of his cock inside me.

"We're going to fix this Hadley." This is his promise to me. He slides his hand underneath my back, lifts me up and threads the fingers of his free hand through my hair, immobilizing me while he kisses me and fucks me mercilessly. I'm done for. I'm stuffed full between my legs and acutely aware of the sound of him slapping against me. His groans and the sound of my wet pussy driving me into yet another frenzy.

"I'm close." He doesn't stop and I know he can hear me. I know he knows what I'm about to do but he keeps going. "Micah", I gasp, trying to wedge my hands between us to slow him down but it's impossible. His grip is like a vice around me, and the realization turns me on.

"This is what your stubborn body gets, Hadley Joanna. Because whether you want to believe it or not, agreement or no agreement, I own you. You are mine. Your cunt is mine. Your mouth is mine. And your ass is mine. Mine to do whatever I please with because I have ruined you for anyone else outside of the brotherhood." His mouth finds mine and I groan and cry at the same time. I've defied him again and this time, I orgasm so hard I'm leaking. It's all over and it feels so good. So dirty. So wrong.

With a growl, Micah finishes inside me and slowly releases his grip on me. Then he kisses me so very gently, bringing us both down from our high.

"It's time for your punishment sweetheart. On all fours. Let's go." He pulls out of me abruptly and I gasp at the harsh exit and my heart sinks at the sudden emptiness. He shifts on the bed, allowing me room to position myself the way he ordered me to. I don't miss how the remnants of his orgasm drip from his hard cock or the glint of satisfaction in his eyes as he waits for me to comply.

# Chapter 12
# Micah

**December 27th 11:45 p.m.**
(Present Day)

Now we're finally getting somewhere. I've always said, if you want to get to know someone…really get to know someone…make them vulnerable. You'll learn more about that person in fifteen minutes than someone who's known them for a lifetime.

I'm looking forward to Hadley's punishment. She had limits that excluded what's to come. And while I get this need met with some of the other women, there's nothing like having access to what you love any time you want it. Her pupils are dilated with lust and her skin is flushed in the most beautiful ivory and pink color I've ever seen. She's satisfied, that I have no doubt. Her cunt came around me so hard I wonder if it hurt her a little.

"You have a total of six infractions tonight. One, you've paid for with the plug. Hesitate much longer and I'll make your infractions a total of seven." She scrambles to get on all fours.

It was clear she wasn't counting. Her eyes widened at the total. Not wanting to repeat this, I'll educate her as she pays for each.

There are a number of things I could do to her, but I decide on a good old fashion spank. She's beautiful on all fours. That blue jewel sticking out of her behind. Our orgasm dripping down the inside of her thighs. What I wouldn't give to have one of the girls here to clean her up with their tongue. I run a finger up the inside of her thigh, capturing our climax with my index finger and bend over her to slide my finger in her mouth.

"Suck", I order, my voice turning stern while she cleans off my filthy digit. "We've both had a long day, Hadley. So, I'll give you a choice. You can give me your ass, or I've got a belt with your name on it." She sucks in a breath, shocked that I've went there. I absolutely love both and since I've done neither with her and they were expressly forbidden in her first agreement, I decide they'll make excellent punishments to get my point across. Do. Not. Disobey. Me.

"If you don't choose I will and I must say, both choices are going to end in me coming all over you. Now which is it?"

"Belt." Her voice is so faint I almost question whether I heard her right. Interesting.

"Grab the headboard", I tell her as I leave the bed to find a good belt for this occasion. I also grab the arnica cream. I purchased a bottle just for her hoping I'd get permission to do this to her over time. I'm curious what her response will be.

When I walk back into the room, she's looking over her shoulder at me. Her eyes widen a fraction when she sees the belt. "Face forward", I tell her, coolly as I climb onto the bed. She's trembling and a part of me gets off on it. A part of me also knows she can call this off at any time so as much as she deserves this punishment, she also deserves consideration.

I'm still painfully hard just looking at her like this and the only question that remains in my mind is how I'll get off. Folding the belt over I give it a good snap, causing Hadley to flinch. Then I run my palm up her backside. I know she's never been spanked before. We discussed it when we drafted her original agreement. I suggested she leave it in with limits, but she was adamant that anything related to BDSM not be included.

"What is your safe word", I ask her, a reminder that even though this is a punishment, she can still safe out.

"Fruit punch", she tells me, and I smile at the memory. When she was a teenager, a boy told her that girls tasted like fruit punch between their legs. She believed it.

I let the seconds tick by. She's beautiful on all fours. I rather like admiring her like this. Like she's a prized steed ready for auction. Right now, she's a bit tense, which I understand. But this wouldn't be a punishment without a little anticipation of the pain to come, now would it? Her breath rises and falls in even deep measure and I can tell she's trying to calm herself.

"Two for speaking without my permission during the meeting this evening", I tell her and land a perfect strike on her backside that echoes through the room, repeating this on the other cheek.

She gasps at the pain, and I take much delight in watching two red marks flame on her porcelain skin. I rub my palm over each mark, soothing the burn and then an idea hits me. I've never done it before but like I said, she's wary of physical aggression and I want to be able to do this again without striking true fear into her.

With my free hand, I grip her hip and then I slide into her so hard she cries out in pleasure. I fuck her. Hard. Deep. Like I'd fuck Emmerson, one of the women who belongs to Mav, also in our brotherhood. Probably like Jonathan used to fuck the whores he paid for in med school.

To my surprise and delight, her tight wet cunt clenches around me. I pull out and deliver the third strike. This time she screams. It was a perfect hit over the already red belt mark on her behind. When I shove back inside her she's tighter still. Fuck me, I'm going to finish.

Through clenched teeth I tell her the reason for the third strike. "Do not hesitate when I tell you to do something."

"Yes, Micah", Hadley says in a thick voice. She's on the verge of tears but that isn't the thing that pushes me over the edge. Hearing her pure submission is the tipping point. I'm lost in the way she remembers to address me with respect. It sounds so sweet coming from her lips that I lose all control and come inside her so hard that I don't realize I've gripped her hip tight enough she's sure to have bruises tomorrow.

She turns to look at me when my thrusts slow. Tears well up in her eyes and I love it. More vulnerability. More layers of Hadley I get to know.

"Who does your cunt belong to", I ask her, pulling out and drawing in a ragged breath as I watch my seed drip from her onto the sheets.

"It's yours, Micah", she says breathlessly.

I nod. "So, when I tell you that this cunt that belongs to me..." I run a finger through her folds and then slide two inside her, pumping lazily as I chose my next words carefully. "...and I do not give this beautiful little pussy permission to have pleasure, and it disobeys me by coming all over my hard cock..." Snap! Snap! Snap!

She lets out a sob and I know I've made my point. I love her with every fiber of my being, and she's shown she can take a punishment when it's due. Being belted is not an easy punishment to receive and she does not use her safe word. So instead of rutting into her, I do more. I cover her with my body, chest to her back and turn her head so I can kiss her. She's got tears streaming down her cheeks and I'm truly sorry for that. But right now, I'm caring for her and I know she receives my care when she pushes her cunt against my hard length, silently begging for more.

"I love you, Hadley Joanna."

"I'm going to come. Please." Her request melts my heart. It's genuine. It's needy. It's submissive and defiant all at the same time which is so beautifully Hadley because she tells and asks as if they're one in the same.

I smile against her lips. "Permission granted." As soon as the words are out of my mouth, she's groaning as she comes around my cock. I milk every ounce of pleasure from her before I release my own pleasure once more.

When I finally pull out of her, she's a mess. I won't allow her to shower. I'm not even sure I'm going to clean her up. I'll dry her tears, but this is how I want her to go to bed. I want her ass a flame and her pussy so wet that this room smells like pure sex when we wake up tomorrow morning.

She stays on all fours, waiting for my direction. I smile as I uncap the gel. She turns to me, her cheeks still we with tears. I let her off the hook and provide an explanation.

"This is for the pain. You won't be as sore tomorrow morning", I tell her, squeezing a small amount of the gel onto my fingers and gently massaging the red spots on her backside. She winces at the contact, and I don't blame her. My aim was flawless. So flawless in fact, it looks like I've only hit her twice. I was an excellent student of Tyler's with Lexi. It's one of the benefits of having this brotherhood. We all come with at least one expertise and we're all very willing to share what we do well and teach the others.

Once I have the ointment rubbed in all the way, I cap the tube and tap on the plug still buried deep inside Hadley's ass.

"This has to come out." I plant a kiss over each cheek's red spot. Then I kiss the small of her back as I slide the jeweled implement out of her. She whimpers at the plug's exit. "Good girl", I praise her, wanting her to know that I see her effort and I am grateful for it.

I grab a tissue and set the plug on the bedside table so I can pull back the covers for her. She's hesitant about getting under the covers.

"I need to use the bathroom", she tells me, wiping the tears from her eyes with the back of her hand. I nod in understanding.

"You can wipe only what you need to. When you get in bed your cunt better be as messy as it is when you went to the bathroom." I give her my stern lawyer look.

"Yes, Micah", she breaths in a stuttered breath.

When Hadley returns, it's clear that she followed my instructions. She's got my cum running down her thighs and it's a fantastic sight. Seeing her like this reminds me of Introduction Night. I want this for her all over again. Perhaps the guys will agree to this once Hadley has an agreement that is accurate.

I make quick work of cleaning the plug for tomorrow. Hadley doesn't know it yet, but this punishment has become the gateway to another first for her. Anal sex was a hard limit for her. I smile at the thought of her being fucked in every hole. I want pictures of her first time. First times are important after all. We should have gotten pictures of Linea but five years ago, memorializing the important milestones wasn't top of mind.

When I return to the bedroom, I find Hadley in the center of the bed, on her side with her eyes closed. Wasting no time, I climb in beside her and pull her against me. Finally, only semi hard, the furious monster is beginning to calm.

"How do you feel?" I burry my nose in her hair and smell that heavenly shampoo she uses. She lets out a deep breath, pausing before she answers.

"Sore and worried...but still relieved." She sounds a little sad, or maybe she's just tired. It's hard to tell.

"Tell me about your relief." I need to hear this. I need to know how she's feeling so I can put another piece of the puzzle that is Hadley back together.

"I could be in my own bed right now."

"This is your bed, Hadley Joanna. At about nine thirty this became our bed."

My hand slides down to cup her breast and she snuggles into me more.

"What about your punishment?" I kiss her shoulder, waiting for her assessment of my belting skill. A skill I'm particularly proud of after much practice. She lets out a chuckle.

"It hurt. A lot. But I couldn't bring myself to use the safe word", she confesses. "I deserved it. I deserve so much more.", she lets out a sob and it breaks my heart.

"You deserve what I give you. Do you not think I'm judicious? Hm? That I can execute a punishment that fits the infraction?"

"I just think..." She sucks in a few stuttered breaths... "...that I won't use the safe word because I don't think I deserve the second chance." She sobs and I hold her tighter.

She shrugs out of my hold and turns in my arms so she's facing me. I believe her. She's at the lowest point she can go right now and the only thing that will fix this is time. "I'm sorry. I'm so, so very sorry." This is the most serious I think I've ever seen her, and it makes my heart stop. She's so sincere. I wonder if her remorse will continue after the implant is inserted tomorrow morning. Only time will tell.

I kiss her on the forehead and pull her to my chest. "I need you to sleep, sweetheart. You have a big day tomorrow." She nods against my chest and within minutes she's sleeping in my arms.

# Chapter 13
# Hadley

**July 21st 12:50 p.m.**
(5 Months Earlier)

Security escorts me to Micah's office. The moment the elevator door pings, I see him leaning against his desk, arms folded over his chest, watching me through the glass walls of his office. He doesn't move a muscle to open the door for me because he's probably watching my face morph with hostility at every second that passes.

The guard opens the door for me, and I glance his way, thanking him and feeling a pang of guilt for being so curt on the way to meet Micah. I don't wait for the door to close before I start my tirade. Because a week by myself with all the time in the world to consider his proposal has given me time to poke holes in some of the things he shared with me in his dining room. He probably thinks I'm an idiot. That I was going to walk in here and declare him God's gift to women and kneel at his feet.

I'm going to castrate him.

"You lied to me." His only reaction is the raise of his eyebrows. It makes me madder. "How stupid to you think I am?" His brows come down and the slight quirk of his lips make me want to tackle him. "I must be super stupid compared to a big shot lawyer like you." I'm standing in front of him in my spa scrubs and he hasn't moved an inch. Truthfully, I wasn't planning on giving him an answer. I wanted to ghost him because people like Micah think they have everyone wrapped around their little finger. It would hurt more if I treated him like vapor. But after the last client I had made a pass at me, I kept my scheduled lunch time and decided to use it to visit Micah and personally tell him to fuck off.

"You were fucking around with those other women while you were with me, weren't you?" Still keeping an arm folded across his chest, he brings a hand up to his face and runs the pad of his thumb over his bottom lip, considering my question. His silence is answer enough. "Oh my God. You're disgusting. You let me believe I was actually dating you and you were actually dating me. All the while, you were with those other women. I mean, no wonder we never had sex. Why would you bother? You could get all the dirty pussy you wanted from your groupies." He chuckles at my insult and his gaze follows my flexing fists tight to my sides.

"I was so wrong about you." And there it was. Tears of frustration that were rapidly turning to hurt. "I have to go. I can't believe I wasted my lunch on this", I say tearfully as I turn on my sneakered heel and swiftly make my way to his office door. I felt like a fool. I hadn't played the part of the dumb lovestruck girl since high school and it's official that for the last month, that's all I was.

"Do you want me to stop you?" His alluring authoritative voice does just that. I freeze, unable to take another step forward because desperately want him to fix this. I nod because I can't talk. He can't see my tears yet and for that, I'm glad. I shouldn't want him to stop me, but I do. The dumb lovestruck woman in me wants him to tell me that everything I just said was wrong. But I'm sure he won't. Because there's no way I could be wrong about this. It's common sense.

The familiar sound of his dress shoed footfalls move toward me and I can feel the warmth of him against my back.

"I can't touch them. I can't talk to them. I can't *see* them. All communication has been cut off. Including texts. So no, I haven't been fucking anyone. When I told you I haven't been with someone in months, I was not exaggerating. I can't possibly find someone I want to call my own if I'm with the others. So, I can't have contact with them until I find *mine*. You're it for me. And for the record, I also do not think you are stupid. I think you're terrified of something different that might just be the best thing that ever happened to you. I do respect your decision, so long as you're making an informed one, but I fear that you are not."

I hear rustling behind me and then his arm extends around me, holding out his phone with his text app up. "Take a look. I have had no dirty pussy since I started my dry spell."

I cringe at the use of my words back at me. Reluctantly, I take the phone and click a few names, clearly seeing the last time he messaged any of them was this past New Year's Eve.

"Do you want to check my call logs? Texts from my brothers?" I can hear the smile in his voice, and I know he's telling the truth.

"No", I quietly answer him, wiping my cheek with the back of my hand.

"Will you look at me?" His voice is so sincere and filled with gentle need, it breaks my heart. I was so mean to him. Reluctantly, I turn to him and hand him his phone. "I will never lie to you, Hadley Joanna. Not tell you things? Yes. Regularly.

But those things won't concern you. And if they do, you'll know when you *need* to know. Not one moment earlier." He looks at his wrist, his fancy watch gleaming in the lights of his office. "You're going to be late. Did you have anything to eat today?" I shake my head, continuing to wipe tears from my cheeks. "I'll have my driver return you to work and have some food delivered." He bends forward and brushes his lips across my forehead. "Thank you for having the courage to come see me today."

I left Micah's office feeling worse than I did when I had arrived. He didn't ask me when he'd see me again and I walked out of his office door and never looked back.

# Chapter 14
# Micah

(1 Year Earlier)

"Mr. Stevenson", Claudia looks down her nose at me, addressing me in the one way that gets under my skin. Mr. Stevenson is my father. I am not my father.

I glare at her like I would an intern when they purposely piss me off.

"You don't scare me. But you know who you are scaring? Your staff. How long as it been?"

"Excuse me?" She's never been so forward with me. I'm taken aback by it.

"No sir, you are absolutely not excused. You asked me to take you off the calendar." She doesn't go further because she's waiting for me to confirm what's happening. "All your friends are going on dates and you're not." She raises a brow at me and when I don't budge, she gets up from her chair, presses a button on her phone and leaves her desk. She doesn't look back or motion for me to follow and for a second, I think that maybe she is going to lunch or to grab coffee except it's a wintery mess outside and she didn't even grab her coat.

I follow her, picking up my pace a bit to see what she's up to but don't follow her too closely because I don't want her to think I'm concerned. I am concerned though. She is my right hand which means she knows everything that goes on here and everything that goes on in my personal life. She knows about the brotherhood because she tends to our schedules, books reservations and everything that goes along with keeping us organized and on point with our women. She does everything but our personal shopping, which is why we hired Suzette. Claudia also knows I'm the last of the men to find *mine*.

*Mine.* That's what we call our woman when we introduce them because that's who they are. It's possessive and neanderthal but we don't care. Because we are possessive and sometimes neanderthal. And despite my halfhearted attempts at finding someone since the New Year's Eve celebration at the Lux, which was my send off for what we call the "dry spell", I've met no one I want for myself.

It's almost February and no one has appealed to me. At the encouragement of Braden I've taken women out. But there's no connection. My heartbeat doesn't pick up the slightest when I see these women.

One could argue that my heart hasn't beat out of my chest when I've weighed in on the women my brothers have chosen, but it's not the same. I have to be so fucking strung out just thinking about the woman that is mine that it's hard for me to function doing the most basic of tasks. In almost a month, no one has come close.

And the reason it has to be that way is once you're in, you're in. The agreement states I cannot just remove the woman who is mine from the brotherhood and any of us can only be voted out by the brothers for violating the agreement. There is a clause that says anyone can remove themselves without a vote but in over five years that hasn't even come close to happening because we love this lifestyle, and we treat our women exceptionally well.

By the time I'm up the stairs there's no sight of her. I walk down the hall casually greeting the people I pass who acknowledge me hoping she's in one of their offices. But as I get further down the hall, I notice her in *my* office. Not only is she in my office but she's behind my desk on my phone.

I have lost my composure as I rush down the rest of the hallway and throw my office door open only to hear her say into the phone, "Blow jobs can't count." I hurry to close the door and whisper yell her name. "No, *you* don't understand. He needs to be the exception. Just send whoever is free to sit under his desk a few times a week. I'll work with the brother's schedule. I could even recommend a schedule." I whisper yell her name one more time with more force and she glances up at me with the same face she'd have if she were talking with one of my clients. I mouth the words hang up.

Claudia does not hang up. Instead, she puts the phone on speaker and Braden's voice comes through loud and clear.

"…if he got out there. I know Micah's not actually trying to find women. There's no way a guy can look like him and struggle. Some of these men found theirs in less than a week. Landon found his in a few hours even though I don't think it was supposed to go down like that. But Claudia, the point is this, get him out of work more and he'll get a whole lot nicer a whole lot quicker."

"Claudia is exaggerating", I say into the line. Braden goes silent. "Hello?"

"You said four words and you sounded like an asshole."

"That's what I'm talking about, Braden. He doesn't even hear it", Claudia commiserates with Braden.

"You're taking care of yourself though, right? I know it's not the same as a woman but damn...it sounds like you haven't blown since New Years."

I hang up on Braden, give a scathing look to Claudia and point to my office door.

"This is also what I'm talking about." Claudia leaves my desk and heads for the door. "You'll have an assortment of lotion on your desk before the end of the week if you don't fix this Mr. Stevenson", she says over her shoulder as she leaves my office.

I sit down at my desk and close my eyes, drawing in a few deep breaths so I don't lose my shit. They aren't wrong. I'm hard up by choice. I've had the luxury of having access to the women my brothers have chosen for over five years. And it's not that I'm out of practice. I can pick up a woman without much effort. The problem is that none of the women I have met even come close to those in the brotherhood and because of the terms of the agreement, there is no way I'm entering a relationship with someone I'm not crazy about. Aside from my own personal sanity or that of my brothers, I have no intentions of introducing a pot stirrer to the ladies or compromising anyone's anonymity by adding someone who isn't one of us into the brotherhood.

Claudia's idea is appealing though. Any of them would do it. Any of them would gladly wait under my desk for me and take care of me when I ordered it. The thought of it makes my pants tighten. Shit. They can't. I love Claudia's suggestion, but she doesn't know these rules. She's never had to know the rules of a dry spell because she's only ever coordinated schedules for new arrivals into the group.

She doesn't know that when my dry spell starts, I can't talk with any of the women. I can't text them, email them, call them, send or receive a voicemail...nothing. It's like they never existed. The point of this practice is that I'm supposed to be more inclined to find someone quickly and find someone who is the best match by cutting myself off from the women. If I'm not getting sex from our women, I'm forced to seek it elsewhere. And even then, I still can't have sex with them. Blowjobs and hand jobs are permitted but intercourse is out. Disease and pregnancy are a no go with the brotherhood. To avoid them, we just don't take the risk.

So that leaves me with either my slicked-up hand and a fantasy about one of the women or my slicked-up hand and a porn. I haven't given myself a hand job in about the last decade because I haven't had to and I'm certainly not going to start now.

I pick up my desk phone and dial Claudia's extension. She picks up on the first ring.

"Mr. Stevenson", she greets me with the coolest tone I think I've ever gotten from her.

"Claudia, can you please lighten my calendar as you and Braden discussed?"

"Of course, *sir.*" The way she emphasizes the word *sir* makes me bristle.

"Please order a nice lunch on me...as a token of my gratitude for you looking out for me and the firm." She clears her throat. "And my sincerest apology for the harsh tone I used with you."

"Thank you, Micah." My first name is how I know I'm back in her good graces again. "Oh, also, before I send your ten o'clock up, the assortment of lube I ordered for you will be here tomorrow morning." And with that, she disconnects the line.

# Chapter 15
# **Hadley**

**August 7th**
(4 Months Earlier)

Twisted Sister's We're Not Gonna Take it blares from my phone on the kitchen counter. Madison. I've ignored all her texts. Now she's calling me. I can't. I just can't. I don't even have words for her right now.

Every day I cry over him. The void he left is that great. I've even tried comparing him to past lovers. This breakup is so much worse.

I was raised in a home that never discussed sex. Not that avoiding the topic was bad. I just don't think it did me any favors. I went out into the world of dating fumbling around. Things that I thought would give me pleasure were considered taboo, like kissing another woman or having sex with more than one person at a time.

I dated men repressing any desire I had for the extraordinary, settling for missionary sex because that was appropriate for a woman to want. Men could want all the dirty things. They could watch porn because that's just what men did. Heaven forbid if a woman watched a porn and liked it...I can't even imagine the names she'd be called afterward.

The men I dated seemed suitable enough. The kind of nice boys a girl would want to bring home to their family. But that's just it...they were boys. At whatever age they were, they acted like juveniles. Anything from not having a good job to not cleaning up after themselves and in some cases treating me like I was their personal secretary. But again, that's just boys being boys because even in today's society, women still play the same role of the dutiful housewife and mother. They just get the pleasure of adding a job on top of it all. And while I don't have children, I shudder to think about what that would even look like with the spoiled men running around chasing after women they have no business even approaching.

Deep down I wanted more from my relationships. I wanted sex. Dirty, toe-curling panty ruining sex. And a man I didn't have to care for. Someone responsible. Someone who would love me for who I am and who I could love for who they are just the same. Someone I was proud to stand next to anywhere and be associated with in the most personal of ways. And before Micah, I hated the relationships I had been in. They weighed me down and sucked the soul from me every day I stayed in them.

And then I met this bartender lawyer who flew every one of my red flags, but he was never an asshole to me. He never mistreated me, took me for granted or brushed me aside as though I didn't matter. Since we met, Micah never let me get him off once. He's only ever taken care of me.

The way he touched me...it was like my body had been made for him. He knew it. In a few short weeks he knew things about my body that men I've dated for several months couldn't figure out. It took him minutes.

And to be fair, it wasn't even the physical stuff that got me, although I have to say it was pretty mind blowing. It was the way he paid attention to me. Like he truly wanted to know every little thing about me. No. He *needed* to know every little thing about me. Because it made him happy to know it. Because he couldn't fathom not knowing it.

I fell in love with him after the second date. He tucked me in after the sweetest kiss goodnight and I just knew he was it. He would be the man who would ruin me for all other men if he fucked up.

And here I am. Ruined. And he hadn't even cheated on me. He just wants to cheat on me. With my consent. And he wants me to do the same to him. Of all the possible outcomes, this was something I would never have anticipated. I'd do all the dirty sex stuff with him, but did he have to do it with everyone else?

Did he fuck up, though? I don't know. A fantasy of mine is being with a woman, and I can't do that if I'm only with him. If he's giving me permission to have everything on my sexual menu, wouldn't my being with a woman, by my own definition be cheating on him?

My alcohol hazed brain is struggling to sort it all out. It's not even noon and I'm pretty tanked. I've gone over this in my spare time. Micah, his lifestyle and how he wants to bring me into it has consumed every ounce of me outside of work.

I keep going over the same questions with no answers. No answers that I like at least.

How could he love me if he's with others? Will he even take me seriously if I'm not the only woman he's with? Who will I introduce as my boyfriend? Would I feel like a whore being given to man after man? What if someone I know sees me out with one of his friends? What if I don't like one of them? Or most of them? Or they don't like me.

I have no real answers. And I'm stuck. Too scared to say yes and too scared to tell him to fuck off. I think if I told Micah to fuck off, I'd never see him again. And that causes a whole new wave of gut-wrenching sobs to bubble up to the surface.

I cry so hard and so loud; I don't even hear Madison enter.

"Oh shit", she says when she sees me. I'm on the couch in my summer pajamas, clutching an empty wine glass. "He wasn't lying."

Her words made me sob harder. She had contact with him. I hadn't even had contact with him. Knowing this felt like the oxygen was being sucked from the room. I couldn't even ask her what he said because I was clinging to my friend, crying into her chest like today was my last day to live.

"Shhh, shhh, shhh...breath, Hadley. Just breath. You're okay", she croons to me. I try to stop my cries, snorting a few times. She hugs me tighter and eventually, I relax, just allowing the tears to silently slide down my cheeks.

"You spoke with him", I manage to get out between hiccups.

"Yeah. I was kidding around and text him that I couldn't get a hold of you. I told him to let you come up for air. He said he hadn't heard from you in weeks."

My sobs start again. This time quieter.

"Hadley, what's going on?" I don't answer her. "Did he hurt you?" I shake my head. "Did he cheat on you?" I shake my head again. "Did he try to put it in you?"

This time I laugh cry. Leave it to Madison to dirty something up at a time like this.

"I only ask because he seemed very interested, and you try to keep those cobwebs at all costs so..."

I shake my head again and pull out of her embrace. I can't hold onto my glass and her while grabbing a refill.

I pour another glass and give her an answer that's close to the truth. Madison is adventurous but I suspect even she would tell me to ditch Micah, despite her interest in ridding me of my cobwebs. And if she told me to cut him loose, I don't think I could handle it. It would feel like I had made a decision, and I don't think I want to make that one.

"It got serious. I didn't think I could be in a relationship that is so serious."

Madison just nods her head in understanding, grabs a glass for herself and that's the last we talk about it.

# Chapter 16
# Micah

**August 20th 12:40 p.m.**
(4 Months Earlier)

Hadley has this way of just showing up without notice. She's like a late menstrual cycle. You know it's going to be messy, but you've never been so happy to have it come into your life without notice.

She'd ghosted me for weeks. In fact, I thought we were over. Never in a million years did I expect her to be requesting my presence. Too much time had passed. But when Claudia called me with that *I know a good secret tone* and no information about my guest, I did what I normally do not do. I let them come up without even knowing who I'm meeting with. I trust Claudia that much. If she ever left me, I don't know what I'd do.

It's almost one in the afternoon and I have a shit load of work to do, but the moment I see her come into view, it's all forgotten. I have to physically fight the urge not to open the door for her myself.

"Hadley Joanna. So nice to see you." I don't offer more than that. She's trying to put on an air of confidence although I can see she's not confident at all.

"I..." It's such a false start for her. A contrast to how pointed she has been every time we've been together. I raise my eyebrows, prompting her to continue. I won't make this easy on her. After all, being without her with not a single word from her for weeks was far from easy for me.

"I want to try." It's all she offers at first, but still I wait. "I miss you." I raise my brow in challenge. "Fine. I miss you and your filthy mouth. And your filthy fingers." I smirk at her humor but she's not quite where I want her. "I missed you." She has tears in her eyes, and I know her admittance is real but it's not good enough. She's lived without me for weeks. She needs to convince me she really wants in.

"If this were anyone else, I'd think they were a creep", she declares in exasperation. I laugh. "I needed time to think without you looking at me and touching me and smelling so divinely like you. Even the tone of your voice makes me want to drop to my knees and worship you. I just couldn't think with you casted over me like some sexy mind-scrambling apparition." I smile at her wit.

"You've never lied to me. I know you'd never hurt me. You'd also never allow anyone else to hurt me. This is a big deal. It changes everything." She chews on her lower lip, still torn over something. "But I'd be yours, ultimately?" I nod. "You call the shots." I nod again.

At this point, I'm white knuckling my desk. I want to rush her, push her up against the wall and fuck her absolutely senseless.

"Anyway...I want you. I love you. I need you in my life. I just needed to see you and tell you in person even though it seems like it's too late." She wipes a stray tear from her cheek and turns to leave.

"You have not been dismissed." How dare she walk away from me after turning my world upside down with her absence, coming in here so God damned pretty, and declaring her acceptance of what we do as well as her love for me. I've never felt so happy and angry all at the same time. She freezes where she stands. "Turn around." My voice booms through my office like I am a God...because I am. I'm her God now.

Hadley turns on her heel, her green eyes lift slowly to meet mine. "From this point forward, you belong to me." She smiles. I do not. "You will follow my rules. You will learn *our* rules." She nods frantically without hesitation. "Sit", I order her, nodding my head towards the large conference table. She rushes to the table while I call Claudia.

"Mr. Stevenson", she answers, with that same sly tone she used on me mere moments ago.

"Claudia, can you send up food? Just an assortment of things. It's going to be a late one."

"Right away Mr. Stevenson. Should I get an appointment on the books with Braden?" I can hear the smile in her voice. She's enjoying this way too much. And she knows everything. She runs our calendar and keeps notes at our monthly meetings. Every stitch of our personal affairs is coordinated through Claudia. She knows every date, sexual preference and difference among the group. Nothing slips past her attention.

"Yes. That would be fantastic. Thank you." She hangs up and I do everything I can not to smile like a schoolboy who just got his first look at a titty pic. She's mine. She's finally mine.

I grab a steno pad and a pen, placing it in front of her. She looks up at me in question. "I'll work there." I nod to my desk. "You'll work here. Everything you like sexually will be on one page. Hard limits will be on another. We'll leave here today with a finished agreement."

And then something else happens that I don't expect. She starts to cry. And for a moment I think she might be reconsidering but then she pushes out of her chair to stand and nuzzles into my chest. Here I am, in the middle of the workday, arms wrapped around a woman for all to see just allowing her to fall apart in my arms.

"What's going on, sweetheart", I croon to her, placing a kiss on top of her head. "Tell me."

"I need…", she hiccups in stuttered breaths between sobs. "I missed…"

I tilt her head up to look at me and nod for her to continue.

"I need to feel you. Control…me…", she begs between sobs and my heart swells at her demand.

I lead her to my desk without the pad of paper and pen. Hadley looks stunned. That makes two of us. But I know what she needs, and it's not control.

Sitting, I take her with me, adjusting her so she's sitting to the side on my lap.

"I want you to get it all out Hadley. I'm not going anywhere. You may sit here with me as long as you like. And when you feel ready, you may take a seat at the table and begin your list."

She sat in my lap for hours before she got up to work at the table. Sometimes she'd cry and sometimes she was so still and relaxed, I had wondered if she had fallen asleep.

I took calls with her on my lap and moved a few meetings back to allow us this private moment. And when she was working quietly at the table by herself, I'd have my staff come in to meet as previously scheduled.

We ended up moving this work to my house. Mostly because when she had composed herself, I couldn't stand watching her take her time over the sexual menu I printed for her after her hard limits had only two items on it and her preference list had five. The sexual tension was so thick I could barely breath. I couldn't concentrate on my work. The only thing I could visualize was Hadley, on her knees for me in my foyer the instant we walked through the door.

"Sucking cock can't be a hard limit", I tell her, glancing her direction as we get closer to my house. I was a little frustrated with her results after sitting in my office all that time. And I get that my conversations in the background with my clients and partners may have been distracting but she didn't exactly leave me with much choice when she showed up at my office. I could have just sent her away, but there was no way I was risking losing her again.

"I don't like it."

"You haven't done it with the right man." I counter.

"I thought you said I didn't have to do anything I don't like", she protests back.

"What don't you like about it?"

"It's degrading", she sighs, sounding like she's halfway to conceding.

"Which part?" All we have to do is make adjustments to the part that bothers her, and this will be a non-issue.

"I don't want cum on me. To be treated like trash." I nod and wait because there's more. With Hadley, there's always more. "Any porn I've ever seen shows a man slapping the woman in the face with it." She shivers. I try not to laugh. She doesn't watch a lot of porn and of what she has seen, it sounds like it hasn't exactly been her pick.

"Then we write that in as a hard limit."

"I can be that specific?"

She doesn't get it yet. "You *have* to be that specific. Over time, the men will just know who you are and what you like but especially in the beginning, you have to write it out as though it's an instruction manual to your body and mind. We won't be giving you a hard pass on things all together."

"Well anal is a hard limit. I need a pass there."

I chuckle. This is going to take so much longer than I thought. "No one gets a pass. Your pussy, your mouth and your perky little ass belong to us. To what degree is what is negotiated."

"It's going to hurt. I'll get no pleasure out of it. And again, I thought you said this agreement was for me."

"It is. And done right, ass play is fantastic." She shivers in her seat. "Okay. For you, you could pick a toy." She shakes her head. "Alright. Fingers."

"*A* finger."

"*A* finger", I repeat, smiling as I cruise closer to home so we can get to work.

# Chapter 17
# Hadley

**August 22nd 3:02 p.m.**
(4 Months Earlier)

Micah taps a key on his laptop with a flourish. He looks victorious. It's Sunday afternoon and we've finally finished my agreement. I don't think I've ever talked about sex as much as I've talked about it this weekend with Micah. Sex isn't something we were ever encouraged to talk about in our family. The topic was treated as if it didn't exist or was unnecessary to discuss. I'm sure Micah noticed when I blushed at some of the terms he'd used.

Fucking. He said that a lot. Pussy was also referenced as though this was common language for him. And when he'd use these words, he'd patiently wait for me to get my wits about me before moving on to the next item of business. All the while it floored me that he had such a filthy mouth and never hesitated once during our conversations about sex. He truly was comfortable with all of this, and I knew that he knew I was nervous. Maybe even a bit skittish.

Sitting behind his desk wearing a t-shirt and jeans, he looks like he's won the lottery. And the lottery happens to be me.

But I'm nervous. I know I can change my agreement later to include the things that I think would turn me on. I just couldn't quite bring myself to say the words rape fantasy or girl on girl or whatever it's called. Even though he had somewhat of a list, I felt exposed calling these out. Like it made me a freak to say I wanted to try one or that the fantasy in my head was a turn-on so maybe the real thing would be too.

He swipes his phone off his desk and taps the screen a few times, then turns it face down, turning his gaze directly on me. He waves me to him as he scoots back his chair and pats his leg. I dramatically lumber out of the plush leather chair and cross the room to him. I'm wearing his t-shirt from last night still. He refused to give me back my panties since Friday night claiming they aren't sanitary to wear more than one day, and he can't possibly do another girl's laundry or send Suzette out to shop for another girl until that girl is official.

I crawl up onto his lap and he pulls me in for a kiss. I love him. I really, really love him and there's nowhere else I'd rather be than in his arms.

Forehead to forehead, we're breathing hard now. And I let the question slip out that I've been holding in since we sat down and got serious about drafting the agreement.

"Why do you do this?" I try to close the gap between us now and start another kiss, but his hands are on my face, holding me there. He gently moves me, so I know the physical stuff is on hold.

He studies me like I might disappear before his eyes. His eyes glitter over every feature from the top of my head to where my lap meets his. Then he drops his hands to the hem of my shirt and lifts it over my head leaving me there stark naked on his lap.

"I'm arrogant, Hadley. But I'm also a realist. I know what I can do well and what I cannot, and the truth is, I cannot be everything to one woman, just like one woman cannot be everything to one man." Micah's palms settle on my waist, sizzling on my skin as I let his answer roll around in my brain. It's so logical. So honest. So Micah. "I know that doesn't mean much to you now, but it will. On introduction night you will appreciate us all differently." Micah's hands slide up my sides, hesitating at my breasts where his thumbs stroke my sensitive skin.

He's thinking. Being careful and deliberate in his words. "I already know who you are for me. And while you don't play every role, you play the most important role for me. If you keep that in mind, everything you thought you couldn't handle gets infinitely easier."

I don't respond. I take a deep breath trying not to panic.

"You're nervous. Maybe even a little scared?" I nod. "Don't be. We'll help you. We'll all help you." His mouth cautiously finds mine as if I'm going to run out of his house stark naked. I allow every ounce of Micah's calm to wash over me when our lips meet. His hands roam freely and somehow, all the worry just vanishes. It's gone as though it was never supposed to exist in the first place.

Later that night, we're back at it again. Micah informs me that I have some questions to answer before all approve of my document. This time, we're in his dining room. He's poured me a drink as he pulls up the draft document on his laptop and what I assume to be questions via email.

I'm thoroughly impressed by how much information the guys want to know. Micah was beyond specific when he reviewed my version. I couldn't imagine there was any room for ambiguity left when he hit send.

"Restraints. If you aren't being hurt, will you allow them?" He looks up from his laptop and further clarifies. "Like in bed. Cuffs? Ties? Ball gags?" He smiles at ball gags because he can anticipate my answer.

"Yes, to the cuffs and the ties. No to the ball gags", I answer promptly so he knows the latter is out of the question with no room for negotiation.

"Blind folds?"

"Yes."

"Candle Wax?" He smirks and I can't tell if he's screwing with me or not.

"No thank you", I tell him with a syrupy smile.

An hour of rapid-fire Q&A and we were finished.

"So, what now", I ask, genuinely curious about this new world I've stepped into and my future in it.

"Now we wait."

# Chapter 18
# Hadley

**December 28th 5:30 a.m.**
(Present Day)

I stand under the hot spray of the shower at an ungodly hour in the morning. It's still dark and all I want is to go back to bed. I've got a welted backside and from my thighs up to my pussy is sticky with Micah and I's release last night. I'm still processing last night. It was nothing like I had anticipated. Who knew I would have outed myself and had come so close to being out of their brotherhood? Most of my experiences with these men have been unusual in that dinner is rarely just dinner and a low-key evening at home is anything but ordinary.

Micah seems to need only a minimal amount of sleep. When he woke me, he looked well rested and had clearly showered for the day. "Go shower. The guys will be here in about an hour. I want you ready."

"Can I wash..." I trail off, feeling strange about asking him if I can wash between my legs this morning.

"Yes. I want you nice and clean for me this morning. Go on." He nods in the direction of the bathroom, and I lumber out of bed as he chuckles and then takes a sip of his hot coffee.

It's a quick shower. I'm nervous and a little jumpy. I do not want a repeat performance of being belted like I was last night. Micah rises when I enter the bedroom wrapped in a towel. He sets his coffee down and meets me in the center of the room, tugging on the towel causing it to fall to the floor. Circling me, he inspects my backside.

"Tender?" He runs a finger across one of the welts and I grimace in response. "I'll put more cream on it before the guys arrive. Lay down on the bed. On your back, please." He leaves the bedroom and returns with the tube of gel tossing it on the bed next to me. Grabbing my ankles, he pulls me forward until my ass is just barely on the bed. He slides two fingers in his mouth and coats them with his saliva, then presses them inside me.

"I love your pussy, Hadley Joanna." He sounds almost remorseful as he makes this declaration. Then he falls to his knees and hooks my legs over his shoulders. "This is me apologizing in advance for what will happen today." He bends forward and kisses my clit, and I gasp at the pleasure. "It's going to hurt." He leans forward once more and runs his tongue up my center, tonguing my clit until I'm squirming. "But it's necessary." His mouth is back on me and now I'm panting.

"I need to…" I can't even form the words it feels so go. "Please", I gasp, wanting to avoid another belting.

"Mmmm…" he hums against my sensitive flesh.

"Micah!" I cannot believe I just yelled at him in bed, but this is serious. My backside depends on his generosity now. He chuckles against me.

"Of course. My apology to your pussy wouldn't be a true apology unless you came."

I grip his head and shove his face into me as he tongues me relentlessly. I'm groaning with wild abandon as I come so hard, my stomach muscles dance with my release. This woman is not me. I would never have done this before. The groaning...the need... It feels so fucking good.

I'm still breathing hard when Micah stands. He tugs on his belt. The same belt he used on me last night. Involuntarily, my pussy clenches.

"I saw that", Micah tells me, eyes trained on my needy cunt. "We don't have that kind of time this morning. However, I'm sure you'll get yourself into a situation where it's deserved in no time", he says as he pulls his hard cock out of his dress pants, not bothering to take off an ounce of his clothing. Wasting no time, he hoists my legs up so my ankles are resting on his shoulders, then spears me with his hard length. "You have my permission to come as many times as you like. In a few hours, you won't want a soul touching you down there."

Just as I'm about to panic, he starts using me for his pleasure. It's such an erotic sight. My feet resting on his shoulders. His dress shirt untucked and unbuttoned at the top. "The things I'm going to do to you." He ruts into me harder, and I can't take my eyes off the place where we connect. He's slick with my need and the sight and sound of us together pushes me over the edge. "That's it. All mine." He slides out of me. "Scoot back." His order is gruff and urgent. Still in a post orgasm haze I comply, my muscles warm and unsteady as I shift backwards on the bed.

Micah climbs on top of me, still fully clothed and cages me underneath him. He secures my head to look at him as he fists a handful of my hair, then he slides inside of me to the hilt and slams his mouth down on mine. My free hands roam his body. His love for me is so vulnerable and raw and I have no idea where this is coming from. It feels like an apology but that couldn't be right. What could he have to apologize for?

"Micah?" I breath out the unspoken question as he looks into my eyes.

"All of this is for you, Hadley Joanna. Do you trust me?" I nod without hesitation because I do trust him. He would never do anything without my best interest in mind. "I need you to be my good girl today, huh?" His eyebrows are drawing together at the same time he gets thicker and harder inside me. "Promise me." He lets out a small groan.

"I will." My hand is on his face now, but he won't allow me to console him. He turns his head and then bends forward and tucks his face into my chest as he releases inside me. I stroke his hair, wondering what has happened. What hasn't he told me? And when he looks up at me, I see apology written all over his face.

He knows that I know something is wrong and he kisses my lips repeating the order to trust him. We share a lingering kiss until his phone pings. It's Braden's tone. I don't know them all, but I know his because they message each other the most.

With one more chaste kiss, he pulls out of me and begins tucking himself back into his slacks. "You do not have permission to clean up. Give me ten minutes and come down with only your robe on." I nod, watching him pocket his phone and leave me, closing me behind the door of his master suite.

I watch the clock as the seconds tick by, my mind reeling with what's in store for me. It's a prototype. They're inserting it. It must go somewhere on my sex because Micah made reference to not being inside me for days. I don't regret agreeing to this but I'm nervous as hell. I wish I had asked more questions. Wait. No. I don't. Because if I had asked more questions, I would have overthought this and I'd be back at my house today, lonely and orgasmless with a gigantic hangover.

It's six. I remember Micah saying they'd meet me at six. So, I open the door and walk down the hall as if I'm trying not to be seen. He just told me to come downstairs. He never told me where they'd be. It's not like Micah to be vague. He's distracted. I don't think he wants this. Whatever *this* is. As I walk down the stairs, I hear the rumble of male voices. Micah's, I pick out right away and while I don't hear him, I know Braden is here by proxy. He's our doctor and anything medical related he's a part of. He's also here to collect his orgasm from me. This is going to be the worst, yet here I am, tiptoeing straight for it.

I follow the voices to the kitchen and as soon as they come into view I breath in a sharp breath at the exact moment the men are silent. They turn to look at me in unison and I freeze where I am. It's an audience, not a private medical procedure.

All the men are there. But when my eyes scan the room, there is one man I don't recognize. Micah and the stranger do not look like friends right now and I want to ask what's going on, but words have escaped me at the moment.

"You must be Hadley", the stranger says, turning away from Micah to cross the room to me in a few powerful strides. "I'm Dr. Kinkade." He extends his hand to me, and I hesitate to touch him, looking over his shoulder at Micah for permission. Micah's jaw ticks and his eyes are hard, but he gives me a curt nod and I shake his hand.

"Nice to meet you", I tell him, even though I'm not sure I mean it. His hand swallows my own and he's much taller than I am. I would guess close to Tyler's height. And just like my boyfriends, he's stunning as well. He has this casual way about him where he seems like he could be at home anywhere. Just to look at him, you wouldn't think he was a doctor. Dressed in jeans and a casual button down, his dark hair is thick and longer on top. It's hair any woman would love to run their fingers through. And his eyes are golden brown pools that make me wonder if he's wearing contact lenses. I've never seen anything like them. His stare lingers a little too long and I pull my hand away feeling unsure of what's expected of me next.

"Dining room", Dr. Kinkade asks the group of men.

"Yes." Even Braden's response is clipped.

Micah cuts through the men and guides me toward the dining room. "Did you wash", he asks me, low enough so no one hears him. I shake my head. "Good girl", he praises me, but I'm so nervous, I can't be turned on by it. Something is disastrously wrong here and the army of heavy footsteps behind me only makes me warier.

Upon entering the dining room, Micah strides over to a chair at the head of the table at the farthest point in the room. He pulls the chair out and nods toward it, indicating this is my seat. Dr. Kinkade sits next to me and pulls a form and an expensive looking pen from his bag, placing it in front of me. The rest of the men file in and fill the seats. Everyone takes a seat, much like yesterday, with the exception of Tyler, Graham and Braden. They stand behind Micah who is standing beside me, his hand resting on the high back of the chair I'm sitting in.

I look around the room and feel like I'm going to pass out.

"Hadley", I flinch in my seat when Micah says my name, nerves getting the best of me. He moves his hand from the chair to my shoulder. "The paperwork Dr. Kinkade has for you is primarily for liability purposes. It states that you are acting of your own free will here today and releases Dr. Kinkade of any and all liability during this clinical trial. The paperwork also indicates how your information will be shared. Dr. Kinkade and anyone in his lab will have access to your results in addition to everyone in this room. Dr. Kinkade will test the device before he leaves to ensure it functions as it should. Afterward, he will check in with you periodically via text and email, which he will also copy me on. Any exchange you have with him, you will also have with me. Understood?" I nod, picking up the weighty pen, flipping through the document to find the spots where I am to sign my life away once more.

"You should read the document before signing", Micah encourages me, stopping the pen in midair from initialing the first line. "Do you want a moment? Alone? Perhaps to read the part about the testing at least?" Micah can feel the uncertainty radiating off me as I try to control the whooshing sound in my ears. And then as if my body was being controlled by an unseen force, I'm signing blindly once again. Once all the lines are signed, I hand the paperwork and pen back over to Dr. Kinkade. He gives me a warm smile and begins thumbing through the document, ensuring the necessary acknowledgements have been given. Then he stows the paperwork and pen away in his bag and pulls out a small leather bag and a sterilized package. My mouth goes dry.

I turn in my seat to look at Micah. He looks concerned, brows drawn together, and lips pressed into a thin line. Braden shifts behind him and the look on his face is murderous.

"Hadley", Dr. Kinkade lays his hand over mine and I turn to him giving him the most incredulous look. He chuckles and raises his hands, palms up, indicating he's not a threat to me. "I can see that you're worried and that's completely normal. This..." He slides the sterile package closer to me. "...is the prototype.

The prototype as he calls it is just shy of three inches long. There's a needle on one end with colorful glass-like bulbs spaced about a centimeter apart.

"It's a simple procedure. I'll clean the area and slide it right through the pubococcygeus muscle. Once the implant is in place, the muscle holds it there and it records your state of arousal. It goes to the app these gentlemen have installed in their phones and with their notes in they enter in the app, we get great data on what turns you on the most. Any questions?"

I turn to Micah once more and he motions to me that I'm free to ask Dr. Kinkade whatever I like. So, I take some liberties despite my audience.

"Is it visible from the outside?" Dr. Kinkade shakes his head. "How is it removed?"

"A small incision is made, and the implant is slid out. It hurts no more than it does when it's inserted", he tells me, anticipating my question all too well.

"Is it safe? I mean, you have other participants I'm assuming. Have there been any issues?"

"None so far. I have a very strong partnership with their primary care provider", Dr. Kinkade looks at Braden. When I turn to look at Braden, he looks no less angry than he did moments ago.

"Okay."

"Okay", Dr. Kinkade repeats reassuringly as he rises and moves to the sink to wash his hands. I turn to Micah once more.

"We'll insert it here", he tells me with the same cool confidence after yesterday's vote.

"Here?" I look around the dining room at the men. They're here to spectate.

"I'll take your chair", Micah directs me, gripping the back and waiting for me to stand so he can slide it out from under me. He isn't negotiating this and the very moment I don't move at his directive, I think I may have earned another belt lashing as a result of my delayed response to him.

Micah pulls the chair back, and the men move around him. It's well choreographed. As though they had discussed everything in the ten minutes he told me to wait in his master suite. Archer takes Dr. Kinkade's seat and Jonathan rises to leave his seat open as Micah grips my waist and lifts me onto the table. Gram and Tyler step forward, taking Micah's place in front of me, and Micah takes Jonathan's vacant chair. Braden still stands off to the side, like a petulant child. I have no idea what's got him so worked up. I understand that he doesn't want me here anymore but it's no reason to pout about it.

It's funny how much the context of a situation matters. Mere months ago, Micah set me on this very table to tell me about the brotherhood. About what he wanted and expected from me if I continued in a relationship with him. I was terrified. But not like this. The two feelings are similar yet completely different. Then I was terrified of the morals I'd be abandoning. Now I'm terrified of pain, this stranger and something I can't quite figure out, but I know I won't like.

I'm taken by surprise when Dr. Kinkade steps up, hands gloved and ready to proceed. Braden steps up in unison.

"I will watch the entire thing. I am your shadow Dr. Kinkade." Braden looks like he could deck this guy. For what, I have no idea.

"As you wish Dr.", he tells Braden as he looks over his shoulder at him and then back at me. "Alright Hadley. I need you to lie back. Tyler and Graham will be helping me here. Spread her wide", he directs his helpers.

My face heats instantly with embarrassment as I look between Tyler and Graham. Neither of them look phased.

"Lie back, Hadley." Micah almost sounds remorseful. I'm half tempted to stop this whole thing and ask him why. But I don't. Because I told him I trust him. And I do. This just doesn't feel right to me though.

The moment I start to lay back, Micah's hand is behind my head, guiding me to the table. Graham and Tyler, still flanking my side, grab hold of my legs. It's like a makeshift gynecological exam. The men holding my legs act as the stirrups as I'm spread for examination.

"I need her cunt at the edge of the table", Dr. Kinkade orders, a satisfied tone in his voice. I've never heard Braden use that kind of language when examining me. I turn to Micah for reassurance, and he grabs my hand as the guys slide me forward. "Perfect. Thank you."

"Breath, Hadley." Archer slides his hand over mine and I grab it like my life depends on it. "You're safe, baby. You're safe", he croons.

I do not feel safe. I feel exposed and vulnerable.

"I'm going to numb you, Hadley. It's just topical." Dr. Kinkade parts my robe allowing it to split down the middle and drape behind my legs causing me to be exposed from the waist down. I tug at Micah and Archer's hands to close my robe, but they don't let me go.

"We're men, Hadley. There's nothing better than seeing pussy first thing in the morning. Let us look." Micah brings my hand to his mouth and kisses the top of it. I relax a fraction. "Good girl", he murmurs.

I suck in a breath as Dr. Kinkade touches me *there*. It's so clinical, which is good. Anything more would be wrong. "Just touching to numb the right spot." His fingers press against my skin, hard enough to find the muscle. There's a snap. "Just a little cool gel", he says as he rubs the numbing agent along my skin.

I close my eyes and take a few deep breaths. I feel like I could throw up. All these eyes on me. This stranger between my legs. He's going to run a needle through my skin.

"Hadley", Tyler barks my name, and I jump at how loud he is. "Eyes open", he orders. I look to Micah again and with his free hand, he wipes a bead of sweat from my forehead, nodding that he agrees with Tyler.

"Who's is this?" Dr. Kinkade looks around the room.

"The cum? That's mine", Micah answers with pride. Low murmurs start around the table. Tyler and Graham are smirking at him and somewhere in all the seriousness, a wide smile appears across Micah's face. "I mean, you're looking at it. If that pussy belonged to you, would you be able to resist it?" I look at Micah, mouth wide open in shock. I cannot believe this conversation right now.

Dr. Kinkade lets out a chuckle. "No. I couldn't. You're clever, Micah. But Tyler and I go way back, don't we Ty?" Tyler winks at Dr. Kinkade and now I'm really confused. I look back at Micah. His smile is gone, and the color has drained from his face.

"Let's begin. Hadley, try to relax. This is going to hurt but it'll be over quick." Dr. Kinkade wipes me with alcohol and blows between my legs to dry it. I suck in a breath at the intimacy of what he's just done.

"Shhh", Micah says, and kisses my hand once more. "Look right here, sweetheart." I look into Micah's eyes, and I relax a fraction, even though Dr. Kinkade is stretching my skin tight with his fingers. I know the second Dr. Kinkade is going to stick me, because Tyler and Graham grip me tighter almost in unison. There's pain. Oh God does it hurt, and I cry out on the table, trying not to struggle against them.

Micah and Archer are both trying to calm me as I give their hands a death grip. I hear shuffling behind me, and I can see the men in my periphery move closer. Chairs scape against the floor as they try to get a better view. I let out a sob because I'm mortified, and the intrusion hurts something fierce. This is a punishment that is almost unbearable. I can't look at Micah or Archer. This is too much. I let out another sob when there's a final shot of pain delivered by Dr. Kinkade.

"It's in. Let's clean you up and test it out, hm? You did good, Hadley. In a few minutes the pain will be a distant memory", he reassures me, patting my thigh.

"Thank you", Micah tells someone and then presses a cloth napkin to my cheeks to dry my tears as Dr. Kinkade wipes me down with more alcohol, blowing on me once more and then wiping me with what feels like a wet cloth napkin.

"Can I go", I ask Micah, my voice thick with emotion.

Micah shakes his head. "We need to make sure it works. We're almost done." I nod at Micah and then look down my body at Dr. Kinkade as he makes room for Braden and Jonathan to take a look. They nod in agreement. "Look good, boys?"

"Yeah", Braden answers Micah, in a tone that indicates they are in a disagreement right now.

"Alright", Dr. Kinkade says as he moves between my legs once more. "Pull up your apps gentleman. You should get a reading of Hadley's state of arousal now. I'd gather is low to non-existent, which is why I test after insertion. I want to show you in real time what happens on the app during arousal and provide compelling evidence that the protype works."

*I test?* Surely, he can't mean himself. Can he?

"Before we begin, Hadley, you need to give Dr. Kinkade consent to make you orgasm."

"She already gave consent", Dr. Kinkade challenges Micah.

"She signed your forms but didn't read them. That's not informed consent and I won't allow someone to be assaulted before my very eyes."

"No." My voice comes out tearful but firm.

"Then I'm afraid I'll have to remove it right away." It's clear by the way Dr. Kinkade throws out this ultimatum, he's had this conversation before. I close my eyes and let the tears fall. I'm in an impossible situation. If I don't let Dr. Kinkade get me off, I lose two votes. And if I lose two votes, I'm done with these men.

"I knew about this, Hadley. You have my permission to let Dr. Kinkade make you come. You have all our permission." Micah tries to sooth me with his rationale, but it doesn't work. "Look around you", Micah tries again. I open my eyes and turn my head as far as I can to see the men have gotten up from their seats. They're all hard. They're all waiting for the show to begin. "They want to see. *I* want to see."

"It's just a moment, Hadley. We'll all help you, darlin", Archer says, rubbing my knuckles over his lips.

"Okay", I tell Archer, and before I can address Dr. Kinkade, his face is between my legs, licking up my slit. I let out a moan and close my eyes at the warm, wet contact from him.

"You two taste delicious", he says, barely looking up from his first taste of me. I can feel his warm breath on my pussy as he talks to no one in particular and then continues licking me. He pauses for a moment, reminding the men to look at their apps, hovering right over my clit.

There's some low chatter behind me but I'm not paying any attention to it. How could I under these circumstances? I'm being tongued by a stranger in front of my boyfriends and with every second that passes, I'm feeling the needle inside of me more and more.

"Hadley." Micah calls my name with such calm adoration. It's then that I realize my eyes have been locked on Dr. Kinkade, rigid with pleasure and nerves. I focus on Micah's handsome face and his smile relaxes me a fraction. "Talk to me. How does it feel?" I let out a pained sound of pleasure as Dr. Kinkade pulls my clit in his mouth and sucks. He slides his finger inside me, and I struggle against Graham and Tyler.

"It hurts", I say, through fresh tears. The searing pain at the intrusion sets my nerve endings on fire.

"Take it out", Braden looks like he's about to come unglued. His eyes are wild, and his jaw is clenched. Time stops as Dr. Kinkade considers his options.

"Hadley, would you like me to remove my finger?" I nod, words escaping me because of the pain.

"Hurry this up or the test is over. That numbing agent only works for a short time and does not numb anything under the skin. This is the only orgasm she gets until I clear her."

"I can't..." I panic, afraid of what will happen if I don't give Dr. Kinkade what I committed to.

"Archer, untie her robe." Micah stretches across the table and covers my mouth with his, stopping my panic with a kiss as Archer complies with Micah's order. The moment I feel the cool air on my breasts I try to pull my hands from theirs to cover up, but they won't allow it.

"I want everyone to see my beautiful girl. Look at you. Being held down by the men who care for you most." His dig does not go unnoticed as things I can't make out are said around the room under the breath of those Micah insulted. "Allowing a stranger to eat your pussy right in front of us. Look at how much Dr. Kinkade likes it."

I look down my body, on display for everyone in the room and when I land on Dr. Kinkade, he looks up at me and tongues me harder. I cry out at how close I am. I'm right there. Right at the edge of release.

"What are you waiting for", Micah asks Archer, his tone incredulous. And just like that, Archer's mouth is on my breast. He's sucking my nipple so hard I'm not sure what feels better, Archer or Dr. Kinkade.

"Where do you want my mouth, Hadley? Hm? Or maybe you don't want my mouth. Maybe you want me to keep talking." I nod. His free hand reaches for my breast and rolls my nipple between his fingers. I whimper at the different sensation. The three of them are almost too much to bear.

"Look at how hard Graham and Tyler are. Should I have you suck their cocks after this?" I shake my head, delirious with pleasure all wrapped up in a thick blanket of guilt. Johnathan walks over to Tyler and there's head nodding and a small smile as Jonathan unzips Tyler's pants and pulls his long thick cock out. He wastes no time pumping it with his fist and I feel Tyler tighten his grip on my leg a fraction.

"Can you come now, Hadley?" I hear a few zippers slide down behind me. Micah looks back and I hear skin on skin and low groans.

"Are they..." I can't even finish my sentence because Archer bites my nipple and at that exact moment, I buck my pussy against Dr. Kinkade's mouth as Micah's mouth finds mine. I'm lost. I'm falling over the edge because I'm being treated like a plaything, and I can't stop my body's response. The moment I orgasm I want to stop. Its pleasure mixed with pain as I feel my muscles spasm around the needle Dr. Kinkade inserted moments ago. But he's relentless as he wrings every last bit of pleasure of out me.

I breath hard as I look around me. Dr. Kinkade licks his lips and nods at Graham and Tyer. The second Tyler releases my leg, Jonathan is on his knees taking Tyler's cock in his mouth. With a low groan, Tyler comes, shoving his cock into Jonathan's mouth as far as he will allow it. Groans sound collectively behind me, and I can literally hear some of them release on Micah's shiny dining room table.

The nipple Archer was sucking on is freezing, now that his mouth is gone, and his saliva has hit the cold air. He still holds my hand, just like Micah and neither of them bother covering me up. Micah's mouth finds mine once more as he kisses me and praises me. *Such a good girl. Mine to show off. Such a beautiful wet cunt.*

We kiss more and I hear shuffling around us. The meeting is over. But not for me.

"Talk to me", Micah prompts, but it's not enough. I don't even know what to say. I can't even process what has happened. What I did… I close my eyes and shake my head, denying him what he wants, knowing I could be punished later. "Are we okay", he asks, with a sense of urgency I'm not accustomed to.

"I think so", I tell him as I kiss him once more. It's the best I can do right now. He wants the truth and really, I don't know yet.

"Okay." He looks down at me with so much concern it hurts my heart. I know he didn't want this. I know he was trying to get Dr. Kinkade to allow someone else to test his device. It backfired and the moment he realized it, he was on edge for me as much as he was on edge for us.

Micah helps me sit up and pulls my robe closed, then he reconsiders, turning to Braden. "Do you want this left open", he asks his best friend, trying to sound casual. Like I hadn't recently driven a wedge between them…like he hadn't just driven a wedge between us because he voted me out.

Braden looks like he could kill Micah. He doesn't answer. The only acknowledgement he gives Micah is looking at him while he ties my robe closed, punctuating that Micah is no longer needed in this room. I look between the two of them and am truly at a loss. These two look like arch enemies and I don't want to be in between them.

Braden takes one look at me, and his face softens more than I've seen it where I'm concerned over the last day. "You can go now", he tells Micah, effectively dismissing him from the room. I swallow thickly as Micah kisses me on the cheek and leaves, closing the door behind him.

Braden steps between my legs causing my robe to ride up. I tense at the mere thought of him touching me between the legs, but he surprises me, raising his hands and cupping my face. "Are you okay?" His deep brown eyes bore into mine and I think I might be hallucinating. I didn't think he cared anything about me since last night. But these are not the actions of someone who doesn't care. These are the actions of someone who is deeply concerned. "Answer me, Hadley. Are you okay?"

"Yes", I nod, his hands moving with me.

"That was so inappropriate. I..." Braden drops his hands and looks away from me. "A good doctor is never supposed to take advantage of his patient. You were under his care."

"I consented." I try to defend Dr. Kinkade, thinking it will calm Braden down, but it does not. In fact, it does the opposite. Braden slams his hand down on the table.

"No! That man is a predator. That is not how a doctor works with his patients. He took from you. You don't take from your patients, Hadley." He shakes his head once more, then pulls me close. "You don't take from your patients", he repeats one last time, hugging me and kissing the top of my head as if he could erase the last half hour just by those gestures alone.

I pull my arms out from between us and hug him back. He looks like he needs it. He sees this differently than everyone else.

"Jonathan didn't seem to mind", I hedge, wondering if Jonathan's actions might get him to see a different perspective. But it doesn't. He pulls back and looks at me, frustration apparent in his features.

"Jonathan's a surgeon. He works on people who are unconscious. And if he sees them conscious, they aren't like that for long. He's hardly my moral compass where this is concerned."

"Don't be mad", I plead with him, sliding off the table, pressing myself against him. I put my hand to his chest and guide him back until the back of his legs hit the chair and he sits, pulling me down on his lap with him. I shake my head and sink to my knees for him. I owe him, and he needs this.

"No. As far as I'm concerned, we're even. Get up."

His rejection stings. I should feel relieved, but I don't. All I can think is that he doesn't want me so much that the thought of me sucking on him is of no interest. Shame floods me. So, I drop my head and try not to cry. He bends forward and tips my chin up.

"This isn't about you. Not like that", he vows, seeing the hurt in my eyes. "Come up here", he tells me, this time sounding gentler and reassuring.

I climb onto his lap, and he wastes no time kissing me. This feels normal. Like I really haven't fucked everything up. He's no different with me now than he was before last night, and my heart soars because now I know I haven't lost him for good.

"I'm sorry", I whisper between kisses.

"I know", he whispers back.

"I love you", I tell him, not caring if I end up dying on the inside because he doesn't say it back.

He chuckles against my lips. "I'd be lying if I said I didn't love you too, now, wouldn't I?" I smile and lay my hand against his cheek. His stubble is rough against my fingers, and I can't help but run my fingertips over the scratchy texture while I look him over. He looks much less angry than he did before.

"You have plans. Suzette dropped off some clothes for you. Let's go grab them so you can get ready." He helps me from his lap, and I can't help but wince at the pain. "There's nothing I can do for you Hadley. It'll get worse as the day progresses. The worst pain will be tomorrow and the following day. You may be out of commission for New Year's", he tells me and then laughs at the displeasure on my face. "I know. I hate it too. I'll check you every day, but you have to take it easy. Okay?"

"I hate this thing already." Braden laughs hard as we exit the dining room and make our way to the kitchen where a few men gather talking to Micah and sharing a cup of coffee.

"Are we all squared away?" Micah looks at Braden expectantly.

"Hadley and I made up." It's the only thing Braden volunteers and a skeptical Micah looks at me, then at my lips. He narrows his eyes a fraction and tilts his head. His tell when he thinks someone is lying to him.

"He didn't want it. So we talked. And kissed." I feel the need to explain even though it's Braden's obligation.

"I need to round on patients. Hadley, I'll check in with you later", he tells me, giving me a kiss on the cheek.

"Is the blowjob transferable", Tyler asks Micah. I can't tell if he's being serious or kidding.

Lifting the shopping bag from the counter, I tell the guys I'm getting changed. I'm halfway to the stairs and I hear the sound of a direct hit. I turn around to see Tyler on top of Braden, blood dripping from Tyler's mouth and Graham holding onto Tyler's arm to keep him from laying into Braden.

"Go", Micah orders me, pointing to the staircase and I scurry to the stairs as fast as my hurt pussy can manage so the men can sort their shit out without me.

# Chapter 19
# **Hadley**

**August 24$^{th}$ 7:45 p.m.**
(4 Months Earlier)

"He's expecting us?"

Micah is holding the door open to a renovated house. The sign in the yard is sturdy, made of wood, whitewashed with black lettering.

DR. BRADEN HART, MD
FAMILY MEDICINE
(860) 392-6966

It's a two-story house a few blocks in from downtown. Just far enough to avoid the hustle and bustle of the community but not far enough off the beaten path to drive away patients, I'm sure. The house looks like a historical monument, with the white wraparound porch and two white wicker chairs sitting on either side of the door. A matching coffee table next to each. Clearly Dr. Hart doesn't mind if his patients stick around.

Micah doesn't answer my question but gives me a stern look instead. I am to trust him. That's what he's saying with the look he gives me now. It's harder than he realizes. At least it is for me.

I'm ushered through the door to find the space looks just as inviting as the porch. Dark hardwood floors with bookshelves and a cabinet of decorative nicknacks. There is a couch and a few plush chairs. In the middle of the room is a large oval coffee table that holds some books. And at the far side of the room is an ornate wood cart with a single cup drink maker, cups and all the fixings. A water cooler sits next to the wooden cart and behind the refreshments, a large window looks out onto the street.

"Just finished up my last patient", a deep voice tells us.

I suck in a shocked breath, surprised there was someone else in the room. I was so taken aback that this place that had all the comforts of home could possibly be a doctor's office, I hadn't even noticed the man standing behind a desk at the other side of the room.

The man chuckles and steps from behind the desk. Speech has left me. This is my doctor? This is Micah's best friend? Blonde hair, brown eyes, tall with a muscular build and a dimple when he smiles.

"Braden Hart." My new doctor extends his hand to me, and I pause before I shake it. "It's a pleasure to meet you Hadley." Letting go of my hand, he shakes Micah's. It feels congratulatory instead of like a greeting.

"Let's get you in a room, shall we?" Braden turns toward a hallway and Micah ushers me forward. As we move down the hallway, it's clear the house has seen a few renovations. Walls and doors have been added to make the space more conducive to a doctor's office instead of a house, but even still, the exam room I'm led to seems larger than what you'd find in a typical doctor's office.

"Thanks for filling out the initial paperwork online. It makes taking a new patient after hours much easier." I nod in acknowledgement. "I have to ask...Hadley, are you coming here of your own free will?"

"I am", I answer, after clearing my throat because the first attempt came out gravely and stressed sounding.

"And you're consenting to the birth control implant today?"

"Yes."

"And you know who I am to you, correct? I'll be one of your boyfriends, but here, in this space, and when I direct you, I play the other role of your primary care doctor."

"Yes. And Jonathan...he's a surgeon and someone you may consult with on my care if needed. He'll also be one of my boyfriends, correct?"

"Very good. The only thing I am to you today is your doctor, understood?" I nod my head.

"Use words", Micah prompts me.

"Yes, Dr. Hart."

"Very good. I've reviewed your chart, and everything looks good. I'll go through a quick exam and then we'll move to the sterile room to put your birth control in."

"Okay." I look over at Micah. He winks at me, and I blush. I know what's coming which shouldn't be a big deal because Micah has seen me naked, but I've never had a man in a physical examination with me before.

Dr. Hart, stands and pulls a gown out of a cabinet, handing it to me. "You can put this on, open in the front. Here's a blanket to cover your lap. I'll get your height, weight and vitals before we begin the exam. I'll step out, just call me when you're ready."

"Breathe, Hadley.", Micah encourages me just as Dr. Hart is closing the door.

I am breathing but it's not helping. My pulse is hammering against my chest and my palms are slick with sweat. I'm so nervous I'm not sure I'll be able to successfully unbutton my own blouse.

Micah stands and takes the gown from my hand. "Significant others do this kind of thing all the time with their partner. You are my significant other." He raises a brow at me similar to how he did the first day we met.

"You're right."

"I know I'm right. Now get changed. We're keeping the good doctor waiting."

The examination goes just like any would. A few awful jokes from a nervous patient about her weight and another about white coat syndrome being the reason for my high blood pressure and then I'm in the thick of the physical exam. To say Braden is thorough is an understatement. He tests my strength by having me grip his thumbs and push and pull various directions. I even get an eye exam. I'm almost through the exam without another round of blushing when he pulls out the table extension and asks me to lie back for the breast exam.

"Hadley, I'm your doctor. This is part of the exam", he gently reminds me even though my face seems to heat more at him calling me out on my embarrassment. "Put a hand behind your head, please." I chose the closest hand to him, and he pulls the robe open to access my breast.

The exam he gives is no different than the ones I've had before except that he talks mostly with Micah about things I have no context to instead of asking me about my weekend plans or what I think about the weather. And when he's done with the breast exam, he covers me back up and steps down to the end of the table.

He nods to Micah and Micah is standing by my side, offering me his hand so I can sit upright without struggling. Braden slides in the table extender and unfolds the stirrups.

"I see from your chart you've had pelvic exams in the past. Would you like me to go over what I'll do here", Braden talks over his shoulder to me.

"Um…no, doctor. That's not necessary." Micah's hand squeezes mine and I let out a long breath of nerves. "I'm sorry. This is just so weird to me."

"No need to apologize. I'd gather it is weird to you. But even still, Micah has a right to be in the room. It will be like this every time we meet, Hadley. Unless Micah gives me permission to meet you without him, of course."

"I know. I just had to get that out, you know?"

Braden nods in understanding while he dries his hands, and then puts on a pair of purple surgical gloves.

"Alright, Ms. McAfferty. Lie back and scoot down until you feel my hand under the paper." I do as I'm told, all the while, Micah holding my hand. He can't take his eyes off me, and I can't stop glancing between the two of them. This type of thing wouldn't fly between the men I've met. It's even wilder to me that these men are friends and have this type of trust in each other.

Braden adjusts the gown on my lap, pulling it up enough for him to see me spread open for him. "Let your legs fall open, Hadley. I need to take a look. It'll be done before you know it", he gently encourages me, flipping on a light beside him and angling it between my legs.

I feel his fingers gently move over my folds. He's focused. In this moment, it's clear to me that there is nothing sexual about this exam. He's really seeing me as his patient.

"Looks healthy." He swivels on his stool to grab a swab. "I just need a sample. It'll test for abnormal cells. Same test as you've probably had before. This one will include sexually transmitted diseases too." I hear a cap close and Braden spreads lubricant on my opening. He slides the specula inside me and opens me further. “A little pressure”, he murmurs as he slides the test swab inside me and scrapes tissue for testing. I grimace a little and Micah squeezes my hand just hard enough for me to look at him and stop focusing on Braden.

“You’re doing great, Hadley Joanna.” I roll my eyes at him and look down at Braden as he’s preserving the sample and then sliding the tool from inside me. He rises to his full height. “Let’s check your ovaries and we can get you dressed”, he informs me as he slides his fingers inside me and presses his hand on my pelvis to examine me properly.

“Everything looks good”, he tells Micah as he slides his fingers from inside me and steps back to pull off his gloves. Micah helps me scoot back and cover up, returning to a seated position. “You’ll have the results of your tests back in forty-eight hours. Your results will go to Micah too.”

I nod, remembering this. It didn’t seem like a big deal at the time but now it seems a bit personal. Braden must see it on my face.

“In order for this to work, there can’t be any secrets, Hadley. I’m sure Micah explained that”, he hedges.

“He did. It’s just that this is also weird.”

“I know. You aren’t the first person who’s shown some pause over this, but I assure you, this will become normal for you.”

When I’m dressed, I’m led to another room. The sterile room. There’s hardly anything in it and it smells clean that’s for sure.

Braden waves me over to yet another leather covered patient lounge chair while Micah stands by my side. The process of hand washing and gloving is done again and then Braden dives right into the procedure. He takes an iodine pad and scrubs the inside of my arm and then cleans it with rubbing alcohol instructing me to stick my arm out at the elbow a bit, so he doesn’t have to clean my skin again.

"This is just a local anesthetic", he tells me, moving his chair to the side of me and hunching over a bit to stick me in the right spot.

We wait again and the guys resume a conversation from earlier having to do with schedules and people I've never heard of. During the conversation, Braden opens a sterile package with what looks like the longest thickest needle I have ever seen in my life.

"Oh shit", I say, without thinking. The guys stop talking and focus in on me. "That's...is that what's going into my arm?"

"You won't feel it", Braden tries to assure me.

"That's huge!"

"Hadley", Micah warns me sternly.

"Alright, alright...if it helps, don't look. Micah, go to the other side of Hadley and distract her. *Talk* to her."

Micah moves to the other side and grabs my free hand. "You want sex, don't you?" Micah dangles the bait in front of me as Braden pulls out a pad for my arm to rest on and twists my arm, wrist facing up. He places one hand on my forearm, securing it to the chair.

"Do not move, Hadley."

"Oh God", I whine.

"On the count of three", Braden informs me. "One", and he slides the implant in. "All set", he tells us, placing the used instrument in the packaging and releasing my arm. "Let me put a band aid on that."

I watch him in shock as he disposes of the instrument and opens the packet to get me a band aid. "No sex for seven days. Understood?" He looks at us like my dad would look at us girls when he was issuing the sternest of warnings.

"Alright, it's been a long day. But before we wrap up, do you have any questions of me, Hadley?"

"Seven long days, huh?" This earns me a laugh from both of the men. And although I was skeptical about how professional this exam would actually be, it helped me to see that these men really aren't looking to take advantage of me at all. They really do care. It's just that their definition of what's right is much different than society's.

# Chapter 20
# Micah

**August 24th**
(4 Months Earlier)

Since I told Hadley about why the fourth of July is my favorite holiday, she's asked me so many questions about camping and what I'd do with the ladies who met me in my tent that I just had to make this a date.

It's only been a few days since she's gotten the implant so it's too soon for us to have sex which is why this date is perfect. I had to improvise on the car ride though. In my youth, I never rode out to the campsite with a woman. That would have implied that we were together and that could never happen.

I took the Audi Q7 because we needed the room for the tent and other camping supplies. It also has more room up front, which means Hadley can spread out for me more. Specifically, her legs. I want her wound tight when we get there, and the car ride is just long enough to accomplish that.

When I arrive at her house, she motions to her outfit before receiving my greeting, which is a nice long kiss and a feather-light caress over backside. “Who do you dress for when we go on dates”, I remind her.

“You”, she says, huffing out a breath while I hold her close to me. Since this trip is like going back in time for me, I want to make sure the details are perfect. So I slide my hand up the side of her skirt to find the cotton panties I’ve provided for her. “I don’t understand you sometimes”, she tells me as I slide her skirt back down, giving her a playful pat on the backside and releasing her from my arms.

“You understanding me isn’t the point. The point is that I’m giving you an experience.” I grab her bag, which is a suitcase, and tip my head to the door, indicating we need to go. “You know we’ll be in the forest, right”, I tease her as she locks the door behind her.

“You should have sent me something to pack my things in then shouldn’t you”, she calls out after me as I head to the car. “Also, it’s a little chilly out here for a skirt”, she complains.

“The girls visiting my tent always wore skirts and managed to keep warm. They also never complained”, I answer back, putting her bag in the back next to the well-stocked cooler. She waits at the driver side door for me to open it for her just as I have since our first date. “I think you’ll find keeping warm will be no challenge at all.” I open the door for her allowing her to get seated and am rewarded with the backs of her bare thighs. She’s appropriately covered on top and is wearing riding boots for the drive out. But her skirt is short. Too short for a forest but perfect for the drive. I have a change of clothes for her when the weather gets cooler. Early fall in the woods tends to get chillier sooner than the city.

When she’s buckled in, I steal another kiss. “You make me so fucking happy. You know that don’t you?” She nods, trying to hide a smile as she leans forward to give me another kiss. I allow it but keep it brief. I could stand out here and kiss her all day without a second thought.

Shutting her in the car and striding around to the driver's side, feeling like the luckiest man on the planet, I pull away from the curb and decide I can't wait to start playing with her. "Slide your skirt up", I order her as I adjust the temperature in the car. Her legs felt a little chilly to me even in her house and I want to make sure the drive is comfortable for her.

"Someone might see. I mean, I know the windows are tinted but, I live here and..."

"Skirt. Up." The skirt isn't very long to begin with, and she only raises it a half inch or so. "More." She makes another half-ass attempt at pleasing me. "I'll tell you when to stop." Hadley makes the slowest display out of baring herself to me. Her efforts almost feel like we're in a test of wills. But I'm not telling her to stop until I see the crotch of those white cotton panties.

"Perfect", I tell her. "The windows are tinted. No one can see in. One of the brothers specializes in security. When I tell you your pussy is secure, rest assured it is. Now recline your chair a bit and take off your sweater." She's wearing a tank top underneath with no bra. I'm so fucking hard right now my cock is ready to tear through my pants.

She does as I tell her, removing her top and setting it on her lap. I grab it and toss it in the back seat. She looks surprised as she adjusts the seat to tilt back so she's at about a one hundred forty-degree angle now.

"Relax your legs." Her legs fall open and she looks up at the sunroof. "Perfect. Are you comfortable, Ms. Hadley Joanna?"

"Yes, Micah."

I start with my hand on her knee like I would driving with her to any other date location. I make slow circles with the pad of my thumb on her skin. It's a three-hour drive to get to our destination and I want to see how wet I can get her before I actually touch it.

She opens her eyes and glances at me occasionally, waiting for me to make another move.

"I like you like this. Maybe I should take the Q7 more often." She lets out a long slow breath, relaxing on the warmth of the seats. "Maybe I should plan dates where the first part is just me admiring your pussy. It is something to be admired. A true gift that you give to me at my request, is it not?" She doesn't answer my rhetorical question but in exchange, the rise and fall of her chest tells me everything I need to know. She's getting turned on.

I slide my hand further up her thigh. "I should warn you that I can't give you the full experience on this trip. That would require you to be nothing to me. So, we'll pretend a little. Would you like that? To pretend with me? You'll come to my tent to be my little toy, hmm? I'll talk to you like I did those girls who meant nothing to me?"

Hadley opens her eyes and nods at me. "Very good. I'll teach you how to suck a proper cock." She nods once more. "Good girls get their cunt licked. Are you a good girl, Hadley?" She nods again. "Let me hear it", I prompt her.

"I'm a good girl." Her answer comes out breathy and she swallows thickly.

The entire car ride is me, looking at her cotton covered pussy, stroking her legs and talking about all the things I'm going to make her do at the camp site. By the time we make it to our site, I can see the moisture on her white cotton panties. I haven't even touched them yet.

I hand her the sweater I tossed in back and she makes herself decent while waiting for me to open the door for her. Opening doors is not a brotherhood rule but a personal rule of mine. I unbuckle her seatbelt and tell her quietly in her ear, "It smells like pussy in here." Then I nip at her earlobe, and she gasps. I give her my hand to help her from the car and she shivers a little at the temperature change.

We set up camp and go for a hike. Nothing too rugged since she's still wearing her skirt. I did have her change her boots. Standing in front of her, she couldn't help looking up at me while kneeling to lace them. Little does she know, that's exactly how she'll be by the fire later.

We go on a nice long hike, stopping by the lake to look at the leaves turning colors on the trees and taking in the peace and quiet. I love the outdoors. The fresh air, the smell of pine and cedar...I need to go camping more often.

At camp, I hand her a cider beer while I start the food. It's what I would have served the teenage girls who joined me, although I never cooked for them.

When the meal is cooking over the fire, I have a seat on one of the folding chairs and motion for her to join me. Her beer is mostly empty, so I reach over and grab another for her out of the cooler, handing her a fresh drink and pulling her onto my lap for a kiss.

Holding the full and almost empty bottle, her hands are occupied while mine are free to roam. "You kiss like a dirty girl", I tell her. She kisses me back with more intensity. "Are you a dirty girl?"

"Uh huh", she breaths onto my lips and starts another kiss.

"Good. Because I want to do dirty things to you. Is that okay", I ask, getting her consent just like I would when I was younger.

"Yes. Please", she pants, going in for another kiss. This time I stop her.

"I want to see something", I tell her before taking my hand and parting her legs. She opens up wider for me, adjusting herself on my lap. "What do we have here, hmmm?" I feign shock about the crotch of her panties still being wet. "Can I touch it?" She nods. "Out loud and with respect, Hadley."

"Please touch me, Micah." I hear the tremble in her voice. The tremble that means she's barely hanging on by a thread. Little does she know, it's about to get worse.

"Since you asked so nicely, I'm just going to take the edge off. Okay sweetheart?" She's nodding but I don't correct her. I have her consent and that's all I was looking for.

My fingers slide up her thighs and start rubbing the top of her panties. She falters and almost drops one of the bottles.

"Ah, ah, focus, sweetheart. Don't make a mess at my camp site." She's nodding frantically and my heart is singing with appreciation and wonder. "Let's see what we have underneath", I murmur, sliding my fingertips under the wet fabric to find her soaked pussy and her swollen clit.

She moans and stiffens in my lap because she's already at the threshold of pleasure and fuck if I don't want to give it to her. But I can't. Because this is how the game goes. At least this is how the game went back then. Have them begging for an orgasm and by the time they slide on top of your cock, you barely have to do anything to get them off.

"Not yet", I tell her as I slide my hand from her panties and lick her arousal off my fingers. Hadley sits there, panting and wide eyed. "Here, I'll take this one", I grab the bottle that's almost empty and set it down between me and the cooler.

"What", she breathes the question, and I ignore it, tipping the bottle up to her lips so she can have the first sip of her beer, then I open the cooler and grab a beer out for myself and I sit there with her, quietly, waiting for our food to finish while she thinks long and hard about what just happened.

I could tell Hadley wanted to say something smart a few times but thought better of it because she'd open her mouth to speak, close it and let out a deep breath. To frustrate her more, I got out a blanket and laid it over our laps, holding her free hand on top of the blanket so she understood quite clearly that nothing more was happening right now.

We eat the grilled chicken and vegetables as she peppers me with questions about the campsite. Is this the same site? Did I have a favorite spot? Will we roast marshmallows? What kind of animals are out here?

I'm not sure if she is genuinely curious or just trying to fill the silence. Funny how the girls I took here were just as chatty years ago.

We finish eating and I clean up, adding more wood on the fire before turning my attention back to Hadley. It's getting dark. Just like in the past, it was the perfect time to teach a needy dirty girl how to suck a cock the right way.

I hold out my hand for Hadley, helping her from her chair. At this point, she's no doubt calmed down from my touch earlier. Now I'm going to rile her back up again. I move the chairs back and drop a folded blanked in front of one. Then I take a seat and point to the blanket.

"Kneel." Her eyes widen, not from indignance but from surprise. I think she thought we were through with our little game. Far from it.

She sinks to her knees, and I take a moment just to admire her. The glow of the fire is behind her. Her long straight hair cascades down her shoulders and her lips part like she's silently begging me to begin.

"Why did you come out to camp with me, Hadley?" I ask as a part of our little game. When confusion flits across her face, I prompt her. "Any of the girls back at my parents' party would have come here with me if I had asked. But I didn't ask them. I asked you." Leaning forward in my chair, I bring my fingertips under her chin and force her to make eye contact.

"I like you", she answers, the simple admittance of a girl, not a woman. She's playing our game now and I love it.

"Do you want to know what I think?" She nods. I don't need her consent yet, so I allow it. "I think you want to know what it feels like for a guy to make you come." Her mouth falls open at how brazen I am, but that's exactly how I would have said it in my youth and not one girl fled from my tent. There wasn't even an ounce of hesitation to stay.

"Do you? Do you want me to make your pussy feel good?" Hadley nods in answer and I pull my hand away from her chin, leaning back and spreading my legs wide for her. "Show me", I order her as I rub the heel of my hand over the bulge in my pants.

She raises up on her knees and brings her hand up to unzip me. This is the first time she's ever put me in her mouth. If I said I wasn't excited and nervous, I'd be lying. Some women don't enjoy giving head. I hope to hell she's not one of them. I *need* it. And when I say need, I mean it.

There's something so filthy and desirable about a woman allowing you to deep throat her. About her wanting your hard cock down her throat because she needs to taste your cum as much as you want her to taste it. I feel worshipped like a god while a woman sucks me to release.

She pauses a moment. My zipper is down. Now all she needs to do is pull me out.

"Do you want my cock in your mouth?" She goes to open her mouth but closes it. "Do you want me to teach you?"

"Yes." She swallows thickly and now I can see clearly, only part of her response is our game. She's either never done this or doesn't like it.

"Go ahead. Take it out", I croon to her as she returns her hand back to me and finds me painfully hard in my boxer briefs.

"You're nervous", I observe. When I stretch my hand out to caress her face, she nuzzles into me, acknowledging my assessment. "Don't be.", I run my thumb over her bottom lip, pulling it down to expose her bottom teeth. "So pretty. Such a pretty little mouth. Will you share your pretty little mouth with me? Where I need it most right now?" I grab her hand as she's pulling it back from my hard length, wrapping her fingers around me to fist me just as I like. "Like this", I show her. She rolls her eyes up to look at me and it's so fucking submissive I have to stifle a satisfied groan. Jesus Christ. If I go slow with her and earn her trust the things I could do with Hadley...

"I picked a good girl to come back to my tent tonight. Good girls get so wet when they've got a cock in their mouth. Would you like to get wet for me? Hmmm?"

I tuck some hair behind her ear, and she shudders at the contact. "Can I dirty you up a little? I can teach you how to be naughty girl." She licks her lips and nods. "I want to hear you ask me."

"Teach me. Please, Micah." Again, with that quivering voice.

"Teach you what", I prompt, again, seeking her verbal consent. "Be specific."

"Teach me how to suck your cock." Her chest is rising and falling in deep breaths, and I'm so turned on right now I'm not sure how I'll make it through this without blowing in her mouth. "Please, Micah", she adds when I don't respond right away.

"Kiss the tip." She bobs forward and gives the tip of my cock an innocent kiss like you'd give on someone's cheek. "I'll tell you when to stop." I watch her gently love on me. Her tongue sweeps out from between her lips, tasting some of my precum. I like that she enjoys it, but I correct her. "Sweet girl. So eager to taste, huh? Look at me", I croon to her. "Does it taste good?" She nods and I stroke her cheek once more. "That's good. That's really, really good, Hadley. But when you kneel for me, I expect you to do exactly as I tell you." She closes her eyes and holds them shut for a moment, perhaps her nerves getting the best of her. "Go on. We're not done with our lesson yet", I gently coax her and now she follows this direction to the letter. "This is how you thank me properly for the privilege of spending time in your mouth", I inform her.

"Do not lick your lips", I warn her. There's something about seeing my shiny cum on a girl's lips. It's like a girl's promise that she doesn't mind getting a little messy, which is a bonus from my standpoint. "Now, take the tip in your mouth. I want you to taste it." She raises up so her rearend is no longer resting on her calves. Before she takes me in her mouth, she looks at the tip. There's a bead of moisture there. "Go on. Taste it. It's for you", I offer, like a God offering a gift to a peasant.

Without further delay she puts her mouth over my tip and swirls her tongue around to taste her God's gift. I stifle a groan as I make quick work to gather her hair into a makeshift ponytail. The ones that left their hair down were always such a turn on to me and as such, I had Suzette add a note to Hadley's package of clothes that told her how I wanted her hair styled.

My balls ache with the pressure to unload and I can feel myself leaking in her mouth even more. Kneeling before me, Hadley is sweet perfection. So unsure of herself but that makes it all the better.

"Do you like it, sweetheart?" She lifts her head to answer when I tap her under the chin. The hand in her hair holding a makeshift ponytail guides her off my hard cock to answer me.

"Yes."

"Do you want more?"

"Yes."

"You're going to have to work for it", I explain to her as I guide her mouth back to me and she opens, taking me in without protest. "That's it", I croon to her when she slides me into her mouth farther this time. "Take your time and suck, sweetheart."

I watch as she carefully bobs up and down on my length. She doesn't go deep enough to gag herself, but she keeps a steady rhythm, her nerves gradually disappearing.

"I think you can take more. Will you try for me?" She answers me by rolling her eyes up to meet mine and hums her approval without missing a beat.

"Very good. Now this time, I want you to take me in your mouth and slide down as far as you're comfortable and suck."

"That's it. Just look at you. So perfect. So beautiful with your mouth full.", I croon to her as she works my shaft slowly and carefully.

I let her suck for a few minutes to get used to this new depth. There's nothing worse than a girl trying to like sucking a cock just for a guy's approval. It's uncomfortable for both of us and quite honestly ruins all the fun.

After no time at all, Hadley has established a rhythm and seems to be enjoying herself. I won't ask her how experienced she is because I can gather, she isn't at all. In the end, it doesn't matter. I'd much rather have her experiences be with me, so she feels good about giving head. It's something she'll be expected to do with the brotherhood regularly. There are no exceptions.

"I'm going to show you how I like it sweetheart", I tell her before I grab her hair tighter and quicken the pace of her bobbing head. "Look at me", I call to her and when she does, I let out a groan. "Oh goodness, look at that. Look at my dirty, dirty girl." She looks back down, clearly self-conscious about me looking at her stuffed full of my cock. "Can I come? Can I come in your mouth? Or right down your throat?" She rolls her eyes up at me once more in answer, those green eyes begging me to do it.

"Relax your throat", I warn her, and then I slide in deeper and hold her there for a second before resuming the depth she's accustomed to. "If you're going to be a dirty girl, you need to choke on it a little. Again", I tell her before she has enough time to prepare for me sliding in deeper.

Her nails dig into my thighs, so I take this opportunity to give her an out. "Do you want to stop?" I move her head so she's free to answer clearly.

"Come in my mouth", she orders me as she wipes a tear from her cheek with the back of her hand. Without a moment of hesitation, I guide her head down and she opens, relaxing a bit more for the intrusion she's about to endure a few more times. We repeat the process and each time I think I'm going to blow, I guide her off me, and then finally, when I can take no more, I have her sit back on her haunches.

"You can tuck me in now." Worry flashes across her features in the firelight and I stroke her cheek with my fingers to comfort her.

Hadley is just as strung out as I am. All we want is an orgasm and I keep bringing us as close to the edge as we can possibly go, stopping it dead in its tracks.

Once she tucks me back in, I have her stand. "Show me your pussy." Hadley pauses and I prompt her further. "Raise your skirt." Looking around as though there were anyone else here but us, she stands before me and slowly raises her skirt, revealing those god damned panties that used to get me so hard in my teens.

This time I kneel in front of her. I slide her panties from her, only to find the wettest pussy I've ever seen. I think we're both at the end of our ropes. But I can't stop the game quite yet because this is what I would have done with those girls. A night to ourselves, no supervision and no interruptions. We had all the time in the world and every night I camped I capitalized on it.

After a few licks, she's aching. I can barely lick her clit, without sending her over the edge. So I focus on the mess elsewhere, staying away from her bullseye altogether.

When I finish, her eyes look wild. She wants it so badly it makes me proud that I haven't lost my touch. I pocket her panties and stand, taking her to her chair to have another beer and talk as the night grows colder. At her first shiver, I stand up and hold out my hand to her. She looks at it like I'm kidding around.

"We should head in for the night, don't you think?" She gets out of her chair so fast she almost nocks it over. I stifle a laugh and lead her to the tent.

When the zipper closes, we're tugging off clothes and groping at flesh like we're starving…because we are starving. We're starving for each other. We're worked up into such a frenzy I decide not to continue the game any longer.

Laying on top of the sleeping bags, I pull her close to me like she's my prisoner. "If this were after the seven-day waiting period I'd show you how those girls and I used each other. Would you like that", I ask her as I bring her leg up over mine and tug her hair, so she has nowhere else to look but at me. We're laying on our sides, tangled up in each other, so dangerously close to fucking that my cock is leaking all over her stomach.

"Yes. Do it. Just pull out", she begs.

I kiss her hard because I want to. Fuck do I want to slide inside of her right this second, but I can't. We'll both be out, and I didn't fight this hard for her or work so hard all these years to build something so utterly fantastic to be kick out. So

I do the next best thing. I slide my cock through her slick folds as she moans in my mouth.

"Don't hold back on me now, sweetheart. After I come, you're going to clean it up with your filthy mouth and make sure my cock is good and empty too." And that right there does her in. She finds her release, bucking up against me as I slide over her relentlessly and I release everything I have between us. My release is all over our stomachs and all over the sleeping bags we didn't bother opening. Such a beautiful sticky mess we made together. Even in this tent with all the fresh air we managed to make this space smell like sex.

We look down at us pressed up against each other covered in our mess, panting and in awe.

The rest of the waiting period is going to be hell.

# Chapter 21
# Micah

**December 28th 6:45 a.m.**
(Present Day)

Fuck! I dab at my split lip with a kitchen towel finally alone in my home with the exception of Hadley. I'm glad she didn't see the rest of what went down between us brothers. It would not have instilled confidence in what we do.

Even still, one look at my lip and my hand will tell her something's up between members of the brotherhood. I flex my hand open and closed, wondering if I broke anything. I dial Jonathan and put him on speaker.

"Hey man." It's how he answers literally everyone. For an emergency surgeon, he's so laid back. I wonder how he does it.

"I think I need an x-ray."

"Of what?" I can hear people talking around him and the sound of metal doors closing. He's either at the gym or in the hospital locker room.

"My hand."

"What happened?" I can hear the smile in his voice.

"I think I broke it on Braden's face." He lets out a long whistle. "And then Tyler's."

"Jesus. What happened after I left?" I hear Jonathan's pager go off. He must be at the hospital. I let out a heavy sigh because a big part of our decisions was a result of testosterone, but the catalyst was emotional.

"Braden came in with Hadley. I knew something was off. Ty made a smart remark to Braden and Braden clocked him. Ty thought Braden had settled down, but he started screaming at us. Said we disrespected Hadley. Treated her like a toy. I hit Braden. Ty pulled me back. Then I hit Ty." There's silence on the line. "Jonathan?"

"Yeah?"

"You think we mistreated Hadley." I said it like a statement, hoping he'd back me up. Because if anyone had a flexible moral compass, it was Jonathan. But he didn't.

"She's your girl, Micah. You're responsible for her. Unless you broke a rule of the brotherhood or lied to Hadley, the only one who can decide if you mistreated Hadley is you. No one else has a right to say shit."

"So helpful", I tell him sarcastically.

"You should get that hand checked. I gotta go, brother." Jonathan hangs up without another word and when I look up, Hadley has manifested right in front of me. As soon as she sees my face, she sucks in a sharp breath and then winces as she crosses the space between us.

Hadley's fingertips are soft and cool as she traces my skin. She's an angel. An angel I may have mistreated.

I grab her wrists, not allowing her to touch me anymore. I can't think with her hands on me right now.

"I'm fine." She looks sad and I know she's blaming herself for my injuries, but I can't have that. "How are you?"

She takes a deep breath and thinks before she answers. It's killing me. I can't tell if she's considering whether or not to tell the truth or if she's just not sure how she is.

"It's complicated. The only thing I know for sure is that thing really hurts. If it's supposed to be worse in the coming days..."

I nod, disappointed that it will cause her so much pain and feeling guilty because I allowed the implant to be put in.

"I know it doesn't seem like it now, but I think you will benefit from it. The pain will subside and then we'll have fun." She looks at me wearily, as though she isn't sure she can take any more of my kind of fun. I smile at her nonverbal response. It's normal to be nervous. "Would you like to see the results? I haven't even looked yet. We could analyze them together?"

"Sure", she says, hesitantly.

I grab my phone and lead her into the living room. It's clear she's uncomfortable. Anyone can see that her gait is off and she's moving gingerly like she doesn't want to cause any more damage than she already has.

I sit on the couch and then pat my knee. I want her right on my lap when we look at the results. I may have questions, and I've learned with Hadley that I get the best compliance when there's physical contact and the promise of a reward. Within a few taps, the app is up on my phone. Hadley's eyes are glued to the screen. I'm not sure if she's trying to interpret the results or if she's panicking. But they're quite good.

The device begins tracking the moment there's any form of arousal. So, when the muscles tighten or the area has increased blood flow, the prototype starts doing its job. What's most interesting about these results is the spike in the beginning. As soon as Dr. Kinkade put his mouth on Hadley, she was being monitored.

"Was it Dr. Kinkade that you liked, kissing your pussy or a stranger?" She looks at me with wide eyes, reluctant to answer. "If you don't tell me I'll have to experiment. And it would take no convincing for Dr. Kinkade to come back to lick that beautiful cunt of yours." Process of elimination would be easy.

"I don't know. He was both." This makes sense to me.

"What turned you on about it?" My phone vibrates in my hand and when I look down, I realize the prototype is reading her right fucking now. Just talking about this is turning her on.

"I..." She starts but can't seem to commit.

"Don't be scared. I want to know this", I urge her. There's nothing I want more right now.

"You held me there. You and Archer. Graham and Tyler too. But you could have called it off and you helped." I wasn't sure where she was going with this. Was I the villain or the kink master here? "The only choice I had was consent. Dr. Kinkade looked at me and he wanted a taste. He looked like he needed a taste." I've been there a lot with Hadley so I can relate.

"So, loss of control is a turn on for you?" She nods. "What else?"

"The audience. Especially when Archer untied my robe." I nod and wait for more. "I was yours to give and everyone got to see how much control you had over me." She lets out a chuckle. "And the things you said to me. About sucking Graham and Tyler off. It was so dirty because I didn't want to. You would have had to have made me."

"So you like having no control. You like being my little toy to loan out as I see fit." The moment I summarize her words back to her, shame washes over her. "There's nothing to feel bad about. Nothing at all. In fact, I have some wonderful ideas for you." I pull her close to me and kiss her. "Who does your pussy belong to", I ask her low in her ear.

"You, Micah." It's shy but it was an answer.

"And your mouth?" She answers that it's me once more. "Convince me", I challenge her, and she's surprised. She didn't think just because her cunt is out of commission that meant I wouldn't have her other ways, did she?

"Madison will be here any minute", she tells me.

"Then you better hurry. Otherwise, you're going to be giving your friend a lesson on how to suck a cock the right way."

# Chapter 22
# Hadley

**December 28th 8:05 a.m.**
(Present Day)

"Stop looking at me like that." Madison giggles in her seat as Steven drives us through the treacherous streets in the winter storm for our breakfast.

"I just can't stop hearing you gag. Jesus, Hadley. How long were you down there? You don't even have any makeup on today. And you're walking like you were railed into the wee hours of the night." I can hear the awe coming from my best friend and feel a sense of pride because for once she might be envious of my sex life. But she's so far off the mark it's ridiculous.

"I'm starving", I tell her, trying to change the subject. She laughs hard at my segue. I smile and roll my eyes.

"I'm sure you are my little Jessabelle", she teases.

My phone chirps in my coat pocket and I pull it out. It's new. I haven't even used it, but I miss my old one. There was nothing wrong with it. But ditching it was part of the deal. That phone was my past. This one is my present.

It's a text from a number I don't recognize. Just as I'm about to open it, Madison swipes the phone from my hand.

"Holy shit! These aren't even out yet. How'd you get this?" She's turning it this way and that as if it were a rare gem.

"Micah replaced my old one", I start to explain but she cuts me off with another question.

"Who's this?" She turns the phone to me, having opened my text.

860-385-2948- How are you?

The words stare back at me, although I have no idea who they belong to. Bubbles dance across the screen, indicating another message is coming in.

860-385-2948- I want to see you.

"Oh my God. Are you cheating on Micah?" Madison looks at me like I'm some kind of ho.

"I don't know who this is." Madison cocks a brow at me. "I don't!"

Madison starts typing on my phone and I panic. She can be honest which I love but she's also been known to piss some people off with that honesty I love so much. She stops typing and waits. Her face scrunches with confusion.

"Who's Linea? And why is she asking you if you're okay?" I start to answer, and she holds her finger up, signaling that I should not answer those questions quite yet. "What does she want to help you with?" Her voice goes flat at the last question. She deadpans as she hands me back my phone. So much for letting her think I've just gotten really good in bed.

"And who's Braden and why is she working on him", Madison asks, using air quotes when she says *working on him*.

"It's...she's..." I stop attempting to respond. There's no easy way to answer her questions without telling her the secret I've been keeping. She's going to think I've lost my mind if I tell her. And if I don't, she's going to think I don't trust her. But the truth is, I don't want to lose her and losing her is a very real possibility if she finds out what I'm up to.

"So you are cheating on him", she states, as though everything has been confirmed by her from a few text messages and my non-response.

"I am not cheating on Micah. Linea isn't even a friend. And Branden...is...complicated."

"What would Micah say if he read those messages?" Despite Madison's sexual prowess, she has the moral compass of a saint.

"He was the one who gave her my number and I'm pretty positive he'd be thrilled." I see confusion on her face and decide to just dive in. "I need your phone number. I only have the guys' numbers in here now", I tell her as I flip through my phone app. "Well, and Linea's." I look over at Madison when she doesn't respond, and her mouth is hanging wide open. "Are you going to give it to me?"

"Guys?" She chokes on the word. "So, you are walking funny because you got railed all night. And Micah knows?!"

I'm not sure if she's excited or disgusted but regardless, her assumption of last night isn't exactly accurate. "I wasn't getting railed all night and Micah had my phone replaced with this one. He put all the numbers in there that I have this morning so yes, he knows everything I'm up to." She looks at me like her head is about to explode. "I need your number, Madison." I prompt her again, slowly, because it looks like she might be having a cognitive event. But before she can answer, my phone starts going off like a slot machine. Madison's eyes widen and I see our friendship dying before my very eyes.

Archer- You were beautiful this morning.

Tyler- I was serious. I'm putting in a request, baby.

Graham- I'm sorry you're in pain sweetheart. Hope you understand it was for you too.

Landon- Heads up. Change of plans for tomorrow because you'll be sore. Low key.

Harlan- I want to make up with you so bad, Hadley. 

Braden- I'll be over to check you before dinner. Call me if you need ANYTHING.

Emerick- Wasn't so hard, was it? 😉 You were a good girl today. Proud of you.

I let out a heavy sigh, knowing I don't have to show Madison these texts, but I also know that my friend will be hurt if I keep these from her. Reluctantly, I hand her the phone and watch her brows get higher and higher as she reads. She turns to me, anger clear in her features and hands me back the phone.

"I have to respond to them", I tell her wearily. She makes an unintelligible noise of dissatisfaction. "It's a rule", I say, in my defense.

"A *rule*?" She says the word as though it disgusts her. "Who are you?"

And that right there is the beginning of the scrutiny I've been trying to avoid. Judgement is what lies are born from. Ridicule is why secrets are kept. Shame is why secrets are protected regardless of the cost.

"We're here", I tell her as Steven pulls up to the curb. She gets out without letting Steven open her door and storms up to the restaurant, the snow and wind swirling around her making her seem like a character in a movie whose superpowers are about to get out of control. I thank Steven and hobble after her, hoping what I'm about to share with her will not tank our friendship or brand me as a freak.

I've never been to this restaurant. Micah picked it. Not because he was controlling my free time, but because he's gone just about everywhere and well...I haven't. It's formal. Or maybe it's just formal for us, I think as I'm being helped out of my coat by the restaurant staff.

"Ms. McAfferty. It's a pleasure to have you and Madison here with us this morning. We have a delightful table for you. And Mr. Stevenson has sent a gift." We're ushered through the dining space, and I can practically feel the hostility reverberating off Madison.

My chair is pulled out for me to sit. Madison is clearly not having any of these formalities and seats herself. The wait staff nods to the envelope at my place setting with my name scrolled elegantly across the envelope. It's for what I assume to be the very expensive bottle of champagne waiting at our table to be opened. I clear my throat to read the card aloud, pulling the thick card stock from the envelope.

*Hadley,*

*Thank you for the spectacular morning. I hope the bubbles will soothe your tender throat.*

*Love,*

*Micah*

The waiter grabs the bottle and with a flourish, opens it for us while I blush uncontrollably in my seat, knowing that everyone at this table knows I got rewarded for sucking cock this morning.

The waiter leaves us after pouring our first glass and Madison raises hers. I follow suit, hoping she'll make the toast.

"To best friends", she says while she extends her glass to mine, clinks it, and takes a healthy swig. Oooookay. That was passive aggressive.

"Madison, just out with it. I know you're mad. Can we just talk about it?" This earns me a kackle.

"Can we just talk about it? We're best friends and I feel like I walked into a movie where my best friend, who I've been trying to get quality time with for months has turned into someone else on the sly."

Okay. That's fair. I'll give her that. She isn't wrong.

"I watched you deep throat a cock this morning. I didn't even know you've ever tasted one. Because the Hadley I know, said that's gross. But this morning, you gobbled one up like you were starving." She cocks an eyebrow at me and I'm not sure what to say. As I predicted, Madison did show up while I was milking Micah and not only am I expected to continue I also didn't want to stop. I needed the contact with him. Him letting me please him when Braden did not was a relief. I don't think I could have taken the rejection of them both.

"It was gross. Before them it repulsed me." Her eyebrows shoot up and I cover my mouth with my hand. Oh my god, what did I just say?

"Them? Would those be the random string of guys texting you on the way here? Who are they?" She takes another angry sip of her drink.

"Yes. And they're not random. I date them. All of them and then some." Her mouth is hanging open as though she's having some sort of brain bleed.

"Mav", she finally asks. I nod my head. "Are you..." She closes her eyes for a moment before she finishes because the words are too hard to say. "...an escort now?"

Now it's my turn to laugh. I can't imagine Micah pimping me out for money. Not even in his most desperate hour.

"No. It's complicated." My phone starts buzzing again. More texts. I turn my phone face down on the table and try to ignore it.

"What in the hell is going on Hadley? I want the truth."

"Okay", I tell her, frustration in my voice. "You want the truth? Here's the truth. When I met Micah, he fell in love with me. And I don't know if you've noticed, but he's pretty hard not to fall in love with. So I fell. Hard. But to be with Micah, I have to be with his brothers." She wrinkles her nose in disgust, and I hold up a palm, stopping her from the commentary I know she's dying to give. "And as it turns out, his brothers are just as easy to fall in love with as he is. I'm in a relationship with all of them." Her eyes go wide. "All twelve including Micah", I answer her unsaid question. "So yes, I gobble cock now."

Madison sits there speechless as I drink my champagne, my phone still chirping away.

"Do you want me to tell you about it? I mean, I'm terrified to tell you because I don't want you to think I'm a whore, but I will because you're mad and if I'm being honest, I don't want to hide this from you anymore." I don't. I wanted to tell her the moment Micah asked me to be with all of them. And I was going to, but I thought Madison might tell me to drop him and there was a tiny part of me that just kept saying *what if*?

"You've been lying to me for months." She lets the statement hang there. It's like a *Scarlet L* for liar.

"I didn't want you to talk me out of trying it. And I thought you would. I thought you'd tell me that what Micah was proposing was disrespectful and to ditch him. So yeah...I lied." Somehow it feels cathartic to say that. I've never lied to Madison and just getting this burden off my chest makes me lighter.

"I would have told you to ditch him. I mean...how is he different from the pervy men you massage?" She holds her finger up to the approaching waiter, signaling we need a minute.

"It isn't all about him. In fact, it's about me first." She tilts her head to the side and squints her eyes in challenge. "He came home from work earlier this week, peeled my clothes off and put his dress shirt on me as pajamas. Then we watched an entire movie on the couch where he fingered me from the opening scene to the rolling credits, giving me orgasm after orgasm. After the movie, he ate me so thoroughly I couldn't say my name and then finally fucked me on the floor in front of the fireplace." Madison's mouth hangs open yet again. "Perverts are in it for them. In Micah's words, he actually *likes* women."

Madison waves the waiter over and before he gets to our table, she says, "The entire movie?" I nod and bite my lip to keep from smiling. "Are they all like that?" I nod again, this time letting the smile spread across my face.

"Are you still mad", I ask, hoping she's more agreeable than she has been in the last half hour.

"Yes, I'm still mad", she says with an exasperated tone. "But mostly because you're with a man who has the finger strength to diddle someone for a few hours and get you off." I laugh. And then she laughs.

"It was so good. I highly recommend watching movies that way."

"Ladies, are we ready to order?"

We weren't ready to order but since we seem to have made up and had more important things to worry about than food, we made some quick selections and were back at the subject at hand.

"How does it work?" Madison is all about the details. As a small business owner, you have to be, so I get it. But the truth is, I don't exactly know how it works. "To be clear, I think they're taking advantage of you. And if you want to change that, you have to fill in the gaps for me."

"There's a calendar and the guys decide who the girls spend time with."

"Girls? Wait. There are others? Is Linea one...of you?"

"Yes. Every guy has a girl. Think of us as the guy's possession." She scoffs at that. "They decide everything for us. This outfit was a gift, specifically for today."

"You can't pick your own clothes?" This blows her mind, and I get it. It took me time to get used to as well.

"Some days I can, but the guys want what the guys want and to ensure they get what they want, some lady by the name of Suzette shops for them."

"What happens if you don't wear it?" Of course, Madison would ask this. She follows no one's rules but her own.

"Well, it depends on who you're saying no to and what your agreement says. I've never flat out refused to wear something; however, I did make an assumption and was taught a very impactful lesson. You tend to be a quick learner with these men." She refills our glasses and motions for me to continue.

"Do you remember how Micah asked me to go to a boring work function with him after our first date?" Madison nods with a sinister smile. The night of our first date, he didn't clean out my cobwebs, but I had never come as hard as I had from someone's fingers alone, my own included. Madison didn't care what he invited me to. He could have invited me to a root canal and Madison would have encouraged me to be there.

"Well, as promised, Micah had clothes shipped to my home. He had everything down to the shoes. Except one item was missing. Panties." She smirks and the dirtiness factor. "And I thought that his shopper made a mistake and forgot them, because after all, she did include a bra for me. So, I pulled a suitable pair from my dresser drawer and thought nothing of it. Micah came in to bring me to his car, but before we left, he did what is a common practice of his. He has me stand still and he circles me like prey. There was absolutely no way he could tell I was wearing panties but somehow, he just knew. And all throughout the night, he would devour me with his eyes or make comments designed to make my core ache with need. By the time he loaded me in his car to go home, I all but spread my legs and begged him to touch me." Madison laughs but it's the honest to God's truth. "Instead, he brought me home and started kissing me before the door even shut. He asked me if I had a good time and if I liked wearing clothes that were chosen for me in between kisses. Of course, I said I did. I had no idea what in the hell those lawyers were talking about, and I didn't care. Being admired by him and the promise of sex later that night…oh my God Maddie it was like a high I don't know that I've ever had before him. Then he asked if I was a good girl today."

"That's hot", Madison tells me, as though I don't already know this.

"I thought I had been, so I confidently said that I was and practically held my breath waiting for my reward. I was so excited when his hand started moving up my thigh and then slid up to grab a handful of my ass. He ran his fingers under the band of my panties and then shook his head. But he slid his fingers between my legs and started stroking me on top of my panties. And then he asked me if my panties were included in the package he sent over. To which I explained that I figured he forgot to add them. He left it at that, bringing me so close I was digging my nails into his shoulders...and then he stopped." Madison's eyes go wide. "He told me that everything he does is intentional. Every order he gives comes with expected compliance. And every behavior that falls short of his expectations comes with a punishment. Then he reminded me that I did not have permission to defile what was his, wished me a good night and left for the evening."

"Oh my god, that's hot. And so mean."

"Yeah. At the moment, I thought I was going to die." She laughs hard. "But rest assured, when I receive my clothes from the men, I put on only what is in the package."

"I bet they don't send you many pairs of underwear", Madison jokes with a laugh.

"That they do not", I confirm.

"What's the kinkiest thing they've given you?" It seems as though judgement has officially left the building.

"That's easy. My first solo date with Archer, he sent me a camel color trench coat with instructions to leave all the buttons undone except the middle three. They ended up having a lot of fun with me that night."

"They?"

"Yeah. We got carry out at Archer's shop. While we were waiting, Archer had me lay in one of his tattoo chairs and unbuttoned my coat to look at me. Then he gave me lessons, in my coat, on how to suck a cock with a Jacob's ladder so I wouldn't chip my teeth or hurt him. After dinner, Archer sent me out to grab him a flash from the front and a few of the guys were laying in the chairs with tents in their pants so big it looked painful. He had me service them and then service him before he took me home and tucked me in." Madison's eyes go wide. "I know Maddie. I'm not lying when I say I come every day and the only time it's from my own hand is when I'm ordered to take care of myself for one of them."

"No wonder you're walking like that", she chuckles as our food is delivered to the table. Suddenly, I'm not hungry.

"What? Did I offend you or something? I mean, Hadley, you're walking like you got railed last night." She laughs and rolls her eyes. "Are you mad?"

"No." My answer comes out clipped. I'm nervous. I don't want to tell her about this morning because I'm still processing it. "Maddie, after this, can we go visit one of them?"

Her eyes practically pop out of her sockets and roll onto the table.

"I need to message him to see if he's free, but I need to talk and I think he'll talk with me." She's still staring at me, so I pick up my phone and start to text Jonathan.

Hadley- I need to talk to you. It's important. No sex.

I add that last part because I've never messaged any of them, so I want to be honest about what I need. There's no way I'm giving another blow job with a witness. I show the phone to Madison, and she nods, still looking like she's in a daze. It's anyone's guess if Jonathan will answer. His schedule doesn't lend for much flexibility.

Meanwhile, my phone continues pinging. I refuse to look at the messages as the total number of unread texts continues to climb. After the morning I've had, I just need some space and knowing that Madison isn't ostracizing me yet is something I'm going to hang onto as long as I can.

We take our time catching up, although I spend the most effort trying to get the focus off me. I've opened the flood gates for Madison's curiosity. Although I know she wants the details, I'm mentally spent and drunk off champagne, so my filters aren't as strong as they normally are.

When we pour our final glass from the second bottle, Madison reminds me that I'm waiting on a response from Jonathan. Reluctantly, I turn my phone over hoping to see Jonathan's name. I do in fact see his name and Micah's right above it.

Clicking on my text from Jonathan, I'm delighted that he can see us. But I have no idea how to round up Steven. Soliciting help from Micah seems practical, so I pull up his text thread. I roll my eyes up to meet Madison.

"What?! What is it? Can we go?" She's practically bouncing in her seat with anticipation.

I look back down at my phone.

Micah- How's your pussy?

Micah- I'm so proud of you.

Micah- Sending Steven's contact info. Just text him and he'll pull around front.

Micah- I love you.

I tap the keys with a quick response, not wanting to delay getting to Jonathan anymore.

Hadley- It hurts. I'm proud of me too. This is scary. Thanks for Steven's number. I love you more.

I fire off a response to Jonathan and then text Steven. Madison and I rush to finish our last glass like our asses are on fire. We flag down the waiter and when I open my new clutch to pay for our meal, the waiter informs us that Mr. Stevenson has picked up the tab. I let out a heavy sigh. He does it so he can see everything. So right about now, he knows that drunk Hadley is on her way to see Jonathan with her drunk friend. I wonder if he's going to be angry. I wonder if Jonathan minds that I bring Madison. I didn't mention that part.

We don't even bother putting on our coats like civilized ladies. Quite honestly, we're drunk hot so the storm outside means nothing to us considering the short distance from the door to the car. Steven is outside waiting for us. His eyes bulge open at the sight of us with no coats on and he rushes to open the door to the car so we can barrel in.

Once in the car, I'm texting Jonathan and making requests of Steven before his seatbelt even clicks closed.

"Steven, we need to visit Jonathan at work", I tell him, not bothering to look up from my phone.

"Oh dear", I hear Steven remark, and realize he thinks we need medical attention.

"It's a social visit." I look back and forth between Madison and Steven's eyes in the rearview mirror. "We're fine. Would you..." I waive him on, not meaning to be rude and apologizing right after I waive him.

"It's not a problem", Steven reassures me, even though I vow never to be so dismissive again.

With the winter storm, the drive is slow, but when we finally do arrive, Madison allows Steven to open the door for her and I take that as a sign that her anger has since passed. All she wanted was to be included. Well, buckle up Madison, because you're probably going to have heart palpitations after this conversation.

We walk in to find Jonathan leaning against the front desk, his white coat over his scrubs a total contrast to his tan skin and dark hair. He's saying something to make the ladies laugh at the desk. Then he suddenly pulls his phone from his pocket, swipes the screen, taps at it and then looks up at us with a heartbreakingly beautiful smile. Before leaving the desk, he says one more thing to the ladies that makes them cackle with laughter and then meets us in the middle of the atrium.

Jonathan is tall. Tyler tall. That's like six feet and some change. And he's a hugger. When he wraps his arms around me and pulls me close to him, I feel blessed. He saves lives and he's giving his love to me right now. I can't explain it, but he's like some mystical creature who's one with God. I always wonder if somehow, he could be a chosen one. But would God choose someone who's bisexual and fucks a ton of women? I don't know. But if it's even possible, I'd say Jonathan was chosen by God to bless every life he comes in contact with.

Now you'd think Jonathan would give Madison a handshake, but he does not. He pulls her into the same hug, and I think Madison feels it too because she lets out a little hum when he pulls her close.

"You two smell like booze. Come back with me. Let's get you in a room", he tells us waiving us to follow behind him while he walks faster than I can hobble. Madison and Jonathan wait for me at the door he's badged open. Jonathan smiles and Madison makes a remark about wanting details on who made it so I can't walk straight. Jonathan tries to give Madison a look that says knock it off, but the good doctor can't pull it off. He has one of the most serious jobs but is in fact one of the least serious people I know. Especially one of the least serious of the men.

He tells who I believe to be a nurse that he's taking us to the last bay. The woman nods and quickly types something in her computer in response. She seems too preoccupied to give more of a response, but it doesn't seem to bother Jonathan, which again, not much that I've seen does.

"Pick a bed ladies." Jonathan motions to two beds in the private room and Madison and I look at each other warily, not moving to select a bed. "I'm giving you some fluids, so you don't have the hangover of a lifetime before noon."

Madison looks green at the thought. "She hates needles doc." Jonathan smiles at how I refer to him.

"Great. We'll do her first", he says, escorting her to the bed farthest away from the door.

"I'll pass out. I swear it", Madison warns Jonathan. What she doesn't realize is that Jonathan isn't asking. He knows what's best for even her in this case. "Can you even do this? I mean, we aren't even real patients here", she objects as Jonathan helps her into bed.

"I assure you I am completely capable of setting up an IV fluid drip. And no, I shouldn't be doing this, but I am because it's the right thing to do." Jonathan rummages around the room for the supplies he's looking for as I lay there watching him in a weightless state.

"Aren't you afraid you'll get fired?" Madison's voice goes up about three octaves when she says *fired*.

"No." It's a simple but sincere answer. Jonathan is a fantastic trauma surgeon. I think it's in part because of this fearlessness he has. I envy him for it and wonder how he pulls it off. "How's your pussy, Hadley? Still sore?" Madison sucks in a breath, shocked that he asked me something so private and

I laugh because I have this feeling that Jonathan is going to have fun with Madison any opportunity he gets now, just because he got a reaction from her. He turns to look at Madison, like he can't understand why she was so surprised at his question.

"It hurts way worse than it did a few hours ago. Can you give me something for it?" I bat my lashes playfully and he chuckles and shakes his head.

"I'm afraid I cannot. First, I'd be breaking a rule. Braden has to give the okay. Second, it wouldn't last long. And third, we need to know how painful it is because pain is often a warning that infection is starting." He sits down next to Madison with the necessary supplies, and she picks this point to challenge him.

"I thought you didn't ask for permission", she says to Jonathan, challenging him on something that she clearly doesn't believe in. Jonathan positions her arm how he likes and starts cleaning off the area he's looking to stick.

"Rules are optional. Except the rules of the brotherhood. Those are not optional. Which reminds me..."

"Ow!" Madison must have just gotten her line put in and looks up at the ceiling while Jonathan tapes it to her arm.

"Hadley, can you get Micah and Braden on the line? My hands are a little tied up." He looks over his shoulder at me and I know what's coming. I've just never seen it play out.

The phone rings as Jonathan sets the drip. I call Micah first and it takes him no time at all to answer. "How are you feeling, sweetheart?"

I don't know what it is, but being in a hospital bed, in pain and hearing his voice makes tears well in my eyes. When I don't answer right away, I can hear the concern in Micah's voice. "Hadley? Are you okay?"

"Hold on. I need to connect Braden." And before he has time to ask any questions, the phone is ringing. Jonathan and

Madison both watch me with concern. Drunk Hadley is an emotional wreck right now. I feel like a blubbering idiot.

"Hey Hadley. You okay, baby?" Braden's warm voice sounds through the speaker and I tell him to hold on as I merge the calls.

"Are you both there", I manage tearily.

"Yes", they say in unison.

"Hadley and Madison are here with me guys." Micah already knew this. He knows where I am all the time no thanks to the handoff reports. "The ladies came in drunk." Jonathan gets right to it. I cover my face with my hand, feeling like a teenager who got caught at a house party after curfew. "I have Madison started on IV fluids to curb the hangover but need the okay to start one on Hadley."

"Is he serious", Madison whisper yells from her bed.

"Yes, he is serious, Madison", Micah answers her question on my behalf. "Jonathan, can you stay with her, or should I come up?"

"No", I interrupt them, full well knowing he wasn't directing that question to me. "I mean, you have plans today and I'd hate to interrupt them over something so silly", I attempt to explain, hoping I didn't hurt Micah's feelings. I know he's a little raw from the last day and I don't want to make him think anything that isn't true.

Jonathan shoots me a look that tells me I've just poked the bear and then answers Micah's question. "I should be able to, barring any trauma that comes in. I'll call you if I have to step away. Braden, what say you", he uses old English to bring Braden into the conversation.

"Go ahead. Micah, I'll message you about checking Hadley out tonight. I'll need to bring Linea over."

"Yeah. That's fine."

The tension between them is clear. I caused this and I hate it. "Don't be mad at each other. Please." I don't know why I say it, but I do. There's silence on the line and when I look up at Jonathan, he's got his hand held up like he's holding a cell phone and he's taking his index finger and poking the palm of his hand, signaling that I should hang up.

"I love you guys. Bye", I tell them, before disconnecting the line. I suck in a few stuttered breaths, shutting my eyes while I sob openly in the bed.

"Hadley?" Madison has no idea what has happened in the last day but she's about to find out. I'm raw. Bleeding out in front of them. And for the first time in a long time, I don't care who sees me like this.

"Let's get your IV in. You'll start to feel better." I suck in a few breaths, openly sobbing. "Feels good to let it out doesn't it", he croons while he preps my arm. "They're going to be fine." He says this like he just knows. "You on the other hand are going to be in a bit of hot water with Micah, young lady."

"Ow!", I wince when he sticks me. "You couldn't have warned me", I ask him imploringly.

"I thought I'd warn you about Micah before this needle. You got drunk Hadley. Without one of us."

"It's not a rule. And he ordered the bottle", I counter, full well knowing that I didn't break another rule so soon after breaking one of the most important ones.

"You are right. Getting drunk is not a rule, but doing unsafe things is. We are accountable for your safety. And if you are doing unsafe things, such as getting drunk, you need to be doing those unsafe things with one of us. Surely you didn't get drunk off splitting a bottle of champagne with your friend, did you?"

I shake my head. He's not stupid. He sees drunk people all the time, which means he knows we each drank about a bottle of champagne. I want to tell him they should be clearer but reconsider. Now is probably not the time to be a smart ass.

"What type of hot water are we talking about? Like...spanking?" I can hear the smile in Madison's voice, even though I can't see her because Jonathan is blocking my view.

"That's up to Micah. I know what I'd do if you were mine though." He gives me a devilish smile.

"Oooh. What would you do?" I groan at Madison egging Jonathan on.

"I'd lick you up to orgasm and stop...over and over and over again. Then I'd make you give me head and tuck you in for the night without letting you come."

"Jesus Christ", Madison says at the same time I tell Jonathan he's so mean.

"What about friends. Can they get punished", Madison inquires with hope in her voice.

"Maddie", I whisper hiss her name, chastising her for inferring she wants the guys to touch her.

"I'm afraid not. We can't touch anyone other than our woman or those belonging to our brothers."

"That's so hot. So like, you just do what you like with these women? Like you could call Braden back and tell him you want a piece of Linea, and he lines it up?"

"Kind of. It's a little more complicated than that and respectful. But I guess if one of us really wanted time with someone we'd find a way to make it happen. But just because you ask for sex doesn't mean you're getting it."

"Of course. I mean, she has to consent..." Madison trails off to herself.

"Yeah...kind of. The truth is, if I called Micah up and told him I wanted to eat Hadley out right now, he could tell me no. In fact, he could withhold her pleasure as a punishment and order her to please me."

"Order her?" Madison seems appalled.

"Yep. And Hadley has to have a real good reason for declining otherwise she's expected to comply." Jonathan motions to the front of his pants and Madison's mouth hangs open. "Fuck me. We have to talk about something else or I might call Micah back and ask him for your mouth." He looks serious so I decide now is the perfect time to ask him my question about Micah.

"Okay. Can we focus? I've already given head in front of Madison once today so maybe I could not do that again?" Jonathan just shrugs at my admittance as though there is nothing awkward at all about giving head in front of your friend. There's no easy way to ask this so I just come right out and say it. "Micah didn't want me to have the prototype, did he? That's what this argument is all about."

Jonathan lets out a heavy sigh, searching my face before he answers. "Why would you say that?"

"Well, he told me not to wash between my legs and then came inside me this morning before coming down to meet you all." Jonathan nods solemnly waiting for me to continue. "I also overheard you two talking." He cocks a brow, and I rush to clarify. "I wasn't snooping. I was right in front of him. He had the phone on speaker and was so caught up in the conversation he didn't notice me standing there. I didn't know what to do, so I waited." He tilts his head at me. "He never tells me anything", I say in defense of myself. Even I know it's a weak defense.

"Um, excuse me. Protype", Madison asks from the opposite side of the room. I still can't see her, and I know Jonathan is doing this on purpose. Neither of us answer her.

"It wasn't the prototype. He knows that's a fair trade for your dishonesty. We'll all leverage it to help you, and he will be fair when he recreates your agreement." Jonathan offers nothing else. We're in a standoff. Once again, I want information and once again, information is being kept from me.

"Hellooooooo? What. Prototype."

I let out a heavy sigh before I'm out with it. It'll probably come out better when I'm still drunk anyway. "I'm testing a device that measures arousal. I got it this morning which is why I'm walking funny. Not because of the sex."

Madison snort laughs, not believing me. When no one joins in, she knows we're not kidding.

"It's in you", she asks, suddenly serious.

"Yes. Under my skin on the left side, just inside my opening." She doesn't say anything and I'm not sure if that's a good thing or a bad thing. Her brain is probably going a million miles an hour and I get it. I can't say my own mind has slowed down much since this morning too. So her reaction is justified in my book. And then it dawns on me. Something I thought Micah was ordering me to do because he was being dirty was actually engineered to keep me safe. But it backfired.

"He kept me messy on purpose. Not to be kinky but to keep Dr. Kinkade from testing the device." Jonathan nodded.

"Micah knew Tyler and Dr. Kinkade were friends. What he did not account for is that Tyler and Dr. Kinkade had been *very* good friends many years ago." I don't follow so Jonathan clarifies. "Dr. Kinkade swings both ways. Micah thought if Dr. Kinkade saw you with a pussy full of throat yogurt..."

"Ha ha! Throat yogurt!", Madison snorts and laughs.

Jonathan and I look at Madison as she interrupts our serious conversation.

"Oh, come on! That's funny!", Madison defends herself from across the room.

Jonathan and I return to our conversation, deciding not to egg her on. "...he'd let someone else get you off. But Micah didn't realize that his plan wasn't a deterrent at all for Dr.

Kinkade. Micah lost control over the one person he committed to protecting with every breath he has. The brotherhood had no authority to step in and stop things, especially since you remaining with us hinged on you having the prototype inserted by not one but two votes. And he had to watch it in front of all his friends. He had to watch you in pain. Then he had to watch you cry when you gave consent for a stranger to get you off. He had to encourage you to come. If you didn't finish, that prototype would have been disabled. He would have lost you."

"What the fuck is going on?"

I can't answer Madison's question because I'm on the verge of another crying spell. I hadn't once considered what happened from Micah's perspective. I had put him through the wringer and for some insane reason, he still wanted me.

"I wasn't there for the fight, but knowing the guys like I do, I'd guess that a combination of Micah being held hostage to another's rules and then handing you off to his best friend who voted you out so you could give him head was probably the catalyst to his aggression. And after the tick in his jaw last night when Tyler gave you a conditional yes, Micah's probably been fantasizing about landing a few hits to Tyler since then."

"He's worried he crossed a line with me." Jonathan nods. "You didn't give him an answer."

"He knows if he crossed a line", Jonathan answers me without missing a beat.

I roll my eyes at him. It's so typical for him not to answer my implied question. It's these men's motus operandi.

"When you were alone with Micah after the guys left, did you feel safe", he asks, even though I know he knows the answer. I nod.

"Did he have to drag you to your knees?" I shake my head. "He wouldn't have chosen what happened this morning for you. If he had any control at all he wouldn't have picked most of that. But Hadley…" He reaches in his lab coat and taps on his phone, turning the screen to me to prove his point. "You came. Hard." I blush at the memory. "And there's nothing wrong with that. You were beautiful this morning. You were terrified but you were absolutely stunning on that table."

"Give him time. He'll work things out", Jonathan says, pocketing the phone.

"All of you get that report from the prototype?" He smiles and winks at me. "So you'll know in real time that I'm enjoying myself from wherever you are?"

"We'll know a lot more than that. Who's getting you off. What they're doing. If you thought your pussy belonged to us before…this is next level. There's a notes feature in the app." He looks smug just mentioning the science behind knowing my pussy's every quiver.

"Can you see that I'm in pain? Does your little meter tell you that?" He chuckles.

"I can see that you are not aroused in the least, which is not surprising. I'm going to message Micah and Braden that I want to check you before you leave." He pats my thigh, and I blush. He's going to do this in front of Madison. I have so much explaining to do.

When Jonathan steps out of our room, my buffer is gone. Madison clears her throat, noisily, reminding me that she is owed some answers.

# Chapter 23
# Micah

**December 28th 12:15 p.m.**
(Present Day)

The elevator pings and I stride down the hall with authority. I'm changing more lives than just Hadley's today, and I need to get my head in the game. Impressions are everything. *Trust* is everything.

Once a year I change a handful of students and their family's lives by giving them something they never knew they could have. Education and money. It's one of my favorite days of the year because it's a big ol' fuck you to dad.

Every year, my siblings and I get funds through a trust to help the needy. My father, the adulterous philanthropist, put this fund together. Each of his children are given a fresh bank annually. The only stipulation is that it has to be spent on the needy.

The first few years, I donated my money to women's shelters. I received not a word from him. But when I became more established and started my own firm, I decided to give back and leverage my gift. And when he received the details of my donation to the community, he lost his shit.

My father is a judge which means he sees criminals of all ages and walks of life. He looks down on them. Wouldn't piss on them if they were on fire. So I knew I'd get his attention when I picked juveniles to send to college and then added my own money to give them a little boost. The student and their immediate family were given wellness coaches, personal trainers, investment brokers with funds to invest, petty cash and a little trip to relax and actually enjoy life all courtesy of me. I couldn't help but to include those little details of how I had personally given back. His call to me was terse at first and then downright explosive. I smiled the entire fucking time and then hung up with him because I "had to go into court". Really, I was waiting on Linea to give me the blowjob of a lifetime. Fuck...it was a good blowjob too.

Today, my assistant, Claudia gets to send the certified package to my father detailing the gigantic *fuck you* I've bestowed upon him yet again. This is by far the best part of my day.

The meeting goes how they normally do. There's hesitation and skepticism. I get it. When people get something good, they want to know what the gimmick is. But then one signs realizing getting something too good to be true is better than getting what they've always gotten and the rest follow suit. And voilà! I have four future lawyers who will be able to work at any one of my many firms across the country. With years of hard work, support and the best training in the business, these people will be unstoppable. Their parents won't have debt. Instead, they'll be financially literate and have investments. And their health and wellness will totally turn around for the better.

"Emmerson's ready for you", Claudia tells me after the last youth has signed. Her outstretched well-manicured hand is holding out a room key for me. She hesitates for a moment, and I know what's coming. "Are you okay?" She visibly blanched when she saw my split lip and the bruise starting to form on my cheekbone when I entered the conference room at the Lux.

I take the key without hesitation. I need this release and Mav so generously gave Emmerson to me for the afternoon. I need someone to take my mind off all the shit that's transpired, and Emmerson is perfect. My head clouds with the possibilities as I consider her agreement. I just need to clear my head. That's all. And Emmerson can help me do that without any emotion whatsoever.

I swat Claudia's hand away as she reaches for my face and shoot her an irritated look. She's like a mother to me and I know she cares but I I'm irritated none the less. I'm a grown fucking man with a split lip. I don't want it cared for and I sure as hell don't want to talk about it. "Fine, fine Mr. Stevenson", she mocks me, knowing I hate it when she calls me that. I shoot her another look as she shoes me out of the boardroom telling me she's got everything handled from here.

As I exit, I think of Hadley and wonder what she's up to now that she's sober. I got the text from Jonathan not too long ago that he released them, and they were doing well. I don't even have the strength to consider a punishment for Hadley at the moment because I'm still not sure that I did the right thing allowing that doctor to lick her to orgasm.

Without a sound, the elevator doors glide open. I step inside and it's just me, surrounded by mirrors. I try not to look too closely at myself, but I can't help it. My reflection is everywhere. I'm scared and angry. Scared of losing Hadley and angry at society for pushing norms on people that are ridiculous. Angry at Hadley for not trusting me and not letting her guard down. I'm also tired. I can see that without a doubt as I straighten my posture and roll my shoulders back. The day has just begun. Perhaps I'll sleep in the suite for a bit after Emmerson and I are done.

The doors slide open, and I'm relieved I no longer have to look at myself as I step into the hallway, bathed in the soft light, a difference from the bright light of the elevator. The room is a few doors down and with every step I take my cock starts to swell. Even he knows he's getting relief.

Swiping into the room, it's quiet. I deliberately make my presence known, not wanting to alarm Emmerson. At first, I hear nothing, and I question whether she's in here. Then I hear the confident murmur of her foreign tongue.

Stunning when she steps into view, she's wearing all black. A pencil skirt, form fitting long sleeve cardigan and black stilettoes. Her hair is pulled up into a sleek ponytail and her red lips mesmerize me as she responds to someone over the phone.

Emmerson is speaking French and although I can't understand a single word, I'm captivated by her. Her dark brown eyes look me over while she talks.

God, she looks like such a bitch. I can't help but smile as she looks me over like I'm nothing to her. It's her way. I think it's how she protects herself. As if she looks like she doesn't give a shit about you then you'll require less of her. But I know the truth. She cares even though she looks like she doesn't.

I have no idea how long she'll be. She's working and no matter how engorged my cock is, I won't interrupt her. I respect her work ethic. I'm a workhorse but still managed to carve out some rest time before the holidays. Emmerson has no regard for the ordinary and I happen to be a big fan of that.

She talks faster, the tone of her voice raising, her eyebrows slant, showing she is displeased. When she's near me, I think she's going to walk right by, but she doesn't. Instead, she doesn't even look at me when she stops at my side, responds to the invisible person on the phone and palms the bulge in my pants. She rubs me on top of the fabric, continuing the conversation over the phone.

Emmerson likes treating others like sex is just a job and wants the same treatment in kind. The fire in her eyes when she feels like she's being used is remarkable. She loves it and I'm happy to give her that kind of joy even though I don't understand it. After all, understanding the fetish isn't the point. Supporting it is.

She continues her conversation like I'm not important, then steps back and moves in front of me. I don't make a move to pull her close. She would not be impressed and would fuck with me so much I'd probably cum before she even touched me.

So I pretend I'm unphased by her behavior. She wants to be treated like I hired her for a fuck and that's quite alright with me.

Sinking to her knees she unbuckles my belt and frees me from my pants. I see a small smile form on her lips as she listens to the caller. She grabs my length in her well-manicured delicate hand and strokes me. I throw my head back, fighting a moan. *She's working. She's working. She's working.*

Her tongue licks my tip, and I gasp. *Fuck.* She looks irritated when I look down at her and after a moment, I understand why. I leaked precum all over her skirt. I want to tell her I'll buy her a new one, but I don't. She's still working.

More French flies from her lips. It's frantic and angry and she continues to stroke me like this is nothing more than a service she's getting paid for. Then she slides me into her mouth, working me over when she's done with her rant.

I want to hold onto her head, but I don't because she's not hanging up this call and she's going to get me off at the same time. She's in control. When is Emmerson not in control?

It's probably been just over a minute that my cock has been free, and I could blow. Her eyes roll up to look at me. She manages to look defiant and sexy. Like she wants me to know this act doesn't matter to her. Maybe it doesn't. Maybe it does. But it's Emmerson and she's nothing like the others in a way that's alarming if I'm being honest. Even Grace shows she cares in a way that showcases her annoyance but Emmerson? Sometimes I expect her to vanish as though she was never here. She plays into nothing. Ever.

Her hand strokes my cock as she responds to the caller. This time when I leak, she lets me, not finished with her thought and unable to stop to catch the stream of arousal dripping from my tip. She looks thoughtful as she watches it stream out of me. At the soonest available moment, she takes me back into her mouth and slides me as far back as I'll go without gagging herself. She hums in answer to the caller, and I almost blow my load right there. I feel that hum all the way to base of my spine and the fact that the caller is likely none the wiser to her actions on this call is hot as hell.

Pulling me out of her mouth again, she responds to the caller. It's an abrupt back and forth between them and when they're done sparing, she laughs, her mouth mere millimeters from the head of my cock. I can feel her breath puff out onto me and that does it. I grab her ponytail, securing her for my pleasure, take my hard length in the other hand and finish the job, all over her face.

White hot spurts of cum stream onto her beautiful face and into her hair. I'm so full of cum it feels like I'm never going to stop anointing her. It takes every ounce of strength I have to be quiet as stream after stream jets onto her tan skin. God it's everywhere on her face and I fucking love it.

She takes me in her mouth, not bothering to wipe her face off and sucks on me more. She swallows the fruit of my aftershock and then sits back on her haunches, letting me slide from her mouth.

She caresses a word in French, and I know she's disconnected the call because she's looking up at me, expectantly. I smile down at her, wipe a smear of cum off her cheekbone with the pad of my thumb and slide my thumb between those beautiful red lips. She sucks as I regard her with awe.

"Beautiful." She bites down on my thumb, and I chuckle. Emmerson can't take a compliment for shit. "I meant, beautiful cum covered whore."

She chuckles and I hold my hand out for her to help her stand. "Wash up. I'm not done defiling you yet."

# Chapter 24
# Hadley

**December 28$^{th}$ 1:03 p.m.**
(Present Day)

"I cannot believe he licked you in front of me", Madison announces with much excitement as we leave through the doors of the hospital we trudged in through not long ago. I shrug. Any of them would have. None of them are shy. Least of all Jonathan.

"Jonathan is the most laid back of all the men. He does what he wants, says what he wants and feels zero remorse about it because he can justify all of it. Not all the men are like that. Some of them don't want anyone to know about their sex life. I think Jonathan has seen too much death to even care what people think of him at this point", I try to explain the rules to Madison but fail miserably because I only know mine for sure. I can guess at theirs based on their behavior and practices with me, but I have nothing to compare their behavior to, so I have to say I haven't put much effort into figuring it out.

When it comes to privacy, Micah told me I could tell anyone I wanted about what I do. I just couldn't reveal others in the brotherhood. And although Madison met Jonathan, there's no way she'll meet anyone who wants to stay anonymous.

Micah must have allowed Jonathan to check my implant. He never actually said, Micah gave me permission. He just said he was taking a look at me to make sure infection wasn't starting. Then he slid my pants over my hips and down my legs, along with my panties.

"His tongue is magic, Madison." I tell her when we're in the car lost in the memory of him kissing one knee and then the other. Giving me a quick check and commenting to himself that I need ice packs. Then slinging my legs over his shoulders to take a taste of me. It was brief. A few well-placed kisses and flicks of the tongue. I groaned in frustration when I realized he wasn't going to finish. He laughed, knowing full well what he was doing. Then he helped me back in my clothes and got us on our way.

"So, where are we off to now?" Madison and Steven both wait for me to have a plan. I just look between Madison and the rearview mirror, not quite knowing what's next.

"I think I want to go home and use these ice packs. We can regroup and do something else in a bit?" Madison nods and Steven pulls away from the hospital in the direction of Micah's.

"Unless your driver has another way of getting you home, I think he's going the wrong way", Madison tells me. The look on my face says it all. "Did you move?" I nod my head and give her one of those nervous emoji smiles. "And you didn't tell me?"

"It just happened last night." She cocks her head to the side. "I did something." I let it hang there, unsure of what I wanted to tell her right now. I had no idea if Micah was home, and I knew she'd confront him if she thought I was being taken advantage of.

"Well what did you do you naughty little girl", she asks, her voice thick with sarcasm.

"My agreement was a lie." She looks as me as though I'm speaking a foreign tongue, because where we come from, the men we date don't have agreements. They have debt, irresponsibility and want a second mommy. "We have sexual agreements. Think of them like a menu for our pleasure. The men can't do anything that isn't on that agreement. I wasn't honest about mine. So I was given an ultimatum. I'd have an open agreement, the prototype that's currently killing my crotch and be under Micah's thumb for the foreseeable future. This all went down last night. I almost lost them all. To keep them, I had to concede to these things."

"So you live with Micah now because you lied? People lie all the time. I don't get it. This doesn't seem like that big of a deal."

"It's one of the worst things someone in this group could have done and I did it." She's shaking her head. "You can't lie to these men. Madison, this is like stepping into another world. Every norm you'd think they'd value, they don't. They're not like all the rest of the guys out there. They're...different." As soon as the words leave my mouth, I feel like I've just used the tag line that's helped men get in women's pants for decades. *I'm different, baby. You'll see.*

Madison laughs next to me. "So he's watching you?" I nod. She rolls her eyes.

"I use his accounts, live in his home and every stitch of arousal is recorded from that prototype."

"And you *want* to live like that?"

"I can't be without him. I tried that. For weeks, remember?" Her mouth falls open. Now she knows the real reason I was so upset when I thought things were over with Micah and I this past summer.

"You told me you were afraid to get into another relationship." She searches my face for answers. "And you weren't lying. You just didn't tell me why you were afraid to get into another relationship."

"I missed him so much Maddie. When I walked into his office, I fell apart. And then everything was okay. He led me to his desk where he sat me on his lap and answered emails." She gives me a curious look. "He'd kiss me on the shoulder as he looked through the most boring legal jargon I'd ever seen in my life, all the while, letting me cry and then settle and then cry and then settle. He was getting me reacclimated with him."

"He moved around his entire afternoon for me."

"To draw up your agreement?" I nod and smile at Madison. "Did he make you give him head at his desk?"

This time I laugh. "No. He brought his laptop over to the large mahogany table and we talked. He scrutinized what little I did have written out like he was going to court about it the next day." When the words leave my mouth, I realize that I think he was going to court with my list. Court with his brothers.

"What is it", Madison asks, picking up on my sudden epiphany.

"I have to call Micah." His number is the first one in my phone. I love that. I love him, I think as I touch the call button.

"Hi Hadley." There's a smile in his voice. Like he's proud of me.

"Hi. You're on speaker." I hear a slosh of water in the background. "Are you home?"

"No." He doesn't give me more than that. He never gives me more than that. I chance a look at Madison, and she's raised a brow. That answer would not fly with her.

"I won't keep you. I just need to know...that day you sent my draft agreement to your brothers...was it court?" He chuckles. "I don't mean court like a sentencing but a final vote? Like a jury?" His brothers were approving my agreement. They were finalizing me being added to their brotherhood and I was none the wiser.

"It was. Yes." His muffled voice sounds annoyed as he says something to someone else in the room. I can't quite make out what he says just the same as I can't make out what the female voice says in response. I chance another glance at Madison, and she looks pissed.

"You're busy. Sorry for interrupting. I'll see you later, Micah." I try not to sound hurt because I know what's happening. I just don't know with who.

"I'm going to have Steven bring you both by the Lux instead of back home. Ask for Graham when you get to the desk. See you soon, Hadley", he signs off before disconnecting the line.

"You're kidding. Right? He's fucking someone."

"Yes. He probably is."

"That's so disrespectful, Hadley. How can you allow that?"

This time I laugh. "Jonathan licked me between the legs this morning. Who do you think gave him permission to do that? That's what this is. And I wouldn't be surprised if Graham had something up his sleeve when we arrive."

"So he's somewhere in the Lux fucking another woman while we're on our way there? That's fucked up. You know that, right? And who's Graham?"

"He owns the Lux." Her mouth falls open and I'm satisfied by her shock once more. "I told you. These guys aren't run of the mill."

"What do you think he wants? What could he possibly want when he's with another woman?"

"I don't know. It could be anything where Micah is concerned." I wince as I shift in my seat.

"What does the implant look like?" Madison sounds uncomfortable just thinking about it.

"The actual implant looks like a needle with a few glass beads on it. But if you're asking what my bits look like, I have no idea. I don't even know if I want to look down there to be honest."

"As your friend, you know I love you right?" I nod, knowing what's coming is going to be bad. "And that's why I wouldn't be your friend if I didn't tell you how wrong I think this is."

My heart sinks at her unsolicited opinion. I want her support. She's the only one outside of the brotherhood who knows what I do...kind of. And she isn't behind it. I have officially out kinked the kinkiest person I know.

"I'm choosing this, Maddie." I look her dead in the eyes when I say it. In no way do I want her to think she or anyone else gets a vote.

"They're treating you like a whore", she says as though her word is truth.

That stings...a lot.

"No. They're treating me how I've asked to be treated. And now, they're treating me based on my body's response to them. This is different." There's that phrase again. I can practically feel her eyeroll, but I don't blame her one bit. Even in this context it sounds ridiculous.

The car stops at the valet and our doors are opened immediately by the attendants. We just stare at each other for a few minutes, like it's a game of who blinks first. Much to my satisfaction, Madison looks away and exits the vehicle before I do. When I get out, I notice Steven's window is down. When I look at him, he winks at me. I forget he's able to hear our conversations. Driving around with Steven is so commonplace I don't consider editing what I say around him. In fact, if he weren't driving with me, it would be weird.

"Message when you're ready Ms. McAfferty", he addresses me formally before I head for the hotel entrance.

When I enter, I see that Madison is already at the desk talking with the attendant. Once the attendant sees me coming, she scrambles to call someone and says something to a coworker that causes her coworker to rush off.

"What did you say to them", I ask Madison when I finally make it to the desk.

"I just checked us in like Micah said." She seems as perplexed as I am.

I've never come to the Lux to meet Graham personally. While he takes immense pride in his hotel, he would never bring me here for a date.

I look around while we wait, just taking in the view. It's fantastic. Just like it was last night. We're in the main hall and there are sweeping staircases everywhere with strategically placed chandeliers. The grand staircase has three sections to it that lead under arched ceilings punctuated by more chandeliers. The ornate ceiling is beautiful, and every detailed feature is polished and pristine.  I smile at its beauty and see Graham written all over this place.

"Ladies", Graham stands behind us, greeting us warmly. "You must be Madison." He extends his hand, and Madison wastes no time shaking it, practically drooling over the sight of him. Funny how she just said moments ago that she thought they were treating me like a whore, but she has no problem touching the very offenders that treat me so.

"Hadley", he addresses me, and then steps up to kiss me on one cheek and then the other. My face heats from the gesture, even though he could do this with a complete stranger, and it would mean nothing more than a warm welcome.

"I'm afraid my office is a bit of a walk from here. Are you up for it?" He eyes me with genuine concern, and I give him a nod without delay. He's never called me here like this so I'm curious and I want nothing to stand in the way of what we're going to be doing. There's nothing sexual about our meeting so far. He seems all business in his navy suit and polished shoes. However, I've been in this situation with Micah. Tables can turn quick if you know what I mean.

With a hand behind my back, he guides me next to him as Madison follows behind us. I feel a little guilty with Madison walking in our wake, but I think she should see how I'm treated. Despite what she thinks my commitment is, I'm treated like a queen.

"I have mixed feelings about this morning", Graham tells me as we walk through the pristine halls. It surprises me that he feels regret for his vote being contingent on the implant. He seemed very resolute last night. "You didn't return my message."

I let his observation hang there as I recall the first time Micah told me about the rule regarding communication. *You will not intentionally refuse to communicate. We will not tolerate the silent treatment in any way. When you're asked a question, you will respond. When you are sent a message in any form you will promptly participate in conversation. Understood?*

"Then you got drunk." My stomach sours. Jonathan told them all. I felt weak. Like I let life get the better of me and went off the rails.

"She is an adult and of legal age you know", Madison pipes up behind us.

Graham stops in his tracks, causing me to do the same. Then he looks over his shoulder at her and then over at me. His look is stern. Like one I'd imagine he'd use with a misbehaving employee...or maybe even Morgan if she was testing his patience.

"I had every intention of answering you", I respond to which he arches a brow, calling bullshit without saying a word. He doesn't move and I realize he's waiting for a response now. I pull out my phone and find his text.

Graham- I'm sorry you're in pain sweetheart. Hope you understand it was for you too.

"I'm not sure what I would even say to this", I start, not wanting to be rude after rereading his message.

"What do you want to say? What was the first thing that crossed your mind", he prompts me, still not moving an inch.

"That I don't believe you are sorry. And that this feels more like a punishment than anything that could possibly benefit me." There. He wanted to know. So now he knows.

"I see." He nods and looks me over as if he's trying to see some hidden meaning on my face and then guides us forward once more.

"You asked." Now I felt like a snotty kid.

"I did in fact ask and I appreciate your honesty, even though I do not like the answer in the least."

"So this was your idea", Madison asks behind us.

"No. It was not. Although I'm sad to say it. The idea was brilliant, which is why my vote was contingent on her compliance as well." We turn a corner and I'm not sure if I'm sweating because of the pain or stress from this conversation.

"Vote", Madison asks, confusion clear in her question.

"Yes. I'm assuming you know that Hadley and I are together, yes?" Madison lets out a grumble at his casual mention of us. "Well, she lied, and brotherhood rules dictate we take a vote on her participation with us going forward. While the implant was not my idea, I was one of two votes that made her compliance non-negotiable. Thus, my text, concerned for her well-being."

"So you forced her?" I winced at her words and accusing tone. They were sparing. In public. In front of me.

"No." Graham looks over at me and smirks. He knows her game. He knows she's trying to pick a fight. "Our women always have a choice. Hadley made hers and she will be rewarded in due time", he says simply, finally stopping in front of his office door and swiping his card over the badge reader.

Graham could care less who knows he's involved in the brotherhood. I'd say Jonathan cares the least and Graham is a close second. Jonathan doesn't give a shit what anyone thinks about him. Graham makes money and has connections. He doesn't need anyone's approval, and this is apparent in everything he says and does. He takes up every space he's in like he deserves to be there. Like his presence is a gift to those around him.

He ushers us in and the recent memory of Linea sucking on Micah slams into me like a freight train. When I stop in the doorway, I feel Madison bump up against me, not anticipating my sudden stop. It's like I can see her kneeling there in front of Micah. I feel instant panic. As if Braden is restraining me again.

"Hadley, you will do it again. Right here in this office. To change the memory. It will be a test. When it will happen, I have no idea, but it will." He seems so sure. As if they've already discussed it. I can't even imagine. "No one is getting in the way of living a truly liberating life more than you are right now, Hadley", he tells me as he guides me into his office by sweeping his arm around me, effectively forcing me into the room. Madison stands beside me as he rounds his desk. I can see her looking at me, peripherally, and do not turn to her. She wants answers. I don't want to give them. Not right now. Now while I feel like I'm suffocating at the memory of Linea sucking Micah off. Feelings of betrayal and anger flood me suddenly, as if I have no control of my own body. And it's only when Graham calls my name, I realize I've been looking at the floor, with fresh tears threatening to roll down my cheeks.

"These are for you", Graham tells me, presenting me with a small envelope made of fancy paper and the embossed logo of his hotel. "Two tickets to the New Year's Eve ball. You may invite who you like."

"Oh. Okay. Thank you." It's surprising he's allowing me to invite someone to his exclusive party. Even more surprising he called me here just for that. My voice is thick with emotion at the memory of what this room means to me. I can get nothing else out other than the short sentiment.

"Micah will meet us upstairs in the penthouse suites when he's available. In the meantime, I'll show you your options and perhaps you'll have them narrowed down when he joins us." I'm truly perplexed.

"Options? For what?" I'm thoroughly confused as his pointed look cuts right through me.

"For your new life, Hadley. You've shown such great commitment to us this morning, we've decided to reward you as we have some of the others. I had hoped Micah would have been here to start the discussion with you, however, some things take more time than we anticipate", he says with a smirk. I try to stifle an eye roll. He's talking about sex. Whoever he's fucking, he's doing so at his own pace. Thoroughly enjoying her. I hate it.

"Stop it", he chastises me, irritation clear in his voice. "Jealousy looks absolutely vile on you." He rounds his desk and steps up to me, his cool gaze landing on me as he clucks his tongue to get me to look up at him. This is business for him. I've never met his business side before, and I don't like it. I want fun Graham right now.

"I cannot wait to see who you become, Hadley." His eyes glitter with excitement and I can't help but to feel a little nervous. "You don't have limitations anymore. So, stop acting like it." He looks angry and I feel like a petulant child. But he's right. I should be grateful but all I can think of is Micah. I want to know who he's with and what they're doing and if she's better than me at it.

"Shall we", he asks, arching a brow.

"Yes, Graham. We shall", I mock him, and his lip twitches in amusement.

As we make our way through the quiet halls, Graham gives us a little history lesson about the establishment. It's an older hotel but has been thoroughly renovated and updated to have the most lavish amenities. It took an act of God to get the historical society to allow it, but since, they've been grateful, considering the amount of revenue the iconic hotel has brought back into the area. Graham hints at another large project he's working on behind the scenes involving yet another historic hotel in the area, however, gives us no real details. Madison still follows behind us and is oddly quiet. I can't tell if she's about to explode, run out on us or give me a discrete wink of acceptance.

Graham pushes the button to take us to the top floor. Upon the doors opening, it looks like we're in an entirely different building. We've moved from white and open to navy walls and chandeliers hanging from the ceilings. Stepping out of the elevator is like stepping into another world. The floor is a beautiful polished red brown set in a herringbone pattern and the doors to each room aren't hotel room doors. They're doors with a big, frosted glass pain and a gold name plate highlighting what is to be behind the door. There's an interior designer, a yoga studio with a sign that indicates they're moving and an event planner.

"We have several vacant spaces for you to choose from. Elena will help you design the space to your liking. She's a master at procuring just the right touches. Depending on what you're looking for, you could be up and running in a few months", Graham informs me as if I know what he's referring to as he hands me a key card. "Go ahead. Look around. I think you'll find a number of these spaces suitable", he tells me before motioning to the door we're standing in front of.

"I don't understand", I respond lamely, making no move to open a door.

"A space that's yours. For your personal endeavors. Perhaps it's a business. Perhaps it's pleasure. But it's yours. A gift from Micah and I", he tells me, nodding at the door with encouragement.

"He just took all my freedom away. Now he's giving me a space of my own?" This time Graham laughs and now I'm thoroughly confused. Is this not what this is?

"It is yours overseen by us. In other words, perhaps you want this space for nothing more than to get some time to yourself. That is perfectly fine. But it will be monitored. You will be monitored."

I huff out a breath of air and extend the card back to him, the petulant child in me returning with full force.

"Perhaps you want your own business. Maybe a massage business. Something that allows you to set your own rules regarding client behavior? Something that allows you to secure top talent and protect them from the men who couldn't get a decent woman if they actually put effort into it?"

Suddenly, my petulant child disappears. "I…you…" Graham raises his eyebrows dramatically as if saying, *looks like we're not so bad after all are we?*

"Open a door, Hadley", Graham impatiently orders me.

I turn to Madison and she's looking at me like I'm crazy for delaying. When I don't move, she yanks the card from my hand and swipes it across the card reader. The lock clicks open, and she pushes through the door, holding it open with her foot while flipping the light switch.

"I like her", Graham says to me as he holds the door open for me to walk through.

"I'm not so sure about you yet", Madison calls over her shoulder, full speed ahead to assess the space. "This suite is okay. If you have your own massage studio, you'll need more rooms. Hadley are you taking clients or focusing exclusively on the business side of things", she asks, as though I've already decided that I'm going to take these men up on their offer and know exactly what I'd like to do with the space.

"I don't know", I answer, still in shock over the men's generosity.

"What?" Madison whirls around on me. "You don't know? What do you mean you don't know? It's simple. What do you want to do?" Graham steps up beside her wearing a full-on smile and I'm shocked. They're ganging up on me.

"It's not simple. It takes thought. And planning. And some soul searching", I reply as if my logic is truth.

"No", Madison deadpans. "It's literally this simple." She puts her hand to her chest. "I *love* cupcakes. Most cupcake places are boring. *I* am not boring. I believe that bakery is art and if you're eating the calories, they better taste fucking amazing. I want to make cupcakes other non-boring people will love as much as I do. I am going to own a bakery." She gives me a pointed look and raises her eyebrows at me. "And then you own a bakery", she finishes sarcastically.

"Can we look at the next room?"

"Oh my God", Madison says under her breath as she pushes past me to leave the suite.

"That, Hadley Joanna, is how it's done. Grow a backbone", Graham encourages me as he ushers me forward.

Since when did Graham and Madison become friends? Every door that is unlocked they discuss the space and what could be done with it. Sure, they involve me in the conversation, but each time, I give them an indecisive answer they look at each other like *there it is*. It isn't until Graham's phone goes off that the spell is broken.

"I'm afraid Micah will not be joining us. He sends his apologies, Hadley. He wants to hear your ideas over dinner tonight. And he'd like Madison to join you."

I huff out another breath of frustration.

"Oookay...I wasn't planning on staying for dinner so it's no big deal", Madison starts.

"I'm sorry. It's not you. It's just...a lot. Today has been a lot and...you know what? If I pick a room right now, just to have as my own do I get access to it immediately?"

Graham nods in understanding. "I'm afraid not. Either way, cameras will need to be installed. However, if you are ready to select a space and know what you'll be doing with it, I can schedule time on Elena's calendar with you to start preliminary designs. How's that?" He answers me like he's placating a child.

I grumble in frustration and both of them look at each other and snicker. I'm not so sure I love this newfound bond they both have.

"I like suite number one." They both smile at my decisiveness. "For a business. No other employees but myself." Graham raises a brow. "It's my business so it's my choice", I remind them. "I'd like to have dinner here tonight. If I have a choice. In suite number one."

"That can be arranged if Micah is agreeable. Check your phone. And Hadley, respond to your messages", he warns me as he leads us from the final suite we've finished touring and back to the elevator.

When we're back down in the lobby, I see Graham in a whole new light. He's pushing me. It's terrifying but I like it.

"Graham?" He looks at me, a small smile playing on his lips. "Thank you", I tell him, and then lean forward to kiss him on the lips.

"I meant what I said, Hadley. Let's see who our girl will become." He kisses me back and then releases me, nodding his head before turning around and heading to his next mission of the day.

When I look back at Madison, she's grinning ear to ear.

"You can't go to dinner looking like that. Let's go", she tells me and loops her arm in mine as we head to the main entrance.

This day is almost too much I think to myself as we head back out into the winter storm. But how can it be that a day of complete overwhelm feels better than the life where I was merely just following along and blending in?

# Chapter 25
# Micah

**December 28th 1:20 p.m.**
(Present Day)

Emmerson is taking forever to finish her shower. I've had enough time to fill the hot tub and check my work email. I swear she knows all the little ways to get under our skin and push us to the limit with complete indifference.

I'm about to go in after her when I hear a door open. I hear her approach by her heavy sigh. God, I love how bitchy she is. It's so entertaining to me. Typically, it wouldn't be a turn-on but there's something about her that's over the top and I love it.

My phone rings. I normally don't check my phone when I'm with another woman, but I'm on hyper alert because of Hadley. She's had a hard morning and I'm not exactly sure we're going to make it through this. When I asked her if she was okay, she said she wasn't sure. I'm glad she was honest with me, but I wished her answer was different.

"Hi Hadley." My chest swells with love knowing she's reaching out to me. I look up and Emmerson is entering the room, stark naked.

"Hi. You're on speaker", she warns me. I smile. I couldn't give a shit who hears what I say, least of all if Madison hears. I don't answer to her so what she thinks of me makes not one bit of difference. "Are you home", she asks.

"No", I answer simply. She doesn't get details and I'm curious if this will push her over the edge after all that has happened in the last day. I suspect she can hear the water in the tub.

"I won't keep you."

My assumption was right. She can hear the water sloshing around in the tub.

"I just need to know...that day you sent my draft agreement to your brothers...was it court?"

I chuckle at her question. Leave it to Hadley to dissect every social part of the past. She's dying to know how we work things in the brotherhood as if knowing will help her. I assure her it will not. In fact, it might make it harder for her to assimilate. She isn't like Linea. She doesn't have the time in. In fact, no one will ever be like Linea. She knows more because we evolved around her, Grace and Kelly. We made our biggest mistakes right before them and they stuck with us through it all. They've earned the right to know more than the others because believe it or not, they had it tougher than Hadley ever will. And the reason they had it tougher was because we didn't have all these rules when they started with us. Our rules keep the peace, and we created them when peace was a thing of the past. More women...more complications...

"I don't mean court like a sentencing but a final vote? Like a jury?"

"It was. Yes." Again, that's all I offer her. She doesn't need to know that she would have been turned away if there were things in her agreement that seemed disingenuous. Or even limitations that were too strict to enjoy her and her enjoy us. I hold the speaker of my phone close to me to muffle the sound and address Emmerson. “Get in.” When Emmerson opens her mouth to speak, I give her a warning. “Do I need to teach you a lesson in following directions, Em?” She rolls her eyes and says something in French that I don’t understand, and I shake my head, turning my attention back to Hadley. She does not get in the tub but there’s something about her defiance that I’m interested in letting play out.

“You’re busy. Sorry for interrupting. I’ll see you later, Micah.”

She doesn’t sound upset, which is good. But she does sound uncomfortable. I don’t want that for her either, but I’ll take what I can get, considering all the changes she’s gone through.

“I’m going to have Steven bring you both by the Lux instead of back home.” I have a surprise for her. One that might help her make this life more of her own and not a life of just complying to our rules. “Ask for Graham when you get to the desk. See you soon, Hadley.” I disconnect the line and turn my attention back to Emmerson.

“Dearest Emmerson, will you kindly join me in this hot tub? I would love nothing more than to hold you in my arms, rub you down with oil and make you come around my fingers before I take you with my cock.”

She’s holding back a smile. Even she knows her behavior is ridiculous sometimes. I hold out my hand and she takes it, climbing into the tub to get her reward.

“Why are you so difficult, Em?” I pull her against me and bury my face in her neck. She laughs and struggles in my arms causing water to slosh over the side of the tub. “Hmm?”. I kiss her shoulder as she relaxes in my arms. She’s just over a year in with us and gives us a hard time at every turn. She doesn't answer me. I really want the answer to my question.

"Have you considered that I'm not difficult at all?" I laugh because I put Emmerson right up there with Lexi and Grace. Three of the most hardheaded women I've met in my entire life. We separate them quickly at events. Not because we think they'll argue. We just don't want them joining forces.

"I have not considered that." Laying back against me, she reaches behind her and pats my face with her hand. A silent gesture of condescension. "You were on a work call when I came to fuck you."

"And?" She doesn't even get riled up.

"And..." I start, pausing momentarily to cup her breast and sink my teeth into her neck, watching her nipples pebble in response. "...you were completely unphased while sucking my cock during your conversation. Weren't you at all concerned the person on the other line would know what you were doing?"

"Are you ever concerned the person on the other line knows what you're doing when I'm riding you in your office?" I can hear the smile in her voice. She makes a good point and she's well aware of it.

"That's different", I tell her, sliding my hand down between her legs.

"Oh, is it?" She laughs out the question. "I think it's different for you because you're a guy. A powerful guy. Me? I'm a beautiful fucking flower." She says the words so sweetly now I'm chuckling.

"You are a beautiful fucking flower", I confirm, sliding my fingers through her folds. "What were you talking about?"

"What do you talk about with my boyfriends?" She groans as I slide two fingers inside her. She's so tight. Fuck. I want to be inside her.

"A whole host of things", I answer, sliding my fingers in as far as they'll go and putting pressure on her G spot.

"Same", she says, barely getting the word out as her body goes limp on mine.

I decide to leave it. I know she doesn't harbor resentment against us, but I do know she's making a point. It's like she's saying, *anything you can do I can do better*. She's a spitfire and I love it.

"You were speaking French." She nods in answer, words hard to come by as I continue to bring her closer to the tipping point. "Will you teach me something?" I'm surprised when she doesn't dismiss my request, giving me something in French right away.

"J'aime le sexe", Emmerson caresses each syllable

I repeat her words, and she chuckles.

"We'll work on it", she reassures me.

"What did I just say?" I stroke her clit with my thumb.

"I love sex", she whispers, turning her head so I can see her face. Eyes hooded. Mouth slack. She's so beautiful, especially when she's about to cum.

"I do", I confirm and put more pressure on her special spot causing her to arch into me.

"But that's not all you love, is it?" She isn't wrong but I'm not entirely sure what she's getting at. "This is more than sex. It's more than sex for all of you. You just don't advertise it." I roll her nipple between my fingertips with my free hand.

"Very observant", I tell her as I reward her for her astuteness. She moans in response.

"I'm not in it for the sex either", she tells me. "Or the dates." Her chest rises and falls as I pump my fingers into her. She's so close.

"Tell me", I prompt her. She's never bothered to have this conversation with me and if my fingers between her legs is a distraction to help her tell it, then it is what it is.

"You..." She pants, reaching back to grab onto my neck, her other hand gripping the side of the tub. "I don't know how to say it. Aaah." She's so fucking close it's killing us both. I stay quiet because I don't want her to stop talking and if there's anything I've learned with Emmerson, one false move will turn the tables in a second.

"When you give us away..." More panting. "Oh god."

"Tell me Em", I croon.

"It's for love. You give us away to be loved. Oh..."

She's speechless as she clenches around my fingers.

"That's it. That's it my good girl. There you go." I slow my speed to match her body's rhythm, but before she's done, she twists in my arms, forcing me to slide my fingers from her so she can face me.

Her mouth is on mine and she's kissing me like she's never kissed me before. I wrap my arms around her and kiss her back while exploring her backside with my hands. My cock is anxiously awaiting her entrance but she's having a moment, and I want to understand it. She normally doesn't get swept up in emotions and this definitely feels like more than a post orgasm kiss.

"Thank you", she tells me when she breaks the kiss.

I smirk at her because it's not the first time I've given her an orgasm and I know for a fact she's cum harder than she just did on my fingers.

"For what?" I knew Emmerson had an arranged marriage planned before getting involved with us. Because of that, we almost didn't allow her into the group. I wasn't aware arranged marriages happened anymore but apparently being married into the right circle was very important to Emmerson's family and the marriage was arranged when she was in her early teens.

The best way to describe Emmerson is covertly defiant. She's the one who breaks the rules quietly while no one's watching. See, it's the quiet ones who you have to watch out for. They're always underestimated, which is how Emmerson wound up in Mav's restaurant after returning from abroad to study. She wasn't supposed to be back in the states. Emmerson was supposed to be in Spain, and she flew back, not because she didn't like it there. It was purely a test to see if she could get away with it unnoticed. And she did.

That's the point where I assumed all bets were off. Her family had cared enough to secure her a future in the right social circle but not enough to know where she was or what she was doing. All she wanted was for someone to care. That's how she found Mav.

Emmerson told her waiter that her food wasn't right. When Mav saw her plate come back, he immediately went out to talk with her just like he would any customer who sent a plate back...which was rare.

Mav told us that she criticized the dish, specifically detailing why it was wrong stating it wasn't accurately advertised because the dish is made much differently in France. She told Mav he should take it off his menu if staff weren't going to make it right and continued to look through his menu ticking off dish after dish that may as well be removed too as a result of his team's incompetence.

She got under Mav's skin in the biggest way. No one had ever been that forward with him and he was determined to prove this little pain in the ass wrong. So, he brought her a glass of wine and asked her to wait, telling her he'd comp her meal and then one by one, brought every dish out that she had openly criticized to his face.

At some point during her tasting, she starts talking in another language. She doesn't even realize she's doing it, and Mav is sold. There's no one else he'd consider but her. They shared a kiss. It was literally one kiss, and it led to Mav begging Braden to put her birth control in before she was vetted, and her agreement was finalized. But rules are rules, and they had to wait.

Emmerson is a good woman. She just needs to be watched closely, or she gets into mischief. It's how she grew up and has become a part of her. We're her challenge now because we actually pay attention to her. It makes it harder for her to outsmart us. It's almost a game.

Emmerson doesn't answer my question, but instead sinks down on my hard length. I throb inside her. She feels fucking amazing.

"I hate hot tubs", she tells me as she kisses down my neck.

"I know. I was hoping we could change that." Her assault happened while she was in a hot tub at her house. Her fiancé raped her, and her own parents let it happen. Well, they didn't encourage it, but they knew what her ex-fiancé was there for. They knew she wasn't interested, and no one stopped it.

"Everything we do right now is your choice. You run the show Em." I lean forward and kiss her lips. They tremble and I know she's remembering. "You're safe." I kiss her again. "Despite the challenge you bring us, I love you." I kiss her sweetly again. "Really love you, Em."

It's the truth. I do love her. If she walked away today, the others included, I'd be saddened. I'd miss her covert defiance and the challenge she gives us with just a stoic look and a slight tilt of the head.

One of the beautiful things about this arrangement is that we do make closer connections with some than we do others. Take Linea for example. She was first. She only had Tyler, Jonathan, Braden and I to choose from. At first, she was terrified of Tyler and loved to hate me. No one hates Jonathan ever so there wasn't an issue there. But when we first met Linea, she was attached to the hip with Braden. When Linea fell apart, it was Tyler that got her through it as we all sat back and watched helplessly, praying every day that he healed her. And by some strange cosmic event, Linea ended up being both my friend and my lover. Something she doesn't have with anyone else. Today, Linea minds Tyler without complaint but challenges Braden almost regularly, willingly taking her punishment from him afterward. And even though it will never be allowed, Linea is the only woman that comes close to making decisions or weighing in on behalf of the brotherhood, just like she did last night during the vote. These are relationships we'd never have if the brotherhood didn't exist.

Em lifts off my hard cock, bringing me out of my quiet contemplation. I slide out of her, and I think I may have pushed her too hard. But she lines me up with her backside.

"Em..." I start to protest but she won't allow it.

"If you want me to like hot tubs then change the memory", she challenges me.

I let out a heavy breath because I won't make a new memory for her like this. "Has Mav had you like this?" I know he hasn't. He'd like to but hasn't broached the subject with her yet. She shakes her head.

"I don't have permission to take you this way." It's true. I don't. While I have absolute say over Emmerson's wellbeing in this moment, I am bound to abide by the limitations set by her owner, which is Mav.

"No one will know", she tells me. It's a poor attempt even for her at manipulating the situation.

"You aren't ready for that yet. It isn't what I was asking you for." She looks totally rejected and I hate it, but she isn't ready. If I did what she asked, not only would it violate the strict code we live by, but she'd be an emotional mess.

She feels a connection to me because Mav called me when she wound up at his restaurant a sobbing mess. But I don't understand why she wouldn't want Mav to make a new memory for her. Regardless, I'll never be the reason a woman feels violated. Never. Not even by accident.

"Let me take you to bed?" When she nods, I kiss her. She doesn't always have to be so tough, and I like that she's surrendering to me right now. It's a form of trust and takes a lot of courage on her part.

Holding onto her tightly, I stand and lift her over the edge of the tub. Water goes everywhere. Neither of us bothered with towels. I get out of the tub and then scoop her into my arms making my way to the bed.

This is more than sex. It's more that getting relief. All of it is. She's mine to care for right now and in a few moments, we're going to be caring for each other. It's spiritual. We'll never give anything less to these women because when we give, we get back ten-fold. It feels fucking amazing. I doubt people in traditional relationships can say the same for long. I've been in this brotherhood for over six years and yeah, it's as good today as it was the first day.

Emmerson, in her typical challenging style pushes at my chest to be let down. I smirk at her and gently set her on her feet, curious about what she's up to. She turns abruptly, and walks to the bed. I watch her with curiosity. She's always been uncomfortable letting people care for her. Sometimes, even as impassive as she is, I think she struggles with us. It's more of an internal struggle to allow herself to just let us swallow her whole. To love her without pretense.

She's dripping wet as she walks to the bed. I love the sight of her. Long dark hair dripping down her back. Water sliding down her skin over her perfect ass. She's freezing but you wouldn't know it by the way she carries herself. She's the picture of self-control and I wonder what would happen if that self-control came undone. What would Emmerson be like?

I've seen a few glimpses of it, but she's so guarded even the lifestyle change of the last year has barely chipped away at the walls she's probably put up her entire life. And although I don't make a habit of comparing women, when I think of Hadley, even with this misstep I see more of Hadley's true self than I do Emmerson's.

Emmerson looks over her shoulder at me and pauses before getting into bed. It's like her final act of pretending she isn't dying to get underneath those covers. She gives me an appreciative smile as her eyes slide down my body. I want to worship her. Right now, is not the time to take care of myself, even if I'm dying to be selfish. I have her for the afternoon so there's time for that later.

When I step up behind her, she relaxes her body into mine. Her skin is cold. "Get in bed", I order as I kiss her shoulder. She complies immediately without a word.

Everything that follows is lazy. It's the slow burn that happens in bed when you know you have hours and nothing to do but explore your partner. I get lost in her and she gets lost in me. There isn't a word spoken. The only sounds are kissing, stuttered breaths, and the wetness between her legs.

She's soaked. I make her finish twice before I finally slide inside her. Once with my fingers and then with my mouth. This is love. We move in unison without a single word being exchanged.

I'm on top of her. Missionary gets a bad rap, but I like the control. I like seeing these helpless women trapped under my large frame. The best part is feeling their orgasm. That, combined with the look of pleasure on their face...I have to think of anything not to cum. I want at least one more from her before I finish, and I want it this way.

Leaning down by her ear, I give her one more order before I resume. “Let go. Emmerson, let go.”

She nods and I kiss her. The kind of kiss that leads to a chemical explosion between us. It was two words in an order and she’s unraveling. Thrusting against me and gripping me wherever she can get leverage. She’s never responded like this, and I love it. This is what I want from her.

It takes her mere minutes before she’s pulsing around me and when she does, I let go too. I feel like I’ve accomplished the unimaginable by getting her to loosen up. I rain kisses all over her face after I’m done spilling inside her and she smiles and chuckles while I do.

I stay inside her and give her a brief kiss on the lips and her body stiffens under mine. It’s so slight I question whether I imagined it but when her eyes open, all I see is pain.

Her beautiful brown eyes stare up at me, welling with tears. They aren’t happy tears.

“Em? Did I hurt you?” I would never forgive myself if I did.

“No”, she answers, with a chuckling sob.

“Talk to me.” And that does it. She sobs harder. All I can do is watch her fall apart. I have no idea what’s going on. Mav hasn’t shared anything out of the ordinary and with the exception of her setting control aside during sex, I haven’t picked up on anything either.

I wait until her sobs quiet, wiping away tear after tear.

“Let me clean you up”, I tell her. She lets out a deep breath, closing her eyes. I’ve never seen this side of her. This is the second girlfriend whose fallen apart on me today and I’m not sure what to make of it. If I wasn’t questioning my own judgement as of recently, I’m really starting to question it now.

Not wanting to leave her alone for long, I quickly grab a plush hotel issued robe and prepare a warm washcloth for her.

When I return, she's still crying silently just like I left her. I lay the robe down next to her and climb into bed.

"Let me take care of you, Em", I tell her, before spreading her legs wider to wipe her down. My mess is everywhere, which doesn't surprise me. I knew it would be a lot and between her release and mine, and I'm glad she's letting me clean her up.

When I'm done, I place a call to room service for drinks to be brought up while I'm rinsing out the washcloth. She needs something to take the edge off.

I redress to be decent for room service. This was not what I had in mind for this afternoon, however, this day has gone anything but according to plan. When I return to bed, she's in the robe, looking like a beautiful mess. I climb in and just hold her while we wait for room service. We don't say a word. Sitting in silence is a relief for her, I think.

It doesn't take room service long to deliver my order. I take the tray from the attendant, not wanting him to step inside so I can ensure Emmerson as much privacy as I can. Tipping him well, I prepare a drink for her. Whiskey on the rocks. I ordered a bottle to avoid multiple calls to room service, but I would not partake. Not right now anyway. Being clearheaded for our conversation is important. I don't want to misunderstand a thing.

She smiles when she sees me enter with a drink in hand. She reaches for the drink I hand her while she wipes away another tear. I don't press her. It's clear to me she needs some liquid courage to talk about what's on her mind.

"I can't stop thinking about it." She doesn't look at me when she says the words. I don't have to clarify because I know she's talking about the worst day of her life. "It's like I'm there all over again." She takes another sip of her drink.

"How long has this been going on?" If I could erase that memory for her I would. I'd do anything to help her. I really would.

"Since the anniversary of…" She trails off, not needing to explain further. It's been months. She's been dealing with this for months and she hasn't told Mav. I know she hasn't told Mav because he would have told all of us as soon as she told him. It's an expectation of the brotherhood. We exchange information freely and continuously to ensure the best for the women we care for. Holding information is unacceptable and could be punishable by being released from the brotherhood for good.

"I hear his voice. Feel his touch. It's like I'm right back there." She shudders and grips the glass.

"And the hot tub was a trigger?" I hadn't thought about it.

"No. It's been like this every day", she tells me through tears.

"Crying?" She nods her head and tries to hold back a sob, snorting when she does. When she starts to cry harder, I take her glass and pull her into my arms and just let her find her release. This beautiful woman was so wronged by the people she should have been able to trust most. I'm still angry on her behalf and I hope her ex-fiancé rots in jail and her father burns in hell because of their actions.

"I need you to talk to Mav, hm?" I rub her back as her sobs quiet. "I'm surprised you haven't yet. Will you tell me why?"

She pulls back and gives me a teary smile. "Mav is sunshine and smiles", she explains with a heavy sigh. I laugh because she's right. Sunshine and smiles is exactly how I would describe him.

"Sunshine and smiles can handle it, I promise you. What he might not take well is that you've kept this from him." She looks down and I tilt her chin back up to look at me. "Tell him.

If you want my help creating a new memory that overshadows the bad one, tell him that too."

"You're going to tell him about this aren't you", she asks me, even though she knows the answer. I nod and she rolls her eyes. As disrespectful as it is, I'm glad to see Emmerson is still Emmerson.

# Chapter 26
# Hadley

**September 1st 8:35 p.m.**
(4 Months Earlier)

My phone pings with the text from Braden. I almost drop my phone because I'm so excited to open it. It's permission. I've been waiting in the car with the man Micah hired to get me from point A to point B and the only instruction I received from Micah was to let myself in immediately after receiving Braden's text.

Braden- Have fun

It's all the permission I need and without hesitation, I reach for the door handle.

"Joanna", Jones calls to me from the driver's seat. Micah told him to call me by my nickname so he does, despite my attempts to tell him that Joanna is in fact not my name and he should call me by Hadley, which is my real name. It's like talking to a brick wall because I'm not scary like Micah and I don't deposit money into his account. Micah's driver, Steven, would never call me Joanna.

I drop my hand from the door and wait for Jones to let me out. Thankfully, Micah lets him wear street clothes to transport me. I'd feel so out of place if Jones wore the same outfit Steven does to cart Micah around in.

Jones opens my door and extends his hand to help me from the car. Every time he does this, I feel like some kind of dignitary. It's so weird.

Once out of the car, I start to tell him he can leave but then I realize I'm not sure what's going to happen in there. Other than sex. Sex is happening in there. Sex better be happening in there.

Jones raises his brows at me as if to say *I'm waiting*. I respond with a quick thanks and hurry up to Micah's front door.

It's chilly for being so early in September and a shiver runs through my body as the wind whips around me. While the outfit Micah chose for me looks ordinary and covers my body, it's the furthest thing from a barrier to the chill of the evening. The cold cuts through the thin fabric like I'm wearing nothing at all.

The door clicks open when I press the lever on the handle. It's silent. And dark. For a moment, I hesitate. Someone who wasn't driven by hired help might think they got the location wrong by how still the house looks.

I step over the threshold and the only sound are my heels on the hardwood floor. I close the door and prop myself up against it for a moment, just to catch my bearings. I've been waiting for this moment for months. It's finally here and I can hardly believe it.

Still, there's no sound coming from anywhere within the house, so I take a cautious step forward allowing my heels to announce my presence. I'm not sure what's louder. My pulse in my ears or my footsteps.

I don't bother turning on lights, even though his house is dark. Micah is neat and clean, so a trip hazard is unlikely, and I don't think he's trying to frighten me by any means.

There's a light coming from the living room. A fire. He lit a fire. I've never dated anyone with a fireplace but seriously how romantic is that?

I quicken my footsteps to get to him and when he comes in to view, I stop in my tracks. Micah is sitting in one of the armchairs, dressed in a black suit. One arm rests casually on the arm of the chair while the other hand holds a fresh glass of whiskey, resting on top of his other hand. The way he looks at me makes me want to kneel. No. Crawl right to him but instead, I just stop and take him in. Clean shave, dark hair, dilated, hungry eyes. In my entire life a man has never looked at me like if I fled, he'd give chase and when he caught me, he'd never let me go.

Micah looks me over, assessing the clothes he had Suzette purchase for this occasion. To my surprise, there's nothing sexy about what I'm wearing, unless you count the fact that he didn't supply me with any undergarments. There were three items in the package. An eggshell blue pinstriped shirtdress, a tan belt and a matching pair of tan heels.

Micah takes a drink savoring the alcohol before swallowing. I watch him swallow and I can't stay silent anymore.

"What do I do?" He normally orders me around and I find that without his direction, I'm lost.

His lips twitch as he fights a smile. He knows he has me. I'm well trained and it feels so freeing. He was right all along. If I just let go I would never want a relationship another way.

Micah stands, his eyes never leaving mine as he crosses the room to where I stand. He's like a king in his castle and I am nothing more than his loyal subject, merely trying to remember to breathe in the king's presence. With two fingers, he tilts my chin up and blesses me with a kiss. When he pulls away from me, he closes his eyes and takes a few deep breaths before answering my question.

"You'll do whatever I tell you." He strokes my cheek with the pad of his thumb, and I close my eyes, relishing his touch. Then he drops his hand to my hip, holding it there until I open my eyes.

He's clenching his jaw and his chest heaves in a breath of air. Then he steps behind me, moving his hand from my hip to my stomach, pulling me against him.

"Who are you here for, Hadley?" He doesn't use my nickname. This is serious.

"You."

"Who do you obey", he asks as his lips trail down my neck.

"You."

"Who do you give yourself to from this moment forward, freely, without protest or restraint?"

"You, Micah."

He hands me his glass and I freeze where I am, breathing in his scent and feeling his hands work open the latch on my belt.

"If you'd like a drink, I'd take it now", he warns with an edge to his voice I've never heard before.

I bring the crystal glass to my lips and take a sip, relishing the burn as it warms me from the inside out.

Micah slides the belt over my shoulders so it's hanging around my neck, freeing up his hands so he can slowly unbutton my shirtdress. His fingers graze against my skin as he opens the garment, exposing my nakedness.

"Slide off your shoes", he orders me, pulling back the neck of my shirtdress so it gaps open further in front but doesn't quite fall off my shoulders.

I step out of my heels as he plants a kiss on each shoulder causing my skin to erupt with goosebumps. Then he takes the glass from me and finishes the rest of his drink.

"Don't move", he orders me as he sets his empty glass down and steps in front of me. "I love the way you look in the firelight", he tells me, bringing his hand up to his mouth and running the pad of his thumb over his bottom lip like he does when he's thinking.

"I want to show you something. Something I've never allowed anyone to see. Would you like that?" I nod my head in answer.

"Out loud, Hadley", Micah corrects me, stalking around me.

"Yes. Please. I want to see it." I don't know what it is but if it leads to sex then yes, I want to see anything he wants me to.

"After you", he motions to the stairs leading to the second story of his home.

As I pad down the hall in bare feet with my dress open, I feel his fingers at the collar of my dress. With a gentle tug, Micah is sliding the garment down my arms leaving me completely naked with the exception of the belt that still hangs around my neck. I hear the fabric land on the floor behind us but I'm too nervous to turn around.

He says nothing as he walks behind me up the stairs. There's enough room for us to walk side by side but why would he walk next to me when he could have that kind of view from behind?

Once up the stairs, I'm not sure where to go. He has one of those upper levels where there's a hallway circling the staircase. Multiple rooms surround us.

"End of the hall", he calmly orders, never once stepping in front of me.

My pace slows a bit. Now I'm hesitant about what's behind that door. What could I have agreed to? It must be good if he's never shown it to anyone else.

We stop at the door and Micah comes around in front of me. Taking the belt from my neck he issues a firm order. "On your knees."

When I don't move immediately, he levels me with a glare, and I sink down into the plush carpet as he ordered me. Bowing my head, I wait for his next order, breathing through my nervous anticipation about what's to come.

"Arms up", he commands, and I waste no time complying.

With no explanation, Micah wraps the belt around one of my wrists, sliding the end through the buckle sinching it tight, then secures my other wrist just the same pulling them so they're bound together. A final loop secures the binding with absolutely no give.

He starts to gather my hair just like he did that night at the fire. "You are mine." He licks his lips as he looks down at me, briefly making eye contact while tending to my hair once more. "Tonight, you begin a commitment with me. I own you. From this moment forward until you no longer desire to be part of this brotherhood you will do as I say."

He unbuckles his belt after securing my hair to his liking. "You will swallow every drop and be grateful that I have decided to give it to you." Micah grips his hard cock and releases my hair just enough for me to bend forward to kiss the tip as he taught me at the camp site. Except this time, he doesn't allow me more than one kiss.

"Open", he orders and when I do, he slides to the back of my throat.

I gag on him as he throws his head back and groans. There's nothing I can do. He's got a tight hold on my hair and my hands are bound so tight my efforts would be uncoordinated at best if I tried to fight him.

When he pulls out of my mouth I gasp for air. He looks down at me, chest heaving, his eyes alight with victory.

"Do you want out", he challenges me.

"No", I rasp, because I know what's to come is going to be amazing.

"Good", he answers me, sliding to the back of my throat once more. He goes deeper this time, and I think I might throw up. "You're okay. You're okay", he croons, and then pulls out of my mouth while I gasp for air. "Shhhh, shhh, shhh", he quiets me, wiping the tears from my face with his free hand. "And now?"

"More", I whisper, my voice hoarse from the intrusion. I can feel the spit dripping down my chin and avert my eyes, embarrassed by how I look.

"Don't do that, Hadley. You're so beautiful like this. Such a messy beautiful mouth", he compliments me before sliding back inside me.

He goes in farther yet and I cough around him, hoping nothing comes up. Micah moans when I swallow out of reflex, and I notice the gagging isn't quite as strong anymore. I can't help but to feel a sense of pride over swallowing while Micah's cock is down my throat.

"Such a good girl", he compliments me, pulling out of my mouth just enough to give me relief but not enough to free me of him entirely.

"My favorite thing in the entire world is having my cock sucked, Hadley. Do you want to taste your new God? Hmm? Do you sweet girl?" He's fucking my mouth so there's no way I can answer, but if I could answer, I'd tell him that I do. I do what to taste my new God. In fact, I'd kneel for my new God all night if that's what he required. Because no man has ever used my mouth like this and where I thought it would be a turn off, I was wrong. It turns out that it's only a turn off if the man using your mouth doesn't know how to use it properly. It's only a turn off if he doesn't know how to say all the dirty things a girl needs to hear to practically come while getting her face fucked. And it's only a turn off if he doesn't force her to look up at him and let her know that she's got nowhere to go and she damn sure isn't getting up until he finishes down her throat.

Suddenly my God stops. "Show me." His hand shakes a bit when he strokes my face with his fingertips. "Take what I have to give you."

When he loosens his grip on my hair, I bob forward. "That's it", he croons. I do it again because I like the praise. Getting nothing that time I go a bit deeper, overestimating my gag reflex, gagging on his cock. "Oh Hadley. I'm so very proud of you", he croons while I repeat the move. "That's it. Don't forget to suck", he gently directs me, then throws back his head with a groan as I please him, following his order to the letter.

He lets me suck on him at my own pace, all the while showering me with praise and adoration. And then he grabs my face, letting go of my hair and preventing me from bobbing.

"Last chance, Hadley", he grits out, pumping in and out of my mouth. I moan around him because there isn't much I can do. "Blink twice if you don't want this." I roll my eyes up to him and he smiles. "Swallow", he barely gets out, groaning into my mouth as he releases down my throat.

I swallow. And swallow. And swallow...until he starts fucking my mouth again. For a moment, I think we're starting over, but he's just ensuring he's unloaded it all.

He guides my face back, sliding his semi-hard cock out of my mouth and smiles down at me. Then he releases my face and wipes the saliva from my chin with his hand.

I'm hauled up onto my feet by my bindings. They bite into my skin a bit and I wince at the pain, but it's soon forgotten when Micah slams his mouth down onto mine. I'm lost in him.

He's guiding me into the room while we kiss, not breaking even when the door closes behind him. I note the temperature change. It's much warmer in this room than in the hall. When I open my eyes to try and sneak a peek, I recognize the same glow of the fireplace as downstairs.

But then I hear the sound of twigs snapping. Leaves rustling. And then Micah's voice.

*Do you want to know what I think? I think you want to know what it feels like for a guy to make you come.*

I pull my mouth from his as I look around the room. We're in a bedroom. His bedroom I assume.

My mouth falls open at the memory. The camping trip. "You recorded it", I state the obvious. Micah doesn't answer right away. Instead, he lets the recording play.

*Do you? Do you want me to make your pussy feel good? Show me.*

"Consent. I did this for every girl who visited my tent. There was no way someone would accuse me of rape. They knew who I was related to. The sex was mutual. They knew I recorded them. It saved a lot of trouble down the line", Micah explains as he steps back from me, naked and still bound with my own belt.

He begins to undress, draping his shirt over a chair on the other side of the room. "They didn't get a copy. But you? After Introduction Night you'll have access to the recording."

I'm shocked. This man thinks of everything. Even as a teenager he was protecting himself.

"Does it bother you", he asks as he drapes his slacks on top of his dress shirt. I'm not sure how I feel about the recording until I hear Micah once more.

*Do you want my cock in your mouth? Do you want me to teach you?*

My voice is full of nerves. Interested nerves, but nerves, nonetheless.

"I want a copy." It's that quick. There is no more contemplation. This recording is real and raw and us unfiltered. I could never turn down the treasure and oddly enough, I'm glad he didn't tell me about it. "Will you record us tonight?"

"No." He's naked now as he crosses the room to me. "Some people play romantic love songs to sex. I thought I'd play us."

We're having sex to a recording of us almost having sex. Just when I think Micah couldn't get any dirtier than he already is, he surprises me.

"It's a privilege to be in my bedroom", he tells me. If that comment came from anyone else, I'd roll my eyes, but from him, I'd believe it. "No one, and I do mean no one, has ever been in here. Ever."

I scan the room. It's done in greys and black. A large rug is under his very large bed. The bedding is charcoal grey. It's plush with more pillows than I'd anticipate a single man would have adorn a bed. The headboard is covered in a plush deep velvet.

"Are you going to hook me somewhere", I ask, since he hasn't unbound me yet and I don't see any way he could hook me to his bed.

"Do I need to?" He watches me as I take in the rest of his luxury bedroom. The dark wood panels are ominous yet regal and the lights angle down from the tray ceiling in such a way that make me believe whatever occurs in his bed will no doubt be an event.

"No", I look at him, wondering what's next. "Will we..." the question dies on my tongue as I gaze at his bed. I want to know if he'll have me there or if he's simply showing me what could be.

"First, I'm going to take what's mine." He grabs me by my bound wrists and leads me up to a paneled wall.

*So pretty. Such a little mouth. Will you share your pretty little mouth with me? Where I need it most right now?*

The recording pushes him over the edge and he's whirling us around, bracing his back against the wall and sliding me down on top of his hard cock so my back is to his chest.

I groan as I adjust to him, my legs straining against gravity. And then suddenly he's taking over. His hands are at my hips, guiding me up and down on his length.

Micah is all muscle beneath me. He has me bound for his pleasure and for some odd reason I wouldn't have it any other way. I had never imagined Micah being overly romantic in bed but this? I hadn't imagined this either. It's perfect. He's taking care of me and using me at the same time.

"Touch yourself", he orders.

I do as he asks and I'm so close. "Oh God", I groan, not sure if I have permission to finish.

Before my body can decide for me, he's hoisting me up and spinning me around, pressing my chest against the wall and raising my hands above my head. He pulls my hips out from against the wall and nudges my feet apart with his own before sliding into me once more.

*That's it. Just look at you. So perfect. So beautiful with your mouth full.*

I cry out his name as I finish around him as he continues fucking me to the to sound of *us*.

# Chapter 27
# Micah

**September 3rd**
(4 Months Earlier)

"I don't want to do it", Hadley tells me, standing at the foot of my bed, refusing to get in.

"You have to do it", I tell her, motioning her toward me.

"It's not right. And it's cruel." She shakes her head, crossing her arms over her chest.

"Would it help if you knew all of the other women will start doing the same thing today?" She shakes her head. "Will it help if you understand why?"

"We can give it a shot", she answers me reluctantly.

"Bed. Now", I order her, pointing to my lap.

Hadley uncrosses her arms from over her chest and climbs into bed beside me.

"The first time we had sex, were you reluctant?"

"Of course not", Hadley huffs out her answer, stating the obvious.

"Tell me why. Where did your nerves go", I ask her, already knowing the answer as I pull her onto my lap like I did that first night we had sex. She lays her palms on my chest as she considers her answer.

"I wasn't nervous at all." I wave her on. "I needed it. I wanted it so badly I was willing to do anything for it." I can tell the moment she gets it. "You mean I'm *anything*?"

"You are in fact anything. The point is to make my brothers hungry for you. This way, there's no reluctance on their part or yours. It will be hard for you to refuse sex from someone who desires you as much as these men will. And when each brother returns to their woman it will be hard for the one they own to refuse someone who's been denied something they've had unlimited access to for so long. So I'm afraid what I require from you is all too necessary in the process", I reason with her.

"So you want me to bring you to the brink of orgasm and then stop before you finish for the next two weeks?" I nod. "And I can get myself off as long as I do it in front of you?" I nod again. "So I can torture you like you tortured me at the camp site?"

I see the glimmer of excitement in her eyes. It's fun to see her like this. She's got the upper hand and now I know she's going to use it.

"So I can order you around", she asks, her voice hopeful.

"Not quite. However, I will give you latitude on how you bring me close to the edge, unless of course I have a specific request", I tell her, giving her my most devious smile. I lift her on top of my hard cock without any warning. She's wet for me, so it doesn't take effort to slide her onto my shaft. "Fuck me until I stop you. Do your worst. Then I'm taking over for a bit."

Reluctantly, she starts moving on top of me. I didn't even take her out of her silk pajama slip and there's something wildly erotic about seeing her like this. She's fucking me all the while I can't see where we connect. Feeling but not being able to see is such a turn on to me.

"I want to feel you come inside me", she begs.

"No", I sternly answer her as I grab the hem of her silk slip, pulling it up and over her head in one swift move. "Jesus Christ you're beautiful", I tell her as she continues to ride my lap. Hadley leans in for a kiss and I oblige until she's breathless, leaning her forehead against mine. "Get up. I want you on your knees."

She's shocked at how blunt I am, so she doesn't move right away. I lift her off my lap depositing her between my spread legs. She's kneeling in front of me, my wet cock throbbing in front of her.

"I need a minute", I tell her as I close my eyes and rest my head against the headboard. I try to think of anything but what we're doing right this second. It seems as though I've underestimated my willpower. I went without sex for so long and when I finally found a woman I couldn't resist I waited longer. Two days of fucking wasn't nearly enough and now I'm to be purposely tortured for the next two weeks.

One might wonder what the incentive is for me to have pleasure withheld. On Introduction Night, I have to give freely before I can receive. It's about trust. I'm trusting my brothers to take care of what's mine even though they're coming to her unhinged. I can't intervene. Only Hadley can. And if she calls my name for me to stop them, it's over. We're over.

By withholding my orgasms from her during this two weeks, I'm also giving her some skin in the game. She'll miss me just as much as I'll miss her. And even though I'll be inside her, she'll need the sticky mess I leave between her legs, and she'll beg to feel my cock pulse in her mouth as she hurries to swallow my cum. We've had each other for two days. That's not even enough to scratch the surface of our hunger for each other. If she can't go through with this, she can't have me anymore and I can't have her.

Such a tangled web I think to myself as I sit up and gather her hair, fisting it into a makeshift ponytail. "Suck", I order her, needing the brutal punishment she's going to give me.

I don't waste time with preludes. There's no kissing my cock. No acclimating to my size. I simply guide her head down and expect her mouth to take me in.

Hadley does not disappoint as she hums at the taste of herself on my shaft. She swirls her tongue around the head, and I guide her up, groaning at how good she's gotten at giving head in only a short amount of time.

"Dirty girl", I grit out as I set the pace for her. "You're such a dirty, dirty girl."

# Chapter 28
# **Hadley**

**December 28th 5:35 p.m.**
(Present Day)

"Why did we come back to Micah's just to go back to the Lux? It's another trip outside and that hair and makeup can only take so much snow."

We're standing in Micah's kitchen. A rare opportunity to be by ourselves here while Micah is in his home office doing heaven knows what. I need to explain what's about to happen before Braden gets here because I think Madison will have a reaction and I'm pretty sure it won't be a nice one.

"Braden's coming over to check me." Madison cocks her head to the side, processing my comment. "My implant. He's responsible for my health and he's coming here to make sure everything is fine with it. He's my doctor now." She laughs.

"Isn't that a conflict of interest?" Her challenge to me isn't wrong.

"Are you kidding? There are so many hands in this pot there's no way Braden would make a bad call on my behalf. These men scrutinize everything. I can't even fart around here without someone knowing about it." Madison laughs, which causes me to laugh. "It's fine, really. He's just going to look at it and go on his way. Then we'll be off to the Lux with my fancy hair and makeup, and you can pepper Micah with all your questions and share all your judgements with me later."

"I'm not judging you", she starts to defend herself, but Micah walks into the room and interrupts us.

"Yes, you are", Micah says to Madison and then leans in to give me a kiss on the lips. "Beautiful", he says in my ear and then kisses my cheek. "Madison, you were judging her after you saw her give me head this morning."

"That's...true. But when I came in, you didn't even stop her. And she didn't even stop."

"Why would I do that? Her head was fantastic", Micah says with such an audacious tone I wasn't sure if he was being serious or overly sarcastic to get Madison going.

"It's private", Madison counters with an edge to her voice.

"And there it is." Madison rears her head back. "The very woman who wanted me to get rid of her cobwebs doesn't actually want confirmation that she has none. It's like telling a woman she can't be a prude but be careful she isn't a slut. And socially, Hadley is expected to meet your expectations when you're around her because heaven forbid if what she does makes you uncomfortable although it has nothing to do with you."

I feel like I'm watching a car crash in slow motion. The two most important people to me are politely having it out before my very eyes. I lay my hand on Micah's arm. A silent request for him to stop, but he doesn't.

"I think deep down inside, most women would kill to be in Hadley's shoes, but they'll never admit it. Because they're scared and they care too much about what others think to put their happiness first."

"Hello", Braden's familiar voice echoes through Micah's house. Micah and Madison don't move. They stare at each other in silence.

I stand there, watching them, watching each other even more nervous than I was before. Braden and Micah are not on the best terms. Braden will examine me. Micah will watch. Madison will...well that I'm not sure about. This experience is new to me. I've been told about the rules I have to follow to be examined by Braden. That in this moment, he isn't my boyfriend. He's my doctor. And if that is true, nothing sexual will happen. So, I suppose there'd be no harm in letting Madison observe too.

Braden enters the kitchen and my heart stops. He's sporting a black eye and next to him is Linea. What in the hell? I don't realize I take a step back until Braden stops in his tracks to observe me. Linea gasps at his side and I follow her gaze to Micah. And before anyone can stop her, she's gliding across the room, sliding between Micah and Madison to get a good look at his busted lip and bruised face.

"What happened", she asks him, swiping her finger over his injury.

"Seriously?" Madison is looking at me for answers and I say nothing. I think she has a pretty good understanding of what we do now.

Micah grabs Linea's wrist, kisses her fingertips and just shakes his head.

"I have something for you", he tells her. And I swear, the angelic way that Linea already carries herself intensifies. It's as if the aura around her glows and crackles with excitement. I can't see it, but I can feel it.

"Seriously", Madison says again and this time I glare at her, although no one is paying attention to her commentary but me.

"Hadley?" I turn my attention back to Braden. He simply holds out his hand and I can't help but smile as I step toward him and place my hand in his. "Don't be nervous baby. This is business and then you can go about your evening." Braden brushes a kiss across my cheek, and I blush. It's the sweetest I think he's ever kissed me and there was barely any contact at all. He shakes his head when my eyes linger on his black eye. He's telling me the incident is on a need-to-know basis, and I do not need to know.

Micah lets out a full belly laugh, and we all turn to see what's so funny. He's laughing at Linea. She's holding an obscenely large bouquet of the most beautiful roses. They aren't quite white, or cream or pink but a mixture of all three and she's got her face pressed into the bouquet, smelling the beautiful flowers.

"What are these for", she asks him, nuzzling her face into the flowers once more.

"Your vote. Thank you", Micah tells her with such sincerity that there's no doubt in my mind that they mean the world to each other.

Linea throws her arms around Micah, and she must whisper something to him because he nods in understanding. When they break apart, she turns to Braden, all business in her features.

"My condition still stands." Braden huffs out a breath in disagreement. "We never even got that walk in the park. And you know I could help her far better than any of you", she challenges.

"That's enough, Linea. You've made your point, but the decision is not yours." She's shaking her head.

"I heard you." Braden cocks his head to the side, confusion clouding his face. "A few years ago, you thought I was sleeping in Micah's office while you, Tyler and Jonathan were meeting. You said I could know things without knowing things. That I could have a positive influence on the other women. You said I could help. That because I was the first, I could be privy to things others don't know. And they might not mean anything to me in a practical sense, but my degree of separation from the other women could be different."

Braden gives Micah a sharp look. Micah holds his hands up, palms out in a defensive gesture. "I didn't know she'd heard that until today. We agreed on it. She heard it. Unless we're going to change the agreement we made years ago, Linea's contingency stands", Micah explains quite simply to Braden.

"I need a moment with you in your office." Braden turns to Linea. He does not look happy. "You do not have permission to talk about it", he tells Linea sternly. Linea doesn't acknowledge his order. "Linea", Braden says her name in warning.

"Yes, Braden", she answers tersely, then takes another sniff of her flowers.

The guys walk down the hall to Micah's office. I'm too tired to even inquire about the exchange between the three of them. Clearly, Linea knows more than she lets on and I can tell it annoys Braden to no end. When I turn to Linea and Madison, Linea is beaming, and Madison is not.

Linea steps forward, completely unaware of the brooding Madison standing next to her.

"Can I hug you", she asks, concern overflowing in the depths of her blue eyes. Before I can even answer, she's throwing her arms around me and squeezing me tight. "Are you okay?" When I stiffen in her hold, she loosens her arms a bit and moves back to look at me. "I don't know anything. All I know is that Braden makes impromptu visits when one of us isn't well. And he never brings me along so whatever it is, it must be urgent", she explains.

"I'm fine", I tell her, attempting to put her at ease, but then Madison pipes up.

"She's not fine. Her lady parts hurt, and she got drunk with me this morning."

Linea heaves in a sharp breath, still holding onto me. "What happened?"

I look around Linea at Madison and give her the stink eye. She gives me the kind of look my mother would give when I wasn't being honest and then tacks on, "Nobody likes a liar, Joanna", for good measure.

"I don't even know if I can say anything", I start, but Linea interrupts me.

"I won't tell anyone. Including Braden." She's still holding onto me. I swear whatever glittery magic she has within her compels me to answer her. When I give her the high level about the implant, she just nods like it's commonplace. "And the drinking?" She truly looks concerned about this one and I'm perplexed.

"I just wanted to forget about all this. Be numb for a moment."

"That's not a real answer, Hadley. Which is exactly why they need to let me spend time with you."

Madison huffs out a breath and Linea releases me, turning to her. "How rude of me. I'm Linea." She holds out her hand and Madison looks at it, not moving.

"No hug for me?" Madison can be a real bitch sometimes. She's jealous. I rarely see this side of her. But I've never seen her jealous about something that involves me.

Linea drops her hand. "You could make this easier on her, you know. What she does doesn't affect you. Unless you're afraid she'll love it so much that there'll no longer be a place for you in her life."

"That's ridiculous", Madison starts, but Linea cuts her off.

"Is it? Your actions are those of someone who's scared. Fear and anger drive a lot of decisions. Like drinking." This time, Linea looks at me. "Hadley is safe and loved. Just because that doesn't fit society's definition of safety and love with one partner doesn't mean it's wrong."

Footsteps get our attention and I've never been more grateful for their return. Braden and Micah look tense. Micah scans the scene before him. I'm sure when he looks at me, he sees worry, Linea, total and utter peace and Madison, red hot anger.

"Hadley, I'll take a look at you in Micah's office. Given the state of you three, I think you should all join us." My mouth falls open. No. Way. "I'm not putting Linea in the car and your friend…"

"Madison", she grits out.

"Madison. Looks like she could be a hair puller." Madison rolls her eyes and Micah smirks. "Let's go. We all have reservations to catch. This should be quick."

Micah leads the way as we all follow behind him. Braden walks behind us. His actions couldn't convey his distrust of us more. I have to say that I don't blame him.

"Hadley, please sit in the chair. Ladies, you'll sit in the chairs in front of my desk. Hadley, I'll take your pants and your panties."

Linea and Madison sit in the chairs, and I begin to take my clothes off. They're facing away from me, which gives me a degree of privacy, however, there's nothing to stop them from turning around and looking my way. I'll be spread out wide for them and I hate the thought of it.

After handing Micah my clothes, he motions for me to sit in the plush leather chair. The material is cold against my skin and I'm grateful he's only asked me to partially undress.

"Ladies, you do not have permission to turn around", Micah warns them. Even though I don't see it, I can practically feel Madison's eye roll.

Braden moves the matching footrest a bit closer to me. "Alright, Hadley. Scoot down until your ankles can rest on my shoulders." I do as he asks, without hesitation. I want to get this over with and put my clothes back on. Micah appears over his shoulder.

"She's swollen", Micah observes.

Braden takes one of my ankles from his shoulder and moves it down to his lap, bending my knee so I open up for him then repeats the process with the other leg. He doesn't touch me. He just looks.

"It looks fine, considering. But if there's any discharge, a line of any sort or a change in the color of her skin, I need to see her immediately. No vaginal sex", he adds for good measure, even though I think that part is obvious. Braden releases my legs and helps me into a sitting position.

"I'll put time on the calendar for you and Linea to meet." I look over at Linea when she gives a light clap of excitement...or maybe it's victory. I can't exactly tell. Braden looks annoyed and I smile at him because they are in fact a true couple. It's adorable.

"Go ahead and get dressed Hadley", Micah orders me, handing me back my clothes. I do not hesitate to put them back on while Linea and Madison are still facing the front of the room like they're going to get detention or something.

When I'm dressed, Braden pulls me close to him and kisses me. "Sweet Hadley?"

"Yeah?"

"Talk to Micah. *Really* talk to Micah", he orders. He wants me to lay it all out for him. To bare my soul. Not being honest got me into this. Being honest may just get me everything I want…or destroy my entire life.

# Chapter 29
# Micah

**December 29th 6 a.m.**
(Present Day)

One of my favorite things in the entire world is starting my day sinking into Hadley's hot, wet cunt. This morning not only is this not an option, but I can't even bring myself to have her give me any pleasure at all. The shame emanating off both of us is so great, I wonder if we'll get past it.

All I can do right now is look at her. She feels off limits to me. Like I don't deserve to touch her. I've never felt like this about any of our women but her…now…I fucked up.

There's a light knock on my door and then it opens. Braden is there looking at me like I'm some kind of science project. I hold my index finger in front of my lips to signal he should be quiet and slide out of bed without disturbing Hadley. Braden has no shame looking at my naked form. I'm soft. I never get out of bed with one of our women soft. He shakes his head, his lips forming a thin line of disapproval.

Throwing on some sweats and a t-shirt, I exit without waking Hadley, pull the door closed and head to my office.

"I have rounds. We agreed that I'd stop by this morning to check on Hadley", Braden starts one of his occasional child-like rants in my wake. I don't respond to him. I know why he's making a big deal out of this. It has nothing to do with Hadley and everything to do with me.

I walk straight to the hard liquor carafes and pour myself a glass not bothering to offer Braden one because he'll be working soon. "Where are you at today after rounds", I ask over my shoulder. Landon has already changed his plans once. Another change shouldn't be the end of the world.

"Mind telling me what this is all about?" Braden hasn't taken a seat which means he is primed for an argument. Now it's my turn to look him over as I take a sip from my glass.

"I fucked up." I let the statement hang there as I chug what's left in my glass and pour myself another. Braden says nothing. I wish he'd at least throw this in my face, but the fact that he remains silent while my soul crumbles for what I've done to Hadley and my brothers further hollows me out.

"Then stop fucking up", he says simply.

I chuckle.

"I'm serious. Right fucking now. Stop fucking up. You know the rules..."

"And I followed the rules", I roar, not giving a fuck if Hadley hears me or not. "She broke a rule. We voted. She lost." I practically spit the last words about Hadley losing because I'm that fucking angry that I couldn't protect her. Our own system fucking failed her, and I was at the helm of it. "Fuck!" I slam my hand down on the bar and knock back the second glass.

"We all watched that go down", Braden starts again but I interrupt even though I know what he's trying to do. He knows I'm torn up about the implant and Dr. Kinkade putting his filthy mouth on Hadley and he's trying to absolve me of the whole weight I carry. But the truth is, nothing he can say will make me feel less culpable than I do now. Nothing. This is something I'll carry with me forever. Every time I look at Hadley's face I'll see it there. My mistreatment. And not only do I not want to let her go but I can't because I'll be turning her over to the rest of the world after I fucking leveled her.

"*I* was responsible for her. Me. No one else in that room is responsible for what happened but me. And I thought I was getting her through it. I thought she was going to be alright with Archer and I there encouraging her. It wasn't enough. It was the best I had, and it wasn't enough!"

"It is what it is, Micah!"

Something inside of me snaps and I rush him. He strikes me first, right in the gut and then in the groin. I'm doubled over gasping for air in a newly sobered state.

"The system fucking fails people sometimes", Braden says as he bends down beside me. "Don't make this worse than it already is. Help her. You can either focus on the last two days or you can focus on the moments right in front of you." He holds his hand out to help me up. It's a sign of a truce.

I grab his hand and do my best to stand up straight despite feeling like I could throw up.

"Stop attacking me, Micah. I'm your friend. Alright?" He looks at me like I do with Hadley when I don't get an immediate response. Expectant displeasure. We all give the look well...except for Jonathan. He looks for compliance in other creative ways.

"I know man. Thank you." Braden nods.

"Can you wake her? I just need a look. I'll check on her tonight too when she's out with Landon."

I nod, letting out an exhale of relief, waiving him out of the room to follow me back up to our room.

"Landon is one of us. He was angry but he'll do right by her", Braden tries to reassure me.

"I know. I just...today is going to be hard for her. If she doesn't feel like she can trust me to care for her, how can I set her up to make sure her time with Landon is enjoyable?"

"I'd say you could go through Tyler, but he's still pretty pissed at you." Tyler recommended Landon for the brotherhood. They go way back. He'd be able to set my mind at ease, but I can't call on him right now considering how things ended between us. In some twisted way, I feel great about that. It was a good hit.

"You're with Grace tonight", Braden reminds me as if I had forgotten.

"What are you, stalking me now", I tease as we ascend the stairs.

"You've got an easy date. That's all I'm saying."

I nod in agreement. This is why Jonathan and Grace are perfect for each other. They both could give a fuck less about anything other than the here and now. Nothing bugs them. Nothing worries them. It's like they have this way of accepting things as they are and don't bother changing them. Instead, they just move around every obstacle with complete disregard as if the obstacle is nothing to them.

I knock on the door to find Hadley still sleeping. I'm not surprised. She was extremely upset last night and cried herself to sleep in my arms. Last night, I was grateful she even let me touch her. Today will be different. Not easy, but different.

I sit on the edge of the bed and pull the covers from over her head. It's clear she had been awake and went back to sleep by the way she has covered herself. The moment her head is exposed, her eyes, swollen from crying, open looking just as sad as they did yesterday.

"Good morning", I tell her, giving her a small smile. She does not smile back, and I try to not to let it affect me, but it does.

"Good morning, Hadley", Braden says from the end of the bed. Hadley rolls over to face Braden. "Micah let you sleep in a little, sweetheart. Sorry to wake you but I need to take a look at you and head out."

With a nod, Hadley wastes no time slipping from out of the covers and sliding to the edge of the bed. I hate how she regards me compared to Braden. At this realization, I play back Braden's advice. Focus on what you can impact going forward. I have Hadley until mid-afternoon. Over eight hours before I turn her over to Landon. I find comfort in the time I have with her, deciding to personally hand her off before I pick up Grace.

"How bad is the pain", Braden asks Hadley while he gets out his phone and uses the flashlight app to see better.

"It really, really hurts", Hadley tells him, emotion thick in her voice. Braden nods and then looks at me.

"This is how it'll be for a few days", he tells her, offering no reassurance. "You should kiss it. Make it feel better", he recommends to me, then he clicks off his phone and taps Hadley on the leg, indicating he's done.

In Braden's usual way, he walks up to me and holds out his hand. I shake it and he leans forward, speaking only so I can hear. "I'll get Linea over here tomorrow morning. In the meantime, try and change the memory."

I nod at him wondering exactly how in the hell I'm supposed to do that. I'm minus ten guys right now, eleven if you count Dr. Kinkade. This isn't even close to what she went through yesterday. Her cunt hurts and she's upset with me, rightfully so. But he gives me nothing, as though the answer is obvious and leaves the room heading out for rounds at the hospital. I turn to Hadley, and she slips down to her knees, turning her head down to wait for my direction. My well-trained girl. She'll normally end a day like this, not begin it. But because we hadn't had sex, she knows this is the default. Her. On her knees. Ready to please me.

I move in front of her and place two fingers under her chin tilting her head up to look at me. Then I simply extend my hand to her, helping her to her feet and plant a firm kiss on her forehead. No. I will not take from her now. Not like this. Not when she has nothing left to give. Not when the scales are tipped, and I should be working to bring her back to me.

# Chapter 30
# Hadley

**December 29th 6:20 a.m.**
(Present Day)

I take my time getting ready. It's going to be a terribly long day. I'm spending the day with Micah and then he's handing me off to Landon this afternoon. I'm stressed to say the least. My best friend left Micah's car last night as someone other than my best friend. She's worried, skeptical of my choices and likely thinks I've lost my mind. We were barely in the house when I broke down. The two people I had felt safest with were different people to me. It was more than I could bear. And I wanted to be brave and hold it in but instead I was weak and let everything that had obliterated my soul flow from me like an erupting volcano. Because I was different too. I had changed so much since keeping Madison out of my life. And I'd be a liar to say I kept her out of my personal life for any other reason than so she wouldn't be able to scrutinize how different I had become.

And now, I look at myself in the bathroom mirror feeling like a hollowed-out version of myself. I laugh as the thought crosses my mind if the brotherhood's goal was in fact to hollow me out. I allowed Micah to take everything from me so I could create the life I want, and I don't even know what that life is.

"Coffee?" Micah appears from nowhere, setting a steaming mug down on the bathroom counter. He looks different than he did yesterday. Last night, he was controlled and hard. My waves of emotion were nothing to him. Today he looks refreshed and pleasant even when he cocks his head to the side as a silent signal to answer him.

"Thank you", I mumble, averting my eyes for a moment before grabbing the cup.

"I started a fire downstairs. We're staying in until I hand you off."

I don't respond. It doesn't matter because I don't get a say. Instead, I pick up the coffee and take a sip. He wouldn't let me please him this morning. I don't know who's falling apart more. Him or me? It feels like I've disappointed him in such a large way that I'll never get him back. Like I'm no longer good enough for him. He seems sad. Regretful almost.

"Dinner last night was eye opening. I thought we could discuss the space you selected in more detail. Perhaps I could help you with what's to come", he offers while I try not to panic at the formality of him. He's all business. I don't want business, but I also don't know what I want from him. I felt treasured and violated yesterday and he was at the helm of all of it. The more the memory swirls around in my brain the bigger the emotional tornado becomes.

"Hadley", he croons my name, and I realize I've been staring into my coffee cup for heaven knows how long. When I glance at him, it's like looking into a mirror of my own emotions. He's hurting just like I am, and I did it.

I close my eyes and step back from him. This is too much. I hurt the best thing that ever came into my life. I gutted him. Then he gutted me which ultimately ended in him gutting himself.

"I've lost..." I can't even finish the sentence I whisper. It wasn't meant to be said. It was meant to be thought. The weight of the realization that everything I ever knew is gone with the exception of my job and my immediate family comes raining down on me with such ferocity that I struggle to breath. And those things that are left only remain because they haven't been caught up to speed on my new life choices. The scrutiny I'll get from my family could be unbearable and if my boss finds out I'm fucking multiple men she won't care if I'm averse to men hitting on me and asking for sexual favors at work. To her, I'll be experienced. She'll think I deserve it.

Micah's hands envelope my own and I realize why. I'm shaking so badly; coffee has spilled over the edge of my mug.

"Let me", he takes the hot mug from my grasp, and I let him without protest. Without another word, he steps out of the bathroom with the mug and quickly returns with a plush robe wasting no time to cover me with it.

"Stop looking at me like that", I manage through the heartbeat in my ears. He simply nods but doesn't change the expression on his face. "Stop it!" And I lung at him with flailing arms and spitting anger.

He's unfazed as he grabs my wrists and backs me into the nearest wall which happens to be the wet walk-in shower.

"Let me go", I shriek as I struggle against him, my naked body still on display through the opening in the untied robe.

Micah responds by pressing his body against mine and gathering my wrists in one large hand, pulling them up over my head. Then he grabs my chin holds me there to look at him.

"No." He's mad. "No. I will not fucking let you go. Not yet. Not until you can make it on your own. Not until you're put back together so you can stand on your own two feet without giving a fuck about who approves of you and what people think of you."

The mere thought that he's willing to send me packing without so much as urging me to stay with him breaks my heart. Not only doesn't he need me, but he doesn't care who has me. And maybe that's why he let Dr. Kinkade put his mouth on my most private place and commit such an intimate act. Because he doesn't care. I'm one of twelve. He can get it elsewhere.

"You don't want to go", he calls my bluff. "You don't want to go, and you don't want me to let you go."

I struggle to look away, but he holds me so tight in protest there will be bruising on my skin for sure.

"Say it, Hadley Joanna", he orders.

"Stop", I sob.

"No." His voice comes out hard and cruel like he's going to snuff out the last bits of my soul any second. "Say it. Say it all to me." His face is so close to mine I can smell the booze on his breath. He's hurting too.

"I ruined this", I choke out. "I ruined us. I ruined them." I sob openly and heave a deep breath before I come out with all of it. "I bared my soul. In that room I bared my soul to all of you...and I thought I would never be able to pull myself out of the despair I was facing if you wouldn't let me stay. You were willing to let me go. And your First Lady made the choice for you." I let go of another round of sobs at the sheer betrayal I felt from that act. The very woman who helped to break my heart was the decision maker. It was more than evident she was brotherhood royalty. Linea could do no wrong. She was their queen. Their First Lady. Their goddess. Their angel. I was a poser. Someone trying to fit into this world I secretly wanted yet couldn't manage to break free of the grip my traditional life had on me.

"And you knew." I shiver. "You knew what would happen to me and you couldn't stop it. And for that, there's a little part of me that *hates* you." Micah flinches at the word neither of us ever thought I'd use on him. "He licked me. Oh God." I start to sob again but Micah just holds me there. I sniffle and then let out a little chuckle. "And you know what? I hate Archer too. I hate him for helping you. And Graham and Tyler. Oh God...I hate them the *most*."

I didn't even realize I felt all these things. The raw hurt I felt had been overshadowed by the pain between my legs and the constant activity of the day. But now all these feelings were bubbling up to the surface. Each bubble that pops is the truth released and it feels so cathartic to say.

I laugh before I continue. "Graham expected me to answer his text yesterday. I got a lecture from the man who forced this to happen. And all the while I defend you all to my best friend. My best friend who has never done any of these things to me. And now she's gone."

I sob more remembering her last words to me. *I'll see you around, Hadley.* She hugged me at her doorstep as though it was goodbye. We've been best friends since the third grade and my sexual practices were what did us in. I let out another chuckle. It's so ironic that I wasn't even really doing the things that turned me on, and I still lost her.

"And today, you're sending me to spend time with the one boyfriend who openly hates me." I let out another sob. This one is so much different than the others. They were guttural pain. This sob is fear. "Fuck your rules, Micah."

And then the damn breaks. I'm crying so hard I can barely breath. It's like the emotions are being purged from my system and I'm powerless to stop them. I don't even realize Micah has let my jaw go until his face is buried into my neck with my hands still pinned securely above my head.

"That's it. Let it out, Hadley." He kisses my neck and another shiver ripples through my body as I continue to sob. His free hand slides inside my robe, settling on my hip. "Do you want me to fix it? I can fix it all." He kisses up my jaw to my earlobe while I sob at the thought of what *fixing it* would look like. He sinks his teeth into my flesh, and I suck in a breath at the sudden pain.

"I can't take any more", I tell him. It's true. "I...don't trust you", I admit and it's the final confession that very well may break us. I don't bother hiding it because he'll know. My calm exterior is gone. I'm no longer guarded. I'm raw and unhinged. Unable to hide my emotions and at this point, even my thoughts.

"I know", Micah says with his lips against my skin. "I know. And I'll get it back."

I suck in air loudly as I sob. I'm heartbroken and scared. I'm scared of them and scared of my losses being true losses. It feels like everything I was so sure I wanted is crashing down around me. The blind faith I had in Micah is gone and I'm more vulnerable than I have been in my entire life.

Micah's lips find mine through my open sobs. My body shivers again and I kiss his upper lip just briefly between sobs. He kisses me back and my breath hitches with something more than sadness. It's a tangle of heartbreak and love and I'm grateful for it. It's a scrap of affection from the man I obliterated and somehow, within my own shattered heart, I'm able to give him love back even though I feel battered and bruised on the inside.

His strong hand shifts from my hip to my back, pinning me to him while he kisses me more deeply. And the dam of emotions slows. Tears of fear and uncertainty slide down my cheeks. Right now, the tears belonging to heartbreak seem to have vanished. How could they remain with his kisses and his touch? It's impossible. It's like ice staying frozen in a sauna. It simply can't exist like that for long.

My hands find his face, gripping him like I need more. Like I'm some magical villain trying to suck the love out of him because I need it so very badly. So very badly I'm not sure I'll make it from one minute to the next if I don't get my fill.

"I need you", I break the kiss to beg him. Surely, he'll let me have this given how heartbroken I am.

"I know", he answers and then continues the kiss.

He's not getting it. I *need* him. I need him in the only way that counts. Even though Braden forbade it. Fuck Braden's rules too.

I press my body against his and reach around him to move his hand from my back. He allows me to move his hand, slowing his kiss just slightly as I bring his hand to rest on my throbbing wet cunt. My own flesh is so conflicted with the pain of the implant and sheer need for him to be inside me. I let out a small chuckle and it dawns on me that I sound insane. Everything inside of me is at war and I can't even get one thing as simple as sex to be on the same page.

I push the uneasiness away as I palm Micah's hard length straining to get free from his grey sweats. It would be so easy to take him out which is exactly what he doesn't want because his hand leaves my own needy place so he can capture my wrist and move it between us.

"No", he breaths. His rejection hits me hard. It's like he took the rest of my heart and crushed the pieces that could be glued together into powder. "Not because I don't want to, Hadley. God..." He lets out his own stuttered breath. "I want to. I want to disregard my brother and fuck you right here against this shower wall." He's breathing so heavily that I'm worried he is now the unhinged one. He puts my hand back against his erection. "I'll hurt you. I'll knowingly hurt you *again*. And this time it will be of my own free will. And that, Hadley...hurting you of my own free will...disregarding rules set in place for your protection and well-being...that would obliterate what little trust you do have of me."

"I'm not letting you go. I'm holding onto what little trust you have left in me and the love you still feel. I'm going to make those feelings overshadow the distrust, heartbreak and hatred. Your love and trust will grow so much that those wicked, diseased feelings that are so prevalent now become tiny, insignificant fissures that exist between us, occasionally aching during a damp cloudy day."

"I don't know what to do", I confess, dropping my hand from the bulge in his pants in defeat.

"This. Do this. Say what you're feeling. Ask for what you need. Do exactly this."

"You keep telling me no", I sniffle, wiping yet another tear from my cheek.

"I know. I won't break the rules. It won't help you if I do." He grabs my face and gives me a pointed look. "Right now. Other than my cock deep inside your tight wet cunt, what do you want?" He waits, searching my face while I still my tears long enough to try and think clearly.

"I want pancakes." He laughs. "And mimosas." He shakes his head. "I want the fucking mimosas." He shakes his head once more. "You had booze. Probably before you had coffee", I spit back at him.

"I did." He releases me and fumbles around for the belt on my robe, tying it shut with no further comment on the subject of alcohol for breakfast.

"While you make my mimosa I want to wear real clothes." He nods. "That I pick." He smiles at me. "I'm serious."

"I know. I will allow it. Go change", he orders me, nodding to the direction of the master suit. Before I leave the bathroom, I rise on my tip toes and brush a kiss of gratitude on his stubbly cheek.

# Chapter 31
# Hadley

**September 22nd 6:45 p.m.**
(4 Months Earlier)

My first double date. I'm more nervous now than I was during my first date with Micah. He's starting me off easy. I already know Braden. We met after my agreement was signed for my physical and birth control. And then of course during Introduction Night. But now I get to meet his girl. Linea. I have no idea what to expect. What do you even say in this situation? We've had sex with each other's guy and will continue to have sex and do all the things one in an intimate relationship does with another.

Do we talk about it over drinks? Will they leave us alone? Or will they chaperone us the whole time? What if she doesn't like me or I don't like her? Are we expected to be friends?

"Hadley."

All it takes is for Micah to say my name and calm washes over me. He knows my mind is racing. Because that's what I do. I overthink things. I stop fiddling with my wine glass and look over at him.

"They're about ten minutes out. Braden had to make a stop at the hospital." He chuckles at me and then asks, "Are you okay?"

"I don't know what to expect. I've been on double dates before but not like this." Not a double date where I've had both guys cocks in my mouth, and I know Linea is no different.

"It's the same really. Look at it this way. You both have something in common", he rationalizes. I cock my head at him and give him my best glare. He laughs because he knows it's hard for me to be angry at him, or even annoyed for that matter. He's so fucking hot...and he isn't wrong.

"Do we talk about it", I ask, trying to understand how these evenings normally play out.

"You can if you like, but I think you'll find that sex isn't the only thing we build these relationships off. Yes, it's a big part of our relationships but we actually *like* women, Hadley. That's why we do what we do."

I take a sip of my drink and look at him like he has a horn growing out of his head. It's not that I think they don't like women, it's just that I don't believe that's their motive for this whole operation they have going on.

"Maybe you need a history lesson when Braden arrives."

"Maybe."

I spend the rest of the time before their arrival trying to get Micah to tell me anything remotely helpful about Linea, but he doesn't budge. It's one of their many rules. If you want to know about something, go to the source. I feel a little strange about this because the source is literally the first of all the women, which means she's done everything under the sun with all of them, including Micah for years. I don't care who you are, that's a tough act to follow.

The moment they come into view, Micah stands and then holds his hand out to me. Yep...we're doing this. I take a deep breath and put a smile on my nervous face to greet them. Braden moves in to hug me and I hesitate. He stands there patiently waiting as I send a nervous glance to Micah. I feel a pang of insecurity when I see Micah's hands cradling Linea's face as he beams down at her. He looks so powerful, and she looks so submissive...and right now, he's entirely focused on her. I wonder if that's how we look to others.

When I turn to Braden, I feel incredibly awkward. Like I've disrespected him and failed a test.

"How do you greet a boyfriend when you meet for a date, Hadley?" He asks me the question loud enough that I can actually feel Micah's stare from behind me.

"I smile and say hi." Braden shakes his head at me in mock irritation.

"When you greet me, you'll let me pull you into my arms and kiss you wherever I please." He holds his hand out and motions me to step forward. I do, still feeling their eyes on me. Braden pulls me into his warm embrace and nuzzles my neck with his nose. Reflexively, I tilt my head for him to have better access. His warm lips work their way up just below my ear. "Breathe. We're all on the same team here, Sweet Hadley."

When Braden releases me, I know I'm safe. I feel it in his stare and it's so important to me because I don't want to start drama with Linea or Micah, and I realize that I'm out of my league here. I've never done this, and my discomfort shows.

Braden motions to Linea, who takes his side. She's beautiful. The picture of perfection. Her long blonde hair tumbles down around her shoulders in the most beautiful waves. She's wearing an over the shoulder oversized boho knit sweater with a pair of dark jeans. A long gold pendant hangs between her breasts. I try not to stare but I'm dying to know what the charm is. She's gorgeous. An angel that the guys could have pulled straight from the heavens above. Her blue crystalline eyes find mine and I can't help but to look away. Is she wearing contacts? I've never seen such a striking blue eye color in my life, I think to myself.

"Hadley, this is Linea. Linea is mine."

Mine. Linea is *mine.* The power in that one word. Sheer dominance. Absolute control. *His.*

"Linea." I finch at Micah's interruption as his voice breaks Linea's spell on me. Micah touches a hand to my shoulder and continues. "This is Hadley. Hadley is mine."

*His.* I shiver at the possession. The finality in his words. And I feel so completely whole because of his claim on me. It was silly to think this would be a pissing contest. But it's still so weird.

"May I?" Linea directs the question at Micah, and he must give her permission, because before I know what's happening, Linea has me in a full-on hug. I'm stunned but wrap my arms around her half-heartedly so as not to be rude. Braden chuckles then Micah follows suit behind me.

"I have heard...absolutely nothing about you", Linea says with a laugh, when she pulls away from me to talk but her hands still rest on my forearms.

"Rules are rules, angel", Braden gently reminds her, then he rests a hand on her waist, signaling to her that it's time to let me go.

Once seated, Braden and Linea order their drinks and then the guys start to discuss something cryptic about hardwood floors and holidays. I try to feign interest, but the truth is, I have no context to their discussion and it's boring me to tears. But Linea could care less. She's watching me watching them, patiently waiting for my attention. When I turn to her, she looks like she's going to bounce around in her seat she's so excited.

"So, tell me all about yourself." She beams back at me, giddy to get to know me.

I must say, I wasn't expecting this. It's strange because women aren't normally this hungry to get to know another woman that they're being forced to interact with over a set period of time.

"What do you want to know? I'm really not that interesting." Micah must have overheard my comment, and I can see him from the corner of my eye turning to look at me. When I look at him, he squints his eyes a fraction in challenge. So I turn away and give my attention back to Linea. "I'm a massage therapist." She nods and smiles wider. "I...um...like to cook", I offer meekly. Both men shift in their chair and all eyes are on us. Linea doesn't seem to notice or is used to this level of attention, but I'm not. I've never had men pay attention to me at the level Micah does and I'm starting to feel self-conscious.

"I like to relax", I volunteer once more, trying to start the conversation up again. "I go on a lot of long walks. Through the city. Torey Park is my favorite place to walk through. The paths are well kept, and it seems safe."

"Oh yes. It's gorgeous this time of year. We should grab coffee and go for a long walk before it gets too cold." Linea looks over at Braden for permission. Braden nods at Micah.

"I think that's fine. It's well-lit at night and law enforcement has a presence there. Let's just look at calendars and we'll try to make it work before the first snowfall." I don't agree or disagree and for some crazy reason I think my interest will be disregarded but Micah gives me the ultimate say. "Hadley?"

"Oh, um...sure." Maybe this will be more comfortable when we're alone.

"There's the most amazing coffee shop on twenty-second", Linea starts, and then looks at Braden and bites her lip. There's a story with this place for sure. Braden's trying to hold back a smile, but his eyes give nothing away. "Anyway, it's amazing and it's not too far from the park. They have the most fantastic pastries. I bet if I asked Tanner he'd hold a few cinnamon rolls for us." She rolls her eyes and looks up at the ceiling placing a well-manicured hand over her heart. "Caramel pecan", she says to the ceiling and then looks back down at me. "But we'd have to start out at a table for those. If we start early enough, we could walk the whole park." She looks over at Braden and now he's chuckling at her.

"Linea, baby." He touches her cheek, and she nuzzles right into him. "She's not going to disappear."

"I know but I like her." She looks across the table at me and gives me a shy smile. "I think we could be really good friends."

# Chapter 32
# Micah

**September 22nd 11:33 p.m.**
(4 Months Earlier)

"When do I get the history lesson", a groggy Hadley asks against my chest. After we got back to my place, I took her to bed. I was so proud of her. Tonight's dinner marked many firsts she would have with the brotherhood, and it went so well.

Sure, she was full of nerves. I couldn't blame her for that. But she got an easy first double date. Linea is such a sweetheart and she's been after me for quite some time to find mine. When she heard that my dry spell was about to be over, Braden told me she was constantly on him about who I chose. She wanted to know details that he could not give. As much as I was driving her crazy, she was driving Braden crazy tenfold.

I like that Hadley is curious. That we're coming back to this. It's important for her to understand the why behind what we do. And while I can't tell all our stories, I can tell my own, which is probably the most compelling story of them all, so I'm glad to do it for her if she thinks knowing it will help her.

"Every year my father threw a summer luncheon at his house. Anyone who was anyone in the legal system or politics came. My mother cooked. She decorated the backyard. She did everything for these parties my father threw. Each guest had a plus one which in most cases was their spouse. Our backyard was filled with people that my father schmoozed and celebrated.

He was, and still is a judge so he knew a lot of high-profile people around town and his goal was to impress them so during election time, it was a no brainer who these people of influence would elect.

But this particular year, I had become observant. Maybe it was age or maybe I had picked up on something that I hadn't noticed in the past. My mother seemed different this year. She had always been busy during the month leading up to these events but the day of, she seemed high strung. Tense. Worried even.

As my mother bustled about, my father strolled through the house and the backyard and picked apart what she had done. But he didn't do it in a way that was obvious. It was just a question with a tone to it. For example, he would say something like, the table linens, is this the shade of blue you picked? In that one question, my mother understood quite clearly that he did not care for the table linens.

With every exchange I could see my mother fighting for composure. My sisters were all sent on assignments for this or that around the house. I was never asked to do a thing. It was so strange that day because it felt like I was looking in on a house and a family I was seeing for the first time.

So I walked up to the island where my mother was slicing vegetables, grabbed a knife and the washed celery and went to work. The way my mother looked at me...Hadley she looked so relieved. Like I had given her a moment's peace. Like whatever was ahead of her she would have the strength to face.

My father had tried to recruit me to pal around with him, but I politely declined. I could see in his eyes that my answer was not satisfactory to him, but I didn't care. My mother needed me and for some odd reason, I knew it without her even saying a word.

The luncheon went on as it usually did. Guests arrived and gushed about how wonderful everything looked. The men commented on my sisters and what fine young ladies they were growing up to be and my father told them of his plans for me to get into law and politics and how he was sure I had what it took to follow in his footsteps as a judge.

I wasn't sure I wanted any of those things, but I was smart enough to know that voicing that to my father in front of his friends especially that day wasn't the wisest idea. And I figured, did it really matter what he believed? Neither one of us really knew what my future held. Getting into the details of something none of us could predict surely was a waste of time.

Mid-way through the luncheon, my father had waved me over to a table with some men I had recognized from other events. They were smoking cigars and laughing. I humored him and sat down, even though sitting at that table was the last thing I wanted to do. Their conversations were always so boring, and cigars smelled disgusting to me.

I wasn't at the table but a minute until one of the guys commented on my mother. They told my dad how pretty she was and how lucky he was. He was lucky. My mother is beautiful. Compared to all those women at the party, my mom stood out by a landslide. But his reply...Christ, I'll never forget it. He told his friends; beautiful women are everywhere. She's nothing special."

Hadley sucks in a breath in shock and I look down at her, running a finger down her arm so she'd look up at me. "It's not what you think", I reassure her. It would be remarkably easy for her to make an assumption that my thought process was similar to that of my father's and that's the last thing I want. Him and I have very few similarities and for that I am glad. The way we treat women will never be one of them.

"A little later, I had gone in the house to grab something and noticed my mother, rushing off in tears. She hadn't seen me, so I walked down the hall to my father's office. The door was open a crack, so I peeked in. There his secretary was, on his lap, her blouse clearly unbuttoned, riding my father at his desk." Hadley sucks in a breath. "He looked me in the eyes and smiled."

"My father was a pig. He had a wife who he promised to be faithful to and he wasn't. And not only that, but he treated her like she was nothing and he told people she was nothing."

"Micah, I'm so sorry", Hadley starts to apologize, but I won't let her continue.

"Don't be, Hadley. When I started my own firm, I had a talk with my mother about leaving my father. She said she could never do it. She wouldn't know what to do without him and she knew deep down inside, he loved her. Then she reassured me that he just loved differently."

"What", Hadley practically yells from my arms.

"I know. There was no convincing her. She had resigned herself to being treated like she didn't matter. Nothing I offered her would change that. So, I went on about my life and refused to settle down, but I was never dishonest with women. They knew exactly what they'd get with me. A meal, a few drinks and an orgasm. That was it. I wouldn't even take them back to my place. In a way, it felt like a lie. Like if I let a woman lay in my bed, she'd think we were more, and I'd never let that happen. Not because I wasn't interested in a relationship but because I hadn't found the right person to be in a relationship with.

And you're probably wondering how this is better. How what we do is better. I don't lie. I would never expect you to lie. I'm honest about the sex I like and so are you. I would never ever treat you like you were nothing because Hadley, this commitment I made to you means you are everything to me. The fact that you trust me enough to learn this lifestyle and live the way we do means that on some level, you're done with the bullshit too.

I don't want any more bullshit in my life. Lying and cheating? I don't do that. I won't use women like their only means is to run my errands, cook my food and suck my cock. I couldn't let you get me off before you had become one of us or were at least on the path to becoming one of us. This isn't a game to me. You aren't a game to me."

Hadley looks up at me and I fall in love all over again. Even with no makeup on she's stunning. Her flushed post orgasmic glow and those beautiful green eyes...I'm so fucking lucky she said yes.

"You're a good man, Micah", she tells me as she stretches up to kiss me goodnight.

# Chapter 33
# Hadley

**October 30$^{th}$ 7:25 p.m.**
(3 Months Earlier)

This is the fourth time I've had been with Braden. Once for the exam, then for Introduction Night, the double date with him and Linea and now on our very own first date alone. There's something about him that's just so relaxed. I can't say that about all the others. He's a country boy. A sweetheart. Respectful. And he's holding my hand on this crisp fall night.

I look over at him as we walk across the grass at a local pumpkin farm. He smiles at me and squeezes my hand, the dimple in his cheek popping out when he does.

"Sweet Hadley." He lets my name just hang there as we continue through the expansive lawn. "You're going to need protection tonight." He shakes his head as though he's unsatisfied with something.

"Why?" For a moment I'm nervous. I thought it would just be Braden and I tonight.

Braden walks closer to me and looks over at me conspiratorially and says with a serious look on his face, “Don’t you know what happens during a fool moon?” He glances up at the moon casting a silver glow on us and I look up at it too. It’s perfect for Halloween. “Werewolves”, he answers his own question sounding playful as he tugs me against him, wraps his arms around me, and dips me backward as he pretends to bite my neck.

I scream and laugh, not expecting Braden to be so playful. This seems more like Archer’s style to me, though I can’t say I really know any of them all that well yet.

Braden pulls up from nibbling on my neck, his face close to mine when he says, “You going to let me protect you?” I shake my head in response. “Oh, so you think you can do it yourself”, he asks me playfully.

I bring my fingertips up to his stubbly cheek and gaze in his big brown eyes. “What if I want the big bad werewolf eat me up?”

Braden looks away and huffs out a breath, considering my response for a moment. “Well alright then”, he answers, throws his head back and howls at the moon and then brings his head back down and pretends to maul my neck. I’m playfully pushing him away as he continues, hearing passersby comment about how cute we are.

When he lifts me up, he doesn’t even wait for me to recover before he’s pulling me in his arms and kissing me.

“I can eat you up, huh?”

“Yeah”, I answer before he goes in for another kiss. Braden is the boy next door type. He’s nice, a little rugged, funny and has a lot of heart.

“I’d like that very much, Sweet Hadley. Let’s go have a little fun. Then I’ll take you back to my house and show you what werewolves can do.” With a wink, he grabs my hand, and we make our way to the ticket window.

The teenager at the window is all decked out in a version of his own werewolf costume. This place takes Halloween seriously. The staff are dressed up and their makeup looks like a professional did it. I'd imagine that kid is going to be uncomfortable when he has to pull off his fake facial hair.

"We'll get two bracelets", Braden tells the kid.

I look at what the bracelet includes and start tugging on Braden's arm.

"Not the haunted house", I start to object. Braden's only response is looking over at me, his eyebrows downturned as it to remind me I don't get a choice here. He thanks the kid and walks us to the side, pulling up my sleeve to secure the fluorescent green band around my wrist.

"This place closes late. Now, we're going to do everything on that list and if you're good, I'll get you a caramel apple after." When he grabs my hand, I playfully pull away from him. He one-ups me and tosses me over his shoulder. I'm laughing and screaming as he carries me toward the haunted house line.

About a half hour later, we've made it through the haunted house and my nerves are a little frayed to say the least. Braden laughs as he follows behind me a few steps. I'm walking like the ground is crumbling under me with each step I take. My only objective is to put enough distance between me and that haunted house. Braden is laughing at me, and I would too if I were him. I literally screamed like I was being murdered the entire time. I turn around, walking backwards to address him.

"Is that it with the scary stuff?" He shakes his head.

"One more, sweetheart."

I turn my back to him and pick up the pace shaking my head. No way. I can't do it.

"You know, I could hurt my vocal cords. You'd have to answer to Micah, hm? How would you like that? Aren't you supposed to return me in the same condition you picked me up?"

"Not always", he answers back, now matching my strides. I look over at him and he's beaming. "Look, you're going on that haunted hayride with me, but I can give you a little something to take the edge off first."

"Like drugs?" Micah never mentioned I'd be offered drugs. That's a hard no for me.

"I was thinking a little oxytocin and dopamine", he answers, grabbing my hand and pulling me off to the side where the foot traffic starts to thin out. "Come here."

I'm too freaked out to protest, so I follow him without asking any questions. The cold air feels soothing against my hot cheeks. Braden takes a look around. "Run", he tells me, and he tugs me into a sprint. We're running toward a trailer with a bunch of hay bales on it. Braden races up the steps and ducks down as best as he can. "Get down", he orders me in a low voice while he helps me onto the trailer.

The sky is lit up by the moon, but the trailer is loaded with enough bales of hay that we're easily concealed, and Braden wastes no time pulling me onto his lap and in for a kiss. We kiss and he struggles with his jacket, tugging free from the sleeves, finally dropping it next to him.

"Do you know what werewolves like?"

"No", I answer and kiss him because he's so damn kissable.

"Pussy."

I laugh loud and he hurries to shush me. "It's serious. You get a werewolf out here during a full moon and that's all they're looking for." Braden palms my face and looks into my eyes, his face losing its playfulness. "Micah didn't tell you about that recessive gene I have, did he?" I shake my head. "That's too bad because guess what I just caught?"

"What", I whisper.

"I just caught me some pussy", he answers me, popping open the button on my jeans.

I huff out a breath at how dirty he's turned all of a sudden, but don't resist when he slides my zipper down.

"I wish this was cleaner but the beast in me just can't wait, sweetheart", he apologizes, before he hoists me up, slides my jeans down my thighs taking my panties with them and then pulling me back down so I can lay down on his open jacket.

Braden doesn't bother removing my pants the rest of the way. Instead, he lets them bunch up against my boots putting his head between my legs and lifting them up so my legs rest on his shoulders.

It's freezing out here. I shiver and he slides his hands underneath me, lifting me up just far enough away that I can feel his hot breath on my freshly waxed lady parts.

"Don't be loud, now, understand?" I nod and the second his lips touch my pussy my hands are in his hair. He's licking me right down the center. It feels so good, I have not a care in the world. I don't care about the haunted hayride, the cold or the fact that we could get caught. All I'm doing is chasing my orgasm and he is relentless as he helps me get there.

"C'mon, Hadley", he encourages me against my slit before he resumes licking me.

Just looking at him between my legs is enough to push me over the edge. That full head of blonde hair the only thing I can see because his face is buried between my legs...The fact that his mouth is licking me *there*. And we're in public. He doesn't even care if he gets caught.

He looks up at me, those brown eyes full of determination and I'm done. I arch against him, clenching in bliss as he continues to lick me. I want him inside me. How he licked me didn't seem dirty. It seemed like a prelude to more. Like the way a man would lick a woman when he wanted inside her. He plants a few more kisses on my slit and I suck in a breath at the aftershocks.

"Braden?" I run my fingers through his hair once more and he looks up at me, planting one last kiss on my slit. "I really like you." Telling him this seems so juvenile, but I have to tell him because I really do like him.

"I really like you too", he tells me as he slides out from between my legs and helps me put my clothes back in place. Once I'm decent, we just sit there together and kiss. I never did this kind of thing in high school but that's what I'd imagine it would be like. Kissing with the promise of more.

"I can't tell if I want to be in your mouth or your pussy later", he tells me between kisses. I smile, interrupting our rhythm.

"Do I get to choose?"

"No, you do not, Sweet Hadley. Look at you, trying to break the rules. I'll have to review the rules with you back at my place."

"You could review them with me here", I suggest, wondering if he'd have public sex with me.

"No ma'am. I want to take my time with you. Let's go so I can get you back to my place."

We walk to the car with our pumpkins and caramel apples in tow after experiencing everything at the pumpkin farm just like Braden indicated we would. The haunted hayride was ridiculous. Masked men in chainsaws chased after us as the driver pretended to have engine trouble. The louder I screamed the louder Braden laughed. I swear, this evening took years from my life.

We pulled up to Braden's house and it was similar to his doctor office. It looked like a large historic country home.

Something like an old soul might own. It was white with many windows with small latices separating the panes. There were large bushes in front of the porch and an old-fashioned lamplight near the driveway. The front door had a keypad there instead of a traditional door lock even though the doorknob itself was old.

He ushers me into the dark space and flips on the light. It smells like cinnamon and vanilla. By the looks of Braden's home, he's refinished much of the old floors and fixtures. His place is beautiful, and the space feels friendly.

He takes his shoes off and sets them near the door. I do the same, noting a pair of Linea's sneakers next to Braden's. They've made this place their home and a part of me wonders if Micah will ever want that from me.

"C'mon. Let's get this stuff to the kitchen", he tells me, grabbing the pumpkins and nodding in the direction we're headed because his arms are full, and he can't motion with his hands.

Once we're in the kitchen, I can just see Linea perched up on the island, cup of coffee or tea in hand with her bare feet dangling over the side. Even when Linea is gone it's like she leaves a little of her behind here. I don't know why but it feels like this is her safe place. Like this entire place is her haven and she shines light into every corner of it now.

Braden takes the box of caramel apples from me and places them on the counter. "Let me show you around."

I follow him through the expansive house as he shows me room after room. Some rooms are off limits. He simply tells me they're Linea's space and moves on. His house is way too big for someone without a family, which makes me wonder if he purchased this place with the thought of filling it with kids someday. I don't ask. He probably wouldn't tell me anyway, but I also haven't been in his life long enough to know something like this either.

I'm about to walk out of one of his spare bedrooms when he catches me by the hand. My mouth falls open with the realization that this is it. He's going to have me in this room, right now.

Braden must see the glimmer of fear in my eyes. We haven't done this yet. I've done it with a few of the other guys and it was just as scary as it is now. Micah isn't here. It's just us so I have to trust Braden is going to do right by me.

"Hadley", he says my name like he's worshipping a goddess. It's sobering. This isn't just a dirty fetish for him. It's more. "Who am I to you?"

"My boyfriend." It's so weird to say to a grown man, especially when I have Micah but that's who he is to me.

"And as your boyfriend, what do I get from you?"

"Whatever Micah allows." Braden nods and steps closer to me.

"Micah has allowed me to come inside your beautiful, tight cunt tonight. Would you like that?"

I don't answer because it still feels wrong to me.

"Hadley, I didn't ask if you thought it was the right thing to do, I asked if you'd like it if I spent some time in between your legs. We have plenty of time left to spend with each other tonight and I have no intention of carving those pumpkins with you."

"Here?" He nods. "Won't Linea be getting home soon", I ask with a nervous laugh. I don't know why but having sex with Braden here...their home feels like a sacred space after meeting Linea. Like I'd be betraying her in some way. She's so sweet and innocent.

"Hadley", he steps up to me and tucks my hair behind my ear before bending down to kiss me, but I turn my head. It feels so wrong in their home. She *lives* here with him. It feels like crossing a line.

Braden doesn't seem rejected or deterred. He simply kisses my cheek and continues down my neck. And with every kiss my body responds to him automatically. I like him. If he asked me out on a date before meeting Micah, I would have said yes. He's nice. And damn if he doesn't know how to woo a woman.

He knows he has me because he returns to my mouth and this time when he tries to kiss me, I let him. Any apprehension about sex is gone. It's like his lips had some sort of drug on them that made me bend to his will.

When he unbuttons my pants, I start on his. We don't break the kiss. We're simply tugging on clothes under the spell of each other. He has most of my clothes off first. The only thing left is my bra. I however, am not that adept at undressing a man, either that or I was too distracted by Braden's mouth and his hands.

I squat down to slide his pants and boxers off and he steps out of them, kicking the clothes to the side. But when I start to stand back up, his hands are on my shoulders, pushing me down to my knees.

"We give in kind, Hadley", he reminds me when I look shocked by his demand. "Open up", he casually orders, and I settle onto my knees and take the head of his cock into my mouth. I don't do much more than that because I skipped a step. I'm supposed to kiss the tip, but he said open up, so I followed his order without thought which is also something I'm supposed to do. And with Braden, it's so easy to trust his orders because he's such a nice guy.

"Open", he croons, and I do, allowing him to slide back as far as he can go until I gag a little. He pulls out and cocks his head to the side, seeming to analyze the depth of his thrust and my response to it. “Relax”, he gently orders as he slides back in, placing a firm hand on top of my head and the other at the base of my neck, his thumb resting on the front of my throat, near my Adam’s apple.

“Linea.” He says her name in a gravelly voice and then lets out a sinister chuckle. “That girl would come without touching herself if she got to watch this”, he laments, looking down at me as I roll my eyes up to him. “God damn, Hadley. Most newbies would be worried about me holding them like this. I bet this is making your cunt ache. Me holding your head to pleasure any way I want?”

I moan my answer because I can’t speak. It is. Oh my god I can feel how tight I am. If he doesn’t fuck me tonight, I’ll be out of my mind when I return to Micah.

“I know…I know…”, Braden croons as he slides back a little farther, testing my gag reflex. “It’s okay. You’re okay”, he reassures me when I gag a little harder this time. He never let’s go of my face. It’s clear I’m not going anywhere unless he tells me I am and I’m okay with that. I’m more than okay with that.

“If Linea were here, she’d rub it for you. She’d make that pretty little cunt come so hard while I fuck your mouth”, he tells me, and I moan again. Women are forbidden in my agreement but what he doesn’t know is that his words are making me even tighter. “Fuck…I’m going to come down your throat and you’re going to gag a little, sweetheart.” He sucks in a breath through clenched teeth. “Then I’m going to teach you how I want you to blow me.” He increases his pace a bit. “And before I return you to Micah, I’m going to make this room smell like so much sex, Linea can smell it when she walks by the open door to go to bed tonight.”

I look up at him and he erupts in my mouth, sliding back to my throat, groaning as he pulses his release, while I do my best to swallow the gift he gives me.

# Chapter 34
# Micah

**November 14$^{th}$ 6:15 p.m.**
(2 Months Earlier)

“Stop fidgeting”, I reprimand Hadley as I buckle her shoe. Could Suzette have purchased shoes with tinier buckles?

“I’m sorry. It’s just...you aren’t going with me”, she states the obvious.

“If I went with you then we’d both be sharing you. I think it might be a little soon for that, don’t you?”

“All twelve of you shared me for several hours. I think I could handle you and Harlan”, she tells me, her response sounding like a pouty child.

“You could. But Harlan is a lover. And if I know him like I think I do, he’ll want this date with you all to himself.” I finish the last shoe and tap her ankle. “Stunning.” Holding out my hand, I help her to stand.

“This is a little much, don’t you think”, she asks, looking down her dress at how it sparkles, turning this way and that.

"Hadley, there is no such thing." I kiss her on the lips ever so gently so as not to mess the red that Harlan insists she wear.

"Won't you be lonely without me", she hedges.

I simply shake my head. No. The answer is no, and she knows it. She just doesn't know who it's with. She never will. Just like the others, they'll never know who I receive once she's handed off.

The doorbell rings and she flinches. I chuckle because it's funny to see my spitfire so rattled. I crook my arm, signaling she should put her palm inside to hold onto my bicep. Reluctantly, she does, and I walk her to the door.

I can feel her hand quiver on my arm and her gait is slower than usual. I bet her pulse is through the roof.

"Breath, Hadley", I remind her and then open the large wooden door to find Harlan there in a tux, equally as stunning as Hadley. A slow smile spreads across his face as he takes her in from head to toe.

"Turn", I quietly order Hadley and Harlan's appreciation of her backside is the best compliment a man can get when it comes to his girl. When I turn Hadley around, Harlan can't wipe the smile from his face. "Have you reviewed her agreement?" It's a fair question. I'm handing off what is the most important possession to me, so I need to know that he has done his homework.

"Yes, sir", he responds, holding up one finger.

I laugh, knowing exactly what he's referencing. Hadley gave permission for one finger in her back door and that is exactly what she'll get tonight. Harlan is an ass man. We all are but Harlan *really* likes a good ass. He couldn't have been more disappointed when he saw Hadley's limit for her back door. Several of us were but, many of the ladies have modified their agreement over time. Most of the time they ask their owner for something outside of their original agreement. Regardless of who they ask, it's her owner and only her owner that will personally grant her request. After such request is granted, it's at her sole discretion to revise her agreement. If she doesn't like what she asked for then nothing changes. But if she does, we make an amendment. From that point forward, the brothers receive updated agreements with the changes outlined. It's quite simple really.

I put Hadley's hand in Harlan's and get an absolute rush from it. I'm giving her away. Giving her away to someone I trust. He's going to covet her. She's going to feel loved beyond all reason and then he's going to bring her back to me to care for. And when Hadley falls asleep, I'm going to read all about their evening in the summary Harlan sends to me. I'm not sure what I'm more excited for. My date with Grace or receiving Hadley back and reading Harlan's report. It's a requirement of the men to report out on the women. We share a drive and can get updates in real time on all the women. Quite helpful for planning purposes.

My date with Grace goes…as planned. Grace is a dream really. Being the second woman in the brotherhood, we've formed a close relationship. Our playful sparing borders on serious topics, but anything infringing on the strict rules the men are to follow ends abruptly. Mostly with Grace, she wants more information than she's entitled to. Where Linea is sneaky at acquiring information, Grace is straight to the point. Anyone outside the brotherhood would likely give her information solely because they were intimidated. We aren't intimidated by…well anything, really.

Receiving our woman after a date is a process. There are certain formalities we must carry out to ensure we understand their viewpoint on how the evening went. As this is Hadley's first solo date, I follow our process to the letter.

I receive her with affection and take a visual assessment. She looks…tired. I kiss her briefly and she responds like she always does. She wants more. And it's perfect because I want to give it to her. But first, I ask her about her date.

"It was...out of this world. The things Harlan can do with the fancy security system gadgets he sells." I correct her. His team makes them too. It's really quite extraordinary. "I mean, Micah...the things he did to me right in front of strangers and they were none the wiser." I ask her what she thinks about Harlan. "On the outside he seems formal and stiff but really..." She sighs. "...he's romantic. I think he likes me", she tells me, scrunching her nose up and making an overly exaggerated nervous face.

I laugh and she relaxes. "Of course he likes you. He wouldn't have agreed to you being with us if he didn't." I kiss her once more and she melts into my arms.

"And your backside?" I'm still holding onto her face, unwilling to let her look away. This was something she was most nervous about. Ass play. Harlan is good. Out of all the guys, he's the best first experience Hadley could have.

"It has been played with sufficiently", she tells me as she fights a smile. "Okay. It wasn't that bad", she hedges.

"Hadley Joanna", I use her name as I first knew it in a stern voice to tell her I wasn't believing her one bit.

"I liked his finger there better when we were having sex."

Fantastic. I hadn't played back there with her yet but now that she was telling me it wasn't the worst thing, I'd have to experience her tight hole myself.

"I'm not changing my agreement though", she tells me, her wide eyes looking up at me vulnerable and sincere.

"That's fine", I reassure her, not wanting to push the issue. A good experience is a win, and we'll take any wins we can with respect to her backside. "Would you like me to take you home or would you like to stay here tonight?" It doesn't matter to me. Either way the night ends the same. We have sex and I tuck her in. The location of where she sleeps is a minor detail in all of this. She has clothes at either place and her driver will be where he is needed tomorrow morning.

"Can I stay here?" She looks vulnerable. Like she isn't sure if I really want her here.

"Of course. I wouldn't have given you the option otherwise. You're always welcome to stay here." It warms my heart that she would want to stay with me. I assumed as much. This evening might be a little difficult for her, which is why we do what we do after these dates.

Without another word on the matter, I take her hand and leader her to the stairs. She doesn't say anything. Just follows me until we get to the stairs and then I'm behind her. Those shoes are gorgeous but death traps on stairs for sure.

Once upstairs, I undress her. I want her to feel celebrated. I want her to know that she's still mine and I love her beyond measure.

"Do you want me to wash up", she asks me between kisses as if I don't know what's between her legs.

"No." I kiss her and don't give the cum that's in her cunt a single thought. None of us do. Now, I draw a line at tasting her, but many of my brothers wouldn't. The truth is, we've been doing this for so long, it doesn't bother us. Some of the guys are bisexual anyway and as long as she smells good, there's not a moment of hesitation from any of them to lick between one our women's thighs.

I make love to her. Slow, deep and possessing. I want her to know that she's beautiful and she shouldn't be ashamed for going out with Harlan and for them to enjoy each other's bodies. I tell her how much I love her and how beautiful she is. How her pussy belongs to me. And all the while she ruts up into me like she can't get enough until her orgasm sucks the cum right out of me and into her.

I don't bother washing her off. I want to wake up and smell what we did tonight. To see the wetness between her thighs tomorrow when I wake her to shower. To have my sheets washed with the stain of us on them.

With a final kiss on the lips, I say good night to her, turn the lights off and head to my office to read Harlan's report. I've seen reports hundreds of times, but this is the first one on my woman. Excitement thrums through my veins at the anticipation of reading about her.

I see my brothers were curious as well. Most of them have gotten to Harlan's report before me. I'm glad to see this. It means they're interested in her, which is the ultimate goal. We want the people in these relationships to be invested. To truly give a shit about each other. That's the way relationships should be.

**Date Tracker**
**Hadley Joanna**

Hadley did not disappoint. Such a vision in her black gown at the theater. She was tense in the car. I'd expect nothing more for a first date. Once she had a glass of wine in her, she seemed to relax. The dinner was lovely. She actually ate! I allowed her to select her meal but fed her bites off my plate to better understand her tastes in food. I laughed at the face she made when I had her taste an oyster.

It was obvious she isn't accustomed to a formal dinner by the way she paused before selecting each utensil. I like that about her. She isn't hiding who she is. She'll learn in due time. At the theater, she was in awe. It was a pleasure to see her wide eyed at the beautiful building with all the fancy ornate little touches. I'll rather delight in spoiling this one.

At the theater, we had a bottle of champagne. I figured it necessary for the trust I was asking her to place in me. At first, she was uncertain that I could conceal us fucking in the balcony. But there's something about Hadley and sex…it's like…when she gets started and she likes what she's doing, she tunes out the world around her. She's so focused on the act that nothing else matters. I had her on my lap for a bit, just kissing and touching her and when she was wet enough, I fucked her with my fingers. Christ…the sounds this woman makes. I couldn't help myself. I pulled myself out and sat her down on my hard cock, forcing her to watch the play while I fucked her from behind. She was so turned on, she barely fought me when I slid my finger inside her ass.

I want my cock in her backside so badly I can hardly stand it. If there's ever an opportunity, I want to be considered first.

**November 14th 11:47 p.m.- Harlan**

I sigh at the last line. There isn't one of us that wouldn't want to claim that hole, however, I can't see that happening any time soon.

I shut my laptop and pour myself a drink. Finding a woman I love so very much has finally happened for me. And she's doing so well with this.

I feel such an immense sense of pride. She's mine and I vow to always do right by her. I'm going to smooth out all the rough spots…all the shit that society will throw at her. It will happen. It's just a matter of time but I'm going to be here to help her navigate through it. To reaffirm that she isn't alone and that she should be doing the things that feel good to her regardless of what anyone tells her. And that she's not a whore or going to hell or any of those other things people say to get you to live safely in the neat little box society created.

She'll never know a day where she isn't celebrated and loved. Not as long as she has us.

# Chapter 35
# Micah

**December 29th 4:30 p.m.**
(Present Day)

The drive is silent. I can feel the stress radiating off Hadley in the passenger seat. She's worried Landon is going to be cruel to her tonight. I haven't said much to her about her evening with Landon, except that she is going because that's part of being involved with us. She doesn't get to pass on a date, even if there is friction. Even though I know Landon would never mistreat her, it wouldn't do her much good to hear this from me.

I was delighted that she fell apart in front of me this morning. Not because I wanted to see her crumble but because I needed to know exactly where I stood...where we all stood. And part of me took pleasure in knowing that her hatred spread beyond me. That I wasn't the only villain in this fairytale and that the others had some work to do as well.

Her reference to Linea was interesting. She called her the First Lady. While Linea was the first of the women, Hadley meant more than the order in which she entered into our unique family. Hadley was calling Linea out on her notoriety, her trustworthiness and her place among the women in the brotherhood. She was acknowledging that Linea had power. Power she could leverage at any time with any of us to tip the scales in her favor.

Hadley's acknowledgement is only somewhat true. But I think this comes from many things, not just the length of time Linea has spent with us. Linea came to us as a virgin. Can you even imagine a virgin with four guys, one of which is a dom? And I'm not talking a virgin that's kissed a bunch of boys, touched herself and given head. I'm talking the best kind of virgin. The virgin that's so sheltered, so very pure, that all things related to sex are firsts for her. So yeah...Linea was different. We cherished every moment with her because to us, she was like a wet dream who needed direction. Direction we were willing to give, and she was so willing to take it.

But Linea's gone through some serious shit. And we had to figure things out with her. It's not like we were gifted a playbook. We made a lot of mistakes with Linea and those who came soon after her. Mistakes that tested our patience and our will to continue the brotherhood. In fact, at one point, we considered ending it. Things where stressful...heated. It was like being in one bad relationship but with an audience.

Linea stuck through it. And over six years later, she's thriving like the others. There are some things Linea can't unknow. So we give her a little latitude. But Linea also knows the price of sharing things that are not her business to share. And even though she is Braden's, Braden will most certainly let the founders, Tyler, Jonathan and myself, dole out suitable punishments without hesitation.

I hit the button to open the gate at Landon's. Such a pretentious home. I stifle an eye roll every time I come through this gate. His grandfather left it to him along with every cent he had when he passed away. Landon and his grandfather were close. Landon's parents hated Landon's choice not to go to school and make the family proud. Landon's grandfather on the other hand did not hate Landon's choice. He rewarded it because he knew Landon would be a great businessman someday. And his grandfather was right. Not only does Landon own one of the largest fitness centers in the city but he owns several more in the surrounding area as well. He's rolled out another company which provides health supplements and nutritional training to those who want to lose weight but also want their food not to taste like shit. He's done quite well for himself to say the least.

Pulling around to the circle drive out front, I stop the car and turn my attention to Hadley. She doesn't have her cell phone. That hasn't changed since her first date with me. She'll be alone with a man she genuinely believes will mistreat her. What she doesn't realize is that mistreatment in any way is grounds for being removed from the brotherhood. Regardless of how mad he is at Hadley, he loves the brotherhood far and above his feelings of anger. Even Landon wouldn't be that stupid.

I look over at her. A vision with her smokey eyes and nude-colored lips. So fuckable yet so off limits. Her makeup screams sex-kitten and although her clothes don't yet, they will. Landon is going to have fun with her tonight.

"Hadley", I call her attention away from the front door of Landon's home. "It's one evening. He's angry. Allow him this. And remember the rules." I don't want to punish her tonight, but I will if she isn't compliant. We don't make exceptions.

"I hate your rules", she tells me, taking her bottom lip between her white teeth.

"You don't hate all of our rules", I smirk at her. Even though she doesn't return my playful banter, she knows I'm right. The one she hates the most is that she gets no information. All the women hate this one. But we soon learned that the more we told the more they talked and the more they talked the more we started to get sucked into their drama, which drained the fun out of this whole thing. And when I say it drained the fun out of the whole thing, that included sex. One emergency meeting and the first rules were created. They did it to themselves.

The weather is still shit. I don't think it's going to stop snowing until spring at this rate. Muttering a curse under my breath, I leave the comfort of the warm car to open her door. She steps out, the snow swirling around her, and I can see the fear in her eyes.

"Be good. I'll reward you later", I promise her before gently pressing my lips to hers.

The door opens and there stands Landon. The king of his castle looking royally pissed.

"Come", he orders her, holding out his hand.

I feel the need to walk her up the small set of stairs and place her hand in his just like I did her first solo date this past fall.

"Landon", I regard him, my voice holding a sternness every male interprets very clearly. Do not fuck with my girl.

"Micah", he says my name in a way that I interpret as dismissal. I walk down the steps hoping we don't have a problem after this date. If he disrespects Hadley I will blow my top, which is something I don't do often. Her date with Landon is a test of the trust Hadley places in me. If it doesn't go well, we'll be taking yet another step back and I can't afford that.

Another step back means she will fear everyone who voted that she leave this family, and she would be right to.

I head to Grace's house. She asked me to snuggle her a few weeks ago. I did but it was lackluster. We didn't have adequate time, and the place was all wrong. So, I planned a date around snuggling at her place. Her clothes were delivered this morning along with two boxes. Both had notes that instructed her not to open them and where they should be stored. The moment she opened her outfit she was blowing up my phone.

Grace- We're staying in?

Grace- Does this mean a night of cuddles?

I read her messages but don't respond. They don't get to know what we're doing ahead of time. She knows I'm not answering these.

Grace- I'm number two. Just fucking tell me.

I laughed at this text. She's trying to pull rank as the second woman to join us.

Micah- I'll see you around six.

She sends me a gif of a woman pulling her hair and screaming. She's creative, I'll give her that.

It takes me longer than I'd like to get to Grace's house. I'm convinced the Department of Public Works has the night off. There isn't one plow or grain of salt to be seen out here. This winter is barely over and it's getting to me. Perhaps I'll take

Hadley on a trip somewhere warm. Go to my firm in Houston for a bit or just take a vacation. All I have to do is find time when she isn't scheduled with one of my brothers. But if I really wanted to, I could just change the schedule where she's concerned. I have the final say on her. The change would just wreak havoc on the rest of our schedules though. Not only would we have to rearrange her dates, but we'd have to rearrange mine. We've managed before and we can do it again. But perhaps right now isn't the time to uproot her. She needs to be integrated. Not to be pulled away to spend time with only me.

The moment I pull in Grace's driveway she's at the door, holding it open for me, a glass of champagne in the other hand. I laugh at her. I swear this woman drinks champagne every night. I'm surprised Jonathan allows it. Thinking back to how long she's been with us, she has a point. We do give her and Linea more latitude.

The moment I'm through the door she's unbuttoning my coat. I laugh at her, and she smiles wider.

"I have been so excited for this all day." Her light blue eyes look up at me. It's like looking at a clear blue ocean.

"Me too", I tell her, because I really have been.

"Liar", she challenges me as I slip out of my wool coat and let her hang it up, appreciating the way the designer sweats I bought her hug her ass.

"Where's my glass", I call to her.

"You're drinking champagne", she asks, in awe of my choice. I don't normally drink champagne. It reminds me of weddings which I abhor.

"It goes with the snacks", I quip back, winking at her. Grace lets out her signature throaty, mischievous laugh and I busy myself in the kitchen preparing the risotto with mushrooms and cream sauce that will compliment the bottle I sent over nicely. "What is it, Grace", I ask, noticing her looking me over as though she seeing me for the first time.

"We've been together for years and I still don't understand you." She's perched on the arm of her couch, glass in hand, marveling at me as I cook this dish from memory, forgoing any actual measuring tools. "How are you so domesticated but you hate anything domestic?"

"I don't hate anything domestic", I correct her, my mind going to Hadley and our new living arrangements. That is by far the most domestic thing I've ever done. "I hate the roles of domesticity. There is a difference." I stir the rice and cover the pan, then turn my back on her to rummage through the box of food. I whirl around and toss the bag of pistachios at her. She screams in shock, missing the bag and spilling some champagne down her shirt. This time I laugh when she glares at me.

"I could tell you that your place is in this kitchen cooking for me after a hard day's work." She rolls her eyes. "I'm serious. Or I could do worse and never tell you that your place is in the kitchen, tending to my every need but just treat you that way instead. Make your life about pleasing me. Act as if women were put on this earth to do as men say. I could fill your spare time with errands to suit my needs and act as though I'm above doing my dishes and cooking my own meals. You'd have no ability to have a life of your own because you're too busy doting on me. I could treat you like you were my mommy." I smirk at the last bit and Grace makes a gagging sound while she gets a dish to pour the nuts into. "The truth is Grace, there are so many beautiful women who are treated like shit while everyone watches, and no one does anything. Because it's been normalized. While I'll never order you to cook for me, I'll order you to suck my cock. There's a big difference. And you know I give as good as I get. So, let me make you rice, and cheese, and popcorn and whatever the hell else I have planned because I love you so very much that if this is the way I get the best head you can offer before the night is over, I will gladly domesticate myself for you."

She slaps me on the arm, and I beam at her. Then I grab her and whirl her around, pinning her between me and the counter. "Grace." Those glacial eyes look up at me while she fiddles with my shirt, unconformable with me zeroing in on her. "I love you." She swallows thickly but doesn't say anything back. She hasn't said those words to any of us in over five years. That's how badly her ex-husband broke her. She is a product of being domesticated.

"Can I pick the movie?" She presses her plump lips together. I'll get nothing more from her today.

"No." She huffs out her displeasure. "I have a plan. And you're ruining it. So stop it. Please pour my drink, go sit down and eat some nuts while you continue to marvel over my prowess in the kitchen. When I have snacks prepared, *I* will select the movie."

Grace is quiet for a few minutes, doing as I have asked.

"You're a good man, Micah." Her declaration is so sincere it's the closest she's ever come to saying the L word to me.

Now it's my turn not to react. I don't feel like a good man. A good man wouldn't have missed that his girl's agreement was a sham just to finally have her. Looking back, all the signs were there. Her reluctance. Her distrust when she ghosted me. The list she made of sexual preferences that could have fit on a post-it. They were all there and then some, screaming at me that I was about to enter into an agreement with a woman who wasn't ready despite the time and space that killed me to give her.

A good man wouldn't have allowed an outsider to lick her cunt when she clearly didn't want it but verbalized consent. The events of the last two days will haunt me forever because

I messed up and it cost the one person I vowed to protect. *My* girl.

"Micah?" Grace sounds concerned and I feel instant regret at mentally leaving her on her date. "You don't have to pretend with me. Linea told me..."

I don't let her finish. "One more word and I will keep your mouth so busy you won't even know what movie we're watching." She opens her mouth to speak once more but when I raise a brow at her in challenge she closes her mouth. "Grace, stay out of it. And if Linea is going to do something that you know she shouldn't, convince her not to."

Grace laughs and shakes her head. "Be serious, Micah. The four of you can't even do that. It's *Linea*." She emphasizes Linea's name and doesn't even have to explain what that means. Linea makes a decision, that is it. She's unmovable, consequences be damned.

"Stay out of it", I warn her one last time, rounding the counter to bring the snacks over for the movie.

Grace takes a seat on her cream-colored leather couch and pulls a throw blanket over her, snuggling into the corner.

I hand her a plate with a little bit of cheese, olives, bread, prosciutto, nuts...all the fixings. If her mouth is full, she won't be tempted to bring up Hadley. She smiles, taking the plate from me and I find her foot under the blanket, pulling it to me to pamper her. She lets out a moan and I laugh, scrolling through the movie channel for what I'm looking for.

Grace and I have been together all these years, and I have yet to just keep her inside and cover her with my love. I think she needs this more than any night out on the town and I'm so glad to give it to her tonight on this nasty, wintry evening.

# Chapter 36
# Hadley

**December 30th 6:46 a.m.**
(Present Day)

"Linea is coming by for a bit this morning." Micah's voice polishes the words to a soft shine as they flow from his lips. I almost choke on my coffee. "I have an errand to run", he tells me, gauging my response.

"Okay." It comes out meek and powerless. I'm not the same woman he entered this relationship with. I'm someone else. Someone I don't think either of us recognize anymore. All of this has exhausted me. The Hadley that had secrets is gone. Every emotion just comes to the surface unlike before when my guard was always up. I wonder if he'll like this version of me better than the one he met at Mav's bar. I'm not sure if I do. Being open is hard sometimes but surrender feels easy when Micah's there. So maybe this is the best version of me.

"I thought perhaps she could bring you that cinnamon roll you should have had months ago. You two could talk. Get to know each other."

I simply nod before I take a sip from the cup.

"I have clothes laid out for you on the bed." He extends his hand for me to take. Cautiously, I place my hand in his and allow him to lead me from the master bath. "You have a few rules to follow while Linea is here." I let out a frustrated huff of air. "Her past is none of your concern. If she volunteers it, you are to stop her and under no circumstances are you to ask about it."

"Okay." I can't really say I'm that interested in Linea. I'm grateful. But interested? Not really. She's my babysitter while Micah is away. I won't be fraternizing with the help.

"You cannot cut the visit short, and you must be on your best behavior." He turns me to face him. "Be. Nice."

I scoff and look away. Micah answers my disrespect by turning my chin to face him. "Hadley?" I close my eyes and nod. I'm in no position to oppose him. Landon and I's date was strained to say the least. I wonder if the plug Micah put in my backside this morning was a punishment. It wouldn't surprise me if it was. I can only imagine what Landon told him about me.

"I'll see you downstairs in ten." He bends to brush his lips over mine and my heart surges. God, I still want him. I want him in the worst fucking way. The lust I have for this man courses through my veins threatening to level me any moment and I have to wonder if someone could die from this feeling. Because it feels like I am. Like I'm starving myself of something so vital to my being that my heart might just stop altogether.

I'm his. He's mine. I'm theirs. But how do I put the pieces back together, so we all don't feel so fractured? I stand there, sipping my coffee, watching the minutes tick by, looking at the perfect outfit set aside for me. It's a cream-colored knit top with matching patterned knit pants. I know he selected this because it's awful outside and it's comfortable because I'm in so much pain. He cares and I love him for it.

When I slip the sweater on it falls around my shoulders. I smile because he supplied me with panties. He normally doesn't do this but since I'm a little wrecked down there right now, he probably knew it would hurt more if I didn't wear them. When I pick up the panties, there's a pendant underneath them. I hold it up to notice initials. His initials. My heart stutters again. God this man...

It's not that he bought me a pendant. It's that he's still staking his claim. After all the damage that's been done, he's looking past it all and still choosing me. I wonder why. I also wonder if I have the strength and blind faith to do the same thing.

Hobbling from our bedroom, I make it to the stairs and hear Micah's deep laugh rumble through the house. It warms my heart even though that laugh isn't because of me. Laughing so loudly isn't something Micah normally does. He's business. Formality. Strict. I know it's Linea who makes him open up like he does, and I want to make him laugh like that someday too.

As soon as I come into view, Micah looks me over and Linea turns her head over her shoulder to see what has caught Micah's attention. I take pride in this. I want his eyes on me. I hear him ask Linea if she knows the rules. She nods and he bends down to kiss her on the lips, breaking the kiss just in time to receive me.

Linea steps aside and tends to the paper grocery bags on the counter and Micah gives me a small smile. I turn away under his stare. It's too much to bear. But he pulls me back to him when he grabs the pendant laying between my breasts. His fingers stroke the gold letters and like a genie rubbing a lamp, my heart swells with emotion.

"Micah", I whisper, desperation and desire clear in the way I say his name.

He says nothing. He simply drops the pendant, bends down and brushes his lips against mine.

I feel like I just got punched in the gut. Linea got a kiss, and I got almost nothing in comparison. But he pauses and the hurt I feel swirls with hope and desire. A mean cocktail of emotions to course through one's veins. He's making a decision. I know this because it feels like time stops for both of us.

"I want what you have with Linea", I whisper to him, the mean cocktail of emotions out on display for him. He doesn't respond immediately, and for a moment I think I need to be specific. But then he takes my lower lip in his mouth and pulls me close to him, so our bodies are flush and kisses me. His kiss feels like a sacred moment. A moment where he's promising his devotion to me and only me and I feel that devotion from the top of my head to the ends of my toes. His promise washes over me and now I feel like I'm promising him too.

When we pull apart, it's clear we both want more and my heart stutters at the thought of having it in front of Linea. I can feel myself stiffen in Micah's arms. Where I once had protection against sex in front of others, as of yesterday this no longer exists.

Micah must feel me stiffen too and his eyes dance with amusement. "We'll get there", is all he says before kissing me one last time and then releasing me from his hold. "Follow the rules", he says loud enough, giving Linea and I one last warning before he leaves the house.

I turn to find Linea organizing ingredients on the counter, thoughtfully batching them and then searching through Micah's kitchen drawers for the tools she needs. When she looks up at me, I smile sheepishly, feeling like I just got caught spying on her even though that was far from the case. She smiles back and I swear, she glows like she came straight from heaven. Maybe it's the blonde hair, blue eyes and fair complexion. Whatever it is, she looks like an angel.

We study each other for a moment. She chews on her lower lip while I toy with the pendant Micah gave me.

Slowly, a smile forms on her lips, and I can't help but smile too.

"I bake when I'm stressed." She motions to the counter full of ingredients. I just nod, finding it hard to imagine what this heavenly creature could be stressed about. "You don't have to help. In fact, I don't want your help." I'm stunned by her directly cutting me out of an activity while we spend time together. When she realizes what she's said, she quickly backpedals to make it right. "I just meant that I need to keep my hands and my mind busy, and I'd appreciate your company. That's all."

"Okay", I tell her, not really hurt by her telling me to sit and watch. It's probably better this way. I haven't completely forgiven her yet even though she saved me. I want to, but it's not that easy for me.

"Join me?" There's hope in her voice and I swear, if she didn't seem like a saint every other time she spoke, she did now. I couldn't refuse her if I wanted to.

She clears a spot at the counter so I can sit without a pile of ingredients in front of me and then gets to work measuring and mixing, while I sit there watching her as though I've never cooked anything myself.

"Thank you." I never thanked her for voting for me to stay. She could have sent me packing and she didn't. I owed her that much at least. Linea simply nods, glancing up to smile at me. I can see she's struggling with something now and don't doubt for one bit that baking does seem to set her free.

"There must be enough ingredients here for a dozen recipes. What are you going to do with all of this when you're done?" There's no way she's going to eat it. She's a tiny little thing like me. And I can't imagine her baking just to throw it all out.

"The guys will love it", she says, even though her words have some sadness at the edges.

"There's no way Braden is going to let you run around out in this weather." She doesn't say anything. "Is he?" Does she really have that much power?

Linea just shrugs her shoulders, adding some baking powder and some salt to the batter, seeming not to know or to care.

"It's because you were first, isn't it. Is that how long I'll have to wait to feel like you look with the guys?" She smiles at my compliment.

"I wasn't always like this", she tells me, grabbing a spoon and scooping up some chocolate chip batter, holding it out to me as a peace offering. It looks delicious so I take the spoon and have a taste. She helps herself to some batter as well and we're silent as we eat.

"How was it then?" I have to know, but it's clear she won't tell me when she shakes her head. "Is that the past that I can't know about? That you can't tell me about?" She nods and it makes me feel a little better that the one woman in our group that has the most rope still has limits. "Then what do we talk about? All this stuff is in the past", I grumble finishing the batter on my spoon.

"How about I ask you things", Linea suggests, grabbing my spoon and scooping out another taste of batter for me. I wrinkle my nose at her not using a clean spoon and she giggles at me. "There's no point in not getting germs in the cookies. Afterall, we all share germs quite regularly", she winks and hands me back a spoon with more cookie dough than the first scoop.

I laugh and take the peace offering, deciding her logic makes sense. We eat in silence for a moment more, and I decide to bite. The worst-case scenario is that I don't want to answer her questions, so I just don't answer them. The best-case scenario is that I get to keep eating cookie dough and make a friend. She seems like someone I'd want on my side in this group so why not give it a shot? Besides, what could she possibly want to know about me that I wouldn't want to share.

"Okay", I concede, and she beams with excitement. I can't help but to smile at her enthusiasm, preparing for the standard questions one gets asked when they're getting to know someone. But I should have known better because nothing in this group is standard. I just wasn't prepared for this question right out of the gate.

"Tell me about your Introduction Night." Elbows leaning on the counter, her eyes sparkle with excitement as she puts her spoon in her mouth and my brain screeches to a halt. She giggles. "Not everything", she qualifies after chewing a bite of cookie dough. "Just the best parts", she smirks, sliding the spoon back in her mouth.

I'm stunned. She takes the spoon from my hand and prepares another taste for me and when I reach for it, she pulls the spoon out of my reach. "Open up", she sweetly orders me with a twinkle in her eye.

I know what she's doing. She's trying to put me under her spell. I turn my head and huff out a breath. This is absolutely unbelievable. It's also the sweetest most intrusive thing someone has asked of me.

"What if I tell you it was Braden? That he was one of the best parts?" I'm trying to goad her into stopping this talk. Surely, she must realize I could share an experience with him that may bother her.

"Open", she orders once more while swirling the spoon around in tight circles to taunt me.

I let out a laugh and hold out my hand palm up for her to put the spoon in, but she shakes her head. I concede and open up for her, playing into her little game. After my taste, I hold my hand out palm up for the spoon she shakes her head. "One. Best. Part."

The thing is, the best part of Introduction Night was not Braden at all. But it's hard to even pinpoint the best part. There were so many parts that I play over and over in my mind, still finding it hard to believe that I was the woman in that room. It was terrifying and amazing...fun.

"I can't." She throws her head back and lets out a frustrated groan. "It's not for that reason. It's just...It was all so...unreal. I mean...who does that? Who does what these men do? And all at the same time. You do realize I had sex with a room full of men that night, don't you? That isn't normal. It was good but even you know that isn't normal."

"I'll tell you mine", she volunteers, and I am dying to know...unless it has to do with Micah.

"I don't think you can tell me that. Can you? Isn't that part of the past?" This is me, being good and sticking to rules.

"That's not the past they're talking about", she tells me, defiance in her eyes. "I would just tell you. I think you should know. I think it would help you. And I promised to help you", she says in response to my question...maybe. But maybe, she's considering breaking the rule and I absolutely cannot break this rule. Oh my god I don't know what Micah would do. And Braden...

"Archer", I tell her, stopping her oral contemplation. She gives me a small smile and I continue. "He...he was my first out of all the guys that night." Her eyebrows raise. "It was so incredible." She's beaming now. "He still is so incredible." She brings the spoon to my mouth once more and I open for her without hesitation this time.

"Archer is so sweet", she croons. "So intimidating with all his tattoos and piercings but the pleasure he gives is pure sin", she says, pushing away from the counter and grabbing some coffee cups for us. "Tell me anything from that night." I still hesitate. This is so weird to talk about. When I don't answer, she glances up at me and offers her thoughts on the matter. "I'd give anything for another first with Archer. All of them, really. You had it the best out of everyone, you know."

I roll my eyes as I stir cream and sugar into my cup.

"I'm serious. You did. Think about how many women have done what you did. I mean, some of the last women and men to join shared a similar experience but you...you got to be in a room of gorgeous men who were there just for you. Just to make you theirs. I cannot imagine how sore you must have been the next morning." Linea chuckles before taking a sip from her cup and looking up at me to confirm. I just nod, feeling the color rush to my cheeks.

"Okay", I concede once more and she's so excited, she comes around to sit next to me on a bar stool, pulling the bowl of dough between us for easier access. "I'll tell you how it started." She nods eagerly and I begin...

Micah is the most casual I've ever seen him when he enters his bedroom. The smile on his face reminds me of one a groom would give to his bride when she appears at the end of the aisle. This is not a wedding. It's far from it.

He strides toward me wearing jeans and a white t-shirt. It's strange to see him like this. I'm used to suits, loosened ties and rolled up starched sleeves. This Micah has come to play. This Micah scares me a little.

He stops in front of me and gets on his knees. Another first. It's so subservient I can't believe the all-powerful Micah is kneeling before *me*. He takes my trembling hands in his and kisses them, his crystalline blue eyes looking up at me for any sign of life. This is it. Tonight is Introduction Night.

"Do you want this?" It's a simple question. One he told me he has to ask because if he doesn't have consent everything stops now.

I nod. "Take me through it again, please." I don't know why I ask. It's not like anything he's shared has helped me put the pieces together. He rises and places my hands around his neck, then leans forward, placing a sweet kiss on my lips.

"I introduce you and then you answer one question, and we take the rest from there." His hands splay on my ribs. His warmth through my satin robe is searing hot. "Do you want this?"

"Yes." I couldn't bear to never feel his touch again and this is the only way I'll be able to have it.

"You give us your consent to touch you?" He must still sense the hesitation I have to losing control and doing something so crazy I can't even believe it's possible.

"Yes." I swallow hard. This is really happening. I try not to panic, but when he leads me from his room, I tug back on his hand. "I'm scared."

He turns to me and considers his response. "You should be." I blanch at his answer. I wasn't expecting it. I was expecting to be coddled. I was expecting to be told that everything was alright but instead I got Micah, uncut. "You'll never see sex, love and relationships the same again. You will question everything you ever knew and measure it against every experience you have with us going forward. Nothing will measure up. The second you walk through that door your life changes."

I thought this was all just sex. I'm young. It would be something new to try. I'd look back on this time and tell my friends or my kids that I was just sowing my wild oats. It's just sex. It's just sex. It's just sex. Quite possibly the safest sex I've ever had too.

So I take a step forward and then another and my life changes the moment I walk through that door.

The chatter silences almost immediately. Men. I'm surrounded by men. And not just any type of men, but tall, muscular, beautiful men. All here for me. I gape at them. They all wear the same type of clothes as Micah. White t-shirt, jeans, nothing on their feet. Now I'm terrified. These aren't just boys. Confidence pours off them. And they're fucking hard. I can see the outline of their erections through their pants. My estimate is there isn't a small one among the group.

My mouth goes dry as I scan the room. High back benches in a circle with numbers in front of them on the floor. The numbers are large circular stickers where I'd estimate their feet would go.

"Do you want this?" Micah asks me again and I know it's for the group. They need to hear it too. I nod, my voice retreating completely. "You'll need to say it aloud for them to hear you".

"Yes", I croak.

"Yes what?" I know Micah's trying to give me my confidence back. But I'm really struggling. When I turn to him, he doesn't encourage me. True to his word, this has to be my decision.

"I...I want this. I want...you", I address the men. The look they wear is serious. All but one. A tattooed man whose eyes light with delight as he looks me over and his smile stretches to reveal beautiful white teeth. That mouth. The devil made that mouth. The things I'm sure he could do with it...

My heart kicks up a bit, but before I have time to reconsider, Micah turns me toward him. When I hear the guys move and look over my shoulder to see what they're doing, he gently guides my face back to him.

"Your safe word is Micah. Don't use it unless you absolutely need it. If you say it, everything stops. It's the end of us, Hadley." I suck in a breath at this tidbit of information. This is serious. "You cannot refuse things that are in your agreement, however, you can ask to stop. Now, what's your safe word?"

"Micah", I breath his name like it's my savior.

"Very good. Once everyone has finished inside you, Braden will be in control. Right now, I'm running this but I'm just doing the math. Each of them is assigned a number. They know the rules. You don't. Don't try to figure them out. It will just distract you from the experience." I nod and he smiles, knowing I'm not going to heed his warning. It's killing me that I don't know the rules and what's coming next. "Pick a number, one through twelve."

My heart beats out of my chest. This is random but in my control.

"Ah, ah, ah...no looking", Micah calls to me when I try to look over my shoulder to see which man is in front of which number.

"Seven." I swallow hard and close my eyes as the guys grumble at my response. Micah disregards the reaction around the room and lays his hand on my cheek, brushing his lips against mine. I grip his wrist, a silent plea not to hand me over to whoever number seven is yet, but he easily releases my hold on him and ushers me around the circle.

The guys had moved the numbers. They knew I'd look. They knew I would pick seven because I could see seven from where I entered the room. Seven was now five. My palms were slick with nerves as I counted two chairs to the right. Tattoo guy.

"Archer, may I introduce to you, to Ms. Hadley Joanna McAfferty."

"Nice to meet you darlin'", he responds, and then holds his hand out to me.

I regard his tattoos for a moment before taking his hand. His eyes smile but his lips do not.

"Up you go", Archer tells me, as he pulls me onto his lap, so I have no choice but to straddle his legs, my knees settling on either side of his muscular thighs. I'm too nervous to sit on his lap uninvited. He looks up at me, settling his palms on my hips.

The moment I look down at him he smiles. "Our only redhead." I bite my lip waiting for the comment every man has ever asked me about the carpet matching the curtains. Jokes on them. There is no carpet. Hasn't been for years. It's hard to find a great aesthetician to do a Brazilian so once you find them, you never let them go.

A flame licks up his skin, from beneath his t-shirt. I trace it with my fingertip, and he waits patiently. I look him in the eyes again and he smiles. When I avert my gaze, he drops a hand from my waist, reaches behind his head and tugs his shirt up and over his head, discarding it onto the floor behind me.

"There. Now you can see the rest of it", he offers as he places his palm back on my hip. I give him a small smile and resume tracing his skin. As I trace his skin, my free hand resting on his shoulder gradually moves to feel the hair behind his head. It's a fresh cut. Probably for the occasion, I muse to myself.

And before I realize what I've done, I'm hovering right over his erection, face tilted to get a look at his body art. He guides my face to his and plants a scratchy stubble-filled kiss on my lips. I tense but he's prepared.

"Your legs are going to get mighty tired kneeling like that", he advises before continuing his kiss.

I feel like a traitor…a slime ball. *Ho. What a ho.* My mind is relentless with this insult as I gradually start to enjoy

Archer's kiss, yet not allowing myself to sit on his lap. I'm naked under this robe and while he's fully covered it's just...it screams HO!

"Ever kiss someone with a tongue ring before?"

I shake my head and kiss him back this time.

"Fuck me, Hadley Joanna. This is going to be so much fun." He looks over my shoulder to who I assume is Micah because no one else is in standing behind us. "Time."

"Three", Micah calls out, and Archer moves me off his lap and onto the man next to him.

"Hey there, Hadley." It's all I get from the man before he passes me over again. *That man was eight. Archer is seven.*

I'm passed around the circle, clockwise to nine. Another sweet greeting. Then to ten. No more contact than steadying me at my hips to move me on, when I finally stop at three. Oh. Fuck.

I swallow hard, taking the man in that I'm now straddling.

"Tyler. Nice to meet you Hadley." Hands that started on my hips gradually move up my sides until his thumbs swipe the underside of my breasts and carefully move me so I'm sitting on his lap. Tyler's erection is unmistakable. I'm almost afraid to look. Maybe later I won't. It'll just happen, and I'll never be the same.

"N-nice to meet you too." I lay my hands on his chest because it's either that or close to his crotch so option A it is.

"I have one expectation of you Hadley, and that's respect. When you answer me, you can use my name or call me sir."

I look up at him in shock. He cocks his head to the side in challenge and I realize I just failed my test.

"Y-yes Siler...Tilus..." I close my eyes. "Sir." His large hands are on my face and his lips meet mine. I open up to him out of fear alone and accept his kiss.

"You're safe", he reassures me as he continues his kiss. And as big as this guy is, I can't help but to believe him. I am safe. If I weren't, he would have handled me differently by now. He takes his time exploring my mouth. I can't help but to feel how ripped this guy is. How does someone get like that?

Right before he ends the kiss, his hands settle on my backside. "Time." He calls over my shoulder.

"Ten", Micah calls and I'm passed around the rest of the circle in the same way, landing on "ten's" lap. Every number called is like this. I don't know how the numbers are calculated, and I stop caring. Because this is nerve wracking. I'm touching people I don't know. I'm letting them kiss me and soon I'll be doing much, much more. But with every lap I sit on, the ritual seems to get easier and easier.

"Seven", Micah calls. I haven't looked back at him once and he seems completely unphased by my intimacy with his friends.

My heart gallops as I land back on Archer's lap, but when I settle in, I note he's no longer wearing pants. The gallop turns into a sprint, but still, he doesn't push me to sit on his lap.

I wrap my arms around his neck, pressing my chest closer to him than I have any of the other guys. Then I lean down and kiss him. I *like* Archer. Not that I don't like the others, but Archer just has this nonchalance about him. I'm more comfortable with him.

He kisses me back and I decide I do like the tongue ring. Maybe I'll like it other places on my body too.

"Micah's so fucking hard right now." I take in a sharp breath, instantly worried that I've done something wrong. "You're fine darlin. This is how it's supposed to be." I don't believe him, and when he realizes it, he invites me to take a look. "Go on. Have a look", he nods behind me.

Archer loosens his hold around me as I turn to look at Micah. In tandem with my turn, he hooks my robe with his finger, releasing my left breast and takes my nipple into his mouth, sucking hard.

I barely get a look at Micah before I'm groaning, closing my eyes to fully experience the divine sensation Archer is creating between my legs. That tongue ring circles my nipple, and I pull his head closer to me, feeling him groan on my sensitive skin.

When I open my eyes, Micah is looking right at me, mouth parted, chest visibly rising and falling. The sight of him is something I've never seen before. His admiration of me is positively breathtaking. This is the literal moment I understand that this is okay. This is more than okay. This is everything to him.

Archer sinks his teeth into me, and I gasp, turning my attention toward him. He covers me up without apology, winks at me and calls *time*.

As I continue to be passed around the circle, they all get to know me in their own way. Some more forward than others, but all of them gentlemen.

It's when I land on Jonathan's lap that I'm taken aback though. I've been passed over him several times but when Micah finally calls "two" I'm guided directly on his lap. There's no option to hover.

"It's a pleasure to meet you, Hadley. I'm Jonathan." I shift on his lap, trying to avoid his erection but it's impossible. "Careful. Wouldn't want to get my pants all wet, would you?" I shake my head in response. "Do you feel like a whore yet, Hadley?" He moves my hair behind my shoulder, his fingertips lightly touching my skin.

"No." Clearly Micah told him about how concerned I was about feeling cheap the day I visited his office to give him my answer.

"Do you want to?" My mouth falls open at his question. He's serious. I don't even know how to answer that. "Be honest. Because if you want, I'll do it for you. I love a good whore." His honesty all but knocks me back. "Grace is my good little whore. Maybe you two will have that in common." He draws his fingertip down the seam of my robe, then runs it over the fabric scraping his fingertip over my hard nipple.

"Not yet", I answer him. He's trying to get a reaction out of me, so I decide I'll do the same to him in kind.

He lets out a laugh. "Well played. But I know a secret. Do you want to hear it?" I nod and he leans in but doesn't whisper. "The shy girls..." He grabs my backside and grinds his erection against me. "The good girls..." He grinds against me once more. "They're so fucking filthy." He pulls me against his crotch once more as he kisses me, and I swear just from the friction alone I'm close to orgasm. I moan against his lips and return the kiss, completely caught up in his spell. This guy knows things about women. That much is clear. And he appears to know things about me.

"Time", Jonathan calls out in a gravelly voice when he abruptly breaks our kiss.

"Seven", Micah calls out and my heart is soaring. I get to return to Archer. So far there's not one I don't like but I have a connection with the devil I was once so afraid of. He's got me in his trap and I'm willing to sin over and over with this guy.

As I move from lap to lap, I notice the guys are in varied stages of dress now. All are shirtless. Most have lost their pants. But one man stands out among the rest. Archer waits for me completely naked. Tattoos cover his body. He's hard, bare and waiting for me. As soon as he looks over to receive me, the devil's smile appears.

I'm straddling him now. Making no move to sit on his lap and he doesn't force me.

"Johnathan", he calls out to his friend that's out of his view. "Did she make a mess on your pants, or should I check", he asks, the dare in his eyes clear as he zeros in on me. This is where shit is about to get real.

"She made a mess", Jonathan volunteers. I breathe a sigh of relief. The flood gates will open when someone touches me there. "See for yourself."

Archer's eyes light up as though he needed Jonathan's permission to be the first to touch me in this intimate way. He doesn't break eye contact as he runs his hand between my legs. His knuckles run up the inside of my thigh and I close my eyes when he's close. As soon as I shut my eyes he stops.

Slowly I open my eyes to the devil himself as his hand smears the slick mess on my inner thighs. He nods his head, shifting eye contact to Micah for a moment. It was so quick, if I wasn't looking, I would have missed it. Then he pulls me to him and kisses me, while stroking me between the legs.

I moan against his lips and kiss him back. His cock slides between my legs transferring my moisture to him and I know this is it. This is my first act of indecency and I'm so ready.

Archer breaks my kiss and unties my robe. Pushing the fabric aside he looks down between our legs. I follow his gaze and throb harder at the sight. I'm soaked. Freshly waxed, my skin is covered in my own slickness. He is also covered in my arousal, but a silver glimmer catches my attention. He's pierced.

Considering we're probably friends now, I reach to feel his piercing but before I can touch him, he grabs my wrist and calls *time* over my shoulder.

"What?" It's the first word I've spoken in a bit, and it earns me a few snickers from the men.

"Eleven", Micah bellows. And around the circle I go. But this time, almost everyone is naked. I straddle them as I'm passed from number to number. All of them are hard. Most of them are leaking precum which ends up being dragged over my stomach, inner thigh and in some cases my pussy as I cross over them. Their hands no longer guide me by my waist but by my rear end. At every opportunity their hands are on my bare skin.

Every number that's called gets dangerously close to committing the most adulterous act of them all, but no one commits. I'm aching with need and about to beg someone to just do it already when number four calls *time*.

"Seven", Micah says, and I make my way around the circle, this time, all naked men, all with leaking cocks and all marking me with their fluids in the most casually obvious of ways.

By the time I get to Archer, my thighs are so slick I can't tell what's from me and what's from them and I don't really care. All I know is that I want him inside me. NOW.

I forget about Micah. I forget about the audience. I forget that I've never had sex with someone wearing a piercing.

It's the most liberated I've felt in my entire life as I swing my leg over his lap and kiss him like I'm in the dessert and he's my only source of water. He shifts me over his hard length, and I guide him to my entrance while I sit down on him.

I feel each piercing as he slides into me and I pull my mouth from his, adjusting to the sensation.

"Someone's eager", he remarks, a small smile playing on his lips. I wipe the smile off his face when I raise up and lower myself back down. He throws his head back and groans, then pushes my robe off my arms letting it fall to the floor.

If he calls time right now, I swear to God I'm going to punch him.

"Please don't." I say it to him in warning as I move up and down on his lap.

"What?" He smiles at me, trying to feign innocence. "You don't want me to say ti.." I slap my hand over his mouth and look over my shoulder at Micah as I continue to ride Archer. Micah is beaming watching me fuck his friend.

Archer bites my hand and I pull it from his mouth. Then he pulls me to him and kisses me as he thrusts into me in a measured rhythm.

"If you don't cum darlin I swear I'll say it. You're so tight. Don't quit on me now", he grits out. I can tell he's holding on by a thread and he wants this just as much as I do. "Come on, darlin. I want another girlfriend, and I want that girl to be you. Let me be the first make your sweet little pussy cum."

I come undone. His sweet and dirty words all mixed together make me unravel. It feels so fucking good. Too fucking good. Archer must think so too because he swells inside me, his arms holding me down on him like a vice as he groans his release into me.

When he's finished, he kisses me so sweetly and for that moment, it's just Archer and me. No one else is in the room. Until he calls *time*.

After everyone has had their fill, the men line the room similarly to how they did when I entered Micah's spare bedroom hours ago. They're no longer naked. When each man was finished with me, he put his clothes on. They were satisfied now. Having no sex for weeks, they got their fill of me as many times as they liked, however they liked, as long as it didn't violate my agreement. The last man to have me was Jonathan. I hadn't done a sixty-nine until him. If I get to ask for something when we're together, I decide I'm definitely asking for that.

I'm kneeling in front of them, my robe nowhere in sight. Micah stands just in front of me but off to the side so as not to obstruct my view of what looks to be a symbolic moment between the men. Braden grabs a small box off an end table and hands it to Micah after shaking his hand.

Micah opens the box, and I see a flash of silver. Micah slides what appears to be a ring onto his finger and hands the box back to Braden. They give each other a brief hug, slapping each other on the back the way guys sometimes do. The hug is longer than I anticipated between the men, and I realize when Micah laughs, Braden was telling him something.

When they release each other, Micah goes down the line and shakes hands with each of the men.

"How do you want her", Braden asks Micah, referring to me.

"How don't I want her", Micah asks his best friend as the guys all laugh at his response. Then Micah zeros in on me and answers Braden's question. "I want her dirty mouth."

My core aches so much hearing him talk like this to me in front of his friends. I also happen to think blowjobs are dirty. Like a girl should never put her mouth *there*.

"Hadley Joanna, will you let me fuck your dirty little mouth?" I'm nodding without realizing it and Micah wastes no time stepping up to me, issuing orders.

Just like the first time, he had me take him out and kiss the tip. The only thing I could hear in the room was us. It was so quiet, if I couldn't see the men in my periphery, I'd think we were alone.

Micah winds my hair around his fist tight this time and gives my hair a little tug. "Suck", he orders me and as I take him in my mouth, I roll my eyes to look up at him. The guys must like my style because a few of them make sounds of appreciation in the background.

My heart skips a beat at how excited they are at my sexual prowess, but my internal celebration is short lived as Micah slides to the back of my throat, gagging me. He holds me there for a few seconds and then allows me to pull back, winking at me as he gives me a moment to catch my bearings before going in deep once more.

"You have made me so proud tonight, Hadley Joanna", he croons to me as he wipes a tear sliding down my cheek. "Tell me something…who do you belong to, sweetheart?"

He slides out of my mouth all the way so I can answer him as he likes.

"I'm yours, Micah. I'll always be yours", I vow to him.

Micah releases my hair and runs his fingertips down my jaw. "Do you want to taste it?" I nod. "Then show me how you take care of the man who owns you."

Without any more prompting I lean forward and take him in my mouth. It's the only invitation I need because I am hungry for him. I'm determined to milk him on my own. It feels like my gift to him for taking such good care of me from the moment we met. And I'm honored to do it.

Here I am, a woman who couldn't stand the thought of sucking on a cock, kneeling before a man taking the greatest pleasure in it. It feels so right. So natural for me to be on my knees with my mouth full of him.

When I glance up at him for encouragement, he runs his fingertips along my jaw. Such a nice gesture that he seems to make filthy beyond belief.

"That's it. You're almost there. Look at you. So perfect on your knees for me. Do you like my cock in your mouth? Oh, it looks like you do."

I take him deeper and suck a little harder. And without warning, his hands hold my face still as he slides into my mouth to his liking and unloads inside of me. The guys make sounds of their appreciation once more as Micah finishes pulsing into my mouth. I swallow everything he gives me, looking up at him to see the expression of pure and utter pleasure on his face.

I suck and lick on him as I wait for him to tell me I'm done. He takes his time, stroking my cheek as I catch drop after drop of his aftershocks.

When he's satisfied, he extends his hand to me and helps me up. Out of nowhere, Braden is slipping my purple satin robe over my shoulders and Micah is tying it shut.

Holding my hand, Micah leads me around the room, and I kiss each of my new boyfriends briefly before they leave for the evening. Then I follow Micah to his bedroom to finish what we started.

The next morning, a knock on Micah's bedroom door wakes me. The room is still dark because Micah has the best curtains that money can buy. I'm sore and tired and my mouth is so dry my voice resists me.

"Hadley, it's me, Braden. You awake? Can I come in?"

I let out a heavy sigh and try to call out to him, but my words only come out as a whisper. Thankfully, Braden opens the door and peeks through the crack. I shield my eyes with the back of my hand as his warm voice fills the bedroom.

"Good morning, Sweet Hadley", he croons to me. I flop back down into bed, and he laughs. It's a laugh of a family man. Filled with love and gratitude. The kind of laugh that makes your heart melt when you hear it.

I crack open my eyes and roll my head towards the sound of some things being set on the nightstand. Light floods the room as Braden opens the curtains and I roll over, partially exposed to him, to burry my face in a pillow.

"Micah mentioned you aren't a morning person", he observes. His heavy steps cross the room and the bed dips slightly. "But I need a few minutes of your time because I'm in and out of here this morning. I have rounds at the hospital, so my visits are always going to be pretty early I'm afraid."

I say my response into the pillow, and it earns me another laugh from him.

"Now look here. I've brought you a few things. I need you to take these pills." He smiles when I turn my head, so my face is no longer buried. "These…", he palms two white pills, "are an antibiotic. You had a lot of action down there last night so it's better to take these to get rid of any unwanted bacteria that's collected so you don't get an infection. Just a preventative." He holds his hand out to me along with a glass of water. I sit up, taking the pills after pulling the covers up to my chest to be decent with him.

The water feels good on my throat. We'd had champagne to celebrate after everyone had finished inside me. It wasn't much but I also didn't have much water last night. It was literally an evening of sex and in order for that to go well, I couldn't exactly be running off to the bathroom every half hour.

I'm about halfway done with the glass when Braden hands me two other pills. "These you'll take daily. Just a preventative as well. They aren't antibiotics but are good for keeping the good bacteria and getting rid of nasty stuff." I take these without question because I trust Braden. He's a good man. A decent man. A man with morals.

"How are you feeling?"

"Sore. My muscles ache." I've never had good sex. Not like I did last night. I came so many times it felt like my bones were liquified. And the strain on my body from the various positions I held is more than apparent this morning.

"If it gets too bad just take some ibuprofen. Micah has some in his medicine cabinet, I'm sure. I'd like to take a look at you if you'll allow it."

I'm surprised by this. "Doesn't Micah need to be here for you to do that", I gently push back at him.

"Not all the time. We talked in advance about his schedule today and he decided he'd rather have you tended to promptly than to wait till later today. I just want to make sure you're okay. C'mon. It'll be quick." Braden stands and walks to the end of the bed, waving me to come down with him.

"Are you even supposed to be in here", I ask him as I scoot to the end of the bed, taking the sheet with me to stay covered.

"Look at you. You're a rule follower, aren't you?" The way he says it surprises me. Like he dislikes rules. Shocking for a doctor in my opinion.

"I am a rule follower", I confirm, sitting in front of him.

"Now when I tell you I'm going to check you, I want you to lie back and open your legs for me. I don't want to have to ask you every time." He says it in this way that is part playful and part chastising. Like he's calling me out on delaying the inevitable but he's being gentle about it to be tactful.

"Okay", I agree, laying back but remaining covered.

Braden shakes his head when I open my legs, his view unobstructed by the sheet. He lifts the sheet up to find me messy between the legs. "Fuckin Micah", he breaths, frustration in his voice. "Let's clean you up. One second." He holds his index finger up to signal I should remain in this position and returns shortly with a wet washcloth.

When he cleans me, he's gentle. I'd expect nothing less from him. Clean to his satisfaction, he sets the washcloth down on the floor and inspects me. "You're a little swollen but that's to be expected. Hadley, I'm going to take a closer look", he tells me, and then I see his head dip down. His face is no longer visible to me. Just his thick blonde hair. "Just a little closer", his words muffle and then his lips are on me.

I let out a breath, instinctively pulling the sheets up a little higher for us and then I remember that Braden is really breaking a rule now. "You can't do that in here", I pant while he plants kisses along my slit.

"I know. I'm breaking a rule." He plants a few more kisses on me, purposely not landing on the bullseye. "Micah's my best friend. He'll forgive me." And then his tongue finds that spot and I arch into him.

"Fuck the rules", I breathe out, gripping the sheets instead of his hair because I know he needs to look presentable this morning.

He moans as he licks me and flashbacks of being with him last night float through my head. We shared a bed in front of everyone. He made love to me like a husband would make love to his new wife. At least that's how I think it would go. It was slow and thoughtful and loving. All the things you'd see in a romance movie. But later that night, he had me get on all fours while he fucked me from behind and I sucked Mav's cock.

Braden is sweet and filthy and he's licking my pussy in Micah's bed. The thought of how wrong that is pushes me over the edge and I'm coming so hard, nudging myself against his face to feel more. Braden ends his kiss with a gentle peck over my clit and then looks at me over the bunched-up sheets around my waist.

"Tell me another rule, Hadley. What happens now?"

"Pleasure is always reciprocated. It's given in kind."

"Good girl. On your knees, Sweet Hadley." I shiver at the thought of sucking on him. Sucking a cock has always felt like such a lewd act to me. Just thinking about how dirty it seems makes me wet.

I'm on my knees in no time, hands folded in my lap, looking down, waiting for my invitation to begin.

"You're so perfect, Hadley. The moment I saw you I knew Micah was right about you. Scared but such a good girl. All you want is to please and to be pleased, don't you."

I nod in response, not sure if he was looking for a real answer.

"Do you like sucking cock?" I nod again. "Do you like sucking *my* cock?"

"Yes, Braden."

"Ask me nicely, Sweet Hadley. Ask me nicely to have me in your mouth."

"Braden, can I please have it?"

"Have what?"

"You're cock."

"Where, Hadley? Where do you want it?"

"In my mouth. Can I please taste you on my tongue." He doesn't answer me. It's so quiet in this room you could hear a pin drop if the floors were hard wood. "I need it", I add for good measure, because at this point, I do need it.

"Take it out", he tells me with a strain in his voice.

"You're not my doctor right now, are you", I ask, looking up at him from my spot on the floor while slowly tugging down his zipper.

"No ma'am. I most certainly am not your doctor right now. I'm your boyfriend who wants his cocked sucked so he can go off to work with a smile on his face. Go ahead and kiss it. Thank it for what it's about to give to you."

Those words...so innocent yet so dirty. I comply immediately, puckering my lips to gently kiss the tip of him. He leaks a little onto my lips, but Braden doesn't allow me to lick it off. I can't go further than kissing the tip until he allows it. So, I sit here and gently kiss him over and over, my lips gradually becoming slick with his arousal until he says otherwise.

"Look up here, Sweet Hadley." I do as he asks, and he snaps a picture of me. "Oh, shit, sweetheart. Look at those wet lips. What is that, huh? Would you like that in your mouth? I bet it tastes fantastic", he croons to me as I nod my head. "Ask me real, real nice one more time."

"Braden", I swallow, "Can I have you in my mouth now?" He looks me over, then tosses his phone on the bed and brings his hand up to my cheek.

"Suck me dry, Hadley." I slide him into my mouth as he groans. "Oh, sweetheart someone is greedy."

I am greedy. My goal is to see how quickly I can get him to blow. He's leaking in my mouth and I'm aching between my legs.

I take him out for a moment and stroke him, catching some precum that leaks down his shaft with my tongue.

"Oh no you don't. You asked for it in your mouth, sweetheart. Open up." I comply and Braden slides back as far as my throat allows him before I gag, fucking my mouth for a moment before allowing me to take back over. "C'mon Hadley. Make me proud."

I set off to do just that. My pace is relentless and in a matter of seconds I can feel his balls tightening.

"Fuck me, Sweet Hadley. I'm going come." Then his hands come to my face, securing me where he wants me as he thrusts into my mouth, and I try my very hardest to swallow what he gives me. I don't succeed. Some has dripped from the corners of my mouth onto Micah's sheets, but I can't pay attention to that right now. I'm not finished. Not until he says I am.

I suck and suck as he strokes my hair and my cheek. "So beautiful with my cock in your mouth. I think I'm going to come by later for more. Would you like to suck my cock later, sweetheart?" I moan and look up at him, unable to answer yet. "Good. Is it nice and clean?"

That's an expectation. Many times, when Micah fucks me, he has me suck my own juices from him and ends up coming in my mouth. It's so dirty and I love it.

After deciding I've met my obligation, Braden taps me under the chin, his signal for me to stop. I slide him from my mouth and use the sheet to wipe the excess off my chin while Braden tucks himself back in and straightens himself up so he can leave.

"I put my number in your cell. Micah left it on the counter last night."

Oh yeah. That happens today. Each of the guys stop over to see me and put their number in my phone. I was official last night but no one was stopping sex to exchange numbers. They'd stop in at various points in the day to do it while Micah was out.

I should be nervous about being alone with them but I'm not. Not after last night. Micah was right. What I had imagined about Introduction Night couldn't have been further from reality. They weren't using me. They were worshiping me. And I worshipped them in return.

# Chapter 37
# Micah

**December 30th 3:30 p.m.**
(Present Day)

"I only told Hadley about how I lost my virginity to you", Linea says to me as she looks up at me like an angel.

I shake my head. "Nice try." She's trying to trick me into telling her who was the first of us to take her cherry. When we told her she'd never know, we meant it and that's exactly how it will remain.

I get an eye roll and a heavy sigh in response. "What else did you talk about?" I glance at Hadley, assessing her guilt. If anyone can blur a line, it's Linea. If anyone can cross a line, it's Hadley. It was a risk putting them together but one I needed to take while I went to visit Tyler and Braden.

"We didn't talk about what happened after I lost my virginity to Jonathan", she answers, trying again with a smirk playing on her lips.

"Okay." I answer, ignoring her second attempt at figuring it out. But I'm not entirely sure I believe her, so I turn to Hadley. She appears to have nothing to hide but then again, she appeared that way when she lied about her agreement.

I step over to the counter to survey Linea's stress baking. She does this from time to time. Ever since we've known her, she bakes for an army when she's stressed out. Today she has baked for World War III.

"We were thinking we could run around and drop some off for the guys", Hadley explains, interrupting the deafening silence. I swipe a cookie. Peanut butter. She's cute if she thinks I'm letting them go out in this mess alone I think, as I take a bite without answering her.

"Get your coats on ladies. We're going to deliver some cookies." Linea is beaming. Hadley looks hesitant. So I walk over to her and hold the cookie up for her to take a bite. I watch her as she chews and then something inside of me snaps. I'm not sure if it's watching her mouth, knowing what that mouth can do or the mere fact that I've been deprived of her for the last two days. But suddenly, I've zeroed in on her like a wild cat about to attack prey.

"Do you know", I ask, my lips so close to hers you probably couldn't slide a piece of paper between them. She answers that she does not. "Such a good girl", I whisper before slamming my mouth down onto hers.

Hadley kisses me with the same starved hunger, and I can tell her emotions are no different than mine. She's trying to get a hold of them. She's upset and vulnerable and in love. All those feelings mix together to form such an unstable and powerful cocktail. I want her so badly and I'm prepared to take her right in front of Linea, except that I can't. I can't because she's off limits and I'm quickly reminded of how I failed her.

As if Hadley could hear my thoughts, she runs her fingers through my hair, scratching with her fingernails to bring my attention back to her. But I need a second to come up for air. I need a second to look at the woman I failed and to regroup.

Pulling back from her, she looks like she's in pain and I want to fix it. Fuck. I want to fix it so badly, but I don't know how.

"I gave up everything for you", she whispers to me, fresh tears brimming in her eyes.

This is where we disagree. I shake my head and see anger flicker in her eyes.

"You gave everything to me. You didn't *give up* everything. Instead, you gave so you could have what you're owed. What you've been too afraid to take from this life. And we're going to stand by your side while you take it. So, what do you want? Right now, Hadley. What do you want?"

"I want you to take this plug out. I've been punished enough for last night." I laugh.

"You think this is your punishment?" I shakes my head. "We haven't even begun to address your disrespect last night during your date with Landon."

She pales at my words.

"You won't get a choice today, I'm afraid. This is a second set of direct orders you disobeyed. There are consequences. And trust me when I say, you'll thank me for that plug later."

"Micah..." Linea starts but I stop her with a glare, and she quiets. I give her a lot of latitude but how I serve up punishment is not where I will allow her freedoms.

"Let's deliver some cookies, shall we?"

It takes us hours to deliver these cookies in the blustery weather, but we managed just fine. Tyler and Johnathan both understood the undertone of these delightful treats. Linea was spiraling. It's what she does. She did it after her first kiss with Braden and she's done it ever since when she's genuinely upset.

I'm sitting across the kitchen table from her at Braden's, watching her rotate a steaming mug of hot chocolate in front of her. The only sound is the porcelain scraping against the table with every rotation.

"We delivered a lot of cookies today, Linea. What's going on?

"Can't a lady just want to bake?" She drops a few more mini marshmallows into the mug, then systematically dunks them with her spoon, concentrating intently on the marshmallows to avoid looking at me.

"Yes. A lady can just want to bake...but not if that lady happens to be you. Now out with it."

Linea doesn't answer me at first. Whatever this is, it must be big. Linea has confided in me at the absolute worst point in her life. And she loves so hard sometimes I wonder if the way she loves will be her demise.

"Linea." I use my stern lawyer voice. The voice that says I need you to tell me because I've got you and not talking is not an option right now.

"This isn't enough. This was never going to be enough", she tells the marshmallows, instead of answering me.

I don't have to get clarification to know what she's talking about. She's talking about what we arranged with Hadley this morning. It chars my insides. She's not wrong. This wasn't enough. I'm failing her all over again. How can someone like me be so calculated with everything I do but fall short with the one person that matters most?

"I need to *talk* to her, Micah."

I can't say anything. Braden's word is final where Linea is concerned. Even voicing my agreement with Linea is out of line. It's pitting brothers against each other.

"What if I just did it? Maybe I'll just call her and say all the things", she rants.

I let out a heavy breath and she turns my way. *Fuck!* I wish she would have kept that to herself. I'm not their lawyer. I'm not their confessional. Everything they do and say goes right back to their owner. They get no privilege, and they most certainly do not get confidentiality.

I'm so angry with Linea for being defiant I almost haul her over my lap. I consider a tongue lashing, but I'd have no right. It's also something we just don't do. But God do I want to. I want to tell her how epically stupid it was for her to say that out loud. That she knows better. That she's sealed her fate now and there is not a thing that she can do to change it. She'll never get a chance to have that conversation with Hadley and that screws both of us. And then I realize that Linea would never do something to screw me over. Never.

"Linea?" My voice is cold and commanding. Even I can hear the danger in my timbre.

"Yes, Micah", her voice so angelic. So compliant.

She finally makes eye contact with me, looking as serene as the day I met her. Like a halo hovers above her head. Most would only see the halo. I, however, can also see the horns holding said halo up.

"What are you up to", I press her.

She fakes a stunned look and then brings her palm to her chest as though she's been wounded.

"Up to? Me?" She looks ahead. "Would you like some cocoa", she asks, her voice so sugary sweet anyone who didn't know her would know she's laying it on thick.

"Be good. Linea, I'm not asking."

"Yes, Micah", she concedes in words only as Braden and Hadley join us in the kitchen.

It takes all the strength I have in me not to lose my shit. I can already feel her bending the rules. Like she has sonar and she's sending out signals to the others, even though I know that's not true. But she is well connected. She is friends with all the women. Has access to communicate freely with them. She's got the longest leash and right now, and she feels compelled to help Hadley because ultimately, it's helping me.

I don't bother schooling my features when Braden walks in. I have to tell him anyway and I don't want Braden thinking I'm on her side. I have caused enough animosity and Braden and I's friendship is strained as it is.

"What's goin' on out here?" Braden stands next to Linea, looking down at her like a father would eye a petulant child.

"How's Hadley", I redirect the conversation. There's no way we're discussing this in front of the ladies.

"Out of order." I scowl at Braden, and he laughs. "She'll be set by New Year's Day." My mouth falls open and Braden laughs harder.

"Are you fucking with me?" He shakes his head.

"No sir, I am not fucking with you. In fact, I'd say she needs an ice pack and some rest." He emphasizes the word rest, and I know he's referring to the plug.

"Do you need rest, Hadley?" I arch a brow at her and wait for her answer. She's caught in the middle. I'm doing this on purpose to see who's side she takes.

"I think you should follow the rules. What would you do in this situation if you weren't mad at me? I mean, I can't imagine you would leave this choice up to me, now, would you?"

Linea sucks in a breath in surprise and when I turn to look at her, she tries to look like she isn't beaming but I already saw her smile. She may as well stand up and cheer for Hadley at this point.

"Linea", Braden warns, his stern, father-like voice cutting through the room.

"We're going to head out. Hadley, I need a word with Braden."

"Oh, let me give you a tour of the house", Linea volunteers cheerfully, but I won't allow it.

"No. She'll have a tour another time. I'll get you into the car and then I'm coming back in to have a word with Braden." This time, it's Braden's turn to object.

"I'll follow you two out. Linea, go get ready for your date with Tyler." When Linea rolls her eyes, Braden tells her to put her collar on. Worry flashes across Linea's face. Braden isn't fucking around today. Linea's antics are stressing him out. Tyler having her for the evening is going to be good for her, I hope.

Linea rises from her seat at the table and comes over to plant a kiss on my cheek. I won't have it, even though I'm frustrated with her. I feel the need to love on this woman even though she pushes me to the limit of my patience sometimes. I pull her close and scratch my stubble along her neck. She shrieks and tries to push away but I won't allow it. And then I kiss her. I know Hadley is watching and I know it stings but I love Linea. With every fiber of my being, I do love her. It's almost like our souls just knew we'd be together. That we'd love each other.

I look over my shoulder at Braden for permission to fuck his girlfriend, but he shakes his head. "She's got a date to get ready for and Tyler asked for her clean." He wants no sign of another man on her.

Heaving a heavy sigh, I tell her that I love her.

"I love you", she tells me, grinning like a lovesick fool.

"Go. Get ready", I tell her knowing that if she's even a minute late for her date with Tyler he will punish his little sub for it. I think Linea enjoys it most of the time, although none of us are really sure.

I watch as Linea gracefully exits the kitchen, already missing her. I'd love to have an evening with Linea and Hadley, but I'm not sure Hadley would behave.

At the moment, Hadley looks tortured. She witnessed a very intimate moment between Linea and I and I know Hadley is feeling vulnerable and angry.

"Let's get your coat on you and get you some rest", I tell Hadley, feeling the full force of her hurt feelings rolling off her.

"Yes, Micah", she answers, defeat laced in her voice.

I nod to Braden, and she turns to him to say goodbye. No words are exchanged. Braden kisses her on the lips, then palms her face with his large hands and kisses her forehead like a blessing of sorts.

Once Hadley is in the car, I pop the trunk and grab three large bags of cookies out. "Tell me she didn't", he hedges, glaring at the bag of cookies as if the cookies alone made Linea disobey Braden's direct orders.

"She didn't. But she says she's going to." Braden is already shaking his head as I push the bags into his arms. "I know. I know..." I start as I put my hands up, palms facing out as though I'm defending myself.

"I can't let that happen", he reiterates with conviction while snow swirls around us.

I understand why he feels the way he does. He almost institutionalized her. He still blames himself for what happened to her. And he certainly still looks at Linea as though she's fragile.

"How are you going to stop it", I challenge. "You may never know."

Or I may have a kitchen full of peanut butter chocolate chip cookies", referring to the bags in his arms.

"She's considering disobeying you to help me. She thinks Hadley needs to hear her story. To understand that she doesn't have it nearly as bad as she could. To understand that right now, she's been given a gift even though she's scared shitless about it."

"Well, I'm going to remind her that I pull the strings. So if she wants to wait a helluva long time to see you again, or even Grace, she'll do as she's told."

We both know this won't be logic to her. Linea will gladly sacrifice her time with me if it means Hadley gets to stay and assimilates into the group. The only way for Linea to concede to Braden's demand is if she thinks Hadley is coming around. And the only way for Hadley to come around is to rewrite her narrative. Grace is another story entirely. Linea will bide her time.

"Braden? What do you think about recreating the memory of the other day? We make some slight adjustments. Maybe since we're all together on New Year's Eve, we have drinks at my place before heading out to the Lux?"

"As long as Hadley and Linea aren't alone unsupervised, I don't care. Send out the message. Let us know what we need to do", he agrees with a shiver.

Braden sounds exhausted. Linea has about worn him out. I almost feel for her later. Braden is going to set her straight one way or another and I know he's going to clip those big wings of hers. He won't risk her sanity again even if she wants to test the waters in a well-meaning way.

# Chapter 38
# Hadley

**December 30th 5:15 p.m.**
(Present Day)

"Don't you want to hear my side of the story", I ask Micah when we back down the driveway, leaving Braden's place.

"I do." His voice is solemn, but he doesn't prompt me.

"May I tell it?" The question comes out strained. This feels like he's checking a box. Like he really doesn't care what happened from my point of view.

"You may. But might I suggest another time when I'm not so distracted and you've let a little time pass? Like tomorrow?"

"I want you to know that I feel disrespected by Landon and that is the reason I behaved the way I did. So, no. I do not want to wait. If I wait, you could punish me before then." He nods, seeming to accept my explanation, so I begin.

"First, he ordered me to him like I was a dog. He told me to *come*. You were there for that. Then when we got inside, he showed me to a room where had my clothes ready for me. They were absolutely unacceptable given how he'd treated me when you all were voting. He was horrible to me and yet he wanted me to put on this outfit that showed my body off for his pleasure. No way. After he berated me the only way I was putting that outfit on was if I got an apology. I told him as much and he laughed at me. He fucking laughed, Micah!"

"But you did put it on, as I understand it", he prompts me, with a small smile.

"Of course I did. Because he told me that you gave him no limits. How could you? No limits to the guy who openly berated me in front of the people I love?" I'm pissed. I really wanted the answer to this. Why on God's green earth did he think this was okay? But per usual, Micah doesn't answer questions about his decisions. None of these men do. And it makes me even angrier.

"I trusted you", I seethe with clenched teeth, trying not to explode on him during the car ride.

"No. You didn't. If you trusted me, Landon telling you that I gave him no limits wouldn't have gotten the reaction from you that it did. Landon used your distrust to get you to comply. Consider it a kindness, Hadley."

"A kindness? Are you serious right now?" I think I must be hearing things. There's no way he can actually think manipulating someone is kind.

"I am. The alternative was for Landon to call me, tell me that you were not behaving within the rules and to ask for yet another vote about your behavior. He was doing you a kindness."

I'm stunned into silence because I wasn't aware that could really happen.

"You see, Hadley, when we started this brotherhood, every rule was built around preserving each person for exactly who they are. The rules also give the men control because women, in general, overthink a lot of things.

Love…sex…fun…they aren't complicated. That's why when we tell you to do something we expect that it be done. Because we're doing it for you, not to you. You don't get a choice. The expectation is that you let go and trust that what we have planned will not violate your agreement, be disrespectful or abusive in any way. And I can understand why you would be concerned. I understand why you may be hesitant to trust my judgement after what happened with the implant. Even the judgement of those you named seem reasonable to question. But flat-out refusal is unacceptable and will not be tolerated."

I sit there, stunned silent. Landon did me a kindness?

"Hadley?"

"Yes, Micah." I don't even recognize my own voice, because my mind is reeling about how close I came to being out once again.

"Landon, for one reason or another still wants you here. You have to want it just as much, if not more. I'll ask you again. Do you want it, Hadley? Do you want this life?"

My heart cracks wide open. The answer is that I do. I very much want this life, but it terrifies the hell out of me. Giving up control and surrendering myself to not just one but many men? It's almost unheard of.

Being with these men feels so good. But it's the part in between that hurts. When I go off to work and my coworkers want to talk about dating, I can't. I mean, I can. I haven't been asked to keep what I do a secret but if I do talk about it, I'll be branded a whore.

I feel like such a fraud, sitting at my parent's dinner table next to my little sisters, all the while looking at my parents like their commitment to each other, a commitment I once fanaticized about, no longer makes me swoon.

I know I stand out from the norm because I don't follow the dating customs of the masses. My choices are to hide or be scrutinized. Neither have been fun, especially in comparison to being with these men.

The one thing I know for sure is that going back to the men who treat me as though I'm a dime a dozen is not an option. I'm better than that. Even if it means my choices are scrutiny or hiding, I'd rather lurk in the shadows and have happiness during pockets of the day than be miserable and follow society's rules all day.

"I do", I answer Micah, trying so hard not to break down in front of him.

"Hadley?" He sounds like a God when he says my name. His voice cuts through the sound of the snow under his tires and commands attention above all else.

"Yes, Micah?" I hold my breath to keep from crying. This is almost too much to bear.

"Let go. Just like you unleashed on Landon last night, let it go. I don't want you holding back with any of us anymore", Micah gently commands. And with his utmost sincere permission, I let one tear fall and then the next as we ride through the streets toward home.

# Chapter 39
# Hadley

**December 31st 7:47 a.m.**
(Present Day)

The next morning, I feel the bed dip with Micah's weight, and I'm torn between reliving yesterday in my dreams or opening my eyes to today. As it turns out, Micah's order to let it out was cathartic and we spent the rest of the day doing things that couples did. We didn't get home until late. Micah decided to stop complaining about the weather and instead, he surrendered too.

Thankfully, a store nearby had adequate winter gear in our sizes and in no time at all, we were set to walk around the town in this never-ending blizzard hand in hand. The fresh air did us both good and for the first time since that night votes were cast for my future in this group, I felt good. Like I could put all that behind me...until I opened my eyes to see Landon perched on the bed looking thoughtfully down at me.

I suck in a breath of air, shocked to see him in Micah's place. Grabbing at the sheets to cover myself I tell Landon how he's not supposed to be in here. This is a brotherhood rule. Bedrooms are sacred space.

"Micah sent me to get you." Landon licks his lips and waits for me to push back, but I don't. I've lost the fight. And I can't be mad at him for his kindness shrouded in threats. Not after what Micah told me.

"You owe me an apology, Hadley." I simply nod, not knowing where to start. "But first, let me give you mine."

Now I'm wondering if this is one of those dreams where you think you wake up but instead you just flip to a different scene in your mind. This cannot be real.

"Your lies hurt me to the core. When Micah explained your betrayal, it filled me with rage. I interpreted your actions as being too good for our kind. Someone that came to us who wanted to get off but never truly belonging to us. I gave my heart to you. Planned dates with meticulous care. I gave you everything because I assumed I was getting everything in return. And I wasn't. I felt duped. Made a fool."

This does not feel like an apology. It feels like justification, and it takes every fiber of my being not to yell for Micah like a crazy person or tell him to get the fuck out. But then he takes my hand, and my perception tilts a bit. Like this contact from him radiates love and generosity throughout my body and into my mind without him having to say words to make it so.

"I was wrong to hurt you and do it so publicly. And I'm truly, truly sorry." The sincerity in his big brown eyes makes my heart stop. "Sometimes, you need time to put things into perspective. And after that night and a few tumblers of scotch, I realized you were going to have to put your money where your mouth was. You had no idea that next day you'd be hurt, spread open before us and have your pussy licked by a stranger." I shiver at the memory. "And then you had your date with me. I know you wanted to cancel. When Micah handed you off to me, I could see the fear in your eyes. But considering, you did good."

I laugh openly at this. I'm getting punished for that date and Landon of all people made a decision to save my ass.

"I'm serious. I was going to tell you, but then I thought, if I don't tell her, I wonder if she'll show me the real Hadley. That's why I threatened you. Held your agreement over your head. Your behavior was out of anger and fear. I just wanted to see what you would do and when you were stubborn, angry and defiant I was satisfied. Because I was getting the real Hadley which is all I ever wanted in the first place. I forgive you and I hope you can forgive me too."

I nod, still unsure of why he's in here. We have nothing scheduled today. In fact, today is my lazy day with Micah until New Year's Eve tomorrow.

"You came out here so early to apologize", I hedge, wondering if he'll tell me what's really going on.

"No. Since Landon saved your ass, now he gets a piece of it", Micah answers from the door. "On your feet, Hadley. Let's go."

# Micah

Hadley cries out when I slide a finger in her ass. She instinctively tries to move away and it's just one finger. One finger strangled by the pucker of that pink knot on her backside.

"Gather her hair for me", I order Landon as he watches eagerly. This is a moment the others will not likely get. Hadley has so much anxiety about having her ass played with there is no way she'll be aroused. Considering her misstep, this is, in my opinion, a suitable punishment.

Landon does a fine job of gathering her hair and twisting it into a tight rope. "Thank you, sir", I tell him, as I take the rope of hair from him, wind it around my fist and pull back so Hadley's back is almost flush with my chest. I kiss down her neck as I slowly pump my finger inside her.

"Why don't you test a toy on her?" Landon eagerly grabs the lube while he looks over the assortment of vibrators I purchased for Hadley. "Do you know that I can feel your cunt cum through your ass?" She tries to shake her head, but my hold is so tight she cannot. "Speak when I address you", I remind her.

"No, Micah", she grits out, trying to adjust to my finger.

"I want to feel it so very badly, Hadley. Do you want that for me, too", I ask as I kiss her neck. "Landon is going to help you, sweetheart. He's going to help your needy little cunt come over and over again before he gets his turn." She startles when she hears the cap from the lube open. "Relax, sweetheart. You're not going anywhere. It's just us. You have my permission to cum as much as you need. You have my permission to like all of this." I sink my teeth into her shoulder, and she gasps while Landon reaches between her legs.

"Landon is going to make sure you come on my cock and I'm going to do him the same kindness. And then, I think you will have appropriately apologized for your behavior during your date with Landon."

Landon clicks on the vibrator and Hadley stiffens again. "I'll let you know, Micah", he answers with a smirk, brushing the toy against Hadley's pussy. Landon is the youngest of us all. He's such a smart mouth little shit, but the brotherhood suits him quite nicely. It tempers him.

"Ah", she breathes, trying to fuck the toy. Between me holding her hair and the finger in her ass, she's powerless to move.

"Let Landon do it", I chastise her. "Who gives you pleasure? Hm? Who allows your little cunt to cum?"

"You do. Oh my God, Micah."

"Where's Landon's praise. He's doing the real work."

"Thank you", she breaths. "Thank you, Landon. Oh, please", she begs, and I can't help but to smile. The woman so terrified of Landon is about to go off like a bomb with his help.

Hadley is on full display for Landon, and he admires her accordingly. Her alabaster skin is perfect against her pink nipples. I often spend time just running my fingertips all over her body and just looking at her. Every part of her is so beautiful. And when I say every part, I do in fact mean every part. Even her feet are these tiny perfect little things directly proportioned to her. She's like a redheaded doll, except she's not a doll at all.

She's a woman who needs a moment to fucking breath. A woman who desperately needs to create her own expectations outside of society's norms. A woman who should be encouraged to blossom and grow into whatever wildflower God intended her to become.

"Do you see how Landon looks at you? Like you belong to him?" I tighten my grip on her hair and pull her head back when she doesn't answer.

"Yes Micah", she answers me tightly.

"Not quick enough I'm afraid." I pull my finger from her ass and extend two out to Landon to put lube on. Hadley struggles when she realizes she's getting more back there. "You do realize you're getting my cock back there, right?"

"No." It's her plea to stop but I don't listen. She doesn't get a say anymore. She lied. Now the prototype is being honest on her behalf. We'll know just how much she loves or hates having her backside played with and I can't wait to find out what the answer is.

I messily spread the lube around my fingers as best I can with one hand in front of her. I know she's trying not to panic. Landon looks at her with concern, but I pay no mind to it, pushing her body forward to bend at the waist while I press her face into the mattress. She lets out a sound in protest and I slide both fingers in, kicking her legs apart so Landon has access.

Hadley groans when the vibrator is between her legs once more. My cock is painfully hard. I've been waiting for this day since I laid eyes on Hadley. All the possibilities. In fact, it was a sad, sad day when Hadley specifically said no anal sex. While I can have this with many of the others, it's not the same as having it with the one you own. I wouldn't have to arrange anal sex if she had allowed it. I'd merely just be owed the act by virtue of her liking it. Which is why I need this experience to be so good for her. As good as it can be to get it on the map.

She groans and I can feel her orgasm on my finger. I can't hold in my groan at the prospect of my cock being inside her. Landon looks up at me and smiles.

"I get her virginity", I tell him through gritted teeth as Hadley's orgasm slows, "but you can fuck her first."

"Fuck yes." Landon wipes hair away from Hadley's face to get a look at her. There's so much care in this gesture I know I've made the right decision giving Landon this gift. I've had a few texts from the guys wanting to be first but none of it felt right to me. When I spoke with Landon after Hadley's date with him, he made an observation I hadn't expected.

*Hadley thought she was going to be abused. That's why she was so defiant. She was protecting herself. She didn't trust either of us that night. If she trusted you, she wouldn't have had to have the handoff that she did like the first time you gave her to me. If she trusted me, she would have been compliant and willing. I told her I would never hurt her, and I didn't. I need her more vulnerable than just being alone with me. I've never asked you for anything with Hadley, until now. Whatever the thing is that she's most afraid of, if you think I'll do it well, I want that. As retribution for her behavior and to get her trust back.*

There was no question in my mind what that one thing would be. The one thing Hadley feared most was anal sex. That and being hit in any way. I can't say that I blame her. Both require keen attention and restraint. Many men aren't able to do these acts well. We are. That's why we do what we do. We pay attention because we want a free pass to continue coming back for the same thing...or the next best thing.

I leave my fingers inside her and move my free hand from her hair, to feel her naked form. Her nipples are taught, light pink buds that I brush lightly with my fingertips.

"It smells like your cum in here", I tell her, planting a kiss on her backside. "Talk to me, Hadley. How are you feeling?"

"Scared", she answers immediately, her voice quivering with the fear she verbalizes.

"I know", I tell her, because I do. I could see the fear in her eyes the moment she understood what we would be doing with her this morning.

"What would make it better, Hadley Joanna?" I want to know. Short of not doing it, this will be helpful to us.

Hadley groans and when I look down, I see Landon has replaced the vibrator with his finger. Tactically this is brilliant. A peace offering of sorts. He is now the tool to her release.

"If you both were smaller...ah...and shorter."

Landon chuckles but I manage to stifle a laugh. This is serious to both of us; however, her request is of course impossible.

"Okay, just get it over with", she breathes, conceding because she knows she has no choice. The terms of her agreement are specific. Open agreement. And although she can safe out, she can't safe out until she tries it.

"What's your safe word", I ask, needing to hear her say it so I'm comforted she won't forget under stress.

"Fruit punch."

Landon stops fingering her and slides his wet fingers into her mouth. She moans as she tastes herself. She always has liked the taste of her own arousal. It's such a turn on. I see it's a turn on for Landon too as he slides his fingers from her mouth and palms her face, eyes dilated with lust himself.

She shudders when she hears me unzip my pants. Goosebumps appear on her backside, up and down her legs. I release my cock, and it is so hard, so swollen with need it's weeping. For days I've been denied inside her. But now I get to be in the absolute tightest place I can go.

I run my palm up her thigh and over her backside, petting her like a prized steed. My arousal drips onto her skin and she tenses underneath my palm.

"My cock wants you so badly, sweetheart." I slide my fingers out of her and grab the lube once more. She flinches again at the opening of the cap, and I use my free hand to run over her other thigh up onto her backside. "The key is not to tense up." She lets out a huff in response and whimpers when I squeeze some lube on the tight pink hole. I use a generous amount on my shaft, so I don't hurt her when I slide in.

"Just get used to the feel of me back here", I tell her cautiously as I rub my hard cock up and down the channel of her backside. Just doing this act alone may send me over the edge. My cock is leaking more than it's ever leaked before sex in my life and I wonder how I'm going to be able to handle being inside of her at this rate.

"Hadley", Landon addresses her, and she tilts her head to look at him. "I want this to be good for you because I want to be invited back. We'll go so very slow. You have our word." His brow furrows and he reaches down to touch her face. When he pulls his hand back, I see that it's wet with her tears. For a moment, I consider calling this off. But as soon as the idea enters my mind it leaves.

"Hadley Joanna, just breathe", I croon to her as my cock continues running over her backside. I nod to Landon, and he brings Hadley up to her elbows, squatting in front of her on the floor at the edge of the bed. He moves the hair from her face and presses his lips to hers.

"Shh, shh, shh. Don't cry." He kisses her again and I tighten my grip on her hips. "We love you. Let us love all of you." Landon kisses her longer this time, relaxing her enough to begin. When I slid the head of my cock inside her, she cries out against Landon's mouth. "I know, baby. I know. Just feel it back there. It's so hard for you. That's what you do to Micah. He's leaking inside you right now." She shivers and I slide in a fraction more. Hadley's body noticeably tenses so I pause and run my hand up her backside, attempting to sooth her.

"It hurts", she breaths, her voice thick with emotion.

Landon simply nods and kisses her while I slide about halfway in. Hadley jerks in my hold. Landon surprises me by grabbing her face, forcing her to look only at him. "Right here, baby. Right here. You're doing so good." She nods frantically at Landon, and I have to say that I'm impressed. I thought for sure I'd hear fruit punch by now. "Just a little more. You can do it. Look right here. Ah, ah...don't close your eyes. Look right at me. I've got you, Hadley."

And with that, I slide home, balls deep, claiming my girl's anal virginity. She sobs and bucks, trying to slide me out of her, but I pull her to me so hard, I know there'll be bruises before the end of the day.

"That's it, Hadley", Landon says with wonder in his voice. "Look at you. You did it, baby", he congratulates her, kissing her on the lips and wiping away more tears. "That's it. Let it out. Let out the fear, the pain and all that uncertainty." He kisses her once more as she sniffles. "It's okay. You're okay. You're okay."

# Hadley

The moment Micah made me come with a vibrator Landon slid inside me. There was no hesitation. No gradual entry. It was one well timed thrust with the contractions of my pussy, and he was in. The fingers he had inside of me probably helped him time that out. So confident about his prowess, he didn't even utter an encouraging word, until now.

Landon is spooning me from behind, pumping slow but deep. He pulls my leg back over his so Micah has better access between my legs. Landon moves his fingers from my wet slit. He smears my arousal on my cheek as Landon guides my face to his turning my head for him to kiss me. Micah slides the vibrator on my clit, and I moan as Landon slowly, rhythmically moves inside me. He's fucking me from behind, laying here in bed like this is something we just normally do and a part of me likes this with him. He's good. Sweet. Careful.

"You feel so good, baby", he croons to me and kisses me again. "I felt that", he tells me, breaking the kiss momentarily to let me know he can feel the pleasure my pussy feels while he's inside me.

I'm full. Uncomfortably full. But since Micah took my virginity in this sense, the fire my nerve endings felt has dissolved into pressure. A pressure that might be making me wetter.

I appreciate the care they're taking, which makes me feel special and not dirty or cheap. The tears from moments ago were born from fear of pain and degradation. Right now, I only feel cherished.

I kiss Landon without prompting now as his hand wanders over my body. His pace stays the same and I'm grateful for it.

That big warm palm of his caresses my breasts and plucks at my nipples. It ghosts down my stomach and then the vibrator is gone, replaced only with his fingers. This feels so much more personal to me than a toy. So necessary. So very right.

Landon stops kissing my lips and plants a gentle kiss on my shoulder as his hand continues to wander over my body. And when I turn my head, forward, feeling the dull ache in my neck from the strain on my muscles I hadn't quite noticed compared to all the other sensations, I'm looking right into Micah's eyes.

God this man adores me. I can see it in his ice blue eyes. The way the corners of his mouth quirk up the slightest bit…It's like he's silently saying *I told you so*. He touches my cheek with his fingertips, also damp and smelling like my wetness. Then his lips are on mine ever so gently, as if he kisses me any harder than he is now, he'll scare me off.

"Hadley Joanna. You look so beautiful right now." He kisses me with possession. "I want to feel the mess Landon leaves for you and then make one of my own." He kisses me again and I'm done. I come as I moan on his lips. He lays there in front of me, his stiff cock leaking and at the ready to have me himself. Something about the way Landon's fucking my backside and the way they both coddle me makes this okay. The way they handle me takes away the fear.

Landon lets out a low groan, tucks his face into my shoulder and releases inside me. It's funny that as tight as I am back there, I can still feel him pulse with his release. And after he's done, he ruts inside me a few more times, sliding out and turning me to him.

Landon's love right now isn't typical. He's playful but precise, never focusing on one thing for too long. But his kiss is slow and consuming. Like he's patching us back up with no words, just languid caresses of his tongue while his hands roam the other side of my body. He makes me feel proud. He makes me feel perfect. And most of all, he makes us feel okay. You can't fake his actions. Call it a post orgasm high. Call it whatever you want. He's giving it to me, and I feel blessed. Honored even.

Micah waits patiently beside us. No doubt watching. Getting harder and harder as each second passes. I'm sure it's killing him not to be inside me and it gives me great joy. The pure thrill of being desired but not yet touchable. Especially for him. He has all the free passes but now he has to wait.

Landon brushes his lips against my forehead. "She's all yours brother", he offers me to him. "I'm going to go wash up", he tells me, pressing another kiss to my lips and then rolling off the bed.

No sooner is he gone than Micah is climbing on top of me. Settling his large frame over mine and brushing the hair from my face.

He doesn't pause. Doesn't offer me words of encouragement or even praise. Instead, he kisses my lips and slides his slicked-up cock inside my ass. On top of me, caging me in, he slides all the way inside me in a single thrust, not allowing me to pull my mouth from his when I grimace in pain.

He doesn't hold still to give me the opportunity to acclimate to his size. Instead, he pumps lazily inside me while he kisses me without ceasing. So very different than Landon's approach, but oddly, not unsettling in the least. As of a few days ago, he owns me in every way imaginable.

I let go, relaxing under him just like I did with Landon, and I take this moment to appreciate the muscular form on top of me. For every hard divot and plain I run my fingertips over, the more aroused I get. And finally, just thinking about where he's fucking me. It turns me on so much I'm at the precipice of orgasm.

And then I look at him. I look into my God's eyes, blue and dilated with desire. Then down to his parted lips, his pearly white teeth just peeking out for me to see… I feel so connected to him. So utterly and completely his, I see stars as I come. Blinking instead of shutting my eyes because I can't get enough of him. He smiles for a moment and then pulses his release into me.

Near the end of his release, he lets out a chuckle. He isn't laughing at me. "I knew it", he tells me, his smile getting bigger. "God damn baby…you're going to be just fine", he tells me as I follow his gaze next to us where his phone lays on the bed, the app to the prototype on full display. "Harlan is going to be so happy about these results."

# Chapter 40
# Hadley

**December 31st 7:15 p.m.**
(Present Day)

"Ms. McCafferty." Steven's voice is barely audible through the whirring in my ears. I lazily roll my eyes up to meet his, staring back at me in the review mirror of Micah's car. Guilt immediately washes over me. He's working on New Years. "Are you alright, dear?"

I give him a meek smile and a nod. "When you drop me off, you can go, Steven." His eyes smile back at me. Not the kind of smile that means he understands and is grateful but the kind of smile that says *you're so sweet, thinking you make the rules*.

My bones feel like they're made of Jello. My brain like it's been scrambled. Down is up. Up is down. Nothing is as it was before the tasting at Micah's this evening.

I thought he wasn't going to take me to the party. A chuckle escapes my lips. And then I burst into hysterical laughter, quieting when Steven's eyes meet mine once more in the review. I'm an idiot. How could I ever think Micah would leave me at home after all he's done to keep me as his. And I told him that a part of me hates him. But here I sit, in his fur and his gown, wearing his jewels...looking like an indignant princess. A wet, confused, emotional indignant princess.

But before he allowed me to get ready for the New Years Eve party, he had me wait in the dining room in that same pale purple robe I wore months ago on Introduction Night. The short list of the boyfriends I felt hate for filed in with Micah bringing in the rear. They sat me on the edge of the table. The same edge I perched on for Dr. Kinkade just days ago. And then they positioned chairs in a semi-circle in front of me, just waiting for me to air my grievances.

"Hadley", Micah starts, letting out a slow breath before he begins. "As you know we do not tolerate longstanding arguments and resentments." My eyes land on Archer who nods. I suspect this is his rule. "I've shared your statement with your boyfriends and the time has come where we must discuss it."

I zero in on Micah, the fight slowly returning in my veins. "So, you used the word *hate*." He punctuates hate as though he were deposing a witness. "Tell us about that."

"You held me there for him. Like it was nothing. This was just business for you." I look at Graham when I talk about business, but his features remain stoic. "I think you enjoyed it. Seeing me vulnerable like that." This time I turn to Tyler. "Not having another option." I turn to Archer. "And you were there to smooth it all out. Like I could dismiss being licked by a stranger." My voice cracks. "And then you...you've never made me suck you like that. Never." I start to sob and when Micah's hand touches my leg, I pull away. "And you...watched it all go down." He nods. "Hate...is a very accurate word for how I feel about you. Just to varying degrees", I add as if that makes the confirmation land better.

"Okay. Let's resolve it. Shall we?" I wipe at my face, sitting there with my feet dangling before them while they're sitting in tailored suits hanging on my every word. I am again at a disadvantage, and I hate it.

"I want to put clothes on", I address Micah.

"No." He offers no explanation, and I feel trapped.

I slide down from the table, attempting to flee but as soon as my feet touch the ground, I'm being pulled onto Tyler's lap. I wince when I land. I'm still tender where the implant is. "Hadley", Tyler calls my name in a chastising tone. "Everyone in that room had a right to witness your compliance. I would have never let Dr. Kinkade hurt you or have even suggested the prototype if I thought he would."

I look away but he grips my face and turns it toward him. "I will never disrespect you, Hadley." He lets his declaration hang there for a moment before continuing. "That being said, I will not tolerate disrespect from you." Tyler holds my face there for a moment longer than necessary, then slowly drops his hand to my thigh. "Now, where was I?"

"Compliance", Graham volunteers, coolness in his voice.

"Thank you, sir", Tyler turns to Graham for a moment then turns his attention back on me. "You know the rules. They are all within your control to follow. I am here to help you follow them." Tyler glances in Micah's direction. "He is here to make sure you fully understand them." Tyler tilts my chin up to him. "You were not treated inappropriately. You were reacting to your own inappropriate behavior. To getting caught. To feeling loss of control. To feeling pain. The only part we imposed on you was the pain and I do believe you used the word *anything* during the vote, did you not?"

"I'm not naïve to think your hatred will snuff out before we leave this room. But it will soon, Hadley. It will."

Tyler kisses me on the lips. It's brief. Nothing romantic. Just a show of affection in the form of a truce and not requiring anything more from me.

Graham rises and Tyler helps me off his lap, taking my hand and placing it in Graham's. I don't dare look away from these men again. Not because I'm afraid but because Tyler is right. It is disrespectful. They're doing a standup thing by acknowledging my feelings and seeking me out to remedy them. What man does that let alone four?

Graham brings his other hand on top of mine and smiles down at me. He looks like royalty, how he stands with such a noble and entitled stature. "We showed you leniency. A kindness. We all knew you would not view it as such. But the alternative would have been so much worse, would it have not? As you know, these decisions are final. Votes cannot be undone. Time cannot be turned back. Decisions cannot be unmade. You are not mistaken. That vote was business. I am in the business of knowing who I'm shoving my cock into, Hadley." My eyes widen at the crude reference. "Who I spend my precious moments with. Who I let into my carefully crafted circle. You may have desired to be one of us, but you simply were not. So, the kindness was giving you an opportunity to surrender to us. To allow the person you were trying to hide to come out so we can see you. So we can *know* you. This was an extraordinary gift. A huge sacrifice for us. The woman we voted *yes* for was a lie. The woman we've allowed to stay is a gamble."

Graham wipes a tear from my cheek. "If you weren't interested in what we had to offer you, you would have never entered into this agreement. There is not one molecule in my body that believes you don't want this. That is the only reason I gave a second conditional vote to the prototype. If I thought you were battling more than a fear of societal norms I would have cast you out without a moment's hesitation. Perhaps I should have clarified this during the vote, but if I'm being honest, I rather like seeing you this way. The real, messy, Hadley Joanna." I can't help but to smile when Graham calls me messy. He says it with such disgust it's comical. I can't imagine him allowing mess in his world. When Graham taps his cheek, I stretch up on my tiptoes to kiss him. His actions don't sting nearly as much after his explanation.

Graham turns to Archer.

"On your knees, darlin." My eyes roll to Archer, and he smiles in response. He knows I'm angriest at him. "Limits", Archer addresses Micah. Micah shakes his head.

"You cannot be…" I start but can't finish my sentence before I'm being pushed to my knees by Graham. I lay my hands in my lap, casting my head down as I've been trained to do while I wait for my cue to begin.

"The first time we met, I tried to flirt with you at the bar when you were on a date with Micah. It was a test. You passed. You even get extra credit because you don't even recall that was me." I hear Archer shift in his chair and smell his cologne as he bends toward me. "I fucked your mouth because I was pissed. In fact, if we'd have had more time, I'd have made you gag so hard you'd think of me every time you were about to lie from that day forward. How does someone pass a test like being hit on…stone cold turning a stranger down without hesitation… to protect her relationship with another man only to then lie to him later? And you got the rules, Hadley. You knew you broke one."

Archer lets out a heavy sigh. All I can focus on is the tops of his shiny shoes and hope he doesn't punish me again. "Look here", he prompts me, and I lift my head to meet his gaze. "It was a moment." He lets the phrase hang there as I process it. "Just like Dr. Kinkade licking your sweet little cunt until you came. It was a *moment*."

I nod. He's giving himself the same pass that he gave me. My moment to deceive was just that. A moment. His moment to smooth it over was just that. A moment. His moment to punish was just...A...Moment.

Archer reaches for his zipper, and I gasp in shock. The men laugh and he straightens up, extending a hand to help me to stand.

And then Micah rises, his hand warm through the satin on the small of my back. It almost hurts to look at him. I'm his and I want to trust him, but I just can't.

"I know", he tells me as though he can hear my thoughts. "We're going to fix the memory tonight. But you see how I couldn't fix the memory without addressing how you felt about your boyfriends, can't you?"

I'm shaking my head, not sure what he's referring to by changing the memory. I look back and see the guys moving the dining room chairs back into place and for the first time since we've been in the dining room, I hear voices. A lot of voices.

Micah palms my face and tilts it up to look at him. "I've invited the brotherhood and their partners to a preparty tasting. It's never been done before as there is so much to do on New Year's Eve. However, they allowed me this with short notice and I will be forever grateful." Tasting? "All of your boyfriends and their partners are here. We've also invited two special guests. What I need to know from you is will you allow them to participate?"

"Participate? In the tasting?" Micah nods, looking very serious. "I suppose", I tell him, struggling to connect the dots.

"Very good. I'm so glad you've consented to this because I very much want to earn back your trust and I'm confident this tasting will move us in the right direction." Micah nods to the guys still left in the room. I turn as Tyler opens the door and one by one, the men file in with their women. All in suits and beautiful gowns. Here I stand at the head of the formal dining room table in a robe. A short robe at that. Hair dripped dry and not a stitch of makeup on me. I want to hide underneath the table...until I see the guests. Now I want to turn into ash and fall to a pile on the floor.

"Dr. Kinkade and Madison will be joining us tonight. They've signed nondisclosures", he points out to me. "As you know, anonymity for some is of utmost importance."

I have no words for what is happening right now. I'm humiliated. Not to mentioned wrought with emotion about a man who I viewed as someone who violated me and my best friend who left me thinking she wanted nothing to do with me now stand before me...with an audience.

"We have a tight timeline everyone", Micah bellows above the chatter. Voices dissipate to stone silence.

"Thank you for joining me for this tasting. For those of you who have been a part of the brotherhood, this is quite unusual. Generally, we're on our way to the New Year's Eve party. But I thought a tasting would be a fantastic way to end the year. Now, participation is not mandatory but highly encouraged. As such, I'm throwing in some incentive even though I don't think it will be necessary." Chatter erupts from the group and Micah waves to silence them. "The winner will receive twenty-four hours with the lovely Hadley Joanna with no limits." Chatter resumes as I gasp at Micah's offer.

"Now, now, now...quiet down everyone, quiet down."

"What are we tasting", Lexi asks as she looks across the room at Madison who seems just as clueless as I do.

"No cupcakes", Micah confirms as the room groans with dissatisfaction. "It's much, much better...no offense, Madison." He winks at my friend and then hoists me onto the table where I sat moments before everyone filed in.

Breaths are sucked in and collective gasps and murmurs of what seems like appreciation fill the room. "Hadley." The chatter rises at Micah's answer. Micah looks down at me. "Hadley", he says my name once more in that stern pointed way that is not meant to get attention but to answer a question. I'm the answer to the question. He sees understanding register on my face and nods his head, then addresses the room once more.

"You get three minutes if you'd like to participate. No penetration. Just your mouth between her legs. In recognition of their service, Tyler, Graham and Archer will go first. After, its first come first serve." He nods to Tyler and splays a hand on my chest, pushing me backwards to lay on the table. Archer and Graham grab my legs just like when Dr. Kinkade put the implant in. My robe falls over my legs exposing my bare cunt to the entire room.

"Can the girls participate?" I couldn't see who asked this, but I knew it wasn't Linea.

"Thank you. Gentlemen? Any objections to the ladies participating in the competition?" He scans the room. "Going once...going twice...no objections, ladies. You may participate as equal competitors if you so choose. Guests outside of the brotherhood may participate but not compete."

I let out a sharp breath understanding Micah's limits. I can still be touched by Dr. Kinkade and not only is he going to allow it but he's going to orchestrate it?

"Hadley, you can safe out at any time." Micah reminds me.

"Tyler", Micah nods to Tyler, indicating he is free to start. Tyler is seated in the high-backed chair between my legs.

"Braden, would you mind keeping score", Micah calls across the room to Braden, who up until Micah called upon him seemed to be glaring across the room at Dr. Kinkade.

Tyler's fingers brush against my legs to get my attention. I cannot take my eyes off him. Hatred still simmers in my veins for him. His explanation was not nearly as adequate as Graham and Archer's, but I don't break eye contact. He tests me as he lowers his face to my bare cunt and rolls his eyes up to look at me as he takes his first taste. The room erupts into cheers, and I immediately feel my toes start to curl. It can't be for what I feel for Tyler. My only explanation is the audience. The sheer vulnerability of it all. I will my body not to finish for him and I'm successful. There's no way I'm spending twenty-four hours with that man and no rules.

"Graham", Micah motions for him to take Tyler's seat. He looks between my legs, and I blush.

"You can't even notice it now, Hadley", he tells me before leaning down and having a taste of his own. I roll my head over to look at Micah for reassurance. He simply looks at me as though he's observing a science project. Completely detached but with a bit of satisfaction. And then my eyes shift just to the left where Madison stands. She licks her lips, not even noticing that I'm looking right at her. The gesture is so startling I turn my head back down to Graham and run my fingers through his hair. Guests roar again as I groan, seemingly unheard by all the ruckus. It's not long before I'm finishing on Graham's mouth.

At first, I'm beyond insecure about it. I have no idea how I look when I orgasm. And who does something so personal in front of others? Graham kisses the inside of my thighs and then goes back down for more, making the most of his three minutes.

"Time", Braden calls from across the room. I turn towards his voice just in time to see Braden tapping something into his phone.

Warm strong hands brushing up my thighs get my attention. Archer. I wish I had a cock to choke him with. He smirks at me as though he's heard that. I wink at him, and he laughs, confusing our audience.

"It's just a moment, darlin", he tells me as he takes a long lick from my ass to my clit, and I almost levitate clean off the table. I finish twice for him. I couldn't help but wonder if I finished twice for him, what would Jonathan do to me?

After Archer, there's shuffling of feat. Men appear in front of my spread legs, each intent on bringing me to orgasm. Some succeed and some do not. At least I know the ones who do not succeed are out and I can make peace with that.

Archer takes his rightful place by my head and grabs my hand. Micah takes the opposite seat, just like he did days ago when I got the implant. A few more men step up for their turn and then to my surprise, one of the ladies is standing before me.

"Bethany?" Archer says her name in surprise. Bethany is his.

"I've never...and I thought that maybe...", she trails off feeling self-conscious of her decision, turning to walk past, reconsidering this bold move.

"Bethany, darlin, wait. Do you want to learn on Hadley?" Bethany nods and my face flames with embarrassment. "Okay."

"You can instruct her", Micah murmurs and my face flames hotter.

"Alright darlin. Take a seat." Bethany gracefully sits between my spread legs. When she reaches a finger out to touch me, Archer stops her. "Only your mouth, darlin. Don't get disqualified now", he warns and Bethany smiles.

Bethany sits there, waiting for instruction in a tasteful black dress with glitter embedded in the fabric so finely it looks like the dress is magic. Her dark hair piled atop her head in an elegant updo, and her beautiful blue eyes beg Archer for instruction about how to lick a woman.

"Kiss one thigh and then the other." He waits for Bethany to comply. "I like to think of this is kind of a thank you of sorts for letting me feast", Archer clarifies. "You can take your time. Kiss near her slit." He smiles and chuckles at Bethany's face when she finds me so wet. "I know. It's strange isn't it", he encourages her. "But it's good that she's wet for you. You can taste her before you commit to the bullseye." I turn to look at Archer, but he only has eyes for Bethany right now.

He's really letting her do this. Oh my god. Her gentle lips are kissing my wetness and all I can think about is that she's never done this before. She's doing it in public and she's never ever kissed a woman between the legs before. Then she kisses over my clit and every muscle in my body tenses.

"That's it. It's right there. Just like yours, darlin. Now all you gotta do is focus there. Lick it. Kiss it. Just love on it a little and she'll go off in no time", he advises her as she gets more courage to continue her exploration.

I roll my head over to look at Micah. He's looking between Bethany and I with adoration. The room has quieted, except for the sound of Bethany eating me.

"That's it. You're doing so good licking that wet little cunt" he croons. "There you go", he encourages her when she finds her rhythm. "Oh my. What a hungry girl you are." And that does it. I come. Hard. My groan is heard throughout the room and I'm equal parts mortified, and equal parts turned on.

"Time", Braden calls.

Bethany rises, leans over me to kiss Archer and pauses, considering if she should kiss me. Her lips glisten with my wetness. Instead of kissing my lips, she leans down and brushes her lips against my cheek, whispering her thank you in my ear before allowing the next participant access.

Dr. Kinkade steps up and out of reflex, I start tugging my legs free from Graham and Tyler.

"Hadley, Hadley, Hadley", Micah corrects me as I struggle. "You agreed our guests could participate. Now Dr. Kinkade will only use his mouth", he reminds me. "Move your hands down and reach for his face", Micah encourages me. "Hadley", he says sternly when I don't comply.

My hands reach down and Dr. Kinkade puts his face into the palms of my hands. "Now guide him to your needy cunt, Hadley. Encourage him to eat."

We're in a standoff. He can't move until I move him and right now, I'm torn between rubbing the pads of my fingers on his freshly shaven cheeks or gouging his eyes out.

"You're in charge, Hadley", Dr. Kinkade nuzzles against my hand, and I consider it a truce. Maybe even an apology of sorts. "Let me see what I can do in three minutes", he bargains with me. And with a deep breath, I pull him to me and sounds of approval rumble throughout the room.

The moment his mouth is on me I lay my head back and let my fingers run through his hair. And when I close my eyes, Archer pulls my robe to the side and exposes my breast, running his fingertips over my nipple. I'm lost in the sensation of being licked and sucked by a near stranger all over again.

"Look at him", Micah gently directs me. "Look at how much he likes it. How he looks up at you like he wishes he could see your naked body again." Again, more chatter around the room, questioning Micah's comment. We're not supposed to be viewed by anyone outside of the group…I don't think.

"Do you know why I let him lick your cunt last time?" More chatter erupts around the room. "Because I wasn't going to lose you because of a stranger. Or a vote. Or my pride." I'm looking at Dr. Kinkade eat me while Micah justifies what he hasn't yet addressed. It feels so good, but I can't concentrate. Not with the conflict of Micah being so unapologetic compared to the others. Well, maybe not Tyler. But Micah's response was actually worse than Tyler's. And that is something I wasn't expecting.

"Time.", Braden calls and Dr. Kinkade gives me one last peck on my slit before he rises.

"Anyone else", Micah asks the room, turning to scan the thinning audience until his gaze lands on Madison. He's pinning her with a look. He gives me that look often. It's the one that is an order without words or even a gesture.

"I...um...it's not...", Madison stammers, which I don't think I've ever seen her do a day in my life.

Dr. Kinkade crosses the room to Madison, puts his hand behind her head and kisses her, tongue and all with my juices fresh on his lips. There's laughter and applause and I'm speechless. And when Madison kisses him back, I'm questioning if my mind is playing tricks on me. They're making out right in front of a room full of people with *my* cum on their lips.

When the room quiets, a woman clears her throat. I turn to see Linea standing in front of my spread legs. "I'd like a taste", she innocently remarks, this time dressed in red like she took today off to do the devil's work instead of her usual job of an angel's.

"By all means. Please, you'll be our last", Micah gives her permission as he motions for her to sit.

My heart is literally thumping out of my chest. I'm almost panting and I can feel Archer's eyes on me, but I refuse to tear my gaze away from Linea.

"So I can only touch her with my mouth, correct?" Micah nods. "And my time starts when my lips touch hers?"

"Correct."

Linea looks up at me and then her eyes lazily drag down my body until she gets to the bullseye. "I'm not well practiced in this, you know. I mean, you won't be my first", she clarifies as she takes her fingers and runs them up the inside of my thigh. “Such pretty legs”, she says, pulling her red painted lip under her top teeth. “I’d like to eat like this again someday”, she tells Braden, who’s across the room. “Grace’s legs held up like this”, she looks across the room at who I assume is Jonathan when she clarifies, as Grace belongs to him.

“I like how it looks. You’re mine for three minutes.” Linea runs her nose up my thigh. I let out a harsh breath. “Oh my…you smell so good.” She runs her nose right up to my mound but doesn’t commit yet. She takes a deep breath, hovering over me. Her mouth is right there. “Wearing my hair up was such a good choice for tonight”, she says, more to my wet cunt than to anyone else in the room. “I think you would have held my hair for me if I turned out to be good though, right?”

I’m nodding. Why am I nodding? She licks the seam of her lips and she’s so close to me I can feel her breath there. And then her lips press against my wet skin, and it feels like I’m being blessed by something holy. The way she bows her head down to kiss me it’s saintly. And I see Micah nod in my periphery. The timer has started. She pulls back a bit to take a look.

“This lipstick is going to make such a mess”, she turns her head this way and that, considering her options. “Do you mind? Do you mind wearing my lipstick on your wet pussy tonight? I’d like to know that it’s there”, she tells me before kissing me once more, just a ghost of a kiss over where I want it most.

“I’ll make you a deal.” I’m nodding. “If you promise you won’t wash me off, I’ll make you come harder than anyone in this room.” A few men grumble but she seems unbothered.

“Okay. Yes.” My voice shakes and it’s barely even a whisper. So is her reply.

"I'm going to check." And then her mouth is on me, and I can't breathe it feels so good.

"Oh fuck", someone says from across the room. "Look at her toes curling already", one of the women observe.

Linea looks up my body and into my eyes as she relentlessly tongues me. She's a liar. She's had practice.

"Yes", I choke out while the familiar warmth of muscles bunching in my belly is the start of the greatest compliment a woman can give another. An orgasm. She lifts her lips from my slit and then runs her nose back and forth all over my clit, kind of like an owner might do to a puppy who misbehaved but nicer and without the yelling. The tip of her nose is slick and tinged with her own lip color. And. I'm. Done. One more lick and Linea will be the second woman who ever made me orgasm. This is one of the fantasies I held back from the men. I did it because I thought it made me bisexual and I wasn't sure I wanted to know that about myself. But fuck the labels. I want to ask Bethany to come back and beg Linea to never stop.

At the mere thought of another woman making me come, everyone disappears from the room. It's just me, Linea and some pesky asshole who just called *time*.

# Chapter 41
# Hadley

**December 31$^{st}$ 8 p.m.**
(Present Day)

The door to the car opens. I didn't even realize we had arrived at the Lux. Steven talks with a porter as a uniformed man helps me from the car. I had relived that hour in the span of twenty minutes or so and I'm still no less conflicted than I was afterward.

A stranger licked my pussy. Then a man I loathe did the same thing, only to kiss my best friend who I haven't heard from in days. Not to mention that my best friend now knows what my pussy tastes like as if she'd licked me herself. And then Linea made me ache so badly. I didn't finish but I was excruciatingly close. I think that eating was possibly better than anything Jonathan has ever done to me, and he's *known* for is fellatio.

I'm so in my own head I barely notice that the reception desk area is void of any guests, that is until the desk clerk comes to help me out of my coat. She tells me I'll be taken back in a moment, but I could care less. I'm still in shock.

I'm in shock that Micah cleared the room after Linea had finished, pulled my legs up over his shoulders and ate me like a starving man at a buffet. "Your pussy belongs to me. You belong to me. And I will never jeopardize that ever again. My failure to challenge you...to avoid this whole thing is mine alone and it will never happen again. Hadley Joanna you have my word as God as my witness as long as you are mine you will be safe, you will be cared for and you will be loved at all costs."

His footsteps pull me out of the memory of Micah in a suit with is face between my legs. I turn to greet him and he's smirking at me. Micah doesn't smirk. Something's up.

He stops in front of me and tilts my head up with two fingers in the signature way that he does and plants a kiss on my lips.

"You take my breath away, Hadley."

"You're not so bad yourself", I tell him, and he gives me the full smile instead of the smirk, putting his hand to the small of my back to guide me into the festivities.

"You look like you know a secret."

"I do. But not for long", he tells me, glancing down at me with the same smirk he greeted me with.

We stop at a door with two security guards flanking the entrance. Micah nods to them and they let us in. It's completely dark until Micah pulls back a thick velvet curtain to reveal a luxuriously decorated lounge. Candles burn on high-top tables. A bar is in the back with bartenders dressed in suits. There are plush couches and chairs in deep purple and lights that are embedded into the floor.

As soon as we're noticed, the patrons start to quiet. Once my eyes adjust to the light, I see that these are not patrons. They're the very group that just saw me sprawled out on

Micah's dining room table. All of them are more than a few drinks in. Loose but fully clothed.

"They quiet so quickly because they want to know who the winner is", Micah tells me. I had completely forgotten about the competition. Every man had kissed me but only two of the women kissed me. Not everyone made me come so I was only looking at a few contenders. I hadn't minded any of them, although the thought of having no limits is worrisome regardless of who I'm with.

"The winner of twenty-four restriction free hours with Hadley is none other than...Linea."

The moment Linea's name leaves Micah's mouth she's screaming with excitement. I look at Braden and he looks enraged. Micah is the polar opposite. He can't stop smiling and before I know what's happening, Linea is hugging me so tight I have to push against her a bit to get her to ease up.

"Did you wash it of", she asks in my ear. I shake my head, feeling the blush spread across my cheeks. "Good." She leans in and brushes her lips against mine. And with that, she turns on her heel and walks back to her table.

All hail the First Lady.

# Epilogue
# Micah

My desk line rings just as I'm packing up for the day. It's January second and I'm back at work way too soon. All I want is to be inside Hadley. But that clearly, that will have to wait.

"Braden is here to see you." I close my eyes, knowing this was going to happen but hoping the day was too far gone for him to visit me. He isn't ready to talk rationally yet.

"Send him up Claudia. Then head home. I'm done for the day."

"Thank you." I do not know what I'd do without that woman. She keeps my work life sane. I don't know how she puts up with other people's bullshit all day. I make a mental note to pay her more.

Braden will refuse a drink, so I pour one for myself and wait for his arrival. The moment I see him through the glass I know he's coming in hot and unreasonable. His hair is fluffy, even for winter. Like he's run his hands through it several times on the way over here. And he's got a look in his eyes that's so wild he looks like he could come unhinged.

"What's our strategy", he asks me before letting the door close behind him.

"We look at the calendar", I start. He leans in like I'm going to give him some genius plan that will make him more comfortable with Linea having Hadley all to herself for a day. "And then we schedule their time together."

"Okay", Braden prompts me to keep going by the questioning tone in his voice.

"And then we let them have it." I take a sip of my drink and wait for the fit that will come from my best friend. Really, I'm getting it from both sides. Hadley isn't so keen on this either. The only one who is completely overjoyed is Linea. And I'm not sure which one of us Braden is angriest at. Linea for working Hadley up into such a frenzy that she was more aroused without orgasming than she was with anyone else who finished her. Hadley for actually being aroused. Or me, for putting together the competition for Hadley's time with no limits and opening it up to the women. No one thought a woman would participate let alone win.

And I have to say, when I reviewed the results, I wasn't surprised. Linea had sat back and watched her competition dig into Hadley without prelude. Without so much as teasing her. Her only true competition was Bethany because she was a woman, and Archer was teaching her on someone who'd never been eaten by another woman. As hot as that was, Linea fucking with Hadley was so much hotter.

Those red lips coming down on her wet pussy. God...I'm still reliving the memory. I hope Linea wants to eat her again. Christ if they like it, I'd order them to lick each other and just sit back and watch.

"They're going to talk." Braden states the obvious.

"How much talking can they do in a day", I challenge, knowing this argument is not my strongest but a decent place to start.

"They're women. They were born with an Olympic gold medal in talking."

I laugh, take another drink and shake my head. "They have no limits, Braden. And talking is not in anyone's agreement. Gossiping is. But it's not something we can stop altogether, as you know. And Linea won't be gossiping as long as she's talking about herself.

"Then we sit them down and explain the rules." Braden is telling me this as if there were more rules in the first place. "They can fuck. That's what they can do. They can do any kind of fucking they want with whoever they want but there's no talking."

I laugh again. No talking? "That's not reasonable, Braden."

"Fine. They can talk but they can only talk about fucking. Fucking and talking about fucking. That's it." I shake my head. "I won't allow this."

"It's too late. The brotherhood agreed. She won." I slam the rest of my drink. "Braden, she outsmarted us. You should be proud of her. It takes a lot to outsmart all of us. Now if she wants to invite someone to her and Hadley's time together so be it, but a vote is a vote, and a commitment is a commitment. Maybe inviting someone else will be a distraction and she'll end up fucking more than she will talking."

Braden glares at me as I slip on my wool coat. "The system failed you buddy. I know how that feels." I slap him on the back, part rubbing it in and part feeling for the guy. I get it. I was recently feeling what he is. "My one recommendation would be to pick the soonest date available. I wouldn't give that one time to plan. She cooked up that win in what...thirty? ...forty minutes? If I were you, I'd start asking the guys to move things around so Linea and Hadley can have their time together in the next week or so."

At this rate, we're looking at a month out. February second. What I wouldn't give to have a front row seat to that show.

# Check out the Bonus Scene!

**Want to know what happened at the New Years Party between Hadley and Linea?**

**Get social with Darla and ask for the Hadley & Linea New Years bonus scene.**

**Email Darla at darlajmichaels@gmail.com or message her on Facebook to join her group.**

# Sneak Peak
# Linea & Braden's Story

## Prologue
## **Linea**

"Linea!" Braeden calls out to me. I look across the snow-covered yard at him. He's standing outside dressed in a red and blue Christmas-looking flannel and a red vest, jeans and black boots. The only thing that's missing is a cowboy hat, which he could probably pull off but he's no cowboy, that's for sure.

I look down after allowing myself the quick glance. It's just enough to get me by. To tide me over until I fall asleep tonight. Until now, sleep is the only time I've been able to see him in the last two weeks. In my mind, there is no fighting. No parents. No brothers. No religion. No expectations.

"Look at me, baby." His words come out almost pained. He's in agony too. I wonder if he dreams of me like I dream of him. "Linea?"

And that does it. The way he says my name like he cares. Like he wants me to be okay and he knows I'm not. I know I'm not.

It's hard to see him through the tears welling in my eyes. Even though I see the fuzzier version of him, he still looks like a God. I blink and allow the tears to fall wiping them away because this is the only time I've cried in front of him. Well, the only time since we've been together that I've cried at all. And he isn't even responsible for my tears.

How do you choose between family and the man who holds your heart hostage?

Braeden takes a step forward and my brother, Adam, cocks his shotgun. Braeden stops and peripherally I see Adam raise the rifle, pointing it right at his target. My boyfriend. Well, one of them.

My brother is an excellent shot. Living in the country, shooting guns is a rite of passage.

I don't bother pleading with Adam to put down his rifle. He won't do it. Adam is equally as protective of me as he is his fiancé.

"If you tell me to go, I'll go. But I don't think you want that."

I let out a sob and quickly cover my mouth. Go? Tell him to go? Just the words coming from his mouth break my heart.

How could I tell him to go? He loved me. Hell, he still loves me. I don't know one man who would stand there and let someone point a riffle at them like it's a pea shooter if they didn't really care for someone.

"If you just come down here, we can go for some hot chocolate and talk. We can work this out." He extends his arm out to me. I want to bolt off this porch and run straight into his arms.

"She isn't going anywhere with you. Get off our property. This is the only warning I'm giving you and then I'll shoot. So help me I will fill you with bullets if you take one more step towards this house."

Braden doesn't move, but I do. It's one step. The wood boards of the porch creek under my boots.

"That's it. C'mon Linea." He doesn't smile but I can see the excitement in his eyes. He knows I'll never say those words. Even if he won't promise me forever. Even if this arrangement we have ends up being my downfall. I'll never tell him I don't want him.

"If you go to him, you aren't welcome back here." I stiffen at my father's voice. His words are cruel, and his message is clear. Choose the only family I've ever known or make a new one.

# Braden

It breaks my heart to see Linea so upset. Her family forced her to come home so she could finish her fall semester and they could "help her get right again".

Well, I have news for them. They can't bring back her virginity and she was never more *right* than she was with me and my friends.

I can't imagine how awful she must feel. How awful her own family is making her feel. She looks even smaller now than she did the day I met her. Like she's shrinking down to nothing just to avoid her family's scrutiny.

I scan the large white porch. It doesn't even bother me that one of her brother's has a shotgun pointed at me. It should, but the only thing I can think about is getting Linea out of that house. I can feel how oppressive they are. And if I can feel it, I'm not sure how Linea can even breath being surrounded by them under the same roof.

They've made her out to be a horrible person. A sinner. All because she's no longer pure and happens to be in a relationship with me and my best friends.

I admit we have an unusual arrangement. But it works. We love it. She loves it. That's all that matters.

One of her brothers shifts in his seat. There's two on each side making a total of five which makes the shotgun entirely unnecessary. They don't say anything or make a move for me, and I wonder if their sole purpose is to hide my body after the brother wielding the riffle pulls the trigger.

I'm still holding my hand out to her even though her father issued that bullshit ultimatum. Who says that to their own child? The choices she has are to be miserable without me or to be miserable without them? Her own father…the person who is supposed to protect and love her unconditionally gave her misery or more misery to choose from. I could never do that to her.

I shouldn't be surprised. She told me her family was religious. I had corrupted their daughter in more ways than one. Before me, she had only shared a few meaningless kisses with men. Now she's on birth control sharing a lot more than kisses.

In fact, one of her brothers walked in on Tyler and I with her. We didn't hear the knock on the door. Linea's roommate was out so we were having fun with Linea in the living room. Tyler had just taken her pants off and was kissing up the inside of her thighs as I was undoing the clasp of her bra.

"What the fuck?!" A man I had only seen pictures of stood in the living room, angry as hell.

"David?!" Linea pushed away from Tyler and I and we handed her her clothes so she could cover up.

Her brother barreled toward us but as Tyler rose to his full height. It wasn't surprising to me that good old David had a change of heart. Tyler is a beast. The only guys who had the courage to get in his face were either drunk or high. David didn't appear to be either.

"I knew this was a bad idea. Let's go. I'll help you get right again." He looked at Linea like she was an errant child and not an adult. She had just turned twenty and was attending college. A double major in theology and political science. Brilliant, beautiful and mine every night for the last month.

And that was it. It was like a switch was flipped. She was completely subservient to David as she followed him from the house without a single word to both of us. She didn't even look at me as I called out to her.

I should have stopped him. Maybe I could have prevented her return home. I didn't know what the right thing to do was.

But I'm here now because this isn't right. And I know exactly what needs to happen.

Linea's hair blows in the crisp wind and her eyes flutter closed for a moment. She shudders at the chill.

We both jump when David fires a warning shot in the air. Fresh tears stream down her cheeks. This time she doesn't bother wiping them away.

"Don't disappoint God and your family even more", her father tells her, laying his hand on her shoulder.

The most pained sob rips free from her chest and I lose all reason as I start walking toward her through the packed snow.

Her brother cocks the riffle and trains it on me once more. But I don't care. The only person I care about is Linea and I'm sure as shit not driving off without her.

Linea lets out a blood curdling scream startling her father causing him to drop his hand from her and with as much force as she can muster, shoves her brother, causing him to shoot and miss me.

Without pause, Linea runs down the stairs of the porch straight to me. I look up for a moment when I hear the front door open. Her mother stands in the threshold screaming her name as if I just ripped Linea from her womb.

She slams into me, and when I wrap my arms around her, I can tell even in the short time she's been away she's lost some weight. She buries her cold face into my neck, looking for affection, but I don't waste any time. I lift her into my arms and carry her right to my car.

"You're safe now, baby. You're safe."

# Chapter 1
# Braden

**February 4$^{th}$ 4:25 a.m.**

"Do I get my phone back today", my angel asks as I pin her to the mattress, taking the last opportunity I can to convince her to stop this plan of hers to help Hadley. I wait to answer her because I'm not sure. She's been without her phone since New Years. I let her keep it till we left The Lux but as soon as we turned in for the night, I took that phone from her delicate manicured hand, turned it off and she hasn't seen it since.

Hadley is due to be dropped off here early. She'll arrive at five thirty so I can make it to rounds on time and get back here to lurk around. Micah will be here. It's the only thing we agreed on. It changes nothing about the rest of the deal. She can still do and say whatever she wants with Hadley. I'll just get to know what the conversation is about so I can brace myself for Linea to fall apart later.

I'm going to ask you again, respectfully." I let the implied request hang there. It's been the elephant in the room since New Year's Eve. Do not tell Hadley about your breakdown. "I can't watch it again, Linea. Please. If you won't do it for yourself, do it for me."

My request is weak. I know it is. I sound like such a pussy. But if anything ever happened to her I'd fall apart. I couldn't exist without her. I can't watch her walking around broken like she was before.

I run my fingertips down her neck where her collar sometimes hangs. It's an elegant diamond collar as Linea has been Tyler's well trained submissive for most of her time with us. She's earned it by far. He came by last night to remove it. A show of him relinquishing control. But in typical Tyler fashion, even that came with a warning.

With two quick snaps of his fingers, the already kneeling Linea wastes no time looking up at him. Even uncollared she's an impeccable sub. She knows her place with him. There's something about him that she follows without a second thought. I hate to say it, but I'm envious of this part of their relationship. It's hard not to be when I'm pinning my girl down on our bed, pleading with her to keep her mouth shut and all Tyler has to do is snap his fingers for compliance.

"I *am* doing this for you", she tells me, laying her gentle palm on my face. I close my eyes, reveling in her touch. So sure of herself. Which I cannot begin to even understand, considering she went through hell to come back to me and ended up even stronger than she was when I met her.

When I open my eyes, she's smirking at me. "I love you", she tells me, stretching up to close the small distance between us to kiss me. I can't help but feel like this is our last everything. Our last screw. Our last kiss. Our last moment in bed, me gazing down at her as the strongest person she's ever been. And the next twenty-four hours could change all of that. "It's okay", she tells me with the voice of an angel.

"I wish I could believe you, baby." I kiss her on the forehead, which I know she hates. I can't help it. I know better than her this time. Even Tyler wasn't so sure he trusted this plan of hers. As an experienced dominant, she challenged him more than any of the subs before her. She was so sick. He was guessing. And when he finally caught on to something he could work with, he was exhausted and none of us could take over on his behalf. It was a long haul and if I don't want to experience it again, I can't possibly believe she'd want to experience it again either.

"Your phone is on the counter. I doubt it's slowed you down much anyway." The only reason she's getting it back is because I want her to have a lifeline when she falls apart. This is inevitable to me. I've clipped her wings as long as I could. Now I just have to let her fly and see what happens.

"Thank you." She slides her hand under the covers and tries to gain access to my flaccid cock. This little talk came after sex so she's a mess down there and I've basically been laying in it. When I don't move, she begs me with those contemplative eyes. It's like she's convincing me with a look alone. No siren's song needed. "I'll be so busy for the next twenty-four hours", she rubs it in, and I can't help but to laugh.

"If you call it off, I'll keep you busy for twenty-four hours", I tell her. And I would. My favorite thing in the entire world is fucking Linea. I know we're not supposed to favor any of the women, but I do favor her. In every way. She's my home. So if she told me she'd cancel, I'd do everything I could to ensure she didn't regret it.

She shakes her head and smirks. Nothing can change her mind. She won fair and square.

"We have time." She turns to look at the clock. "An hour before I need to get ready." I'm already getting hard against her. "It sounds like a good idea to one of us I do believe." She's smiling now and I know I've lost. I can't go into the hospital thinking about sex, which is exactly what will happen if I don't have her again before I leave. "I'll even clean you off", she volunteers.

"Linea, it's funny to me that you think you have a choice."

# Linea

Braden eyes me as I swipe my phone from the kitchen counter. He has expressed his worry in every fashion possible from threatening me, to bargaining to even withholding things...such as this phone. But all I needed to do was be observant, use patience and be resourceful to get to this day.

If you get upset, they think they've got you. But if you act unfazed, they give in and try something else. Taking my phone did hurt though. If I'm being honest, I'll never look at email the same. It's a lot different waiting on a text compared to an email. It took me a few weeks just to get people in the habit of checking their emails to watch for mine. Which meant mailing a letter might have actually been quicker in some cases.

Even still, I was able to communicate with people to make today possible. Since this is my twenty-four hours, I get to invite who I want, have the food I want and do what I want. Which means I won. I actually beat the men at their own game. And it's so funny how differently the founders have been behaving as a result.

Micah couldn't be prouder. He doesn't even have to say it. The look on his face tells me everything I need to know. In his usual style, Jonathan is just along for the ride. No fight or redirection needed. He is Switzerland. Tyler looks at me as a threat. The jig is up. He knows I'm always watching. And now, he's more careful with what he shares around me. If I'm hearing about something I shouldn't know by accident, it won't be from Tyler, that's for sure. But Braden...he's worried. No. He's terrified. And I get it. I really, really do. But as I've thought about the history of it all, I'm the one who's done the work. That should not go unnoted.

Braden was very supportive, don't get me wrong. But he was so wrapped up in the thought that he failed me, he became an observer. And to this day, over five years later, no one knows what really happened when I went back home.

I couldn't tell them. With every day that passed it got harder and harder to say the words. They know a portion and they think that's what pushed me over the edge. But it wasn't. It wasn't even close. And I couldn't bear to tell them because then they'd never do the thing they wanted to do, which was form the brotherhood. And they certainly wouldn't let me participate. It would have torn them apart because Braden wouldn't have let me go. Either out of love or obligation, I was a non-negotiable for him. And I didn't want to be a burden, which I ended up being anyway. But if Tyler hadn't have helped me, I don't know where I'd be today. Certainly not here and certainly not well.

But now, they have everything they ever wanted. It doesn't matter if they know what really happened during those two weeks of hell when I was away from them. But it will to Hadley. Because she'll see that what she's enduring is minimal compared to what it could have been. That even though she feels betrayed by Micah, me and heaven knows who else in the brotherhood, our intentions are good, honest and true.

So in many ways, I'm doing this for Hadley, Braden and Madison. She's my surprise guest. I won't be given another opportunity, especially if this goes as badly as Braden expects. So, I decided to make her a part of the day because she'll need to know what I do in order to stay the course if this is really a life she says she wants.

"Thank you for charging it", I tell him while he prepares a cup of coffee for me, just the way I like it. Sweet with lots of cream. He nods his acknowledgement and slides the mug across the counter to me as I search through the messages for the urgent ones. I've missed so much, and I suppose I should be upset with him. But really, who was going to reach out to me that wasn't involved with one of the men? My family is gone. My friends gone along with them. This is what I have. It's good. I'm treated very well, and I love them as much as they love me.

I tap on Madison's reply, skimming the message. Then I send her a quick message telling her she can come for as long as she likes. Whenever she likes. But secretly, I hope she makes most of our time here. It'll be easier to explain if we have time together.

On to Tanner. He's agreed to have one of his staff deliver the caramel pecan cinnamon rolls. A dozen caramel pecan cinnamon rolls to be exact.

"That's a lot of cinnamon rolls", Braden says, coming up behind me and commenting on my message before putting his arms around me and snugging me against him. I hear him inhale my scent. He nuzzles into my hair at my neck and then gives me a gentle kiss where my skin is now exposed.

"Hurry back and maybe there'll be one left for you", I tease him, even though he isn't a big fan of breakfast to begin with.

Familiar steps sound down the hall. I'd know that cadence anywhere. Micah. The quiet thuds must be Hadley. I turn around in Braden's arms. "It's time."

"Yeah. It's time, isn't it", he answers me, brushing my hair off my cheek.

For the first time since I won, he looks sad. Like his heart is breaking right here in my arms.

"Do you remember what you said to me before Tyler took my virginity?" He laughs at my shameless attempt at getting him to confirm who actually deflowered me. "You told me to be brave. That it would only hurt for a little bit. But then everything would feel so much better afterward."

"It's not the same, baby", He shakes his head at me.

"It is, Braden. We all need this. Now go. Go do your big shot doctor thing and we'll all be here waiting for you when you get back."

I kiss him on the lips, expecting him to linger, but he doesn't. He takes what I offer, nods at Micah, kisses Hadley on the cheek and walks out of our home without looking back.

I don't realize I've watched him disappear until Micah stands in front of me. He lays his hands on my shoulders. "You good?"

I swallow hard, realizing that not only did I lie to Braden, I also lied to Micah. But I'm not worried about the punishment because I know I did the right thing and I'm better for it. I'm worried about the fallout with my relationship to the founders. But I think of Hadley last month, bearing her soul to a bunch of people she really barely knows, and I think if she can do it, then so can I. And they'll forgive me just like they did her.

Yeah", I answer. "This is just...it's a lot. And I want it. But I really don't want to fuck it up." Micah's laugh fills the room.

"You won't, Linea. You couldn't possibly fuck anything up if you tried."

I pat him on the chest, stand on my tippy toes and give him a quick kiss, knowing full well Hadley is watching behind him.

"Okay. Now if you'll excuse me, I have a date with Hadley", I fake chastise Micah.

"And me."

Hadley and I turn to Madison in shock. There was no way I was expecting her this early.

"You told me to just let myself in. Unless you changed your mind?" She starts digging in her bag for what I'm assuming to be her phone, while I rush to stop her. Hadley stands there as though she's seen an apparition. Micah patiently observes.

"Yes. Oh my goodness I'm so...surprised that you're hear so early. Come in. Let me take your coat." I help her out of her winter coat as she explains.

"I didn't want to interrupt by coming later. And I was able to train one of the staff to open and close for me, so it all worked out. And Erik... I was just encouraged to be here because it's a show of good faith." Madison rambles, clearly nervous about joining Hadley and me.

"We aren't going to have sex. I mean, I don't think we are. Maybe we'll just see where the day takes us." I look between Madison and Hadley and quickly realize Hadley has no idea what Madison has involved herself in. She looks between Madison and I as though she's trying to catch up but with each passing second, she seems to be getting upset.

"You invited her", Hadley asks, motioning to Madison as though she has no right to be in our space.

"I did. I thought maybe you both could know the same things and maybe experience the same things. You'd benefit from them." I usher Madison to the island and grab three coffee cups. When Hadley doesn't move, I nod to Micah, signaling that I'd like his help. Hadley scoffs and allows Micah to guide her to the seat next to Madison, while I make coffee for the three of them.

"I'm sorry", Madison tells Hadley. I don't know her well, but she doesn't sound as strong-willed as she did in the kitchen a month ago while she was sizing me up and judging me for my romantic interests.

"You don't need to be. You made your decision. I can live with that. I'm sure I'm going to have many more people leave my life because they can't condone my behavior", Hadley replies.

"That's not why I haven't been around", Madison tries to explain, while I busily tend to the coffee to let them work this out.

"Is it the awkwardness of knowing what I taste like?" I smile at Hadley's bite, although I don't want them arguing. We don't have time for that.

"No." Madison leaves it at that, thanks me for the coffee and starts adding cream and sugar to her liking.

I hand a cup of coffee to Micah, and he takes it thankfully. He's used to the early hour, but I can see that he looks tired. I don't know the details, but I know that there's strain between Micah and Hadley.

"So what are we doing today", Hadley asks, quirking an eyebrow at me and taking a sip of her coffee. "I mean, if it's not sex. If you're not going to make me lay naked for you to finish what you started, what the hell else could possibly be so important that we're spending all this time together?"

I glance at Micah and he nods in encouragement.

"Well, we all have a past and I thought you should know mine." Hadley assesses me as though she isn't sure whether or not I'm being honest. "I think it will help you both." Hadley looks at me confused once more.

"I'd like to hear the story", Madison prompts. Hadley gives her the side-eye and I take a big drink of my coffee, gathering the courage to start.

I round the counter and motion for them to follow me into the living room where we can get more comfortable. They follow silently, Micah's unmistakable cadence following behind them. His footsteps have always sounded like a warning to me. The way a principle or a teacher would walk down an empty hallway with their dress shoes leaving a measured click or clack in their wake.

We're sitting nowhere near each other. Micah wanting to keep his distance so as not to disturb my time with Hadley and Madison unsure if she wants to be near Hadley.

"Why don't you start from the beginning", Micah prompts me as any lawyer would. And so I begin at the start of my fall from innocence.

# Acknowledgements

In the mid-2000s I had written a list of things that were important to me to accomplish during my lifetime. Writing a book had made the top of my list. Several false starts and a few laptops later, I can finally say that I've achieved this goal.

But my achievement wouldn't have been possible without the unwavering faith of my best friend and my husband. My best friend, formerly known as Michelle's little brother, heard all about my doubts and insecurities while writing this story. I would leave him messages in desperation about an author's plight and he'd answer each message with patience and thoughtfulness even though I'm sure he was screaming at me on the inside. After countless changes and iterations to this story, it's finally finished, and I owe that in part to you.

And while my husband didn't studiously scrub every scene and provide me with detailed feedback, he did something just as valuable. He believed that if I said I was going to write a book then I was going to write a book. He never once criticized me for it taking over a decade to complete my first novel and didn't go running from the hills when he read the first chapter and realized that his wife really, really loves erotic romance. Thank you for taking my word as fact. Your unwavering faith in me means more than you will ever know.

Speaking of scrubbing the content, a huge thank you to my beta readers, Jim (my bestie) and Ana Hantt & Josie Baron from Fiverr. Your feedback was spot on and helped me do justice to the story of Micah and Hadley.

Along this journey I met a the most fantastic cover artist and asked her to put together my cover art for this book. In my opinion she is positively brilliant and a joy to work with. Thank you, Kristina Bates, for paying attention to the little details and partnering with me during this adventure.

To my coach, Clayton Snyder. When I wanted to rewrite this novel three hundred pages in, you strongly advised against it. Through it all you have pushed me not only in completing this novel that I started over three years ago, but you didn't let me flounder with my mindset and fitness practices. Best coach ever. Thank you.

And finally, to my readers...I've always said a good book is like a cheap vacation and the best books are like vacations that you look forward to revisiting. My hope is that this story has provided you some levity and maybe even some inspiration. And if you liked it, there are more stories in the works for the brotherhood so stay tuned!

Thank you for choosing to spend your free time reading the dirty little stories that roll around in my head all day. I appreciate you from the bottom of my heart.

# About The Author

Darla lives in a tiny little town in Wisconsin with her husband and three small children. Her favorite thing about Wisconsin is fall because hello...the beautiful colors, caramel apples and Halloween of course!

Darla is obsessed with everything organic and homemade, natural products, and making her own lotions, scrubs and soaps with herbs and oils. Darla loves cooking, chardonnay and rainy days where everything seems to slow down a little.

A perpetual optimist, Darla strives to inspire others. She wholeheartedly believes that everyone has a genius somewhere within them and anyone can achieve whatever they want if they put in the work and never give up.

www.ingramcontent.com/pod-product-compliance
Lightning Source LLC
Chambersburg PA
CBHW061857310726
48972CB00004B/1066

*9798991717007*